Praise for *Death of a Lesser God*

'Beautifully written and a fascinating insight into
the turbulence of post-independence India'
PETER MAY

'Another exuberant thriller in his award-winning Malabar
House series ... as usual with Khan, an entire era and
community are conjured with quiet panache'
FINANCIAL TIMES

'A sumptuous, brutal, heart-stopping thriller. Vaseem Khan
writes with charm and wit, and an eye for detail that transports
the reader entirely. I couldn't love this series more'
CHRIS WHITAKER

'Post-partition India is subtle, intriguing and
dynamic; the hero, Persis, is brave, intelligent and
charming; the plot is complex and rewarding'
GREG MOSSE

'Blends a grippingly modern plot with gritty and unvarnished
history. A vibrant thriller about belonging – and who gets
to decide who belongs. A superb book and his best yet'
WILLIAM SHAW

'Breathless and brilliant, *Death of a Lesser God*
propels Persis Wadia into dangerous and deadly
new territory. Highly recommended!'
D.V. BISHOP

'Vaseem Khan delivers a masterclass ... Full of tension
and political conflict, Khan brilliantly weaves in history
and a deft portrait of post-Raj life in Bombay and
Calcutta. The result is an immensely rich book'
ALIS HAWKINS

'Tense, gripping and impressively plotted ...
historical fiction at its finest'
WILLIAM

T0204994

Also by Vaseem Khan

The Malabar House series
Midnight at Malabar House
The Dying Day
The Lost Man of Bombay

The Baby Ganesh Agency series
The Unexpected Inheritance of Inspector Chopra
The Perplexing Theft of the Jewel in the Crown
The Strange Disappearance of a Bollywood Star
Inspector Chopra and the Million Dollar Motor Car
(Quick Read)
Murder at the Grand Raj Palace
Bad Day at the Vulture Club

Death of a Lesser God

Vaseem Khan

HODDER &
STOUGHTON

First published in Great Britain in 2023 by Hodder & Stoughton Limited
An Hachette UK company

This paperback edition published in 2024

2

A CIP catalogue record for this title is available from the British Library

Paperback ISBN 978 1 399 70764 0
Hardback ISBN 978 1 399 70760 2
ebook ISBN 978 1 399 70762 6

Typeset in Adobe Caslon by Hewer Text UK Ltd, Edinburgh
Printed and bound in Great Britain by Clays Ltd, Elcograf S.p.A.

Hodder & Stoughton policy is to use papers that are natural, renewable
and recyclable products and made from wood grown in sustainable
forests. The logging and manufacturing processes are expected to
conform to the environmental regulations of the country of origin.

Hodder & Stoughton Limited
Carmelite House
50 Victoria Embankment
London EC4Y 0DZ

www.hodder.co.uk

When the girl looked at me, she asked,
'What are you, a man or a demon?'
I replied, 'I am a human being.'

From *The Arabian Nights*, Everyman's Library
edition translated by Husain Haddawy

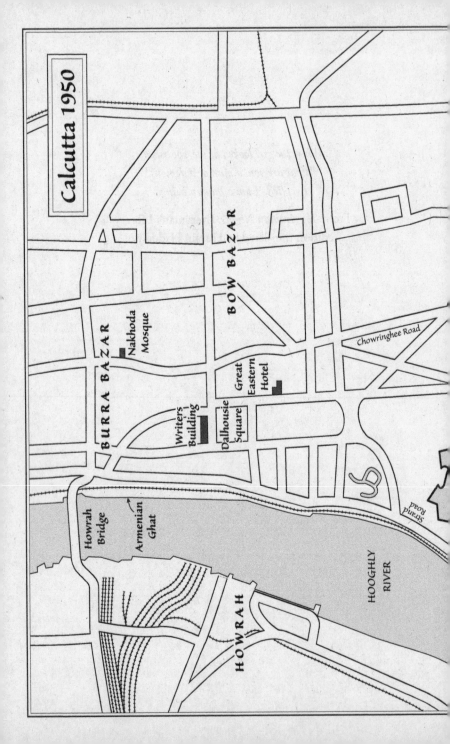

I

Bombay, 1950 – James Whitby

They say that some crimes can never be forgiven.

I don't believe that. If history has taught us anything, it's that notions of right and wrong are a movable feast. Conquest by arms, infanticide, the burning of witches – through the ages, men have found ways to justify all manner of evil.

My name is James Whitby and I have been convicted of a crime I did not commit.

Arora came to see me today. He was dressed in his customary pale herringbone suit, with a tie so heinous it might have frightened Death away. Dark hair, slicked back, a trim moustache, and tortoiseshell spectacles. A neat little man with the grace and bearing of a pianist.

There was something different about him.

I couldn't put my finger on it, at first, but then I got it. He was shrouded in the air of defeat, something I thought I'd never see.

He sat down beside me, set down his leather satchel, and pulled a pack of Woodbines from his pocket. Tapping out a cigarette, he lit one with a silver lighter embossed with the Statue of Liberty. He'd bought it in New York during a law symposium some years earlier.

He offered me the pack. I took out a cigarette and allowed him to light it for me.

We sat in silence for a few minutes, watching the smoke twist into slow-moving dragons in the air.

It was the day after the Supreme Court turned down my appeal.

There's a certain irony to the fact that this man, regarded as one of the sharpest legal minds in the country, is also my sole remaining confidant. Friend would be too lavish a word. Arora is a force of nature and it's damned difficult to befriend a hurricane.

In court, he'd proved his worth. I can't fault him for losing. It was the case that was hopeless, not the lawyer.

There are times I look at him, this man whom I've come to admire, and think: is there a small corner of his heart that believes me to be guilty? He professes not to wish to know, or indeed to care. But no man is an island. No native can exist in the India of today and not feel some affinity for the political sentiments that have wracked this nation for nigh on half a century. In court, he urged the jury not to conflate the evils of empire with the crime that I was charged with. Did they heed him? I cannot believe that a coal of resentment does not burn in the heart of every Indian when faced with a man such as myself. I embody everything they came to hate. I am the ogre of their past; I am the giant with feet of clay.

During the trial, Arora made much of the fact that I too am Indian. Technically speaking. Born in Bombay, I have spent most of my life here, save for the three years I passed at Cambridge. I've walked the same streets as them; I've breathed the same air. But I will always be an outsider. Not because of the life of privilege into which I was born, but because of the colour of my skin.

Arora and I had laughed at that, the sort of hollow laugh men in the trenches share before the whistle blows.

'I spoke with the governor's office,' he said, eventually. 'He won't receive me.'

I flicked ash on to the flagstones beneath my feet. He waited for my response but there was nothing left to say.

'Is there anything I can get you?' Light falling in from the barred window flashed from his spectacles.

'I suppose a revolver would be out of the question?'

My macabre attempt at humour fell flat. He transferred the cigarette to his other hand, then placed his right hand on my forearm. An uncharacteristically intimate gesture. He did not offer me false hope. What would be the point?

When we first met, I asked him outright, 'Can a white man expect justice in Nehru's India?' My question was born of anger; even then I'd felt aggrieved, resentful at the way I'd been treated. Railroaded, as the Americans might say. Indeed, there are moments when I feel like a man who's collided head-on with a train.

He took his time to reply. 'When I was a young man, my father sent me to London, to study law. I undertook my pupillage at Lincoln's Inn. I was by no means the only Indian there, but we were a small group, largely ostracised by our white peers. It occurred to me then that it must be a natural thing to be treated as second-class citizens in another country. But to be relegated to the status of inferior in one's own home ...? That, I'm afraid, is something many Indians can neither forget nor forgive.'

2

The mansion was partially hidden behind a screen of palm trees.

Persis drove the jeep up to the gate, then waited as the security guard, whose moustache looked as if it had recently been ravaged by fire, examined her credentials with boiled eyeballs before ushering her through. She'd been told to arrive at two. She was ten minutes early.

The Whitby mansion was one of the largest homes on the Carter Road promenade, a whitewashed enigma that few had ever been invited to investigate from the inside. A twelve-foot-high perimeter wall, topped with iron spikes, encircled the place, giving it the aspect of a better class of prison.

Parking her jeep on the forecourt, beside an alabaster fountain filled with bottle-green water and with a scarred and pitted statue of Hypatia rising from its centre, she allowed the engine to idle for a moment, looking up at the bungalow's austere façade, a mishmash of overhanging balconies, wisteria, and pale stucco. The type of colonial edifice that, in other areas of the city, had made way for art deco apartment towers and gaudy cinema halls.

She caught sight of herself in the mirror; her forehead was sheened with sweat, her jet-black hair pulled back under a peaked cap. Dark eyes – her late mother's eyes – looked back at her. What would Sanaz make of her now? *India's first female police inspector.* How little such a label understood of her life, so often hostage to the aspirations and antipathy of others, a single woman, an only child, in a country still struggling to find its feet after independence.

The British may have left, but the energies her countrymen had once directed towards revolution were now engaged in endless complaint. The country, many said, had gone to the dogs.

Which was odd because the only ones not complaining were the dogs.

She realised that a man was watching her from the doorway.

Small, dressed in white livery with gold piping, and topped by an enormous turban that swept up like the prow of a ship, he hovered beneath the arch as she exited the jeep and crunched over the gravel towards him. He looked like a busboy who'd lost his way and ended up in a pantomime version of 'Ali Baba and the Forty Thieves'.

She was led through a hallway the size of a football field, up a flight of wooden steps lined by portraits of po-faced white men staring stoically into space, and then through a maze of corridors to a large office where an elderly white figure awaited her behind a desk wide enough to park a car on.

The man was emaciated, lost inside a dark grey suit with a tie ratcheted around a pale throat. A cadaverous face, thin-lipped, with a balding pate mottled by liver spots, and a few wisps of white-blond hair clinging forlornly to the base of the skull like the chin whiskers of a goat. For an instant, she had the impression that a corpse had been propped on a seat and left to greet her.

And then the figure stirred. 'Leave us,' he commanded.

The houseboy abased himself until he was practically horizontal, then shuffled backwards out of the room like a geisha, closing the door behind him.

A rattling cough shook her host. Bony hands gripped the armrests of his seat. 'Thank you for coming, Inspector.'

'Did I have a choice?'

She realised that the chair he sat in was a wheelchair, albeit of a more elegant design than the one her father had inhabited for the past two decades, a dark and fearsome thing resembling a medieval instrument of torture.

His pale blue eyes, beneath ghostly eyebrows, rested on her, an evaluating gaze that instantly discomforted her.

She recognised him, of course.

Charles Whitby. Industrialist. Millionaire. One of those Englishmen who'd chosen to stay on after independence; a man who, if the press were to be believed, had been at loggerheads with Nehru's government ever since. In many ways, Whitby was an anachronism, a creature of India's past who, for reasons known best to himself, had decided to tough it out, instead of heading for the hills with the bulk of his compatriots.

'Would you like a drink?'

'No, thank you.'

He rolled his wheelchair to a sideboard. Selecting a whisky from a cluster of labelled bottles, he poured himself a generous measure. She noticed that his hands shook. Palsy.

Her eyes wandered around the room, a dark, panelled affair, with an old-fashioned recessed fireplace large enough to host a wedding. On one wall, an enormous tiger skin, fangs bared, took pride of place, the beast's glassy eyes crossed with confusion, possibly wondering what it had done to deserve such a fate; on another: a gallery of photographs, arranged in neat rows. The procession of framed prints showed Whitby as a younger man, ageing through the years, grimacing in the company of various luminaries: British and Indian politicians, members of the Indian nobility, film stars and starlets.

A dog the size of a small horse lay panting on a tasselled Persian mat. It raised its head to eye her with an appraising look as if hors d'oeuvres had just been served. Of *course*, Whitby had a dog. No Englishman's castle would be complete without a hound. And a dozen native servants, all of whom ranked several places below the dog.

She held its gaze until it looked bashfully away, collapsing back on to its paws.

Returning to his spot behind the desk, Whitby sipped at his tumbler, watching her over the lip of the glass. She had the sense that he was preparing himself to speak, but needed a moment.

The lacuna forced her to revisit the reason she'd come calling on the man – her earlier encounter with Additional Deputy Commissioner of Police Amit Shukla.

Shukla had caught her outside Malabar House, intercepting her as she'd arrived at the station that morning. She'd only later realised that he must have been waiting for her.

Back in his Buick, he'd ordered his driver to leave them.

'My father purchased this car from a departing Scotsman,' he began, once they were alone. 'Gandhi always said that one day we'd make our own vehicles. He was a great visionary, but he wouldn't have known a good car if it ran him over in the street.'

She waited in silence for him to circle to his point. The cloak-and-dagger nature of the encounter intrigued her. In the short time she'd known him, Shukla had rarely indulged in subterfuge. He was the sort of man who'd happily stab you in the front. And then in the back – and sides – for good measure.

'What do you think of them?'

'Sir?'

'The British. What's your opinion of them?'

'I don't understand.'

'Persis, in my experience, there are two types of Indian. Those who are martyrs to the past, and those willing to embrace the future.'

She coloured, wondering if perhaps he was obliquely referring to Archie Blackfinch, and the complicated equation that now defined her relationship with the Englishman. She was glad Blackfinch was out of the city on an extended tour of the provinces.

It gave her time to confront her own muddled feelings.

'I have an assignment for you,' Shukla continued. 'Are you familiar with the James Whitby case?'

'I'm familiar with the headlines the case has made.'

'Whitby is due to be hanged eleven days from now. When that happens, he will become the first – and quite probably the last – Englishman to be executed by the Indian government.' He paused. 'Did you follow the case?'

'He murdered Mazumdar. The lawyer.'

'Fareed Mazumdar wasn't just any lawyer. He was the lawyer Nehru's government had employed to bring Whitby's father to heel. Charles Whitby is a divisive figure, a man who has made many enemies over the years. Despite this, he retains a great deal of influence. I have no idea of the levers he's managed to pull, but the order has come down that a discreet reinvestigation of the Whitby case is to be carried out.'

'Whitby was convicted. His appeals have been denied. The case is closed.'

'Nevertheless . . . The directive has come from the commissioner's office.'

Realisation dawned. 'Sir, are you asking *me* to re-examine the case?'

'Asking implies a choice, Inspector.'

She startled as a leper leaned into the window, drooling at her like a mad goat, and flailing a bandaged hand.

Shukla barked at the man until he staggered backwards, to be absorbed by the early morning crowd flowing along John Adams Street.

'The task is straightforward,' continued the ADC. 'Go over the case, but do not attract attention. I'm sure you can appreciate the furore should your efforts become public knowledge.'

'I can hardly investigate without asking questions.'

'If you proceed with caution, we can simply say that you are reviewing the case, an internal formality.'

'What if I investigate and it becomes clear that Whitby *is* guilty?'

'Then so be it.' He paused. 'We have a moral conundrum before us, Inspector. Do we seek justice for a man who the press has painted as the *enemy*, or do we allow prejudice to blinker us? Consider this: what if Whitby really didn't do it, and the fact comes to light only after his execution? Can you imagine the repercussions if we were to hang an *innocent* white man?'

'I suspect that you're somewhat confused, Inspector.'

Charles Whitby's voice drew her back to the present.

'An explanation would help. Sir.'

'It's quite simple. My son is due to be executed for a crime he says he did not commit. My political contacts claim they can do nothing. Frankly speaking, they've washed their hands of me. It seems I don't quite command the influence I once did.' He bared his teeth. 'You are my last hope. It has taken a great deal of wrangling even to secure *your* services in this matter. I had hoped for a full-blown investigation by more experienced officers, but beggars, it seems, cannot be choosers.'

She ignored the insult.

It was no secret that Malabar House, the smallest station in the Bombay constabulary, served as home to those who had upset the upper echelons of the force, condemned to pass their remaining years of service in a state of ignominy. But Persis had been sent there through no fault of her own, her crime far more prosaic. In the intensely patriarchal environment of the Bombay Police Service, there were few who wished to work with a creature as exotic as a police*woman*.

Nevertheless, her short time at the station had seen her successfully tackle several high-profile and politically charged cases, elevating her to the status of a minor national celebrity. With fame had come plaudits and brickbats. There were many who considered her sudden irruption into the nation's psyche to be symptomatic of a country changing too quickly for its own good, a drunken elephant on the rampage.

'What is it that you think I can possibly discover that the original investigators missed?'

'James, my son, is a fool. The evidence against him is . . . overwhelming. Nevertheless, it is my duty as his father to do all that I can. He is my only child. If he dies before me, then all this' – he waved a hand at their surroundings – 'will have been for naught.'

'Where is his mother?'

'She left us both when he was still a boy.' Said matter-of-factly, yet she saw blood darken his cheeks.

'You chose not to remarry?'

'No. I had neither the inclination nor the patience.'

She paused. 'If the evidence is as damning as you say it is, why do you think James deserves a second chance? Or is punishment fitting only for Indians?'

The pressure of his gaze was like a hand pushing her backwards. 'There was a time when a native would not have dared speak to me that way . . . My son's life is at stake. You must commit yourself to proving his innocence.'

'I will commit myself to uncovering the truth. If that's not enough for you, you had better call your friend the commissioner and ask him to send another lackey to do your bidding.'

He looked as if she'd bashed him in the face with a tyre iron. Finally, his head creaked forward. 'Very well. You have eleven days. Eleven days to save James. Or, as you put it, to "uncover the truth".'

'I'll need access to the original investigation.'

He reached into a pocket and held out a sliver of white card bearing the name *Vikram Agarwal*. 'Liaise with my aide. He will expedite matters. Resources, funds, contacts – all that I have is at your disposal . . . I expect that the need to proceed with discretion has been impressed upon you? Should word of your investigation leak, there are those who would seek to stop you.'

'I understand.'

'Do you, Inspector? There are many who call me a *colonialist*, a man who made a fortune from the *mis*fortune of others. I refute that description. I built a business and I did what I had to do to achieve success. But I was no better or worse than others; certainly, no better or worse than any of your own maharajas, nawabs, and nizams. I've had dealings with such men. Take it from me: no more corrupt and incompetent a shower has ever blighted this land.' Anger squirmed over his pale features. 'Many have asked me why I chose to stay . . . I've lived here for almost five decades. Longer than most of those who are so keen to show me the door. They want to tear down everything I've built. They want to steal from me in the name of *reparation*.' He spat the word.

She realised what it was he put her in mind of: a hoary old dragon, sitting on a hoard of gold, breathing fire at all those daring to enter its mountain lair. She recalled reading about an unsavoury accusation levelled at Whitby, something he had done during Gandhi's early non-cooperation-movement years that had caused a stink, setting the nationalists against him. They'd hounded him ever since, but Whitby's influence and fortune had held them at bay.

But now the tide had turned, leaving Charles Whitby a lonely and embittered old man, condemned by his own past to live out a future that he could not accept.

3

The monsoon had begun.

Rain in the tropics – as the earliest British adventurers had learned – bore little relationship to the gentle drizzle that caressed the Home Counties or the Scotch mist that enveloped the rolling hills of the Highlands. Monsoon rain came down like a rebuke from the gods, lashing the parched earth with enough force to concuss cattle and drown dreams. This wasn't sophisticated rain; this was the sort of rain that mugged you in broad daylight and left your body sprawled in the gutter.

Persis parked her jeep in the alley behind Malabar House.

Ducking out, she sprinted to the station's arcaded front entrance, splashing past potholes large enough to swallow an elephant, rats squeaking indignantly as they were born along the open drains. A doorman lurked beneath the arched doorway of the four-storey corporate tower that housed Malabar House, holding aloft an umbrella that, in the face of the deluge, looked about as much use as a paper hat under a V2 rocket.

Far above, water cascaded from the mouths of the mildewed gargoyles lining the edge of the building's roof.

As she barrelled into the lobby, spilling water from her peaked cap on to the terrazzo, the receptionist, a young woman in a peach sari, glanced at her in alarm from behind a marble counter.

Ignoring her, Persis headed down into the basement, where the police station was housed.

Wading into the cramped offices, she discovered that only Birla, one of the station's trio of sub-inspectors, was at his desk, chewing on a rod of sugarcane as he perused a report. He stared at her, then said, 'You know, most people tend to take their clothes *off* before they shower.'

She squelched to her desk, reached in and grabbed her spare uniform, then wandered back upstairs to the ground-floor washroom. Here, she took a towel from the rack, dried herself, changed, and then returned to her desk.

'Would you like some tea?' asked Birla.

'Yes.'

He barked at the office peon, sending the boy racing off like a hare pursued by dogs.

'Is Seth in his office?' she asked.

Birla nodded. 'And in a foul mood.'

'When is he not?' she muttered, lifting herself up and heading to the door at the rear of the room.

Roshan Seth, the station-in-charge, had once aspired to greatness in the Indian Police Service.

An intelligent and capable officer, he had, for years, been groomed for a senior post on the Bombay force, with every expectation of achieving it. But all that had come crashing to earth with the advent of independence. As a new guard of native senior officers had taken over from the British, they'd made it a point to root out all those who had shown excessive enterprise during the imperial era.

Seth's name had ended up at the top of a short list.

Before he could protest his innocence, he had found himself shunted to Malabar House, his career taken out into a field and clubbed to death before being shot between the eyes for good measure.

Now, Seth reminded her of a deposed king sent into exile. Shorn of his former influence and the trappings of office, he inhabited his new life with an aggrieved sense of hopelessness, his cynicism manifesting as a late-blooming friendship with the bottle. The man was often in his cups by the early afternoon; by evening, he was practically horizontal on the floor behind his desk.

She found him scanning a notebook laid flat on his cluttered desk, reading glasses perched on the end of his nose. A tall man with a trim moustache and the thoroughbred grace of a racehorse, he seemed too large for his surroundings, like a caged tiger. If it were not for the stink of failure wafting from every surface of the office, one might think Seth was a mover and shaker, hard at work on matters of great import.

'Not like you to be late in,' he said, pulling off his spectacles and waving her into a chair.

'I was sent on an errand.'

He frowned. 'Not by me.'

'By Shukla. He's asked me to take on a case.'

Seth blinked. 'Why wasn't I told about this?'

'You'd have to discuss that with him.'

He ground his jaw. She could see him working out the equation in his head and arriving at an answer that precluded any possibility of confronting his commanding officer. Shukla was not a man to cross; he'd throttled many a promising career, but wasn't averse to stamping on the ashes of a dead one when the occasion demanded it. 'What's the case?'

'I'm not at liberty to say. I simply wanted to tell you that I'll be tied up for the next eleven days.'

Seth's nostrils flared. 'And how does Shukla think we're supposed to cope in your absence?'

'There's always Oberoi.' Her tone was caustic.

Her fellow inspector at the station, Hemant Oberoi, had made it clear from the beginning exactly what he thought of a woman being *allowed* on to the force. That the dynamic between them had recently changed – Oberoi had saved her life and in so doing had taken a life – his first – had done little to lessen their mutual antagonism. They'd spent the interregnum since that case largely avoiding one another.

'Oberoi is away. He's in Pune on a training course.'

'What are they training him in? How to be a human being?'

'Oberoi is being groomed. Malabar House is just a brief sentence for him.'

She knew that Oberoi had ended up at the station because of an indiscretion. It stood to reason that an incompetent blowhard, the scion of a powerful family, would be marked for better things. The thought churned her stomach, but there was little she could do about it. In the short years since taking over from the old imperial police force, the Indian Police Service had already distinguished itself as a bastion of corruption, nepotism, and incompetence, outdone only by the tax office. If Caligula had still been around and inclined to don the khaki, he'd have found himself right at home.

'I'm sure Fernandes can hold the fort for eleven days.'

George Fernandes was the senior-most of the trio of sub-inspectors at the station, a man she'd come to respect, and had worked well with, despite a rocky start.

She realised that Seth was looking at her thoughtfully.

Over the past months, life at the station had begun to change. With the largely negative press coverage heralding Persis's arrival, and her subsequent investigations engendering a further spate of lurid headlines, interest in Malabar House had veered from utter disregard towards alarmist rhetoric. Some portrayed the station as a sordid pit of venality, harbouring a dangerous subversive; others wrote in to express their admiration, a welcome counterpoint to the sacks of rabid fan mail urging her to leap under the nearest bus.

She was aware of a softening in the stance of her male colleagues – Hemant Oberoi excepted – and a gradual, if grudging, acceptance. She suspected that, for a group tarred with the brush of ignominy, it did not hurt to see Malabar House earning the occasional scrap of praise.

Even Seth seemed marginally happier, though that seemed akin to the Grim Reaper taking a day off to visit the pub.

He slipped a hand into a drawer and threw a folded newspaper on to the desk. The *Indian Chronicle*. The top half of the front page showed a blurry photograph of a white man in a morning suit juxtaposed with a photo of an Indian. Beneath this was the headline:

BOMBAY GOVERNOR REFUSES PLEA FOR CLEMENCY. WHITBY TO HANG IN ELEVEN DAYS.

'It's going to be the biggest show since they hanged Godse.'

Nathuram Godse. Gandhi's assassin. A martyr to some; a terrorist to others.

She'd often wondered at the demons that had driven a man like Godse. Surely even he could not have guessed the impact that three bullets would have on the affairs of three hundred million.

With Gandhi's passing, a certain vision of India too had died.

Nehru, finding himself at the Congress helm, had struggled in the wake of his former colleague's legacy. The India he'd inherited following Partition, a plane with its wings shorn off, had proved to be a bumpy ride, post-independence optimism quickly giving way to disillusionment. Buffeted by forces both internal and external

– the clamour of the feudal class, the expectations of the junta, the exigencies of world politics – Nehru had navigated a treacherous path between appeasement and change.

Anarchy was only a badly formulated missive away.

Persis was simply glad that any mistakes the Prime Minister might make would, at least, be Indian mistakes, and not those dictated by the whims of foreigners. And if he crash-landed the plane . . . Well, a five-thousand-year-old culture had little to fear from another revolution. India barrelled through revolutions the way runaway bulls charged through knock-kneed matadors.

'I don't suppose Shukla has you mixed up in *this*?'

She rose to her feet. 'I should go. I have a lot to do.'

'Fine. But remember this: if you *are* involved in the Whitby case, tread lightly. As far as the public is concerned, Whitby is the devil incarnate.'

4

Seth's words stayed with her as she drove to the Arthur Road Jail near Jacob's Circle.

Entering the two-acre plot, she was reminded of earlier visits; the prison – Bombay's principal place of incarceration – had become notorious for its brutal regime and overcrowded conditions, with prisoners often stuffed twenty to a cell, forced to contort themselves around one another like shanghaied yogis in the hold of a slave ship. The place was so bad it made the Black Hole of Calcutta look like a suite at the Taj.

She announced the reason for her visit to the bloodshot-eyed constable on duty at the reception, and was immediately taken to meet with the warden. The man listened stonily to her request and then informed her that visits to James Whitby could only be authorised by the governor of Bombay.

She handed him the card given to her by Charles Whitby. A call to Whitby's aide soon resolved the matter. She suspected that the resolution involved a gratuity; certainly, the warden's demeanour changed from intransigent martinet to accommodating courtesan in the space of a brief conversation.

She was led deep into the prison by a whey-faced guard who looked like an upright cadaver with working eyeballs. Arriving at a wooden door with a barred portal, he opened it with a key chained to his belt, then stepped backwards.

Entering James Whitby's cell, she was surprised to discover that it was a relatively large space, whitewashed, with a cot on one

side, and a wooden table and chair pushed against the other. On a
shelf above the table, a row of books rubbed shoulders with potted
plants. The flagstones beneath her feet had been brushed clean.
The scent of sandalwood infused the air.

She was momentarily taken aback. The room was more hospi-
table than many hotels in the city. She suspected Charles Whitby's
hand. At this rate, the warden would be a wealthy man by the time
they hanged the Englishman's son.

A white man was sitting at the table – James Whitby, she
presumed – eyeing her in astonishment as if a giant turbot had
walked into his presence. He was dressed not in a prison uniform,
but a white, open-necked shirt and cavalry twill trousers.

As she finished her inspection of the room, he rose from his
chair.

Introducing herself, she said, 'I was hoping that we might
speak.'

He flashed a lopsided grin. 'I have little else to do, Inspector.
Please, be my guest.' He waved her into the chair, before walking
across to perch on the edge of his cot.

'Do you know who I am?' she asked.

'Your fame precedes you, Persis. May I call you Persis?' He
didn't bother to wait for a reply. 'I've followed your adventures in
the newspapers. I suppose you're my father's last throw of the dice.
I wonder how much this gambit is costing him.'

His tone was sarcastic, and she sensed a complex undertow of
emotions beneath his words. It struck her that Whitby and his
father did not share a warm relationship.

'He believes that you're innocent.'

He gave a mirthless laugh. 'No, Persis. He doesn't believe that.
My father is simply attempting to ward off the inevitable. I am the
torchbearer of his legacy. Seeing me swing from the scaffold was
not part of his plan.'

She took out her notebook. 'May I ask you a few questions about the case?'

He pulled a crumpled pack of cigarettes from his pocket and stabbed one into his mouth before lighting it. 'Fire away.'

'Last year, on the fifteenth of September, you visited with the lawyer Fareed Mazumdar. Why?'

'I wanted to talk to him about my father's case.'

'You're referring to the case the government has filed against him? What exactly is he accused of?'

'It's a historical matter. Back in the early 1920s, when Gandhi initiated his non-cooperation movement, my father still owned numerous factories and mining operations around the country. As you can imagine, the disruption cost him a great deal of money. He decided to solve the problem in the manner he always solves such problems: by force. The accusation is that a key employee heading up a protest at an industrial plant in Barrackpore was murdered by my father's operatives. On his orders.'

'Did he do it?'

He stared at her in surprise. 'That was very direct. The truth is . . . I don't know. I was a boy at the time.'

She realised that he wasn't much older than herself, though looked infinitely more careworn. His blond hair was cut short, and his face was weathered in the manner of a block of ice left out in the sun. He was clean-shaven, but she saw a cut just above his upper lip. She imagined his hand trembling as he held the razor, staring at his reflection in the mirror, wondering how many more times he would be able to stand there and perform such a simple ritual.

'Did your father send you to speak with Mazumdar?'

'No.'

'Why did you go? What did you hope to achieve?'

'I – I hoped to have an honest conversation with Fareed. My father felt the case against him was politically motivated. By those who hope to run him out of the country.'

'Why would they – whoever *they* are – do that? There are plenty of Englishmen who've stayed on after independence.'

The corners of his mouth turned up. 'Let's just say that my father refuses to accept that the world has changed. He no longer calls the shots, but continues to act as if he does. That sort of arrogance upsets people. To be frank, he probably deserves to be sent packing. The problem is that if he leaves, then *I* might be forced to leave too.'

'You're not beholden to him.'

He grimaced. 'Wealth is a difficult habit to break. And my father controls our wealth.'

She ruminated on this a moment, then said, 'You went to see Mazumdar. A few hours later he was dead. What happened?'

'We talked for a while. And then I left.'

'What did you talk about?'

'I spoke to him about my father's belief that the case against him was manufactured. Our own lawyers reviewed the evidence. All Fareed had was sketchy witness testimony, from an old employee of the family. I asked him to persuade the government to drop the case before it went to trial.'

'But he refused.'

'Yes.'

'Did you argue?'

He hesitated. 'Yes.'

Her pen scratched across the vellum of her notebook. 'What happened next?'

'I left.'

'*Where* did you meet with Fareed?'

'His office. In Kala Ghoda.'

She leaned back. 'How did you end up being arrested for his murder?'

He sighed. 'I decided to take another crack at him. I went to his home – this was a few hours after meeting with him at his office. As I walked into the parking lot below his apartment building, I heard a cry. Then I heard footsteps, and I thought I saw the shape of a man moving away from me in the shadows on the far side of the car park.'

'Did you get a look at him?'

'No. It was dark – the lights were out. At any rate, it took a few moments for me to pinpoint where the initial sound had come from. As I approached, I tripped, and fell on to a body. When I got my bearings, I realised it was Fareed. He'd been stabbed.

'He died minutes later. That was when a scream sounded behind me. A woman – one of Fareed's neighbours – had come down into the car park. She saw me hunched over him, blood on my clothes, and assumed the worst. Her scream roused the security guard. I tried to protest, but neither of them seemed in the mood to listen. And so I ran. In hindsight, that was a mistake.'

'Were you arrested the same day?'

He grimaced. 'I barely made it to the end of the street. I'm afraid I was a little worse for wear.'

'You were drunk?'

He said nothing, instead lifting the cigarette back to his mouth.

'Did you do it?'

The question caught him off guard, as she'd intended it to. She watched him closely, but he gave nothing away. Finally, he spoke, 'No. I didn't kill Fareed.'

'But the prosecution found enough merit in the case to convict you. Or do you think that too was politically motivated?'

His eyes narrowed. 'I suspect my father would be disappointed in your attitude. When he pays for something, he expects to get full value.'

She stiffened. 'Your father hasn't paid me.'

'Don't be naïve. He's paid *someone*.'

A flush of anger burned her cheeks. It was Whitby's turn to scrutinise her. 'You know, when I met with Fareed, he said something to me; it's stuck with me ever since. He told me that you can fight men, but you can't fight history. During my trial, the racial question dominated everything. Being British – and Charles Whitby's son – it's like the mark of Cain. But the hell of it is, they expect me to *understand*. As if, somehow, by convicting me, they're balancing out the worst excesses of the Raj. They'd like me to stop making a fuss about silly little things like my innocence. Tell me, Inspector, is it a condemned man's duty to comfort his executioners?'

His sense of aggrieved entitlement irritated her. 'Shall I tell you what *I* see?'

'Enlighten me.'

'I see a man terrified by the prospect of his impending death. So terrified that he makes light of the efforts of the one person who might be able to help him.'

He smiled coldly. 'What makes you think you can help me?'

'I don't know that I can. But if you really didn't do it, I'll do my best to prove it.'

For an instant, his façade dropped. He leaned forward; his blue eyes, as pale as his father's, drilled into her, searching for the truth in her words. She saw something in him then, a sense of helplessness, the helplessness of a man caught in the arms of a whirlpool.

She stood up. 'Of course, if I discover that you *did* do it, I'll come back and watch you hang.'

5

The lights were still on in the bookshop.

She parked the jeep in the alley beside the store, then walked back around front, stopping to peer through the Wadia Book Emporium's glass façade.

A young woman sat behind the counter, scribbling in a ledger.

Even after a week, the sight was jarring. She still hadn't got used to not seeing her father in his customary spot, hunched over in his wheelchair, with an expression about as welcoming as a Gestapo interrogator.

A week earlier Sam had embarked on a delayed honeymoon with his new wife, Meherzad, a month-long tour of the Himalayan foothills, beginning in the old British summer capital, Shimla. It was the first holiday he'd taken in decades, the first time he'd ventured away from the shop since the death of his first wife, Sanaz – Persis's mother – in a car accident.

It was only recently that she'd discovered that Sam had been behind the wheel of the car in question. The guilt he'd lived with had kept him from taking another partner until Persis had grown to adulthood and found her feet in the world.

When she'd discovered that he was planning a second marriage, it had come as a shock. Her father was about as suited to marriage as Henry VIII.

The wedding had taken place on a blistering March day, with Persis – and a small guest list of the couple's friends and family – in attendance. A part of her had rejoiced that Sam now had a companion, one that he, by all accounts, adored; another part of her was saddened that her own role in his life would now change.

Sam and Meherzad had delayed the honeymoon while her stepmother attended to various family matters.

When they'd finally departed, Sam had seemed less than joyous. The truth was that her father would have happily sent his new wife off on her own – he had about as much desire to leave Bombay for the supposed delights of the rest of the country as a Frenchman had of leaving a good brothel.

She knew that her father's real concern had been the bookshop.

For two decades, he'd reigned from behind the counter, like a soldier manning a gun emplacement. The shop was an extension of Sam's own persona: loud, chaotic, and impervious to change. *Who in the world would run it in his absence?*

It had been left to Persis to find an answer.

She entered the shop, the little bell above the door ringing gently as she stepped inside.

The girl at the counter looked up. A smile spread across her features.

'Hello, madam.'

'Seema.'

The girl tapped the ledger spread open before her. 'It's been another excellent day. We've sold out of the new Agatha Christie. She seems to be very popular!'

Persis shrugged. 'Readers are fickle. Who knows if anyone will remember her name fifty years from now?' She pulled off her peaked cap. 'Have you eaten yet?'

'I was going to carry out an inventory and then close up.'

'You can do it tomorrow. It's already eight.'

'But—'

'No buts.'

She watched as Seema reluctantly locked the ledger away.

The girl had been a revelation.

They'd met two months earlier when Seema had been assigned to her by Roshan Seth as part of a mentoring programme. Following a rocky start, Persis had agreed to take the girl under her wing. She'd been given no cause to regret her decision.

Seema lived with her ailing mother and younger sister in a one-room shack in Bombay's largest slum, the sort of makeshift hut that collapsed with a sneeze. Her father had walked out on them years earlier; as a consequence, her formal education had been blighted by the exigencies of setting food on the table. For years, she'd cleaned railway latrines, educating herself as best she could in the evenings.

Sam had been impressed enough by the girl's enterprise to allow Persis to employ her in his absence. He'd even, grudgingly, agreed to pay her.

What Persis *hadn't* expected was the way her young ward had taken charge. It was as if something long dormant had been awakened in her, and the quiet, self-effacing girl had suddenly been overtaken by the spirit of Genghis Khan.

In the space of a few days, she'd reorganised the bookshop's haphazard cataloguing system, hired a delivery boy so that elderly customers could telephone in orders, and introduced a coffee corner where readers might sip a cup of Darjeeling's finest in between perusing their favourite authors.

The thought of her father's reaction when he discovered these innovations – the coffee corner, in particular, with its chattering gatherings of elderly women – had already given Persis sleepless nights.

In the evenings, after closing the shop, they would take supper together, discussing the cases Persis was working on. Seema's ultimate goal was to apply to the police academy. If her efforts in the shop were anything to go by, Persis was certain the girl would end up running the police service, one day.

The door chime sounded behind them.

She turned to find Nussie, her mother's younger sister, bearing down on them brandishing a copper stockpot. 'Dinner's here!'

Twenty minutes later, she'd showered, changed, and was sat at the dining table in the apartment above the shop, Seema opposite her, Persis' grey tomcat, Akbar, indolently curled up on the Steinway watching them both as Nussie served dinner.

'When are you going to learn to cook?' said her aunt, ladling lamb dhansak on to her plate.

'I'm a police officer. Why would I need to cook?'

'Well, what are you going to do when you marry?'

'What makes you think *I'm* the one who'll have to do the cooking?'

Nussie turned white, as if Persis had suggested she might take up child sacrifice as a hobby, but forbore from commenting.

They talked about the Whitby case, Persis impressing upon them the need for discretion. She was used to discussing her cases with her father; it often helped to have a sounding board as she felt her way through an investigation.

'Why would you want to help him?' said her aunt, aghast. 'He murdered an Indian patriot. In cold blood.'

'He claims that he didn't. That we've rushed to convict him because he's a white man.'

'I've heard of that father of his. Charles Whitby. Nasty piece of work. He moved to Bombay years ago. By all accounts, he's spent a lifetime treating Indians as little more than lapdogs. The apple doesn't fall far from the tree, Persis.'

'Are you saying Whitby doesn't deserve justice because of his father's actions?'

'He's already had justice! He's been convicted by a court and sentenced to death. He should bloody well hang.'

Persis was momentarily taken aback. She hadn't expected her genteel aunt to be quite so bloodthirsty. It was as if Florence Nightingale had announced that she enjoyed bull-fighting on her days off from the hospital. 'And what if they were wrong?'

Nussie sniffed defiantly, but said nothing.

'What do *you* think, Seema?'

The girl seemed pensive. 'I think that justice is a notion for the wealthy. The poor never talk about justice because we rarely see it. If you're asking me whether mistakes can be made, whether prejudice might have biased the decision against Whitby, then yes, it's possible.' She pushed her wire-framed spectacles up her nose. 'I think you should investigate to the best of your ability. If Whitby really didn't commit the murder, he shouldn't hang for it. That would be a stain on our souls. No enlightened nation should want that.'

6

The heat was suffocating.

The monsoon had arrived a month early, at the hottest time of the year, resulting in bouts of torrential rain interspersed with periods of broiling heat. In an earlier age, the British would flee the lowlands and the godawful humidity of the monsoon months to specially built summer retreats nestled in the Himalayan foot-hills. For the ordinary residents of the plains, however, there was nowhere to hide, the air so thick it was as if they were trapped together in a giant sauna – but without the European sense of sweaty, arse-slapping camaraderie.

The next morning Persis arrived at the Bombay police head-quarters opposite Crawford Market with her uniform already clinging to her back, and sweat running down her face as if a faucet had been installed above her forehead.

Parking her jeep, she exited the vehicle, and stood a moment mopping her brow with a sodden handkerchief, looking up at the Gothic edifice that had served as home to the central machinery of the Bombay force for over five decades.

From across the road drifted the cries of fruit sellers and cobra vendors, the shrieks of lovebirds mingling with the horning of taxis and the desperate pleas of dragomen, a racket loud enough to deafen a statue.

The day was barely an hour old and her mood had already soured.

She'd awoken to the postman hammering down the front door. The rat-faced fellow had handed her a letter, then stood there leering at her in her sweat-soaked nightgown until she'd shut the door on his betel-stained grin.

She'd opened the envelope to find a photograph of Archie Blackfinch atop a camel, decked out in the manner of an eighteenth-century explorer, in safari suit and sola topi, grinning to beat the band. Scrawled on the back of the photograph were the words: *Jaipur is an absolute riot!*

As she'd wolfed down a breakfast of kedgeree and orange juice – having overcooked the kedgeree until it had the taste and texture of gravel – she'd found herself dwelling on the Englishman's missive.

Blackfinch, a criminalist with the Metropolitan Police in London, had arrived in Bombay a year earlier, at the behest of the Indian Police Service, to help the Bombay force set up a forensic science laboratory. They'd met when the murder of a prominent English diplomat had fallen into her lap on New Year's Eve.

Her initial impression of the Englishman had been ambivalent.

A tall, handsome man, bespectacled and badly dressed in ill-fitting suits and perennially scuffed shoes, his clumsiness and irritating mannerisms concealed a rare perspicacity, and a sense of humour that had seeped, like floodwater, under her natural defences. He had the disarming look of one of those Englishmen who indulged in newt-mating or amateur theatre, the sort who ironed their newspapers and wore paper hats to ward off the rain.

Something had sparked between them, unexpected, unbidden, but impossible to deny once it became apparent. Against her own better judgement, she'd allowed herself to become embroiled in ... what? 'Relationship' was too grandiose a word for the few moments of closeness they'd shared, a brief affair that had left her confused by her own emotions.

The simple truth was that there was no future in pursuing a romantic entanglement with Blackfinch. India may have made giant strides towards a free and independent future, but the idea of a native woman striking up with a white man, an Englishman at that, was the sort of bad idea that led to whole nations falling out with each other.

It would have been easier for her to have taken up with Adolf Hitler, if he hadn't killed himself and hadn't looked like a human fruit fly.

It had been almost a relief when he'd departed on an extended junket around the country – his mission to replicate his efforts in Bombay by establishing forensic labs in several of the larger Indian metropolises. That he'd taken to sending her postcard photographs from his various ports of call only added to her belief that he hadn't yet accepted that there could never be anything real or lasting between them.

Like many Englishmen before him, Archie Blackfinch believed that the world would simply orient itself to his desires.

She pushed the matter to the back of her thoughts, and returned to the task at hand.

She'd come to the station to meet with the man who'd led the investigation into the murder of Fareed Mazumdar.

In the lobby of the headquarters building, she presented herself to the receptionist, and was duly asked to wait. She took a chair, her eyes wandering impatiently around the walls of the cramped space, alighting on portraits of the various men who'd shaped the city's police force.

Technically speaking, Bombay's first police service had comprised a ragged militia employed in the late 1600s by the city's Portuguese rulers, a band of louts and drunks tasked to prevent garrisoned sailors from plunging knives into each other's backs over games of chance.

The cure had proved worse than the disease; the city's crime rate had actually *risen*.

It wasn't until the collection of marshy islands comprising Bombay had been united by the East India Company's land reclamation project, that a permanent force had been established.

Her gaze lingered on a portrait of the maverick commissioner Charles Forjett.

Obsessed by the notion of native insurrection, Forjett had prowled the streets in disguise, looking for signs of subversion, once arresting two men that he accused of conspiring to blow up the town; he'd had them stripped, strapped to cannons, and blown to smithereens in front of a packed crowd.

Forjett's brand of hands-on policing had set the mould for those who would follow, until the arrival of independence, and the first Indian commissioner, Ranjan 'Tiger' Shroff.

Persis had never met Shroff, but his reputation as a ruthless authoritarian would have made Forjett well up with pride.

A peon arrived to lead her up two flights of stairs, to the office of the crime branch detective who'd supervised the Mazumdar case.

Ranjit Singh was a grizzled Sikh wearing a mango-coloured turban and an unruly beard that looked as if a Scottish terrier was attacking his chin. He scowled as she entered, then pointed her into a seat. His crumpled white shirt was marked with sweat rings emanating outwards from under his arms, like the markings on a tree stump. A heavy stink of tobacco hung in the room.

Singh's demeanour was hostile from the outset. 'So you're reinvestigating the Mazumdar case. Why?'

'I'm not reinvestigating. Simply reviewing.'

'There's nothing to review. Whitby killed the man and now he'll hang for it.'

'And you're sure of that?'

'As sure as I am that a woman has no business wearing that uniform.'

She coloured, but refused to rise to the bait. She needed Singh's cooperation. 'If you can't help me, then perhaps I should be meeting with someone more senior.'

His expression darkened. Finally, he ground out, 'What do you want?'

'I need access to your case files.'

He glared at her as if she'd asked him to saw off his own head and hand it to her on a platter. He picked up a phone, barked into it, then slammed the receiver back into its cradle.

'What else?'

'I want to hear your thoughts on the case. Why are you so certain that he's guilty?'

'Because all the evidence says that he did it.'

'*He* claims that he's innocent.'

Singh snorted. 'He went to Mazumdar's office that day intent on convincing him to drop the case against his father. When Mazumdar refused, he became enraged. He went to a nearby bar and drank. The barman says he was drunk by the time he left. Drunk and angry. He walked to Mazumdar's home, caught up with him in the car park below the building, and stabbed him to death.'

'Were there any witnesses to the killing?'

'A woman, a resident of the building, caught him in the act, covered in blood.'

'Whitby claims he found the body. Tripped over it, in fact.'

'Did he also explain how his prints ended up on the knife?'

It was her turn to pause. Whitby hadn't mentioned that.

'He says he saw a man fleeing the scene.'

'And yet he can give us no meaningful description of this individual. The truth is that we found nothing to indicate that anyone else had been in the car park other than Whitby and Mazumdar.'

'Did you consider any other scenarios?' she persisted. 'A thief, perhaps, who killed Mazumdar just before Whitby chanced on the body?'

'Mazumdar's wallet and watch were still on him. The security guard saw no one pass by. Except Whitby. No mysterious third parties that conveniently vanished into thin air.'

'But there must have been others with a motive to harm Mazumdar?' she persisted. 'He was a prominent lawyer, after all.'

There was no need to clarify her meaning. Lawyers in India generally enjoyed a reputation somewhere below that of vultures and mass murderers. Persis had always felt the comparison was unkind to vultures, who, in the Parsee faith, at least, were considered holy animals.

'We found no one,' he ground out.

A rap on the door. A peon entered and handed over a thick manila folder tied with string.

Singh weighed the folder in his hand, then reluctantly passed it over, as if handing her a kidney.

'And the case evidence? The victim's personal effects?'

'I'll have them sent to you.'

She nodded, then quickly scanned the folder.

It all seemed to be there. Singh's write-ups of the investigation, the pathologist's post-mortem report, the forensic analysis of the crime scene and evidence. A brown envelope lodged at the back of the folder contained a sheaf of photographs.

She decided to review the material later, without Singh snorting at her like a bull in a field. Sikhs had a notoriously volatile temperament, with a tendency to push in the faces of those they disagreed with. It was a wonder the hulking detective had answered any of her questions at all.

'I take it you've met with him?' said Singh. 'James Whitby, I mean?'

'I've spoken to him.'

'He's a very convincing man, I'll give him that.' He leaned forward on his elbows, sending a gust of cologne her way that would have gassed a small dog. 'The Raj is over, Inspector. *We* ended it. You don't have to do what a white man tells you to do any more.'

'I have my orders.'

'My father was a salaryman in Punjab. He worked for a shoe company. He'd tour the country with samples of his shoes, visiting retailers and workshops. One day, as he was passing through a small town on the outskirts of Ludhiana, he was swept up in a Quit India protest. My father was a patriot, but he was no firebrand. He believed in satyagraha, Gandhi's non-violent resistance.

'The protestors headed for a military barracks. They were unarmed. But a British officer decided to disperse the crowd using force. Things got out of hand. My father was shot dead. They found two bullets in his back.' He stopped. 'The British officer was never brought to trial. In fact, they fêted him for putting down a *riot*.' His eyes blazed. 'I don't care who ordered you to do this. You're a traitor to your kind and a disgrace to that uniform.'

7

The Bombay High Court had been around for almost a century, another of the venerable old buildings in the Fort area built in the Gothic revivalist style, one of three high courts originally established in the old presidency towns of Bombay, Calcutta and Madras via letters patent granted by Queen Victoria.

Persis had always found the building a dour presence, reeking of false respectability and a sense of artificial grandeur, like an ageing dowager with an opium habit. With its imposing central turret and gloomy grey-green walls, she'd always been put in mind of a glorified prison.

Marooned atop twin octagonal towers located either side of the central tower, statues of Mercy and Justice looked bashfully out over the city, avoiding one another's eyes.

She could understand why.

Justice and mercy were in short supply inside Bombay's premier place of litigation, where cases had been known to run on so long the plaintiffs had died awaiting a judgement.

She'd come to the court in search of Rakesh Arora, the advocate who'd defended James Whitby during his trial. Telephoning his office, she'd been informed that he was in session at the Bombay High Court, but might be free to meet with her during the lunch recess.

Arriving at reception, her thoughts lingered on her meeting with Singh.

Disgrace.

When he'd called her that, she'd said nothing; but, as she'd stepped out of his office, the word had begun to toll in her mind. Was this how she would be viewed if she continued to pursue the case? What might the fallout be for her career? She realised, with the benefit of hindsight, that she should have discussed this further with ADC Shukla.

Then again, perhaps she was deluding herself.

Shukla had ensnared her with a trap fashioned from her own ambition. He'd known that she would not turn down an assignment for which she'd been hand-picked, a task that he'd told her was of critical importance to Delhi.

At what point would she come to regret her decision?

She was directed through the labyrinthine building towards a courtroom at the rear. Slipping inside, she lurked at the back of the wood-panelled room, watching as Arora spoke from the defence counsel's bench. From the little she could gather, the case was about a long-standing dispute over a cow, two parties laying claim to the same animal.

The judge, a boar of a man, seemed half asleep. She recognised his face from the newspapers. Justice Fraser, a notoriously bad-tempered Scotsman, with a penchant for summarily sentencing members of the gallery to a night in jail for contempt of court, a ruling that could encompass, equally, the punctilios of court procedure or a mistimed sneeze. The long-standing judge was one of thousands of Britishers who remained in the country and still believed in the tenets of *civis Britannicus sum*.

For men like Fraser, the sun had yet to set on the empire, and they weren't about to be dissuaded of that fact by the trifling matter of Indian independence.

Arora seemed in his element, a well-spoken, attractive man, with a flair for oratory.

She listened to him argue his case, chin held at a poetic angle, ending with an impassioned and somewhat surreal plea for the semi-divine nature of the cow to be given due consideration by the court.

Ten minutes later, the judge called a halt to proceedings. Persis moved quickly forward through the press of bodies and introduced herself to Arora.

The advocate conferred for a moment with his junior, then bade her follow, leading her up a flight of stairs to the Judges' Library on the second floor. Here, he ushered her towards a reading table, before sending a hovering peon to fetch lime water.

Taking off his black robe, he slung it around the back of his chair and loosened his collar. Turning his face up to the ceiling fan above their table, he allowed the swirling breeze to cool the sweat on his face. 'Have you been to see him?'

'Yes.'

'How was he?'

'Sceptical.'

Arora nodded glumly. 'I try to meet with him every evening, to keep his spirits up. As you can imagine, it's an increasingly uphill task.'

'Is it true that you've exhausted every appeal?'

'To all intents and purposes. I've written to the president of India. But given that the Bombay governor has refused clemency, there is little chance of the president overriding him.'

'So Whitby will be executed?'

'Barring any new evidence, yes.'

To her surprise, he seemed inordinately saddened by the prospect. In her experience, once a case was decided, most lawyers washed their hands of the matter, consoling themselves with their fee in the event that things had not gone their way. But there seemed something personal in Arora's manner.

'Do you really believe he's innocent?'

'I do.'

'Why? Or are you simply clutching at straws because you failed him?'

His eyebrows lifted in surprise. 'I did the best that I could.'

'Then why the doubt? The prosecution proved their case.'

'It's not as simple as that.'

'Explain it to me.'

He knocked his knuckles softly against the side of his glass. 'Have you heard of the myth of the good Nazi, Inspector?'

She frowned. 'No.'

'It's an ironic term. Meant to deride Germans who participated in the Nazi regime, but claimed they knew nothing of the atrocities being committed in their name. A denial of personal moral responsibility that now colours our view of every German, whether it be true or not.'

'What has that to do with Whitby?'

'A similar dynamic has been at work with the British in India. We find ourselves unable to accept that not every Britisher who lived here during the Raj was a monster.'

'My understanding is that Charles Whitby stands accused of ordering the murder of an Indian in the 1920s, of treating us abominably. It stands to reason that his son might have imbibed similar values.'

'I disagree. James and his father are chalk and cheese. In fact, I believe that James's experience of observing his father while growing up is at least partly responsible for his own view of India.'

'Which is?'

'He is dismayed at the way some Englishmen – including his father – behaved here. But he thinks of himself as Indian, no more or less than you and I.'

'That's absurd.'

'Is it? He was born and raised here. Who gets to decide who belongs and who doesn't? After all, what does a Sikh from the Punjab have in common with a Tamilian from the south? Or a Bengali Hindu Brahmin with a Keralite Muslim? We are a collection of peoples, so varying in culture, customs, language, and history that we may as well be classed as a minor continent. What right have we to treat Whitby as an outsider?'

His impassioned appeal gave her pause. 'Why did he hire you?'

'He didn't. It was Charles, his father, who approached me. He wanted the best advocate in the country, an experienced murder hand.'

'*Are* you the best?'

He smiled gently. 'I'm good at what I do, Inspector.'

'I just saw you advocating on behalf of a cow.'

His brow furrowed. 'The first thing you learn as a lawyer is never to take anything at face value. The cow in question belongs to a temple complex. Deciding its ultimate owner will have major repercussions for the devotees of the temple, tens of thousands of individuals.' He picked up his glass of lime water and sipped at it. 'I'm glad that you're reinvestigating the case. But if you're to do so with any hope of success, you must keep an open mind.'

She sat back. 'There can't have been many advocates willing to defend an Englishman accused of murdering an Indian lawyer.'

'I looked at the case, not the man. I believed I could win.'

'And the publicity would not have harmed your reputation, I suppose.'

He looked peeved. 'I don't need the publicity. I had a thriving practice before Whitby approached me. If anything, taking on the case has cost me clients. Not everyone is as enamoured of my commitment to the cause of justice. I even received word that Delhi was keen to see James Whitby convicted.'

She scoffed. 'You think Nehru rigged the case?'

'No, of course not. But juries are hardly immune to public sentiment or political rhetoric.'

She decided to change tack. 'Did you know the victim?'

The question seemed to catch him by surprise. 'Mazumdar? No, not really. I mean, I knew *of* him. He made his name in Bengal. He'd only moved here from Calcutta after the war. He was considered something of a nationalist – another excuse for the press to fan the flames against James. "White oppressor murders patriot lawyer."'

'You make it sound as if the situation was hopeless.'

He hesitated. 'I confess this case has affected me more than most. I've come to admire James. His stoicism in the face of being wronged. But soon, he will be gone. A smudge left in our collective memory. Who will care? Who will remember the man that he was, rather than the political pawn that he became?' He waved his glass around, indicating the building they sat in. 'This court was built at the height of the Raj. Men such as Gandhi and Jinnah practised law here. During the Quit India years, innumerable freedom fighters found themselves in the dock facing trumped-up charges of sedition. And yet, in spite of everything, this is where justice must prevail, or else what value is our freedom?'

She allowed the lawyer's moment of philosophical grandstanding to lumber its way out of the room, then said: 'I'd like a copy of the trial transcript.'

'Of course. I'll telephone my office and have it sent over immediately.' He made a show of checking his watch. 'Forgive me, Inspector, but I must return to court. Please feel free to call me at any time should you need further assistance.'

8

Curiosity killed the cat.

Perhaps this was true in other parts of the world, but in Bombay, curiosity could have skinned the cat alive and roasted it over a slow flame and it would have done little to dampen the natural inquisitiveness of her countrymen.

Persis arrived back at Malabar House to discover that Singh, in spite of his hostility, had been as good as his word. The physical evidence from James Whitby's trial had been delivered to the station in several small crates. The crates had temporarily hypnotised Birla, who hovered around them, as if, perhaps, they might house gold bullion or the lost treasure of the Incas. He'd astonished her by asking if she needed help; Birla was usually as likely to volunteer for additional work as he was to place his head inside the mouth of a crocodile.

His curiosity reached fever pitch as a runner arrived with a folder of the trial transcript of *Case No. 335 (1949): The State of Bombay vs James Whitby.*

She decided to work in the interview room, the only private space in the station aside from Seth's office.

She hauled the crates on to the rickety interview room table, and laid out the case file and the trial transcript folder beside each other.

This was where an investigation really began. Assembling the building blocks of a case, seeing how they might fit, recognising where the gaps might lie. She felt a gentle excitement pulse through her, like sap rising through the veins of an unfurling flower.

First, she went through the case file and the trial transcript, making notes as she went.

According to the chronology, James Whitby had met with Fareed Mazumdar at around four in the afternoon, leaving Mazumdar's office an hour later. He'd then visited a nearby bar where he was seen by several witnesses. He left the bar at around seven, and walked the fifteen or so minutes to Mazumdar's private residence. At approximately seven-fifteen, he entered the car park below the building. It was here that the state claimed he'd chanced upon Mazumdar returning from his office. The prosecution had speculated that Whitby, incensed by Mazumdar's pursuit of his father, enraged by the lawyer's earlier intransigence, and having steadily drunk his way to a heightened sense of aggression, had initiated an argument, one that had ended with him stabbing Mazumdar to death in a 'frenzy of murderous rage'.

A witness, a Mrs Mathur, had walked in on the scene. Her screams alerted the watchman, Ram Tilak, who'd arrived moments later. According to the pair, Whitby had stood up, his shirt soaked in Mazumdar's blood, and had then taken off. Tilak had given chase.

Moments later, Whitby had tripped, fallen, and all but knocked himself unconscious.

Tilak had raised the alarm. A crowd had gathered, and detained Whitby until the police had arrived to take the Englishman into custody.

He was fortunate not to have been lynched on the spot.

The murder weapon, a knife, had been found at the scene. Later, Whitby's fingerprints had been discovered on the hilt.

She took out the sheaf of crime scene photographs and went through them.

The body of Mazumdar was shown from various angles, dressed in a dark suit and white shirt, blood blooming brightly across his chest. The knife was found just a couple of feet from the body.

She picked up a photo of the knife.

The weapon had an unusual design, with a gold-coloured, H-shaped hilt fashioned to be grasped in a clenched fist. The blade was broad at the hilt and tapered to a sharp but thickened point. On one side, the top of the blade bore an inscription in what looked like Sanskrit; on the reverse, there was a decorative heraldic design featuring a shield and a trio of falcons.

There was no mention in the accompanying note as to what the Sanskrit might mean.

She knew from the trial transcript that Whitby had denied possessing such a knife.

But if the knife was not his, then how had it arrived at the crime scene? Who had used it to murder Mazumdar? And why leave such a distinctive weapon behind?

Her gaze lingered on the body.

She recalled the lawyer Arora's words – namely, that Mazumdar had only moved to Bombay after the war. A nationalist lawyer from Bengal whom the Indian government had used as their attack dog in a bid to bring Charles Whitby to heel.

This thought led to another: namely, that she knew very little about the victim.

Working back through the case file, she made a note of Mazumdar's addresses, both office and home, and the contact details of his former aide, a Victor Salazar.

Her eye snagged on a minor detail. A reference in the case file to Mazumdar's personal effects. A curious note that had been discovered on his person.

She rose from her chair, opened the evidence crates, and steadily went through them.

Inside she found the victim's clothing, neatly labelled, the shirt and left lapel of the blazer still heavily encrusted with dried blood.

The murder weapon was also in the crates.

She held it a moment, balanced on the palm of one hand. It was lighter than she'd expected, with a strange heft to it, and an elegant beauty that belied the murderous use to which it had been put.

Mazumdar's briefcase had been with him at the time of his death.

She went through it, but found little of interest: a copy of that morning's *Times of India*; a brace of case files; several ancillary documents relating to court motions he was drafting.

A cloth bag contained the contents of Mazumdar's pockets at the time of his murder. A wallet with exactly one hundred and fifty-two rupees; a packet of Capstans; a lighter; and a note, on soft blue vellum, discovered in the breast pocket of his blazer.

The edges of the note were darkened by blood.

She unfolded it carefully. Curiously, there was no writing on the letter-sized sheet, merely a drawing:

The Star of David.

She knew the symbol, of course, though was hazy as to its exact meaning.

Why had Mazumdar, a Mohammedan, been walking around with a Jewish symbol tucked into the pocket of his blazer?

She went back into the case file and the court transcript and quickly realised that neither the defence nor the prosecution had touched on the note. It had been deemed irrelevant to the matter at hand. In all probability, this was true, but something about it bothered her. She hated loose ends, and hated more the fact that in a case that had decided the outcome of a man's life, no one had bothered to chase down this thread.

She looked up at the battered interview room clock and saw that two hours had vanished.

She rubbed the back of her neck, easing out the dull ache that had begun to collect at the top of her spine. She needed food, and a shower. She was conscious of the fact that a noxious odour emanated from her, as if she'd spent the day rolling around in a dung heap.

She carried on working.

Taking the pathologist's report from the case file, she saw that it had been prepared by John Galt, the predecessor to Bombay's current chief pathologist, Raj Bhoomi. Galt had been the man in charge when she'd first arrived at Malabar House, a year earlier, but had died shortly after, his heart giving out during a visit to a local brothel.

The death had shocked her, not least because Galt had always seemed to her a patrician presence, tall, emaciated, monosyllabic, and with the general look and demeanour of an accountant. The idea of him cavorting with a member of the opposite sex had never entered her mind.

Later, she'd felt a sense of restless guilt at the sense of disapprobation that had instinctively overcome her – who was she to judge a man like John Galt?

Even accountants had urges.

She'd just never supposed they'd find anyone willing to accommodate them.

Mazumdar's autopsy listed the cause of death as exsanguination due to multiple stab wounds. Seven in all, all to the front torso, centred around the heart and stomach. Galt had determined that the principal wound had penetrated the precordium – the chest wall over the heart – and the heart, leading to catastrophic injury. Other wounds had penetrated the thoracic cavity and the abdomen into the right lung, the stomach, and the thoracic aorta. All the wounds were consistent with the knife found at the scene.

The prosecution had made much of the fact that no defensive wounds had been found on the victim's hands. This, they claimed, demonstrated that the victim knew his killer, and had allowed him to get close. James Whitby had then launched a frenzied attack, giving Mazumdar no opportunity to defend himself.

The scenario seemed to fit the facts.

The only question was whether Whitby was the one holding the knife, or an innocent victim of circumstance, as he claimed.

9

Bombay in the evening was no less a frantic ant heap than it was in the daytime.

Weaving her jeep through the crowded streets, she was acutely aware of how the city had grown in the past years. With the influx of refugees following Partition, and the constant stream of starry-eyed hopefuls, drawn, like the dazed victims of a vampire, to India's city of dreams, Bombay's population continued to skyrocket.

The city was bursting at the seams, pushing out in all directions like an out-of-control hernia, while slums sprang up overnight on the smallest patch of waste ground. The municipal authorities spent their time chasing their own tails, with neither the resources nor the experience to deal with the problem, bulldozing and building in a frantic delirium.

And yet, this was a city of wealth and glamour, home to the nation's premier film industry, where captains of industry rubbed shoulders with sportsmen, politicians, and international celebrities in the glitzy jazz halls of five-star hotels. In the streets beyond the gilded ballrooms, beggars, lepers, eunuchs, and a limitless supply of the disenfranchised and the dispossessed existed in a sort of rude democracy of the damned.

She arrived at Tamarind Lane in Kala Ghoda, parking directly outside the complex where Fareed Mazumdar had leased office space.

A sugarcane stall was doing a brisk trade beside the entrance to the building, despite the vendor's pungent body odour, and a torn vest that looked as if he'd recently crawled through barbed wire. A yellowing poster advertising Nehru's Congress Party pasted to the wall behind the stand had been defaced with an anti-government slogan, depicting Nehru as a sycophant of King George VI, erstwhile emperor of India.

With the country wracked by civil unrest and economic uncertainty, the post-independence honeymoon was well and truly over.

In the building's open doorway, Mazumdar's aide, Victor Salazar, awaited her anxiously, a small, hunchbacked Goan, with a toothbrush moustache and a dark, puffy face. He was dressed in a badly fitting suit, and a tie that seemed painfully close to throttling him.

Salazar seemed unhappy at being summoned so late in the day.

He led her into the building, past a wooden plaque listing the various lawyers leasing offices on the premises, and up a flight of steps stained red by betel juice.

On the third floor, he halted outside a door barred by two planks of wood nailed across the front. A yellowing police notice was tacked to the planks. Salazar carefully removed the notice, then produced a chisel from his suit, like a magician pulling a dove from a hat.

She watched him as he levered the planks away from the door frame, allowing them to clatter to the floor in an explosion of dust.

'The office has remained untouched since Mr Mazumdar's death.' His tone was disapproving, as if, perhaps, like the grave robbers of the Egyptian pyramids, Persis was about to defile a sacred place.

Unlocking the door, he led her inside.

The dead man's office was smaller than she'd expected. One wall was given over to green-bound legal volumes and copies of the *Indian Law Review* running all the way from 1900 to the present day; the opposite wall was taken up by large bay windows, obscured by chick blinds, and, presumably, overlooking the street below. On the rear wall, a series of photographs catalogued the independence struggle, Gandhi and his compatriots prominent – a means, she suspected, of impressing Mazumdar's nationalist bona fides upon prospective clients.

In the centre of the room, a trio of desks were arranged in a horseshoe, Mazumdar's the largest, an old-fashioned roll-top, French-polished to a honeyed sheen, and with a high back that would have all but obscured the lawyer when he was sat behind it. The other two desks, Salazar informed her, belonged to himself and to Mazumdar's junior, a young Welshman named Owain Price.

The tambour of Mazumdar's desk was drawn.

She rolled it up and began to methodically go through the various drawers, pigeonholes and compartments, Salazar squirming on the spot in an anxiety of sweat and incipient panic. 'May I ask what you're looking for?'

'I'm trying to reconstruct the day that he was killed. What was he doing? What was preoccupying him? Who did he meet with, aside from James Whitby?'

'I can answer some of those questions.' He walked to his desk, opened a drawer, and took out a ledger. Leafing through it, he placed a finger on a page, and read from it. 'He had two appointments that day, including Whitby. In the morning, he was in court. He returned in the afternoon. Just before he met with Whitby, he had a meeting with Professor Alok Shastri. Shastri is a friend; they often play bridge together.'

'Were they discussing a case?'

'You'd have to ask Mr Price.'

'Where can I find him?'

He reeled off Price's address, and she scratched it down in her notebook. She detected something in Salazar's manner. 'Is there something about Price you'd like to tell me?'

He seemed to freeze, then said, 'Owain Price was a poor lawyer. I was surprised that Mr Mazumdar put up with him for as long as he did. They argued frequently. In fact, I believe he was due to dismiss him just before his murder.'

She absorbed this. 'How long have you known him? Mazumdar, I mean?'

'He came to Bombay in late 1946. He hired me a month later when he opened this office.'

'What about family?'

'I have a wife, two children. How is that relevant?'

'I meant Mazumdar.'

He coloured. She realised that he was a man who lived off his pride. As a hunchback, no doubt he would have faced innumerable obstacles; professional success and a productive marriage meant a great deal to him. He was intolerant of mistakes, particularly in himself.

'Mr Mazumdar was a confirmed bachelor.'

'In all these years, he never once stepped out with a female companion?'

'If he did, he did not discuss it with me. In the office, he preferred to concentrate on the task at hand, rather than waste time in idle gossip.'

'Did he mention any family in Calcutta?'

'No.'

'You were never curious?'

'It was not my place to be curious,' he said, stiffly.

'What sort of man was he?'

He seemed to consider the question. 'He was dedicated to the law. He believed it to be an instrument by which the injustices of our society might be redressed.'

'Did he have enemies? A disgruntled client, perhaps?'

He drew himself up, or as far up as was possible given his physical encumbrance. 'Our clients were never dissatisfied with our services.'

'But he lost cases?'

'Hardly ever.'

She realised that talking to Salazar was pointless. The man was as likely to divulge Mazumdar's secrets as an Italian was to admit to an affair. If there were skeletons in Mazumdar's closet, they would remain blissfully hidden for the time being.

She finished going through the desk, but found nothing to shed any further light on her investigation.

'There's one more thing,' said Salazar. He hesitated. 'A day after he was killed, I received a call from a journalist. He said that Mr Mazumdar had been in touch with him prior to his death. He wanted to know if Mr Mazumdar had left anything for him, notes, written testimony, that sort of thing. I told him I had no idea what he was talking about. Mr Mazumdar had not mentioned anything about him to me.'

'Who was the journalist?'

'An Aalam Channa, at the *Indian Chronicle*.'

She cursed under her breath. Channa. A newshawk who'd set himself against her from the moment she'd arrived on the force.

The last time they'd met she'd almost broken his fingers.

She took out the note that had been found on Mazumdar's body, bearing the Star of David.

'Do you recognise this?'

'It looks like a Jewish symbol.'

'It was found on Mazumdar the day he died. Can you think of a reason why he'd be carrying this around?'

He seemed mystified.

'Did he have any Jewish clients?'

'No.'

'Any Jewish acquaintances?'

'Not to my knowledge.'

She completed her search of the desk, then allowed Salazar to lock up and lead her back down into the street. It was almost seven and evening had fallen. 'How far is Mazumdar's home from here?'

'A ten-minute walk.'

'On the day he died, did he walk home or drive?'

'He drove.'

'Did he drive himself?'

'Yes.'

'Was that usual?'

'Yes. He often drove the short distance from his home to the office. He enjoyed driving. When he had to go further afield, he would use his driver.'

She thanked him for his help, and turned to climb back into the jeep.

IO

Fareed Mazumdar had lived on the first floor of an apartment tower in Fort.

Arriving at the complex, she first noted that it was gated, with a security guard out front. Leaning out of the jeep, she asked the man if he was the same guard who'd been on duty the day Mazumdar had been killed.

The scrawny fellow bounced up from his stool and launched into a passionate disquisition, part-defence, part-testimony, recounting how Mazumdar had arrived that day and driven down into the car park, and then, moments later, a wild-eyed James Whitby, smelling strongly of liquor, had turned up on foot, demanding egress. The guard, Ram Tilak, being a simple man, had not had the temerity to refuse the Englishman, something he would regret to his dying day.

Moments later, he'd heard a scream emanating from the car park.

He'd raced inside to find Whitby standing in a pool of blood, the body of Mazumdar at his feet. According to Tilak, the Englishman had been poised to launch an attack on the defence-less Mrs Mathur of apartment 102. Sizing up the scene, Tilak had leaped to her aid, frightening Whitby into making a run for it. Tilak had given chase, heroically apprehending the murderous villain, a fact he'd detailed with considerable relish in court.

Persis drove down into the basement-level car park, got out of the jeep, then spent a few minutes going over the crime scene.

The car park was expansive, with concrete columns dotted around the space at regular intervals, and populated by a stable of upmarket vehicles, a riot of glistening chrome, whitewall tyres, and snarling radiator grills.

There was nothing to mark where Mazumdar had fallen.

At the back of the car park, a narrow passageway, screened by a thin wall, led to the rear of the compound within which the apartment tower stood. A wall, approximately seven feet high, encircled the plot. She judged it to be little obstacle for an athletic and determined intruder. If Whitby had been telling the truth about seeing a figure fleeing the scene, then perhaps this was how the man had gotten in and out without having to negotiate the guard out front.

She took the stairs up to the first floor.

Lavinia Mathur was in her early fifties, a tall, severe-looking woman with short grey hair that fitted her head like an iron helmet. She wore square-framed spectacles and had a mole above her upper lip. She walked with a slight limp, wielding an elegant cane with an ivory handle in the shape of a bird.

'I lost my husband just over a year ago,' she said, leading the way into her apartment. 'He died at our home in Jodhpur in Rajasthan, a heart attack. It's why I moved to Bombay, to escape his memory. So it wasn't that I hadn't seen death before. But when I walked into that car park and saw Whitby leaning over Mazumdar, all that blood, it was simply too much. I'm not the sort of woman who normally screams, you understand.'

The apartment was spacious, with high Victorian ceilings, curtained bay windows, a gleaming parquet floor, and the sort of heavy, claw-footed furniture that wouldn't have looked out of place in the Palace of Versailles. A sideboard was littered with objets d'art including an ornamental silver spittoon and a replica of Gandhi's three wise monkeys in brass.

A white Pomeranian yapped at them from the top of a grand piano, a dancing ball of fluff on legs. On the wall behind the piano, a lugubrious elderly gentleman dressed in a regal Rajasthani outfit and turban looked gloomily down on the scene, as if trapped inside the frame of his portrait.

'Did you actually *see* Whitby striking Mazumdar?'

'No. But it couldn't have been more than a few moments after the stabbing that I walked in on him.'

'Was he holding the knife when you saw him?'

She frowned. 'All of this was in the testimony I gave at the trial.'

'I'd like to hear it from you.'

She picked up the yapping dog, and sat down on the sofa with it, clasping it tightly to her bosom in a strangler's grip, muffling its bark. 'The scene is burned into my mind. I walked down to my car – well, it was my husband's car, to be truthful. He used to call it his pride and joy. He was gifted it by the maharaja of Jodhpur – my husband worked for his administration. It was a running joke between us: you know, that he loved that car more than he loved me.' Persis followed her gaze up to the desolate portrait of the former Mr Mathur and wondered briefly whether the man had actually been joking. 'I stepped into the car park and there was Whitby, crouched over Mazumdar's body. And yes, the knife was in his hand. I screamed instinctively, and his head snapped around. That's when he dropped the knife.'

'Did he say anything to you?'

'No. He advanced towards me, but then the security guard, Tilak, arrived. Thank God that he did, otherwise there might have been two bodies in the car park that day.'

'How well did you know Mazumdar?'

'Not that well. He was a very private man. Kept himself to himself. I tried my best to be neighbourly, invited him to several

social functions, but he would always excuse himself, citing work.'
She sounded miffed.

'Did he ever speak about family or a female companion?'

'Not to me.'

'Did you ever see anyone visiting with him?'

'Not that I can recall. Now that I think about it, the man was
something of an enigma.'

I I

Fareed Mazumdar's apartment had remained untouched since the day of his murder.

The authorities had searched it cursorily, discovered nothing of significance to the investigation, and, in due course, returned it to the building's owner, a superstitious real estate magnate who'd decided not to place it back on the market until after the case had run its course, and enough time had elapsed for the spirit of his former tenant to find peace.

A key to the apartment, discovered on Mazumdar's body, had ended up in the case evidence log.

Persis now used that key to enter the apartment, Lavinia Mathur watching her nosily from the doorway of her own apartment at the far end of the corridor, her Pomeranian still clutched tightly to her chest, the poor creature turning blue in the face as its paws paddled ineffectually in the air.

The apartment was identical in layout to Mathur's, but that was where the similarity ended. Whereas Mathur had stuffed her place with seemingly every conceit invented by the mind of man, Mazumdar's home was bare, as Spartan as a monk's cell. The whitewashed walls were devoid of paintings or portraiture; a few functional pieces of furniture graced the living room; and the bedrooms – of which there were two – were as characterless as motel rooms.

In the kitchen, the fridge and cupboards were all but empty, stocked with a handful of out-of-date items, including a Gruyère cheese hairier than the average Greek grandmother and a stick of salami so tough it could have been used as a cosh.

This was the apartment of a man who spent very little time at home. She'd seen prison cells with more personality.

In the master bedroom, she opened Mazumdar's wardrobe to find several suits hanging in the darkness. Shoes, shirts, under-clothes, a range of dark ties – all had been left undisturbed.

Her eye was caught by something sticking out over the lip of the uppermost shelf. She reached up and pulled it out.

A slim manila folder.

What was it doing here?

She walked to the bed, and sat down.

Inside the folder, she discovered several newspaper cuttings, together with a series of envelopes, addressed to Mazumdar at his home, postmarked with dates in the weeks before his death.

Collectively, the cuttings detailed a case from October 1946, the trial of a Calcutta gangster, Azizur Rahman, accused of murdering two people during the Calcutta Killings – an Indian woman named Rita Chatterjee and a black American soldier: Walter 'Kip' Rivers.

It became clear from the articles that the advocate who'd defended Rahman had been Mazumdar.

The case had stirred up controversy, with Rahman – a promi-nent local figure in the Calcutta Muslim community – accusing the authorities of manufacturing the case against him because of his Mohammedan beliefs.

Ultimately, Mazumdar had prevailed, proving his client's inno-cence in court.

Picking up the envelopes, she guessed that someone had been mailing these to Mazumdar. But why?

There were four articles and five envelopes. What had been in the fifth envelope?

She made an intuitive leap.

Taking out her notebook, she lifted out the note with the Star of David. Folding it along crease lines prominent in the sheet, she discovered that it fit perfectly into the last envelope. There was no guarantee it had been mailed to Mazumdar in that envelope, but it seemed a safe bet that that had been the case.

Again, she asked herself: why?

What had the Star of David to do with the Rahman case? And why would someone send these cuttings to Mazumdar?

The fact that he'd been carrying the Star of David note in his pocket on the day that he'd died proved that the matter had been weighing on his mind.

A mystery, much like the man himself.

She wondered why the folder was still in the wardrobe. The answer came to her immediately. The police had searched the place as a matter of routine, but with no real expectation of discovering anything useful. With James Whitby already in custody, they'd dismissed any relevance of the folder – and its contents – to their investigation.

They had their man and that was all they needed.

12

'They're trying to kill me.'

Her father's voice was unusually subdued. At home, Sam's natural tendency was to bellow, as if everyone he came into contact with was either an imbecile or a foreigner.

Persis had arrived back at the shop, helped Seema close up, shared a hasty supper with the girl, and then sent her off in a rickshaw.

After Seema had left, and unable to still her brain as it churned over the unfurling investigation into Fareed Mazumdar's death, she'd poured herself a glass of sherry from her father's cabinet, set Brahms's Piano Sonata No. 3 on to the gramophone, and then settled on to the sofa to work through her case notes.

Akbar, her grey Persian, stirred beside her, uncharacteristically complaisant.

She suspected that the cat was missing Sam, though why he'd miss a surly old man who considered him a worthless rug on legs, she couldn't begin to fathom. Her father seemed to have the perverse knack of eliciting warmth in those who came to know him, without appearing to reciprocate.

Before she'd managed to make much headway, the phone had rung.

Sam and her new stepmother, Meherzad, had driven from Shimla to Parwanoo, another of the hill stations that dotted the Himalayan foothills, out on the border between Himachal Pradesh and Haryana. Here they'd visited apple orchards, flower gardens, and spent time taking in the stunning valley scenery.

Not that you would have known it from the way Sam was complaining.

Her father appeared to find everything disagreeable, from the size of the fleas in his bed, to the food, to the coolies who pushed his wheelchair up and down the slopes of the hamlet. He claimed that one of them had tipped him over, to almost tumble to his death in the valley below.

Persis could almost sympathise with the porter.

'Papa, it's your honeymoon. Can't you just enjoy it?'

She held the phone away from her ear as Sam launched into another tirade.

When he'd finished, she took a deep breath, and said, 'This isn't just about you. Have you considered what it must be like for Meherzad to spend her honeymoon with an old grouch?'

'Grouch?' Her father seemed mystified. 'Who are you talking about?'

'I'm talking about you!'

A silence drifted down the phone.

'Do you really think that's how she sees me?'

'If the shoe fits, Papa.'

They ended on that somewhat discordant note.

Afterwards, she'd picked up her glass and returned to the case, allowing the facts to settle in her mind, like sediment drifting to the riverbed.

Fareed Mazumdar: a nationalist Calcutta lawyer who'd moved to Bombay late in 1946, had been hired by the Indian government in 1949 to build a case against industrialist Charles Whitby for ordering the murder of one of his employees back in 1921.

Shortly afterwards, Whitby's son, James Whitby, had visited Mazumdar's office in an unsuccessful bid to convince him to drop the case. Hours later, Whitby had murdered Mazumdar.

At his trial Whitby denied murder, though admitted that he'd gone to Mazumdar's home that evening to reargue his case. Whitby had been convicted of the killing and sentenced to death, a death that was now only ten days away.

Prior to *his* death, Fareed Mazumdar had received several envelopes containing press cuttings relating to a 1946 murder case in Calcutta, in which he'd defended a prominent Calcuttan charged with a double homicide. One of the envelopes had also contained a drawing of the Star of David.

She presumed that the drawing and cuttings had been sent to Mazumdar anonymously – certainly, there was no clue on the note, articles, or envelopes as to who had sent them.

How were they related to James Whitby's case, if at all?

She was still mulling over the question when sleep found her an hour later.

13

As one of the oldest law firms in the country, Dinshaw Mistry & Co. boasted offices in Bombay, Delhi, and Madras. Located on the ever-busy Colaba Causeway, the firm rented the top four floors of a building with a basalt sandstone façade and an enormous billboard crowning the roof emblazoned with the glowing face of the firm's founding partner, Framji Dinshaw, a pioneer in the Indianisation of the country's legal profession.

Dinshaw's status as a patriot had been cemented back in 1934 when, at the age of seventy, he had been killed at the height of the independence struggle. A young postal worker had made his way into the central courtroom at the Bombay High Court where Dinshaw had been acting as defence counsel for a man accused of distributing revolutionary pamphlets; thirty minutes into the session, the postal worker had taken a grenade from his pocket, removed the firing pin, shouted an anti-British slogan, and then lobbed the missile at the bench, where the presiding judge, Justice Jonathan Harper, a staunch defender of the Raj, had spent the better part of the morning glowering at the accused.

Fortunately for Harper, the amateur insurrectionist's aim had proved wayward; the grenade had caught the ceiling fan and ricocheted down on to the defence counsel bench. The resultant explosion had killed Dinshaw on the spot and severely wounded his junior, as well as effacing the moustaches of several august members of the public sat within the blast radius, a crime some considered more heinous than the old lawyer's death.

Persis arrived at the firm's offices at just after ten, parking the jeep out front.

Around her, the street shimmered with heat; the humidity was already high enough to drown fish. Worker ants stumbled along in a daze, faces glistening. The traffic on the busy thoroughfare was a typical Bombay morass, a conga of cars, trucks, rickshaws, buses, bicycles, handcarts, stray animals, and a river of careless pedestrians with as much regard for the rules of the road as a bull elephant in heat. The air held a bouquet that was practically Bombay's trademark: a heady perfume of shit, urine, and sewage.

She made her way past a turbaned watchman, announced herself to the wilting ground-floor receptionist, climbed up to the offices of Dinshaw Mistry & Co, announced herself to a second receptionist, and was duly led to a meeting room and asked to wait.

A ceiling fan stirred the boiling air around the room; the windows had been left open, letting in more warm air and the cacophony of the street below. The room was plushly appointed, with oak panelling, a fresh coat of paint, a gleaming boardroom table, a royal blue carpet as thick as elephant grass, and a striking painting of a muscular Zarathustra posing heroically on a mountaintop.

Below the picture stood two pedestals on which roosted a pair of marble vultures. They reminded her of Hector and Achilles, the stone vultures that rested on a plinth above the façade of her father's bookshop. Early customers of the shop had found the minatory avians somewhat disconcerting, until it had been explained to them that the birds were merely symbols of the Parsee faith.

Framji Dinshaw, like herself and Sam, had been a Zoroastrian.

The door opened behind her and a short white male entered. His dark hair was scraped back over a high forehead and his brown eyes were closely set. A scruffy moustache flowed over his upper lip, like algae washed up on a beach. A grey waistcoat enclosed a pinstriped shirt, the sleeves rolled up to the elbows.

She had the impression of a great labour interrupted.

'My name is Owain Price,' he said, in an accent she'd rarely encountered, melodic, with the vowels drawn out almost to breaking point, like prisoners on an inquisitor's rack.

The Welsh, she'd been led to understand, were a peculiar breed of Britisher – patriotic when the mood took them, neither quite at home with the shortcomings of empire, nor overly demonstrative against its excesses. To many Indians, they were kindred spirits, having made a holy animal of the common sheep, reminding them of their own reverence for cows.

'I understand that you wish to speak with me?'

She introduced herself and quickly recounted the reason for her visit.

The young man – she guessed him to be in his mid to late twenties – frowned. 'I'm afraid that I don't see how I can help. Yes, I worked with Fareed, but I have nothing new to say on the subject of his murder.'

'Nevertheless, I'd like to ask you a few questions.'

A protest began to form on his lips and then he seemed to change his mind. 'Very well.' He lowered himself gingerly into a chair like a man who'd recently been caned on the bottom. 'What is it that you wish to know?'

'How did you end up working for him?'

'He advertised for the post of a junior. I applied and he hired me on the spot.'

'This was back in late 1946?'

'January 1947. He'd arrived a couple of months earlier from Calcutta to set up a practice here.'

'Why did he leave Calcutta? I mean, by all accounts he was successful there.'

'I'm afraid I don't know. I asked him, of course. He said that he simply needed a change of scenery.'

'Did you believe him?'

'I had no reason not to.' He paused. 'Of course, I began to suspect there was something more to it. He seemed never to want to talk about the place. Strange, given that he'd grown up in the city, and, as you say, made his name there.'

'You worked closely with him?'

'Yes, of course. I was his junior. We discussed cases and I would help prepare them.'

'Did you advocate in court?'

His hesitation spoke volumes. 'No. Fareed didn't trust anyone else to present his arguments.'

'I suppose that led to friction between you? Being held back, I mean.'

His eyes became flinty. 'No. Fareed was an excellent lawyer and I learned a great deal from him.'

'Victor Salazar tells me that you frequently argued. It's his belief that Mazumdar was planning to dismiss you. My guess is that would have made it difficult for you to find another position. A young, inexperienced advocate, a white man, thrown out by a renowned Indian lawyer.'

His cheeks burned. 'Salazar's never liked me. He's had a chip on his shoulder since the day Fareed hired me.'

'Why?'

'Why do you think? I was never *Indian* enough for him.'

She shifted in her seat. 'Why did you stay? In India, that is. Why not go back to Britain and practise there?'

He gave her a defiant glare. 'Have you any idea how many times I've heard that? How can I go *back* to a place I've never been? I was born here, in Surat. My father was a Welshman who worked for the railways. I did my law degree in India, and qualified at the

Madras Bar. My father's retired now. Has a home in Pondicherry. He moved there after my mother passed.' He spoke in a sputter of sweat. 'My childhood was a happy one, Inspector. The upheavals of independence didn't affect us in the slightest, other than colour the average Indian's perception towards people like myself and my father – the "stayers-on", as I've heard us called. The truth is that I have no desire to live in a country I barely know. India is my home and if you want me to leave, you'll jolly well have to drag me out of here, kicking and screaming.'

His tone revealed a strength of feeling she hadn't anticipated. In many ways, his words mirrored those of James Whitby, sentiments she'd rarely heard expressed. It seemed a unique irony that the British, now vastly in the minority among the Indian multitude, had become voiceless in the very country where they'd once suppressed the voices of the native inhabitants.

'How did you feel when Mazumdar took on the Whitby case? Charles Whitby, I mean?'

'It was another case, no more, no less. The Indian government alleged that Whitby had ordered the death of a senior employee during the non-cooperation-movement years. It was our job to prove it in court.'

'Charles Whitby believes the case has been manufactured. A means of wresting his assets from him.'

'Not by our reckoning. We have – *had*, when the case was ours – a witness. If it had gone to court, I'm certain we would have won.'

She hesitated. If Price's confidence was not misplaced, it simply underlined James Whitby's motive in the murder of Fareed Mazumdar. If the Englishman genuinely thought Mazumdar would be able to convict his father, his emotions might easily have slipped out of control that fateful evening. Perhaps Mazumdar had even revealed his hand, setting out the strength of his evidence, convincing Whitby that he had to act.

'Where is the case now?'

'In hiatus. The Centre will, no doubt, find another firm to prosecute Whitby, but I believe they decided to postpone proceedings until after Fareed's case is settled.'

'You mean after James Whitby has been hanged.'

He didn't bother to reply.

'Did you feel a conflict of loyalty?'

He frowned. 'What do you mean?'

'Charles Whitby was British. As are you. Yet here you were, attempting to prosecute him on behalf of Indians.'

His brow darkened. 'I suppose you're one of those Indians who believes that the colour of my skin means that I cannot be trusted?' He thrust himself forward, elbows grinding into the tabletop. 'I don't have to justify myself to you. I do my job and I do it well. Race has never come into the reckoning. At least not for me.'

She weathered his glare, then said, 'I suppose you had to look into Charles Whitby's background quite thoroughly. Tell me about him.'

He pouted for a moment, like a sulky schoolboy, before responding: 'Whitby was the second son of a Nathaniel Whitby, a civil servant who came out here in the late 1800s. At some point, Nathaniel quit the Indian Civil Service to go into business for himself. He started with jute, then moved into cotton. Around the turn of the century, he became ill and was set to hand the business over to his eldest son, William, but fate intervened. William was killed while out hunting. Mauled to death by a tiger, if you can believe that.

'Charles inherited the business at the tender age of twenty. Everyone expected him to fail. He didn't. Instead, he expanded into sugar, coal mining, and iron production. He engineered an incredibly profitable concession in Rangoon. He had a sharp eye for a deal and was, by all accounts, utterly ruthless at the negotiating table – the sort who, if he'd been a soldier, would have enjoyed bayoneting the wounded.'

'Why was the case against Whitby being handled in Bombay? The murder he was accused of orchestrating occurred in Bengal.'

'Whitby's been in Bombay a long time. He moved here in 1922, though he often flies back to Calcutta for business. They tried to get him to go back and stand trial there, of course. Whitby refused. Claimed infirmity.' He gave a sharp laugh. 'It doesn't matter where he's tried. If the Centre wants you, they'll get you in the end.'

She reached into her pocket and took out the Star of David note. 'This was found on Mazumdar's body. Does it mean anything to you?'

Price looked at the note, then handed it back. 'No.'

'You had no Jewish clients?'

'None that I was aware of.'

'Salazar tells me that Mazumdar had been in touch with a journalist at the *Indian Chronicle* just before his death. Did he mention anything about that to you?'

'No.'

'I went to Mazumdar's apartment. It hasn't been touched since the police conducted a search of it just after his murder. I found this there.' She reached into her notebook and took out one of the cuttings she'd found in Mazumdar's wardrobe. 'He was sent several of these before his death, all pertaining to the same case, along with the Star of David. Did he ever mention these or this case?'

He examined the cutting, then shook his head. 'As I said, he rarely talked of his Calcutta days.'

She paused, then said, 'How was his demeanour in the days leading up to his killing?'

He considered the question. 'To be frank, he seemed agitated. I asked him what was bothering him, but he said it was nothing.' He hesitated. 'I'm not the kind to talk out of turn of the dead, but he was drinking. Heavily. It went on for months, to the point where it began to affect his judgement.'

'Is that one of the reasons you argued?'

He sent another sharp glance her way. 'Frankly, yes. He'd never been a big drinker, but in the weeks or so before he died, he was all over the place.'

She absorbed this, then: 'Can you think of anyone who might have wished him harm?'

He snorted. 'We're lawyers, Inspector. Enemies are an occupational hazard.'

'Anyone in particular?'

'As far as I can make out, the case against James Whitby is ironclad. But if you're serious about looking for alternative suspects . . . There was a case we took on a couple of months prior to Fareed's death. We defended a chief lieutenant of Youssef Sabri. Do you know who that is?'

She nodded. Sabri was a prominent member of the Bombay underworld.

'We lost the case, a rarity. At the last second, a key witness came forward that strengthened the prosecution's hand. Sabri blamed Fareed. He even threatened to kill him.'

She straightened in her chair. 'You heard this threat?'

'Yes. He stormed into the office and tore into Fareed.'

'What did Mazumdar say about it?'

'He told me it was just Sabri's way. The man was blowing off steam. Fareed was confident we'd remain his first port of call the next time he got into a scrape.'

'Did you tell the authorities about this after his murder?'

He pursed his lips. 'They never asked.'

She had the urge to shake him till his teeth rattled. Tact had always eluded her, but in the year since she'd arrived on the force, she was learning that it was sometimes better to bite one's tongue.

Of course, biting one's tongue was a lot harder than simply shouting at people.

'Doesn't it bother you that James Whitby might be innocent?'

He seemed taken aback. Reddening, he said: 'Doesn't it bother you that he might be guilty?'

They stared at each other, until, finally, she spoke. 'Were you in the office with Mazumdar that evening just before he left for home?'

'No. I was in court.'

'The high court isn't far from where he lived, is it? I mean, it wouldn't take long to walk from there to Mazumdar's home.'

He frowned. 'What are you implying?'

She swept up her cap and got to her feet. 'If I have further questions, I'll be in touch.'

14

Her next stop was the Institute of Science on Madame Cama Road where she'd scheduled an appointment with Professor Alok Shastri, the man Mazumdar had met with at his office on the day of his death, just prior to his appointment with James Whitby.

It had been years since she'd last set foot inside the Institute.

She recalled a lecture delivered by a visiting American economist back during her years at the University of Bombay, just a few hundred yards to the north. The American, a large, florid man who'd reminded her of a water buffalo, had confidently predicted the end of the Raj, claiming that it would soon become economically unviable for the British to continue in India. He'd underlined his analysis with a colourful remark that had stayed with her: 'Running a colonial enterprise is like raising an elephant. It's hard work, costs a fortune, and sooner or later the elephant craps on your head.'

The Institute had changed little. Another colonial-era building, funded by philanthropic donations following a call to arms by the then governor of Bombay, Lord Sydenham – amateur scientist and Fellow of the Royal Society, London – the Institute had received its own royal imprimatur following a visit by the king-emperor in 1912.

Shastri had asked her to meet him in the Cowasji Jehangir Hall.

As she walked through the botanical gardens set before the hall, she couldn't help but note the statues of various British luminaries that had graced the Institute over the years and how they contrasted with the dull smattering of Indians on display. Even in their statuary the British seemed to radiate an innate sense of their own destiny; it was a wonder the Indians didn't climb down off their plinths and offer to shine the marbled shoes of their erstwhile rulers.

Shastri turned out to be a tall, rake-thin man, balding and bespectacled, and dressed in the uniform of the absent-minded professor – a rumpled shirt with worn cuffs, a mismatched tie, a sweater, and a blazer that looked as if it had been stolen from a tramp. She wondered that the man hadn't broiled inside his outfit, but he seemed not to be bothered by the turgid heat.

Greeting her effusively, he led her through the cathedral-like hall and to an office on the Institute's second floor. The office appeared to have been struck by an earthquake; Shastri cleared a space on his cluttered desk by the simple expedient of sweeping a teetering pyramid of notebooks on to the floor. He ushered her into a chair and then threw himself into a seat on the far side of the desk. He seemed a bundle of nervous energy, as if he'd been struck by lightning and it had somehow become trapped inside him.

'A part of me is glad that you're reinvestigating the case,' he said. 'I've never really believed in an eye-for-an-eye. Then again, another part of me thinks that perhaps Fareed deserves his measure of justice.'

'Doesn't James Whitby deserve the same?'

'Yes, of course. Assuming that he's innocent.'

'How exactly did you know Mazumdar?'

'We met at the Radio Club. We were both members. I suppose the fact that we both grew up in Calcutta gave us something to talk about. Birds of a feather, so to speak.' He grinned, revealing a full set of white teeth.

74

'My understanding is that he was a very private man.'

'Yes. Fareed was as guarded in his own life as he was loquacious in court. But we found common ground. I think he was intrigued by my calling.'

'What exactly is it that you do?'

'I'm a theologian, Inspector.'

'You study religion?'

'There's a little more to it than that. Theology seeks to understand how we, as humans, *experience* faith. Religion impacts us profoundly, to the point that it can short-circuit all our other senses. Witness the horrors of Partition. Men who'd lived peaceably alongside one another for centuries driven to a murderous frenzy merely on the basis of their differing faiths. By understanding religion, I believe we can glimpse our hidden selves.'

'Is that what you and Fareed talked about on the day he died?'

'Among other things.' He smiled disarmingly. 'To be frank, Fareed *was* somewhat consumed by the subject. I believe that his experiences in Calcutta coloured his thinking about the place of religion in our modern, supposedly enlightened society. He became particularly engaged with the subject of evil, of sin and redemption.'

'How do you mean?'

'Well, it's the reason he left Calcutta.'

'I don't understand.'

Shastri bounced on his seat like an overexcited child. 'Fareed was in the city on Direct Action Day. He saw things that . . . Well, I'm sure you can imagine.'

Direct Action Day, 16 August 1946. The day of protest called for by Mohammed Ali Jinnah, future Prime Minister of Pakistan, one-time Congress Party comrade of Gandhi and Nehru, and agitator-in-chief for a separatist Muslim homeland. Jinnah's call had been heeded by Muslims across the nation. Fuelled by long-simmering communal tensions, the initially peaceful protests eventually sparked the powder keg of racial tension, unleashing murderous rioting in the city and, from there, across the country.

Calcutta had witnessed the worst of the slaughter, the old colonial capital registering some four thousand dead in the space of three days; men, women, and children hacked to death as Muslim, Sikh, and Hindu gangs roamed the streets unhindered, killing with gay abandon. The city's British overseers had chosen to observe the carnage safely from the sidelines like referees at a bad-tempered football match.

'It's my understanding that he didn't leave Calcutta until the end of that year. In fact, he tried a case linked to the rioting.' Slipping out her notebook, she handed him the newspaper cutting she'd discovered in Mazumdar's bedroom. 'Someone was sending articles about this case to Mazumdar just prior to his death. Do you know why?'

He scanned the article, then shook his head. 'I have no idea, Inspector. But I do know that this case had something to do with Fareed leaving Calcutta.'

'How so?'

'He mentioned it once. Obliquely. He won the case, but he appeared to be unhappy that he had done so. Can you imagine that? A lawyer dissatisfied with winning a case!' He almost clapped at the absurdity of it.

'He didn't say why?'

'I'm afraid not. It was one of those blind spots from his past that he refused to talk about. I learned not to pry. *Hic sunt dracones!*'

'Did he say anything about the individuals involved in the case?'

'Not that I can remember.'

She next showed him the Star of David note. 'He also received this.'

76

'The Star of David?' He pursed his mouth in confusion. 'I'm afraid I have no idea why someone would send this to him. He certainly wasn't thinking of converting to Judaism.'

She decided to tack in another direction. 'Did he mention anyone who might have wanted to harm him?'

'Not that I recall.'

'What was his demeanour that day? And in the days leading up to his killing?'

He scooted around on his seat again, as if he were trapped inside a bobsleigh hurtling downhill. 'Well, now that you mention it, he seemed troubled. I assumed it was the usual lawyer's travails. Fareed was committed to his chosen vocation, sometimes too committed for his own good.'

'I'm told that he'd begun drinking heavily in the months before his death.'

Shastri nodded. 'That's correct.'

'Did he mention anything specific, something that might have caused this change in behaviour?'

'No. I asked him, of course, several times, but he said he'd simply not been sleeping well, the stress of work, and so on. Alcohol helped him to sleep. In all honesty, I'd only arranged to meet with him because I was hoping to convince him to take a day off and go to Brabourne Stadium with me to watch the cricket. But he said he was too embroiled in the Whitby investigation. No time to blink, let alone recuse himself to enjoy a day of leisure.'

'Did he mention the case?'

'As a matter of fact, he did. He said he had Charles Whitby in his crosshairs; he told me nothing would give him greater pleasure than to "pull the trigger on Whitby in court". I remember it because it was out of character for Fareed. He was usually dispassionate about his cases, whether he was prosecuting or defending. But he seemed to have a genuine loathing for Charles Whitby.'

'Why?'

'Well, aside from the obvious – that Whitby appears to be the very paragon of everything that Fareed stood against: an arch colonialist, a white profiteer, a man of little or no moral worth – I suspect it was also because he'd known the man in Calcutta.'

She blinked. 'Are you saying that Mazumdar knew Charles Whitby *prior* to taking on the case against him?'

'Why, yes. Didn't you know? It's one of the reasons the Indian government chose him to prosecute the man.'

15

A heavy shower overtook her as she reached the station.

She watched a bedraggled eunuch lumber past the jeep, lifting up his sari as he splashed around a quivering pie dog. The dog looked about as wet and miserable as a goldfish in a toilet bowl.

She got out and sprinted towards Malabar House. The rain struck her from all sides, like a careless pickpocket being slapped by the many-handed mob in a crowded tram.

The station was deserted, blissfully silent, and then Birla and Haq, two of the station's three sub-inspectors, came rattling into the basement like a mariachi band.

Haq, a hulking, morose man who wouldn't have looked out of place playing Frankenstein's uglier understudy, lurched into his seat. She heard the rustle of a newspaper; the smell of just-fried samosas drifted across the room.

Saliva flooded her mouth. She hadn't eaten in hours.

'How's your mysterious case going?' said Birla, walking over to her desk.

He reached into his own twist of newspaper and crammed something into his mouth. Watching him eat, her stomach began to complain like a short-changed brothel madam.

'It's going well.'

Her eyes dropped to the newspaper in his hands.

'Would you like some? Your stomach is rumbling loud enough to bring down the roof.'

She rewarded his concern with an icy look. He shrugged. 'Suit yourself.' Turning on his heel, he went back to his desk, leaving a waft of fried spices and cheap cologne in his wake.

She took out her notebook and flipped through the pages, seeking to impose a sense of rudimentary order on the facts she'd uncovered, while they were still fresh in her mind.

Fareed Mazumdar had known Charles Whitby in Calcutta. Mazumdar's theologian friend, Shastri, had given her the basic details of that acquaintance, but she would need to speak with James Whitby to confirm that information. If Shastri had told her the truth, then it cast Whitby's conviction in a whole new light.

In 1922, Charles Whitby – together with his son – had moved to Bombay.

In August 1946, Mazumdar, now a prominent lawyer, had still been in Calcutta and had witnessed, first-hand, the Direct Action Day riots. Later that year, he'd defended a man accused of using the rioting as cover to commit murder. According to Shastri, something about that case had driven Mazumdar from Calcutta to Bombay.

And in 1949, just over two years after Mazumdar had arrived in Bombay, the Indian government had decided to prosecute Charles Whitby for ordering the murder of an independence agitator at one of his factories back in 1921.

They'd chosen Mazumdar to head up the prosecution.

Whitby's son, James, had tried to convince Mazumdar of his father's innocence. He'd ended up being convicted of Mazumdar's murder.

Prior to Mazumdar's death, someone had been sending him press cuttings of the 1946 trial that had driven him from Calcutta, as well as a note marked with a Star of David. Why? What possible connection could that trial have to Mazumdar's murder?

Perhaps there *was* no connection.

She picked up the telephone and asked the receptionist to place a call to the *Indian Chronicle*. Moments later, she was connected to Aalam Channa.

'Inspector, to what do I owe the pleasure?'

The man's enthusiastic greeting momentarily derailed her. After their last encounter, she'd expected hostility; she'd forgotten that Channa was shameless enough to embarrass a colony of nudists.

'Just before he died Fareed Mazumdar was in touch with you. I want to know why?'

A textured silence drifted down the phone. She could hear the gears moving inside the journalist's head. 'So would I, Inspector. Mazumdar left a message stating that he had a story for me. I was unable to get back to him for several days. And then he was murdered.' He paused. 'Why are you interested?'

She put down the phone.

Sitting back, she listened to the fan clicking above her.

She realised that she was in danger of drowning beneath an avalanche of information.

Her task was to determine whether James Whitby had killed Fareed Mazumdar, not to lose her way down rabbit holes.

She opened her notebook to a clean sheet and condensed the thrust of her investigative efforts into several simple questions:

Who was the shadowy figure James Whitby saw in the car park just before he discovered the body of Fareed Mazumdar?

Who sent Mazumdar the press cuttings and the Star of David note?

Why was Mazumdar unhappy about the Calcutta case mentioned in the press cuttings, despite winning?

She paused, examined what she'd written, then added:

Was Charles Whitby guilty of ordering the murder of an Indian activist back in 1921?

Who else had a motive to harm Mazumdar?

This last question lingered in her mind.

Her thoughts looped back to the meeting with Mazumdar's former junior counsel, Owain Price. The Welshman had stated that the gangster Youssef Sabri had threatened Mazumdar following the loss of the trial of one of his key henchmen. Sabri was the kind of man who took things personally. He could easily have sent a trained killer to vent his displeasure – perhaps the figure that Whitby had seen in the car park?

Excitement quickened inside her.

She knew that what she had was razor-thin – there was only James Whitby's testimony that the shadowy figure he claimed to have seen was even real. But if the Englishman *had* been telling the truth, then, coupled with Price's account, she now had a credible alternative suspect for Mazumdar's killing.

The question was: what did she do next?

Given the semi-clandestine nature of her investigation, she could hardly demand a full-scale police assault on Sabri, hauling the man in for an interrogation. Nor could she simply send along an intermediary to question the mafioso on her behalf.

All of which meant that she would have to tackle the matter in a more direct manner.

16

Organised crime in Bombay enjoyed a reputation somewhere between notoriety and quaintness.

The general consensus was that it was neither particularly organised nor so criminal that the authorities were ever prompted into actually tackling the various gangs carving up the city between them, and who now existed in a sort of unhappy peace, like daughters-in-law forced to live under the same roof. Indeed, in the eyes of many, the most organised criminal enterprise in Bombay *was* the police force.

Gangsters might routinely push each other into the harbour with chains tied around their ankles, but at least they tended to leave the average citizen alone, which was more than could be said for Bombay's policewallahs, many of whom could have comfortably made it onto the country's Most Wanted list.

Persis knew that Youssef Sabri maintained offices in the midtown Mazgaon district, on Gunpowder Road, near the pier.

She parked directly in front of the office, a rundown, warehouse-like building with a billboard above the door and another on the roof that made it look as if it had just committed a crime and was trying to hide behind a moustache and a hat.

A pair of foot-soldiers stirred like big cats spotting an overcurious gazelle. They were pale-skinned, from Bombay's Afghan Pashtun community, tall and broad-shouldered; shaved apes in safari suits. Their matching attire gave them the look of store clerks, though she doubted most store clerks were capable of snapping a man's arm in two as Sabri's lieutenants were wont to do, usually when they were bored.

'I'm looking for Sabri.'

One of the brutes, a toothpick sticking out of the side of his mouth, said, 'He's not here.'

'Where can I find him?'

The man exchanged a glance with his colleague. This was the sort of question that classified as higher-level thinking in the Bombay underworld.

'I have information for him.'

The Pathan's eyes brightened. *This*, he understood.

Corrupting police officers was Sabri's stock in trade.

'He's in Chinatown.'

The Mazgaon district had been home to a vibrant Chinese community for decades, many of whom had been transplanted from Canton to Bombay by the East India Company, in a bid, some said, to shame the local labour force into making more of an effort. The Indians were considered lazy, incompetent, uppity, and prone to sitting around drinking chai and chatting about the state of national politics or the fecundity of cows, when they should have been getting on with the underpaid and back-breaking jobs assigned to them.

The Chinese, on the other hand, had proved themselves in the Opium Wars, with a monomaniacal tenacity that impressed even the most demanding British overseer.

Shoemakers, tailors, carpenters, hawkers, opium den madams: the Chinese had added another dimension to the city's ever-evolving mosaic, and now crowded the warren-like streets around the Mazgaon railway station.

She walked the short distance from Sabri's headquarters to the Kwan Kung temple on Nawab Tank Road, a two-storey building fronted by a door painted in peeling red and gold.

A whiskery Chinese methuselah lay comatose in front of the door like the world's ugliest welcome mat.

She stepped over him and into an empty vestibule, then began to climb a flight of stairs in the corner.

She arrived in an altar room, a tiny, incense-filled space, adorned with wind chimes and paper lanterns, with a hulking statue of what looked like a Chinese soldier.

The sound of chanting floated in from an open window.

Padding over to it, she saw that the temple overlooked a cemetery. A group of people, mainly Chinese, moved as one body around the plot, their voices carried up by a sultry breeze.

Footsteps behind her.

She began to turn, but before she could complete the movement, something thudded into the side of her head.

She fell, reaching awkwardly for her revolver, struck the back of her head against the windowsill, and whirled into blackness.

When she came to, she was lying on a small cot, her hands trussed behind her.

A man in a fine white suit and tie, with blazing white shoes to match, was sitting in a chair and regarding her with a steady gaze. He had a thick head of dark hair, slicked back over a gleaming forehead, and a slim moustache. A cigarette was held in a manicured hand.

Youssef Sabri.

She struggled upright, attempted to get to her feet, felt a rush of blood at her temples, and fell back again, collapsing heavily against the wall.

'Careful, Inspector. You've had a nasty blow to the head.'

'Untie me,' Persis ground out. 'Detaining an officer of the law is a criminal offence.'

'My men merely tied you up for your own protection,' said Sabri calmly. 'They didn't want you to wake up and do something rash. There's a price on my head. It's not beyond the bounds of possibility that a member of our sterling police community might attempt to collect the bounty.'

'If I wanted to kill you, you'd be dead already.'

He smiled disarmingly, then waved his cigarette at a hulking flunky. The man stepped forward, blotting out the light. Pulling a butterfly knife from his pocket, he snapped it open and leered at her.

She yelped as the brute lunged at her, took her roughly by the arm, swept her around, and cut the cord binding her wrists, all in one practised movement.

She turned back to Sabri, eyeing the man warily.

'Would you care to join me for lunch?' he said.

They ended up in a small but lavishly decorated Chinese restaurant a hundred yards from the temple. A birdlike woman, barely tall enough to make it to Persis's shoulder, harangued a staff of waiters like a general ordering men around a battlefield.

'Did you know that today is a special day in the Chinese calendar?' Sabri remarked. 'A day for visiting graves and paying respect to one's ancestors.'

'Is that what you were doing?' Her scepticism dripped on to the red tablecloth.

He smiled broadly, revealing the perfect white teeth of a racehorse. 'I am a river to my people, Inspector.'

'You're nothing but a common criminal.'

'I'm a businessman, no more, no less.'

'Smuggling. Gunrunning. Racketeering. Extortion. You have an intriguing sense of commerce.'

The corners of his lips turned downwards. 'Why did you come looking for me?'

She hesitated, then plunged. 'In September of last year, the lawyer Fareed Mazumdar was murdered. A month prior to his death, you were witnessed threatening to kill him.'

He held her with liquid eyes. 'I believe the Englishman James Whitby is due to be executed for that particular crime. Are you suggesting that I somehow helped him?'

'Not helped.'

He smiled with all the warmth of a crocodile grinning at a wildebeest. 'I had nothing to do with Mazumdar's death.'

'But you *did* threaten him?'

'I am a passionate man. Occasionally, I express myself in ... regrettable ways. But Mazumdar was in no danger from me.'

'You were disappointed in the way he handled your lieutenant's trial,' she persisted. 'He lost the case and your second-in-command was sent to prison. *That* cost you a great deal of money.'

'Take a walk around Mazgaon, Inspector. You'll soon find out how I spend my money. As for my lieutenant ... Yes, I was upset by his incarceration. But not because of any financial loss. It's because he is my friend.'

She sensed the sincerity behind his words. Could she believe him? 'How well did you know Mazumdar?'

'He arrived in Bombay with a reputation for defending those the government sought to defame. When my lieutenant, as you call him, found himself in trouble, I called upon Mazumdar.'

'But he failed you.'

He picked up a gold demitasse spoon, tapped it gently on the table. 'I dislike lawyers, Inspector. When I was a boy my father ran a bicycle repair shop, right here in Mazgaon. One day he fell afoul of a local politician who wanted to move him out so that he could build a tenement on the land. My father refused. The politician tried everything: threats, blackmail, police beatings. But my father was an honest man. A man of integrity. And so, in the end, they used the law against him. They dragged him into court and drained him to the point that he had no choice but to sign away his livelihood. A week later he jumped into the Mazgaon dock and killed himself.' His features hardened, and, for an instant, she saw the killer behind the mask. 'Honest lawyers, honest policemen, honest politicians . . . I suppose they must exist, but I've personally never had the pleasure.'

A phalanx of waiters descended on the table, leaving behind enough dishes to feed a small army. Persis realised that she still hadn't eaten anything since the morning; hunger was hammering at her insides like the seven dwarves inside a cave lined with gold ore.

'You're not going to make me eat alone?' In the darkened restaurant, he seemed to loom larger than life. Against her better instincts, she found herself admiring his fine features, his obvious charm, his sense of the debonair.

She scraped back her chair. 'I have to go.'

He looked genuinely disappointed. 'A shame. I hope we can meet again soon, under different circumstances.'

'I can't imagine the circumstances that would force me to willingly seek out a criminal. Other than to arrest you, of course. I'm still not convinced that you played no part in Mazumdar's death.'

'Don't expect me to weep for a dead lawyer, Inspector. The fact is, I've never killed a man who didn't deserve it.' He locked eyes with her. 'You've killed too, haven't you?'

She stiffened. 'That was different.'

'You eliminated those who needed to be eliminated. If you hadn't, you might not be standing here today. It's no different in my line of work.'

17

She stopped at a roadside eatery and ate a late lunch. Meat soup, though the meat was largely a matter of hoping for the best.

Her thoughts roamed back over the encounter with Sabri. The confrontation felt like a wasted effort. She'd learned nothing new. Sabri's denial had to be taken with a pinch of salt.

And yet . . . she couldn't shake the feeling that he'd been telling the truth.

And if that was the case, it meant that she was back to square one.

With the Sabri thread seemingly at a dead end, she returned to the other elements of the case that had raised unanswered questions.

By the time she'd finished eating, she'd decided to redirect her efforts to the mysterious Star of David note found in Fareed Mazumdar's pocket. She felt sure that the person who'd sent it to him – and, presumably, sent the cuttings about the old case in Calcutta – had done so for a reason that wasn't to Mazumdar's benefit. If so, then there was a good chance they might have had something to do with the man's death.

With no Jewish friends to call upon, she trawled her memory. Her knowledge of Bombay's Jewish community was limited to the institutions left behind by the legendary Sassoon family, a legacy that encompassed the Sassoon docks, libraries, innumerable buildings dotted around the city, and a host of philanthropic endeavours.

Her thoughts eventually alighted on a visit, in the company of her mother, to the 'oldest synagogue in Bombay' – the Gate of Mercy synagogue, just ten minutes south of Mazgaon.

It seemed as good a place as any to start.

It took her a while to find Samuel Street.

She parked the jeep at the top of the narrow avenue, then continued on foot, walking past a tea stall, an open-air barber's, and a sewing machine repair shop. A man with a fly swatter waved flies from what looked like rectangular blocks of excrement, but which, on closer inspection, turned out to be slabs of tamarind, dark as tar.

The sun had scorched the last wisps of vapour from the sky. The heat clung to her like a lovesick octopus.

Asking directions, she found her way to a decrepit-looking building tightly wedged between two equally careworn edifices, like a drunk being held up by friends in a bar. The synagogue's exterior was painted in yellow and blue, the paint faded and cracked. The doors – prominently marked with twin Stars of David – were flung open, but there seemed little sign of life within.

She stepped over the threshold, passed through a small ante-room, and entered a spacious inner chamber. The walls were a pale, frosty blue. She laid a hand on the nearest wall; it seemed to perspire beneath her fingers with the cooled-sweat feeling of a desert cave. Weak light entered from shuttered windows, picking out wooden benches and old-fashioned lamps suspended from a high ceiling.

As she stood there, the sounds of the street faded away. Dust motes seemed to gather in the light and dance, like the murmuration of birds. A vivid sense of deceleration overcame her. She was transported into the past, her mother's shade hovering at her shoulder, whispering into her ear: *Sometimes faith is all it takes, Persis. Just a little faith.*

Religion on the subcontinent had always seemed a combustible enterprise to her.

Growing up in a small but influential Parsee community, Persis had once naïvely imagined India to be a sort of democratic religious marketplace, where vendors of all feathers shouted out the merits of their wares, and those with the loudest voices or the most beguiling message garnered the most adherents. Everyone was essentially free to choose. A happy fraternity of the willingly deluded.

The Partition riots had shattered that illusion.

At the very moment of India's independence, as she'd listened to Nehru articulate the nation's secular ideals, her thoughts had turned to the reality of the past years, a reality that had put the lie to his words even as they were uttered. Something had been unleashed that couldn't be put back, a sense of animal hunger that could only be satiated by the devouring of the *other*.

And yet, the power of faith persisted. You couldn't throw a stick five feet without hitting a swami, sadhu, saint, mullah, pandit or fakir. In other countries, religion was relegated to the margins, evoked only at funerals, christenings, or in dimly remembered prayers when life's bicycle ran headlong into the eighteen-wheeler truck of fate. Those who openly displayed their religious tendencies were considered mad, stupid, deluded or naïve.

In India, symbols endured. From the calcified remains of Christian saints, to the soaring architecture of Muslim conquerors, to innumerable Hindu pilgrimage sites dotted around the place, to the rumours that Jesus had once walked the mountains of Kashmir – presumably in something more than a sackcloth robe – religion had left behind stories that twisted and flapped through the populace, attaching themselves to susceptible minds.

She'd tried to find the meaning that sometimes took up residence within such systems, but all she saw was half-formed truths, used by men – and it was *always* men – to incite a belief so dense it refused to allow doubt.

Her father had once told her that a man without doubt was a danger to himself and to others.

As with most things, Sam had been proved right.

The spell was broken by the sight of a man shuffling into the room from a door at the rear. He spotted her and stopped, taking in her uniform, and the saddlebags of sweat under her arms.

She felt acutely self-conscious beneath his gaze.

He was elderly – ancient to her eyes – dressed conservatively in a white shirt and dark trousers, his hair, what remained of it, as white as the down of a goose, and scraped back over a skull that curved upwards like the dome of a mosque. His eyes were a crystal blue, the colour of icy mountain lakes; they looked out from a burnished face, glowing like miniature lanterns.

She introduced herself, and the reason for her visit. 'I was hoping someone could help me understand a little more about Bombay's Jewish community, and how Fareed Mazumdar might have been linked to it. Are you the rabbi here?'

The man shuffled forward. 'My name is Benjamin Samson. I am the hazan – the priest here. There are no rabbis in India, though occasionally we are visited by rabbis from America and, more recently, Israel. Come.' He led her to one of the wooden benches. Lowering himself on to the polished wood, marked by the faint graffiti of ancient scratch marks, he faced her. 'What would you like to know?'

She hesitated. 'Anything you can tell me. I'm afraid I have no idea what I'm looking for, and my knowledge of Judaism in Bombay is limited.'

He grimaced. 'That doesn't surprise me. In a nation of three hundred million, we are but drops in the ocean. Even when I teach the history of Indian Judaism to young Jews, they find it difficult to find any passion in such a meagre tradition. Perhaps that's why so many have moved to Israel now. How can I possibly compete with the promise of the Promised Land?' The question was uttered with a soft exhalation of bitterness. 'The Jews have been on the subcontinent for two thousand years. The first wave, the Ashkenazis, came to Cochin, in the south, fleeing persecution in Judea. Centuries later, another group was shipwrecked off the Konkan coast, just south of Bombay. They are the Bene Israel, Jews that took on local customs and integrated with the society they found themselves in, a society of Muslims, Hindus, Sikhs, and Christians. In the nineteenth century, a third wave of Jews arrived from Iraq – the Baghdadi Jews. They were traders and merchants, many of whom became fabulously wealthy.'

'David Sassoon was a Baghdadi Jew, wasn't he?'

'That's right. He was once the treasurer of Baghdad, and worked closely with British merchants in India. His success encouraged other Iraqi Jews to migrate here. Traditionally, the Baghdadis and the Bene Israel have never gotten along. The Baghdadis look down on us as not quite Jewish enough. We're too native for their liking, despite the fact that Bene Israel means "children of Israel".'

Phlegm rattled in his throat. She sensed a quiet anguish; not anger, but a sense of opportunity squandered. Clearly, even within the Jewish community, factionalism was a source of tension.

'Mazumdar was a Muslim. How would you describe the relations between Jews and Muslims here?'

'Until a few years ago, I would have told you there had never been a problem. We respected their faith and they respected ours. The fact is that we both hail from the same fountainhead, two rivers springing from the same source. Our prophets are their prophets and vice versa. It's only a minor difference in interpretation that makes me a Jew and Mazumdar a Muslim. Consider this.' He waved at their surroundings. 'This synagogue would never have been built but for a Muslim. During the Anglo-Mysore Wars, the Mohammedan king Tipu Sultan captured several East India Company officers. Among them was a commander named Samuel Divekar. When asked his religion, Divekar replied that he was a Bene Israel Jew. Under normal circumstances, Sultan would have put Divekar to death – not because he was a Jew, but because he fought for the East India Company. But Sultan's mother overheard the remark – she immediately expressed her pleasure, telling her son that the Bene Israel tribe was mentioned in the Quran, which spoke well of the Israelites. She convinced Sultan to spare Divekar's life, and when he returned to Bombay, he built this temple in gratitude to God.'

He stopped, and she was forced to prompt him to continue. 'And now?'

'Now, I'm no longer certain. With tensions in Israel between Muslims and Jews in the news, it has prompted debate and disagreement. But I am no expert in such matters. My concern is the upkeep of this place and the traditions that I have known all my life. Once there were forty thousand Jews in Bombay. Now, with so many making aliyah, there are barely a tenth that number. Yom Kippur and Rosh Hashana are no longer the festivals they once were.'

Persis reached into her pocket and handed him the Star of David note. He opened it with withered hands, his ghostly eyes taking in the symbol. 'Yes. That is the Magen David – the Shield of David. It has been a symbol of the collective Jewish identity since at least the seventeenth century, though the Seal of Solomon from which it is derived is much older.'

'The Seal of Solomon?'

'Yes. The original seal attributed to the signet ring of King Solomon, builder of the First Temple in Jerusalem. In the traditions of Jewish mysticism, some believe that the ring was given to Solomon by the archangel Michael, engraved by Yahweh, and imbued with the power to summon supernatural forces, forces that subsequently helped Solomon build his temple.'

'Can you think of any reason why someone would send this to Mazumdar?'

He shrugged. 'Solomon is one of the forty-eight prophets of Judaism, son of the legendary David. Muslims too recognise him as a prophet. They call him Sulaimān ibn Dāwūd – Solomon, son of David.'

With nothing to anchor it to, the information was useless to her.

He seemed to sense her frustration. 'I'm sorry I cannot be of more assistance. But you say this man was a lawyer? Perhaps I can direct you to an acquaintance? Someone who may have crossed paths with him. A fellow lawyer. He may be better placed to shed light on any possible connection between Mazumdar and this note.'

18

The cadaverous jailor was in a good mood.

She followed the man as he whistled his way into the depths of the prison, jauntily turning into corners, ignoring the curses and various personal attacks impugning his mother's virtue drifting from the cells.

She found James Whitby crouched over his table applying glue with a spatula to a balsa wood aeroplane.

'What do you think?' he said, as she entered the room. 'It's a Tiger Moth.'

'I need to ask you some more questions.'

He leaned back in his seat. 'You know the most difficult thing about these last few days? Time seems to have slowed down. I try and distract myself, but the truth is, anything I do is akin to a man trying to avoid the avalanche bearing down on him by turning his back to it.'

'You lied to me.'

He crossed his arms, frowning. 'Explain.'

Before she did so, she first took him through everything she'd discovered, the meetings with Owain Price and Youssef Sabri, chasing down the possibility that Sabri might have had Mazumdar killed, the notion that Price too had held a grudge against his former employer.

Whitby's eyes quickened. 'Do you think there's a chance either of them could have done it?'

'I have no evidence to support such a theory.'

'But there's a possibility?'

She felt the heat of his desperation. The temptation to offer him hope was overwhelming. 'Without concrete proof, I can't connect either of them to the killing. I'm sorry.'

He deflated, the sudden gust of optimism leaking away like air from a punctured tyre.

'It would help if you could remember anything more about the man you saw in the car park.'

'That's always been the problem. It was dark. The lights had been smashed. All I saw was a tallish figure in the shadows, dressed in black, with a hat pulled down low over his head. I think he was wearing gloves too.'

'Did you get a look at his face?'

'No. He had his back to me.'

She paused, then: 'Your fingerprints were found on the murder weapon.'

He blinked. 'Yes. When I fell over the body, I reached out. My hand found the knife. I pulled it out of him. It was an instinctive reaction. I didn't know what I was doing.'

She waited a moment, evaluating his steady gaze, then changed tack. Taking out her notebook, she handed him the cutting she'd found in Mazumdar's house, along with the Star of David note. 'Someone was sending cuttings of this case to Mazumdar before he died. According to those who knew him, he was agitated in the weeks leading up to his killing.'

He seemed bemused. 'I have no idea what these mean. What has this got to do with me?'

'Mazumdar's friend Shastri told me that this case was the reason Mazumdar left Calcutta. Something about it didn't sit well with him. Perhaps someone was reminding him of whatever that was. Someone who didn't like Mazumdar very much.'

He saw where she was headed. 'Another potential suspect?'

'Possibly.' She stopped and looked directly into his eyes. 'He told me something else. He told me that your father *knew* Mazumdar, back in Calcutta.'

He froze. Silence spread around the narrow cell, thick and choking. Finally, he spoke. 'Yes. We knew him.'

'Why didn't you tell me?'

'It didn't seem important. It's not relevant to my case.'

She bit down on her tongue. 'Shastri gave me the basic details. But I'd like to hear it from you.'

'Fareed's father worked for us. His name was Shabaz. Shabaz Mazumdar. He was one of my father's key aides, a man he employed to liaise with his workforces up and down the country. Shabaz was educated in England. He was an incredibly competent man. My father used to joke that if he painted Shabaz white, he could practically pass for an Englishman. I never understood how insulting that must have been for him until much later.'

'And Fareed?'

'Fareed and I knew each other as boys – we were the same age. His mother had died during childbirth and his father hadn't remarried. Shabaz was around our house so often that Fareed and I became friends. Of a sort.'

'Your house in Calcutta?'

'Yes. My father has residences in all the major cities and spent a lot of time away from home. It was usually just me and my mother at home. Until she left us.'

'Why did she leave?'

His gaze flickered. 'My father says she was flighty, always hankering for more. He says she ran away to America to pursue a career in music.'

'But you don't believe him?'

'I think she left us because she finally realised the truth about him. About the sort of man he was.' There was a note of sadness in his voice that gave Persis pause. 'The funny thing is, I think he actually loved her. Possibly the only thing he ever did love. He was never a sentimental man – or at least, he never allowed sentiment to rule his actions. But my mother leaving him sent him into a paroxysm of emotion. For the first time, I saw him less than sure of himself. I genuinely believe he would have gone after her if his pride hadn't stood in the way; a day after she left, he planted a tree for her in the gardens of our home in Calcutta. A pomegranate tree – it was her favourite fruit, you see. The tree was the gesture of a romantic fool, grasping at what he'd allowed to slip through his fingers. I sometimes wonder how differently my life might have turned out if he *had* gone after her, pleaded with her to return, begged for her forgiveness. Then again, I doubt my mother could have been persuaded to walk back into hell.'

'And *you* never sought to find her? Later?'

'Why would I? She abandoned me to my father. Oh, I think about her sometimes. I know she's out there, somewhere. I imagine she has a new family; perhaps I have half-siblings. I have no wish to know them; I have no wish to see her again.'

She sensed the brittle nature of his words; they rang hollow to her ears. 'Did you get to know Fareed well during that time?'

'As I said, we met occasionally. Until the age of seven.'

'What happened then?'

He paused, his gaze drifting back into the past. 'Fareed's father was murdered. He'd just become the chief staff officer at our plant in Barrackpore. He's the man whose death my father has been accused of orchestrating.'

19

Bombay, 1950 – James Whitby

Do you believe in monsters?

It was a question I put to Arora soon after my father first hired him. He looked at me quizzically, not quite understanding what I meant.

When we are young, we're presented with dark creatures from the forests of our imagination – ogres and trolls, krakens and gorgons, werewolves and vampires; it's only as we grow older that we understand that the only real monsters are the ones we carry inside us.

My father was a tyrant. A man who viewed the world in a particular way, through the lens of his own arrogance and the heady mist of his relentless ambition. Some men pass through life with little understanding of where they wish to go; they stumble along, buffeted by circumstance and the whims of fate, forever at the mercy of their own weaknesses. But my father was never like that.

He knew exactly what he wanted and stopped at nothing to get it.

'Does he ever mention my mother?'

Arora took off his spectacles and wiped them with a handkerchief. 'No.'

'My mother's name was Mary. Mary Elphinstone. She was blonde, hazel-eyed, and as beautiful as a summer's day in the Alps.

She loved chamber music – she was classically trained, a coloratura soprano. She met my father at a function put on by the Grand Opera House in Calcutta. I don't think she came out to find a husband, but she was one of those Englishwomen who romanticised the subcontinent. Something about my father must have appealed to her. He wasn't traditionally handsome, but he was rugged, wealthy, and had the air of an adventurer about him. He needed a wife and she fit the bill.

'I have no idea how soon after they were married she realised her mistake, but it couldn't have been long. I remember as a young child witnessing her unhappiness. She'd sit at the piano, our home a mausoleum to their marriage, and play, but it was as if she was expressing her sadness in the form of music. Later, I would think of her as an exotic bird, trapped in a gilded cage. The caged bird might sing, but sooner or later it loses the will to live.'

'Perhaps they were simply badly matched?'

I smiled grimly. 'Let me tell you about my father. One day – I must have been about five – I discovered a stray dog, barely older than a pup, in the gardens of our Calcutta home. I have no idea how the poor beast got in, but it was clearly injured. I took it to my mother and together we tended to it. I asked my mother if I could keep the animal. She agreed, but impressed upon me that I, and I alone, must take responsibility for its well-being. She thought it would be a valuable learning experience for me. My father was away, in the Punjab. He'd been having problems up there with the local labour; terrorists had burned down one of his factories.

'I named the dog Odysseus; I spent every waking moment with him.

'When my father returned, the dog bounded out to greet him. He was the friendliest creature you could possibly imagine. My father recoiled, then asked me what the dog was doing in our home. I explained. He stared at me for the longest moment, then went inside. When he came back, he was carrying his hunting rifle. He killed the dog in front of me.

'He told me that the dog was a native. It would eventually turn on me, like the rest of the damned country. He wouldn't allow a dog like that, a stray, to live under his roof.'

Arora seemed momentarily shocked.

'That's my father. In some ways, I don't blame my mother for leaving us.'

'Even though she was willing to leave you behind?' His tone was mildly critical.

'I suppose she convinced herself that she had no choice. My father would have tracked her to the ends of the earth if she'd taken me with her. In the end, she just left. I remember it vividly. It was a few days after news reached us that Fareed's father had been murdered up in Barrackpore. My mother had heard a rumour that my father had been behind the killing. I heard them arguing. He denied it vehemently. I guess she didn't believe him. Or maybe it was the excuse she'd been waiting for.' I paused. 'The next day she was gone, her wardrobe cleaned out, her suitcases vanished. I found my father in his study. He'd been drinking heavily. "She's left us," he said. "It's just you and me now."'

At first, Arora didn't know what to say. For a lawyer, I suppose that's a rare occurrence.

Eventually, he rose to his feet, brushing imaginary dust from his trousers.

'I don't know if your father ordered the death of Shabaz Mazumdar or not. He denies it. As his lawyer I must take him at his word, just as I take you at your word that you didn't kill Fareed Mazumdar. What I do know for certain is this: you are a good man. Unfortunately, good men don't always get the fate they deserve.'

20

The promenade in front of the Whitby mansion was frenetic with activity. A film shoot was in progress and she was forced to park further along the road.

Walking up, Persis saw an overweight leading man with a handlebar moustache dancing around a rickshaw parked in the middle of the road, a slender, sari-clad young woman smiling demurely at him as she leaned out of the rear. The rickshaw driver, a rat-faced fellow with a mouthful of improbably white teeth looked on, tapping his feet in time to the music floating over the set.

She saw that traffic had built up on either side of the shoot. In other countries, she supposed this might have been cause for irritation. In the city of dreams, it was merely an excuse for a small crowd to gather, drivers getting out of their cars to gawk at the spectacle.

As she approached, the leading man suddenly yelped, grabbed his haunches, then pirouetted smartly to glare at a grinning urchin standing by the side of the road. The urchin waved a catapult at him, then scampered off down the street, the leading man in hot pursuit.

The director rose from his seat, bellowing at his crew. The heroine cursed, pulled a packet of cigarettes from her sari, lit one, and began to smoke.

Persis was led through the mansion by the turbaned houseboy who'd greeted her on her previous visit.

As she entered Charles Whitby's office, Whitby's hound leaped up from his rug and bounded towards her, a slobbering, carnivorous mass on four legs.

She recoiled instinctively, but a bark from Whitby, seated behind his desk, brought the dog to heel.

The beast stared at her, disappointment evident in its eyes, then lolloped back to its spot.

She saw that James Whitby's lawyer, Arora, was standing by the desk, in a pale suit with a bow tie. Herons flapped across the front of a colourful waistcoat.

It was Arora who'd called her that morning to tell her that Charles Whitby wished her to visit with him.

'Well, Inspector? What have you found out?' The Englishman seemed agitated.

Ignoring his brusqueness, she launched into a brief summation of her efforts.

'I've heard of Sabri,' growled Whitby, when she'd finished. 'The man's a rogue.'

'But you have nothing tangible to tie him to Mazumdar's killing?' Arora looked at her with his hands in his pockets.

'No.'

'In the old days, we'd have hauled him in and beaten him black and blue until he confessed.' Whitby's voice boomed around the room.

'I've come across this lawyer you mentioned, Mazumdar's junior, Owain Price,' said Arora. 'An intense young man.'

'If Mazumdar really was about to dismiss him, then it gives Price a motive,' she said. 'But I find it difficult to believe that that motive would incite one lawyer to murder another.'

A silence settled on the room; the only sound was of the slobbering hound.

'Why didn't you tell me that you knew Mazumdar from his Calcutta days?' she said, directing herself to Whitby.

'I didn't *know* him,' the old man replied. 'I knew his father. Fareed was just a child. I barely registered his presence.'

'His father was the man whose murder you're now accused of orchestrating.'

He thumped the table, startling her. 'Damnable lies!' The hound raised its head and looked quizzically at its master. 'Nehru and his cronies have the scent of blood in their nostrils. They think they have a tiger in their sights and they'll stop at nothing to bring me down.'

'So you deny killing Mazumdar's father?'

He incinerated her with his eyes.

'Why wasn't it front-page news that Fareed Mazumdar was the son of the victim in the case he was pursuing against you?'

'Because neither he nor the government wanted the obvious conclusion to be drawn. Namely, that this is a malicious prosecution.'

She watched him seethe at the perceived injustices that India had inflicted upon him. Could he be so blind to the irony?

'Did you speak with my son?'

The question caught her off guard. 'Yes.'

She expected him to ask after James, but he said nothing. 'Don't you want to know how he was?'

He said nothing for a moment, then: 'In our Calcutta home, there's a German grandfather clock. I won it in a game of chance as a young man, from a business rival. I spent many hours in that house listening to the ticking of that clock. It tolls in my mind now as I count down the hours to James's death.' He opened his eyes. 'You must work faster, Inspector. Find something, anything. Save my son.'

Arora accompanied her out of the house. They stopped by the fountain. The pitted marble of the Hypatia statue seemed to glow in the sunlight.

'What will you do next?'

'I want to chase down the link to the press cuttings Mazumdar was sent before his death. I suspect I may have to go to Calcutta to do so.'

'Do you really believe they have something to do with his murder?'

'I don't know. But there's a reason someone was sending them to him. I want to know that reason.'

He rubbed his chin. 'Very well. Mr Whitby has a private aeroplane. His aide can arrange a flight as and when you require it.'

A momentary silence. 'He's a difficult man to like,' she remarked.

'No more so than many Indians I've worked with.'

'You're dogged in his defence.'

He shrugged. 'He's right about one thing – if he wasn't who he was, if he wasn't a white man, an Englishman, our government would not have bothered to prosecute him for Shabaz Mazumdar's murder. They have very little evidence. A single supposed eyewitness, from nearly three decades ago.'

'One is all it takes.' A thought occurred to her. 'I'd like to talk to him. This witness.'

He hesitated, evaluating the request. 'It's a her. And she lives in Calcutta. She's the Whitbys' former housemaid. I will send you her details.'

She turned to look directly at him. 'Do you really think James is innocent?'

'Yes.'

'You'd stake your reputation on it?'

He smiled gently. 'You're not alone, Inspector.'

She frowned. 'I don't understand.'

'There are few in India who would deny our right to feel aggrieved at men like the Whitbys.'

'I don't feel aggrieved. I just don't think they should be allowed to escape justice because they're white. We beat them fair and square. They have to live by our rules now.'

'*Our* rules?' He raised an eyebrow. 'The irony in all of this is that it was the British who introduced the rule of law here. Their mistake was in placing themselves *above* those same laws. You see, we Indians don't mind a little bit of degeneracy – after all, our nawabs and maharajahs practically invented it. But the British decided to rub our noses in the dung and tell us how wonderful it smelled.'

'Then it's about time they realised their mistake.'

'We didn't beat them by convincing them they were mistaken, Inspector. We beat them by convincing them of the futility of carrying on. We made it seem a Sisyphean endeavour to continue to stand against the tide of our moral outrage. But now, we're so blinded by the desire for vengeance that we're at risk of becoming the very thing we fought against. If we believe that a white man deserves less consideration *because* he is white, we will be no better than them.'

'Do you really think a man like Charles Whitby will ever treat you as his equal?'

'Whitby has three centuries of unlearning to do. He's like an old oak. He will break but he won't bend.' He pulled a handkerchief from his pocket and wiped his mouth. 'The British were *raised* to see us as inferiors and thus made little effort to appreciate our culture. Our scriptures are thousands of years older than their own. We were building cities in the Indus Valley when they were still living in forests. The British in India believed themselves a race of gods – lesser gods, but gods nonetheless. They consider their fall to be against the natural order of things.'

'You sound as if you admire them for it.'

'I don't admire, but I understand.'

'I can't say I agree with you.'

'Allow me to paraphrase the Bible. "What does it profit a nation if we gain our freedom but forfeit our soul?"' He looked up at the scarred statue. 'James and I have become friends. I want to save him. Not as a lawyer, but as his friend. I believe in his innocence. More importantly, I wish to preserve *ours*.'

21

A crowd boiled in front of the entrance to Malabar House, blocking her entry to the side street where she usually parked. She could hear chanting, but couldn't make out exactly who or what they were worked up about.

The gathering had the tenor of most morchas on the subcontinent, a mass of fist-pumping and slogan-shouting, three parts denunciation to one part protest, with an underlying hint of jamboree.

A barrel-shaped man with a head like a mouldy apple stood on a stool, bellowing through a loudhailer in Hindi. Sweat glistened on his forehead, and his thick beard leaped about like a conductor's baton at every jerk of his head.

She parked the jeep and got out into the midst of the melee.

A high sun steamed the sidewalk. The air was as thick as soup.

As soon as she stepped towards the Malabar House arcade, she knew that she'd made a mistake.

With the instincts of a predator, the crowd registered her arrival, and turned on her as one man. The man with the loudhailer aimed it at her like a rifle, then lifted it to his lips. 'There she is! Ghaddaar!'

Ghaddaar. Traitor.

The chant was taken up by the crowd. She saw now that some of them were wielding bamboo sticks, beating them against their legs in a tuneless rhythm.

Instinctively, her hand drifted to her revolver.

And then, without warning, they were crowding in on her, shouting, cursing, red-eyed with the mad lust of zealots.

She snatched the revolver from its holster, and then gasped as a lathi struck her wrist, clattering the weapon to the floor.

She was pushed back against the jeep. A hand reached out and yanked off her cap. Another tore at the front of her khaki dress shirt.

She fell to her knees, did her best to protect herself with her arms as blows rained down. A cry escaped her as a sandalled foot found her side. Coherent thought vanished.

She saw a grinning ruffian waving her own revolver above his head.

And then, an instant later, the revolver was ripped from the man's grasp, and he dropped to the floor like a sack of flour. In his place stood Karim Haq, a head taller than anyone else, as wide as a carthorse, Gulliver in Lilliput, wielding a cricket bat.

Beside him was Birla; behind them were the station's two constables, the office peon, and Roshan Seth.

Seth pointed his revolver into the air and fired two shots.

The crowd fell back. The man with the loudhailer swooned off his stool, hitting the ground with an audible thump.

'Come on,' hissed Birla, bending down to her ear. 'Let's get inside before they realise he's not actually going to shoot anyone.'

'Here, take this,' said Seth.

He handed her a handkerchief. She looked at it in stupefaction.

'You're bleeding,' he said, indicating her nose.

She took the proffered cloth, and dabbed at her face. The handkerchief came away imprinted with a scarlet butterfly.

Seth went back behind his desk, picked up a folded copy of the *Indian Chronicle* and threw it down in front of her.

Her eyes picked out the headline.

BOMBAY POLICEWOMAN SEEKS
TO UNDO WHITBY CONVICTION

Beneath was the subheading: 'Malabar House Officer Conducts Rogue Investigation To Free Patriot Lawyer's Killer.'

The image was accompanied by a trio of photographs: a large one of her, and two smaller ones, inset – one of James Whitby, the other of the body of Fareed Mazumdar.

The byline revealed that the article had been penned by Aalam Channa.

She mentally nailed the journalist to a barn door. Then took potshots at him. With a blunderbuss. Perhaps she should have expected it. Channa wasn't the type to volunteer information without expecting something in return; any interaction with the journalist was an unspoken bargain with the devil. And woe betide you if you didn't deliver your side of the deal.

'Who were they?'

'A local chapter of the Indian Union Muslim League.'

Her brow furrowed. She couldn't remember coming across such an outfit.

Seth sat down heavily. 'The IUML is the Indian arm of the original All-India Muslim League. That was disbanded in 1947 once the Leaguers achieved their goal – a separate home-land for Muslims in Pakistan. But the Muslims left behind in India decided they needed a voice in the new reality and so they created their own offshoot. They've had a bumpy ride, with many questioning the need for them to exist at all. The Partition riots have made communal tolerance about as rare as good Scotch.' He reached into his desk, drew out a bottle, poured himself a drink. 'You could use *stuff* to dissolve metal.' He gulped down the glass with a shudder, then looked at her. 'When you shake a few branches you have to expect the occasional tree to drop on your head. You should have told me.'

'I was asked not to.'

'By who?'

She hesitated. 'ADC Shukla.'

'In that case, perhaps you can explain this mess to *him*. You've been summoned to HQ.'

22

A second visit to Bombay police headquarters in the space of a few days was not one she had anticipated.

She arrived with her nose still throbbing. A stray hand must have caught her during the fracas outside Malabar House. The thought of the attack sped up her heart, flooding her thoughts with a mixture of anxiety and rage as she made her way up to ADC Shukla's office.

As she moved through the corridors, eyes followed her. She sensed their judgement. She knew perfectly well – through the example made of Roshan Seth – that the police service was more than capable of throwing out the baby with the bathwater. And then shooting the baby.

She entered Shukla's office to find the ADC behind his desk. A second man was in the room, pacing the floor agitatedly like a man whose wife had just given birth to triplets.

She recognised Ravi Patnagar, head of the state CID – the Criminal Investigation Department – of which the crime branch unit at Malabar House was a part. Technically, Patnagar was Roshan Seth's superior – and thus hers – but she'd only met the man once, and the impression made had been less than favourable. Malabar House was considered an embarrassment by the rest of the CID, the butt of jokes, and the place where investigations – and careers – went to die.

An elephant graveyard for police officers.

Patnagar rounded on her, waving a copy of the *Chronicle* in her face like a man flagging down a cab. 'What did you think you were doing, Inspector?'

She flushed. 'My job. Sir.'

His neck seemed to expand. 'On whose orders did you reopen this investigation?'

She turned her gaze to the ADC. Shukla seemed lost in his own thoughts, and then, leaning back in his chair, said, 'Inspector, you must understand that rogue investigations cannot be tolerated. Where would our criminal justice system be if we second-guessed every conviction? Your actions have caused the service a great deal of embarrassment.'

It took an effort of will to prevent her jaw from hitting the floor. It suddenly dawned on her that she was being left to swing on the scaffold. Shukla was denying all knowledge of her investigation, let alone instigating it.

Perhaps she should have anticipated this.

She was not so naïve as to not have realised that Shukla's manoeuvring, his wish that she tackle the case alone and unheralded, spoke to machinations beyond her own rank.

She understood, instinctively, that if she wished to salvage her career, she would have to play along.

'Sir,' she managed to grind out.

'You understand that this constitutes grounds for dismissal?' Patnagar had come uncomfortably close, his moustache dancing above his lip. She recalled the rumours that he and Roshan Seth had once been contemporaries, now turned bitter enemies.

'Ravi. Why don't you step outside for a moment? I'd like to talk to the inspector alone.'

Patnagar seemed confused for a moment, as if the floor had given way beneath his feet and he was working out whether or not to allow gravity to take its course.

Finally, he stepped backwards. 'Yes. Of course. Sir.'

He stalked out of the room like a man wearing boxer shorts made of sandpaper.

As the door closed on him, Persis found she could no longer contain herself. 'Sir. This is – is—'

Shukla raised a placatory hand. 'I warned you from the beginning not to attract attention.'

'I was following orders. *Your* orders!'

He folded his hands over his substantial stomach. 'Your efforts have stirred up a hornet's nest that I hadn't anticipated. The commissioner is … displeased.' His fingers tapped out a rhythm on the desk. 'I think a few days out of uniform should placate the mob.'

'You're suspending me?' Her disbelief was a tangible thing.

'On paper, yes. But I'd like you to continue the investigation. And report only to me.'

'I don't understand.'

'The situation hasn't changed. James Whitby is still due to be executed. If there is any chance that he is innocent, then we must prove it.'

'Sir. Please explain to me why we are doing this. How did Charles Whitby convince you to reopen the investigation?'

'Whitby has been around a long time, Persis. A man like that … Let's just say he understands the principles of leverage.'

She sensed his meaning. Charles Whitby had a hold over someone in the police chain of command that had allowed him to push for this private investigation into his son's conviction. Who was the compromised party? Shukla? Or perhaps the commissioner? She couldn't begin to guess at the secrets Whitby had accumulated over the years.

In the end, it really didn't matter. The juggernaut was in motion, and, if she wasn't careful, she might be ground to dust beneath its wheels.

'Why me?'

Shukla's silence spoke volumes.

'It's because I'm expendable, isn't it? Far easier to get rid of the only woman on the force if things go wrong.'

The ADC didn't bother to correct her.

She felt the betrayal like a knife between her ribs.

For the first time, a sense of hopelessness overcame her. What was the point of fighting on in a place where she was so clearly resented, so openly undermined? Was it worth it? Was her self-respect worth it?

And then she thought of James Whitby, alone in his cell, counting down the days, hours, minutes to his execution.

Her shoulders straightened. 'I'll complete the investigation. But after that I shall tender my resignation. Sir.'

Shukla continued to regard her, his face an impenetrable mask. 'What have you discovered so far?'

Disappointment coursed through her. She'd expected – what? A plea that she reconsider? A few words of praise? What was the point of making a grand gesture if it was going to be utterly ignored?

She swallowed her embarrassment, and quickly brought him up to speed with her efforts, then said, stiffly, 'I need to travel to Calcutta to find out more about the case described in the press cuttings sent to Mazumdar.'

Shukla was nodding. 'That might be for the best, in any case. Defuse the Muslim Leaguers, defuse the situation. I have a colleague in Calcutta. I shall give him a call.' He paused, evaluating her. 'You may not realise this, but the Whitby case has become something of a cause célèbre in Britain. There are some who are pointing to us and saying: *See, this is what happens when you give the natives their head.* The suggestion being that we are petty, vindictive, unable to exercise the rule of law – at least not in the way the British believed they did. They're still finding it hard to reconcile themselves to the fact that Gandhi turned turning the other cheek into a weapon. They consider their ousting as a grand betrayal. The Whitby case is a test, for us all. We cannot afford to make a mistake.'

23

David Sassoon's hands were raised in supplication, a dreamy look in his eyes.

The marble statue stood at the foot of a flight of stairs leading upwards to the library's reading room where Persis was due to meet the man referred to her by Benjamin Samson, the priest at the Gate of Mercy synagogue.

Sassoon's statue depicted him in his bearded and turbaned avatar, regally swathed in robes. The image, no doubt, had caused a certain degree of spiritual confusion to the casual onlooker – Sassoon could easily have been mistaken for a Muslim, a Sikh, or a Hindu fakir. The fact that he remained Bombay's most recognisable Jew was a testament to the imprint the Sassoon family had made upon the city.

Samson had guided her to a lawyer by the name of Adam Hyam.

She'd called Hyam's office. His secretary had arranged for her to meet the man at his afternoon haunt, the David Sassoon Library in Kala Ghoda.

She announced herself to the security guard, a scrawny fellow who looked so bored he could have doubled as a store mannequin, and then jogged up to the reading room. Here, she met with a librarian, who pointed a finger towards the back of the space.

She weaved her way between the desks. Towering bookshelves in Burma teak loomed on either side. A small, wiry man made his way perilously up a ladder with a small broom in one hand, as if ascending the north face of the Eiger.

Hyam looked up as she approached. She opened her mouth to speak, but he raised a finger to stop her, then pointed at a sign nailed to the wall behind him.

DISCUSSION STRICTLY PROHIBITED IN THE READING ROOM.

Leaving his papers behind, he bade her follow, then led her back downstairs and out into a small garden at the rear of the library, a verdant oasis amid the tumult of the city.

He waved her into a cane chair, then took one opposite her.

'Your notoriety precedes you, Inspector,' he said jovially.

At the age of eighty, Hyam retained a spare frame, and a head of petrified grey hair that stood vertiginously upright as if he'd been frightened by a ghost. Square-framed spectacles sat in front of eyes full of mischief. He was the sort of old man she'd heard described as *spry*, boundlessly energetic, leaping from steering committee to Rotary Club meeting like some sort of bureaucratic mountain goat. He'd achieved everything he wanted to in life and could now do exactly as he bloody well pleased.

In that respect, he reminded her of her father, without the jolly demeanour.

She took his comment to mean the incendiary article in the *Chronicle*. She was about to respond, but he spoke up. 'I say good for you. I have no idea if Whitby is innocent or not, but I know a hatchet job when I see one. Personally, I wouldn't line my dog's kennel with the *Chronicle*. Channa is an unprincipled hack.'

She explained the case to him, and the reason for her visit, handing him the Star of David note. He examined it, then handed it back.

'I knew Mazumdar. Not well. He was relatively new to the Bombay High Court, whereas I've been in and out of the place for almost sixty years. A quiet man, measured. Not exactly unfriendly, but neither did he court attention, no pun intended. Of course, he was a lot younger than me.'

'Did he have any dealings with the Jewish community?'

'Not to my knowledge. Of course, I can't speak for every Jew in the city.'

'My impression was that there aren't many left.'

'More than you'd think. But you're right. Most have made the journey to Israel.'

'But not you?'

He smiled wryly. 'I've thought about it, of course. But I'm eighty years old. I was born in Bombay and have lived my whole life here. My late wife is buried here. My practice is here. India is my home. I don't believe that my Jewish identity is compromised in any way by not making aliyah.' His eyes crinkled behind his glasses. 'Besides, it doesn't really matter where we are buried, does it? It only matters what awaits us after we die. And none of us truly knows the answer to that. A lot of people are in for a nasty surprise, Inspector. After all, we can't *all* be right.'

'Perhaps we're all approaching the truth from different sides of the same mountain?'

His eyebrows lifted in surprise. 'Wise words. One doesn't usually hear such sentiments from the young.'

'I *feel* a lot older than I look.'

He reached out unexpectedly and tapped her warmly on the arm. 'If you'll take some advice from an old man ... Ignore what others think. The only thing that matters is what *you* think. Follow your conscience and it will rarely steer you wrong.'

An unexpected warmth rose to her cheeks. Hyam had an extraordinarily comforting manner. She imagined his calm, avuncular demeanour had helped him win numerous cases over the course of his career. Denying him would be like kicking a puppy. With steel-toed boots. 'Mazumdar was a prominent Muslim. Could that have been a source of tension with the Jewish community? Because of Israel?'

He considered the question. 'You have to understand that India has been good to the Jews. We've never encountered any real anti-Semitism here. Oh, there was a minor flare-up around the time of the Balfour Declaration, but no scars were left. And the Jews that came over in the Farhud from Iraq – the pogrom following the end of the Anglo-Iraq War in 1941 – carried some of their anti-Muslim resentment with them, but that soon dissipated. As for the Bombay Zionist Organisation ... that never had more than a few hundred members at its most popular. When Israel was established, again, a few noses were put out of joint, but daggers remained sheathed. The truth is that once the exodus began, most of our Muslim neighbours were sorry to see us go.'

She sat back, disappointed. Hyam's words seemed to indicate a dead end in her pursuit of a Jewish connection to Fareed Mazumdar's murder. 'Can you think of *any* reason that someone might send a Star of David to a Muslim lawyer?'

'Perhaps it's just a coincidence? Or an elaborate joke, one whose punchline we can only guess at.'

24

She could hear voices floating from the rear of the bookshop.

It was past seven, but it felt later. The day's events, culminating in her suspension, had taken their toll. The fact that she was now forced to look over her shoulder, watchful for fanatical protestors, only added to her sense of bitterness.

Her thoughts strayed to the Muslim League bandleader who'd whipped the crowd into a frenzy earlier that day. How vociferous would he be with a bullet in his knee?

That was the problem with fanatics. They were as brave as lions with an army at their backs. But on their own, facing a woman who knew eight different ways to kill a man with her bare hands . . .

Seema was on the sofa at the back of the shop with Mrs Elsa Randall, a long-term customer. A strong smell of coffee floated in the air.

She paused for a moment, just out of view behind a bookshelf, listening to the pair talk about exotic flora. Mrs Randall had served as a biology teacher at the Cathedral Girls School for almost three decades – Persis remembered her from her own time there. She ordered textbooks by the dozen, but her real passion was botany, a subject with which she could bore a donkey to death – as she herself had put it.

The two women, young and old, conversed using a mixture of English and Hindi. It seemed a happy compromise. Seema's English was, at best, passable, and Mrs Randall's Hindi was of the sort British tourists used when dealing with foreign waiters, largely a matter of bellowing the same word over and again, accompanied by crude hand gestures.

But at least she'd made an effort. In that, she was a rarity, Persis thought. She'd encountered so few foreigners who'd bothered to learn the native tongue. Beyond arming themselves with the limited vocabulary needed to bully servants and rickshaw drivers, they'd never felt the need.

Her thoughts returned to the Whitbys.

For men who'd tried to convince her that they belonged here, she wondered just how much effort they'd made to assimilate. But then, wasn't that the difference between conqueror and conquered? The British, wherever they had gone, had done so with the belief that they were exporting their own enlightened creed. It had rarely occurred to them that the places they'd ventured, armed with navies and cannon, might have their own storied histories, their own cultural palimpsests. They barged in like drunken fathers-in-law, demanding things be done their way, and shooting anyone who disagreed.

It hadn't always been thus.

She'd read of the earliest British traders, who'd taken on local customs, married native wives. They'd woven their own thread into the great Indian tapestry. Others had managed the same feat: her own Parsee ancestors, the Jews. Men like Adam Hyam, who retained both a Jewish and an Indian identity, and wore both with equal pride.

But there had been failures too.

If he hadn't been murdered, Gandhi might have died of a broken heart at his inability to prevent Partition. Indians were no angels; they'd given in to communal bickering, allowing themselves to be seduced by the rhetoric of blood and vengeance. Perhaps there was something deep in the human psyche that made such fissiparousness inevitable, a sliver of darkness that would always end in the same place: division and death.

* * *

After Mrs Randall had left, they'd gone upstairs.

Aunt Nussie had arrived armed with food, warming it up while Persis peeled off her uniform and showered.

Afterwards, she stood in her bedroom, wrapped in a towel, her long black hair damp against her back, looking at the discarded uniform where it lay forlornly on the bed like a spurned lover. The idea that it had been stripped from her, after everything she'd gone through to earn the right to wear it, sat in her stomach like a lead dumpling.

Eventually, she picked it up and threw it forcefully into the laundry basket.

A yowl rose up to greet her.

She reached in, plucked Akbar from the basket, and set him down on the bed.

She dressed, then carried him to the dining room, where Nussie was ladling chicken soup into a bowl for Seema.

'I see you've made the newspapers again,' said Nussie, with the sort of faux cheeriness a wife might employ when told by her husband that he was off to Paris with his pretty young secretary in tow.

Persis was in no mood for another fight with her aunt. She'd decided not to tell her about the rioters outside the station. Nothing good would come of it. Nussie had never understood her desire to enter the police service, considering it about as suitable an occupation for a woman as coal mining or bareback bull riding.

Before she could answer, the phone rang.

It was her father. Sam appeared to have reached some sort of telepathic agreement with her aunt. 'I leave for a few weeks and you manage to find a way to set the whole country against you!'

'Papa, you're exaggerating.'

'Am I? You're assisting a convicted killer, a *white* man who murdered an Indian patriot. Have you any idea what people are saying?'

'Haven't you always told me that people are idiots?'

Silence drifted down the phone.

'Look, I appreciate that you're concerned. But the fact is that I've been *tasked* to do this. And the more I look into it, the more I think there's no smoke without fire. Tell me, Papa, if Whitby was Indian would you still ask me to step aside, knowing that an innocent man might be sent to the gallows?'

His voice was subdued when he next spoke. 'I just want my daughter to be safe. Is that too much to ask?'

She enquired about his ongoing honeymoon, believing, mistakenly, that this might prove safer ground.

A bout of gastric disturbance had kept Sam – and thus most of the hotel staff – up all night. He bemoaned the fact that Meherzad had slept through it all, as if perhaps he'd expected his new wife to assume a duty of care for his troublesome bowels as part of her marriage vows.

'Papa, please don't be so dramatic.'

'Dysentery is no laughing matter, young lady.'

'What will you do now?'

Seema was at the sink, soaking the dishes. After Nussie had left, Persis had told her about the attack at the station. The girl had taken it with an equanimity that belied her years.

Persis glanced at her. 'You know you don't have to do that, don't you?'

'I don't mind.'

Persis was spooning cat food from a can into Akbar's bowl. The grey Persian looked on from his perch on the Steinway. As soon as she'd finished, he leaped from the piano, dive-bombing the bowl like a kamikaze pilot.

'Your father has a point.'

She stiffened and turned to stare at the girl. 'You too?'

'I mean, they care about you. They're going to worry. If Partition taught us anything, it's that even ordinary people can become monsters at the slightest provocation.'

Persis walked to the sink, picked up a towel, and began to dry the dishes. '"The enemy is fear. We think it is hate; but it is fear." Do you know who said that? Gandhi.'

'Gandhiji is not the one who was almost lynched today.' Steam billowed from the sink. 'Besides, all his wisdom couldn't stop Godse's bullets.'

For a while there was only the sound of the running tap. 'So . . . what *will* you do now?' Seema repeated.

'I'm going to Calcutta.'

The girl's shoulders straightened. 'You didn't mention that to your aunt.'

'No.'

'I've heard that Calcutta is a wild place.'

Persis said nothing.

'Were you planning to go alone?'

'Who else would I go with?'

The girl's hands sank into the water and emerged with another plate. 'I've never been to Calcutta.'

Persis stared at her. Ambition was one thing . . . Then again, the idea of navigating Calcutta on her own, out of uniform, riding into town with a storm at her back, courtesy of the *Indian Chronicle* . . .

'You understand that I'm not going there for a holiday?'

'Of course. It's an investigation. I could help.'

'You're not a police officer.'

'But I will be. One day. Isn't that the point of *you* acting as my mentor?'

'A mentor isn't supposed to place their mentee in harm's way.'

'Am I not old enough to make the decision for myself?'

She looked at the girl with grudging respect. 'You're sure about this?'

125

'Yes.'

Persis hesitated, then nodded. 'Very well.'

A smile of disbelief. 'Do you mean it?'

'I do.'

Seema allowed herself a moment of adulation, before her euphoric expression was replaced by a frown. 'I made a commitment to your father.'

Persis set the plate down. 'We'll just have to find someone else to take over for a few days.'

It was Seema's turn to hesitate. 'May I make a suggestion?'

'Of course.'

'I think Aunt Nussie would be more than happy to help.'

Persis's jaw went slack. The idea that her aunt, Sam's sworn enemy, might be placed in charge of his beloved bookstore would never have crossed her mind.

Thinking of Nussie, she realised that any discussion with her aunt about Calcutta would inevitably lead to a discussion about Darius.

For the past several years, her aunt had energetically pursued the notion that Persis might choose Nussie's only son as her life partner. The idea of *keeping it in the family* appealed to her aunt in a way that had defined the Parsee community for generations. Persis had put paid to her aspirations the last time Darius had visited Bombay, by effectively telling him that she'd rather marry a cross-eyed baboon.

Her aunt, nevertheless, had not quite given up hope. No doubt she'd insist on Persis meeting up with her cousin, something that Persis herself had as much desire to do as she had to climb into a lion's cage and poke it in the eye with a sharp stick.

And then she thought of the look on her father's face, telephoning the shop to find Nussie on the other end of the line.

'That's a wonderful idea. I'll speak to her right away.'

25

Bombay, 1950 – James Whitby

Growing up in Calcutta as an only child, I became aware of an intense loneliness, which only heightened after my mother left us.

My father, never the warmest of men, withdrew.

I had few friends. Like many of the British who'd made India their home, we'd always socialised among ourselves – our own little islands of Englishness – and treated the natives – even our closest allies – with, at best, a lukewarm tolerance, at worst, outright disdain.

My mother had enjoyed Calcutta's social scene, but my father despised his peers. He maintained a berth at the Calcutta Club for the express purpose of promoting his business interests, but, once his wealth and influence outgrew the need for such vulgar politicking, he refused to set foot in the place and would happily have bulldozed it back into the swamp from which it had been raised.

At the age of eighteen he packed me off to Cambridge. The relief on his face as I departed was palpable.

I was a fish out of water in England and was treated as such. Many of my peers seemed to hold me personally responsible for the unrest on the subcontinent, tales of which were greatly exaggerated by the local newspapers, Indians agitating for independence portrayed as rampaging killers and the sort of indiscriminate sexual predators who'd ravish a lamppost.

There was a lot of flannel about not sparing the rod, teaching the natives a lesson they'd never forget, like Leopold in the Congo. To my ears, these would-be saviours of empire, the wet-eared spawn of English lords and ladies, seemed every bit as fanatical as the Bengalis I'd heard campaigning in Calcutta, but with considerably less charm.

Whenever I dared to venture the opinion that the British had spent three centuries fomenting division, had turned a blind eye to our own mistreatment of the locals, and thus couldn't complain if our chickens were now coming home to roost, they looked at me as if I was a priest who'd stripped nude in the pulpit of their Sunday churches.

I think what angered them most was the fact that we'd spent three centuries breeding Indians to docility and now they had the cheek to turn that very docility against us. Had the Indians fought properly, we could have justified going in and giving them a damned good thrashing.

But how do you fight a population so underhanded that they simply refused to hit back when you slugged them full in the face?

It was like trying to fight water.

I suppose that was when I realised that I too was a child of empire, for I had been born out there, in the crucible of our ambition. Why then had I remained immune from the desire to subjugate the world?

I returned to India and tried to explain this to my father. He looked at me as if I was a failed investment into which he'd already sunk too much of his capital.

He gave me a meaningless job in his own empire, and a salary that allowed me a measure of freedom.

It would mean nothing to say that we drifted apart; we had never been close.

Years later, when the war began, I would come upon him, tuned in to the bellicose commentary on the radio. He would try and impress upon me the importance of the struggle, of Churchill's noble fight to save Britain from the plague of Nazism.

I, out of simple curiosity, listened to Gandhi, imprisoned for inciting the Quit India movement; Gandhi – and his fellow revolutionaries – accused us of harbouring double standards. After all, if *we* were morally entitled to fight against an evil that sought to oppress us, to take from us our freedoms and the values we held dear, then how could we deny Indians the same right?

At times, I felt as if a fight for my very soul was taking place inside me.

It would be years before I understood that the fight was with no one but myself.

26

'Are you afraid of flying?'

Persis turned towards her companion with a neck as stiff as an ironing board. A sheen of sweat had erupted on to her forehead. 'What makes you say that?' she ground out from between gritted teeth.

Seema looked down at her wrist, currently clamped in the older woman's vice-like grip. 'It's just that I think I'm losing feeling in my hand.'

They'd arrived at Santa Cruz aerodrome, in mid-town Bombay, at just after ten, where Charles Whitby's aide awaited them.

Vikram Agarwal was a lean man, clean-shaven, with a thicket of black hair parted with geometric precision, and a suit so crisp it looked as if it could have stood up and marched off on its own.

He led them swiftly through the airport and out to the airfield where a Douglas DC-3, a monoplane with twin propellers, awaited them.

'They were used by the Indian Air Force during the war,' he said conversationally. 'Mr Whitby bought several once the war ended and a glut of military aircraft hit the market.'

Sunlight glinted off the plane's grey fuselage, emblazoned with the logo of Charles Whitby's company, the Erebus Corporation.

Persis retained enough of her classical schooling to recall that Erebus was the Greek god of the underworld, ruler of Tartarus, where the shades of the dead went before their onward journey to Hades. A strange choice of name, she thought, but perhaps that said more about Charles Whitby than the company he'd built.

Agarwal introduced them to the aeroplane's pilot and crew, and then handed Persis an envelope. Inside, she discovered a bundle of cash. 'What's this for?'

'Expenses,' he said.

She pushed the envelope back into his chest. 'I don't want Whitby's money.'

He blinked, momentarily nonplussed, then nodded. 'Nevertheless, if you should need it, give me a call and I'll wire it to you. Time is running short. Mr Whitby has stated that every possible resource is to be made available to you.'

The flight had been delayed by an hour, by which time her anxiety had had time to peak.

She'd only flown once before, on a postal plane, with tin buckets for seats and a goat for company. She'd been left less than enamoured of the experience.

Seema, to her astonishment, seemed to be taking the whole thing in her stride. The girl had never been near an airfield, but acted as if she'd been born on the wing.

The flight was all but empty, the twenty or so seats occupied by only two others, a pair of grey-haired and grey-suited executives who paid them no attention, engrossed in their own conversation.

As the aeroplane juddered off the tarmac, Persis closed her eyes.

Beside her, Seema cooed with pleasure. 'Isn't this wonderful!'

Almost five hours later the plane landed on the tarmac at Dum Dum aerodrome, some ten miles from the centre of Calcutta.

As she set foot on terra firma, Persis had to resist the urge to prostrate herself and kiss the earth, as Columbus was said to have done upon reaching the New World.

They walked towards the airport on rubbery legs, a low white-washed building glinting in the late afternoon sun.

Inside, they found a bearded taxi driver awaiting the twin exec-utives, who barrelled past them without even a cursory nod, as if they'd just been forced to spend the past five hours with a pair of lepers, or, worse, their mothers-in-law, and couldn't wait to get away.

Persis scanned the arrival hall, a roiling mass of natives and whites, mixed in with uniformed airport staff, and flight crews cutting a swathe through the press of bodies as if on the way to invade a small country. A poster of Amelia Earhart emblazoned across one wall declared that the American aviator had passed through the airport in 1937, on the return leg of her tragic attempt to circumnavigate the globe.

Her gaze finally landed on a large woman dressed in a sunhat, jodhpurs, and a beige blouse, bearing down on them like a charging elephant, waving madly, and bellowing at the top of her lungs.

'What ho, ladies! Welcome to Calcutta!'

Dinaz was on fine form.

Persis recalled the four of them – Dinaz, Persis, Jaya, and Emily – back at the Cathedral Girls School in Bombay, first encounter-ing each other, and then against all odds, becoming and remaining friends as they passed over the precarious bridge linking adoles-cence to adulthood. They'd weathered the vagaries of life – and the turbulence of the Quit India years – together, their quartet only splitting up when Emily finally returned to England with her parents once the anti-British violence began to spiral out of control.

A year later, Dinaz too had departed, to take up a position on the other side of the country, in the Sundarbans, just south of Calcutta, working with the Forest Management Division.

They'd stayed in touch.

Once Persis made the decision to come to Calcutta, she'd given her old friend a call.

Charles Whitby had been right about one thing.

Time was running short, and Dinaz's local knowledge would prove valuable in the coming days.

She regarded her old friend out of the corner of her eye as Dinaz barrelled her vehicle, a bright red Lancia, through the thronged Calcutta streets.

Dinaz was the sort of woman often described as a *galleon*. Tall and broad-shouldered, with the build and demeanour of a concrete pillbox, she was possessed of a razor-sharp intelligence, and a never say die bloody-mindedness of the sort common to army officers tasked with exhorting men into battle by threatening to shoot them if they refused.

Over the past few years, she'd made a life for herself in the 'city of palaces', as Calcutta had once been known. In her regular letters, she'd been effusive in her praise of the former capital of the Raj, if not always of the locals that inhabited it.

Persis had never ventured this far eastwards.

Her scant knowledge of Calcutta came via her late grandfather, Dastoor Wadia, who'd woven bedtime tales for her from the several years he'd spent out here in his youth, around the turn of the century.

The problem with Calcutta, he'd explained, was that it was full of Bengalis – or rather, the sort of Bengalis who were so supremely in love with themselves that they'd convinced anyone who would listen that they and they alone were the torchbearers of art and literacy on the subcontinent, the doyennes of culture, poetry, political rhetoric, and fish.

It's what made them such rabble rousers, he'd suggested, willing to go to war over an incorrectly worn dhoti or a poorly spiced hilsa. They'd eventually proved more troublesome than the local mosquitoes, forcing the British to up sticks and move the seat of governance to Delhi in 1911.

Though Dastoor had seemed disparaging, Persis had detected an underlying fondness in her grandfather's words.

He'd eventually confessed that he'd always maintained a soft spot for the irascible Bengalis, with their love of disputation and their lofty ideals; he admired, too, their adoration of the written word, for which they'd gladly have given their lives – had they not been so averse to the sight of blood.

Indeed, it was in Calcutta that he'd first become infatuated with the notion of opening his own bookshop.

The city itself remained strategically important – half of India's sea-borne traffic passed through the entrepôt, its location a critical stopover for routes from Europe and North America to East Asia and beyond. Once a pestilential riverine swamp, infested by bamboo jungles where tigers roamed freely, snacking on unsuspecting locals, the city was, in part, an invention of the British, who'd purchased the rights to the local land and the villages that sat upon it.

One of those villages had been Kalikata, from which it was said Calcutta took its name.

Over the centuries, the British had raised the city in their own image, the way some men felt obliged to do when far from home; hulking great Victorian buildings, beacons of British India, continued to sit on the city's chest, weathered by generations of Calcutta sun and rain.

In recent years, Calcutta's population had swollen. Refugees had poured in from Burma, following the Japanese World War Two campaign there, and, later, during the Partition years, from the eastern half of Bengal, now renamed East Pakistan.

Like Bombay, the city struggled to deliver the ideals of the new nation, with a boisterous population demanding food and a fair wage, ever willing to set alight anyone and anything that appeared an obstacle to the fulfilment of such desires.

If Bombay was said to be the city of dreams, then Calcutta was where dreams came to grief against the shoals of political reality.

27

The Great Eastern Hotel in Dalhousie Square had been built more than a century earlier, when Calcutta was still the most important city in the eastern reaches of the British Empire.

Charles Whitby's aide had explained that the Erebus Corporation held a standing account at the hotel and that he'd taken the liberty of booking two suites for them.

The hotel sat halfway along a bustling thoroughfare, a pandemonium of bicycle-tongas, taxis, cars, handcartwallahs, and foot traffic. If there was one thing Bombay and Calcutta had in common, Persis thought, it was the mind-boggling chaos that was the hallmark of both cities' tarmacked capillaries. In a way, it was almost reassuring to be in another metropolis where traffic rules were considered mere *suggestions*.

Powering down the street, Dinaz revved the Lancia's engine, almost mowing down a hapless bicyclist, before screeching to a stop directly in front of the hotel.

A pair of porters sprang at them like gorillas in heat, vying for their suitcases.

Persis looked up.

The Great Eastern's exterior façade shone a brilliant white. A balustraded balcony situated at first-floor level ran the length of the frontage; above, rows of brown-shuttered windows opened on to the street.

They entered a tastefully appointed lobby. Glossy wood panelling, marble floors and rich red carpeting winding up a central staircase gave the impression of a plush gentlemen's club or the better class of French brothel. A chandelier that wouldn't have looked out of place on the *Titanic* hung from a ceiling high above.

In the centre of the lobby, an orange-faced white man with sandy hair was bellowing at a liveried bellhop in an American accent; the boy had his shoulder pressed against a luggage cart so overloaded with suitcases it resembled the Great Pyramid of Giza.

Behind the reception counter, a duty manager welcomed them with a practised smile that had worn grooves either side of his mouth. He had a childlike face which made the thin moustache under his nose appear to have been scribbled on by a painter's filbert. His morning suit and cravat ensemble, however, was impeccable, as was his cut-glass Home Counties accent.

Persis waited while the gentleman confirmed their reservations.

Placing a bound ledger on the counter, he opened it, and then ran a finger down the page with great ceremony, as if perusing the Domesday Book. He beamed at them. 'The rooms are all set for you, madam. However, I'm afraid your maid will have to stay elsewhere. Our servants' quarters are completely full at present.'

It took a moment for her to grasp his meaning. She risked a glance at Seema, but the girl was standing rigidly beside her, brown eyes blinking rapidly behind her spectacles.

Before Persis could say anything, Dinaz leaned over the counter, looking ready to blast the martinet with a blunderbuss. 'That is *not* a servant. She's one of your guests, you halfwit.'

The man wilted inside his morning suit like a slug doused with salt.

The suite was high-ceilinged, decorated in shades of maroon and gold, with a four-poster bed the size of an imperial barge, a wardrobe that could have housed an elephant, a Chesterfield arrangement reeking of new leather, and a carpet so thick that tribes of pygmies might have become lost in it.

She picked up a hotel guidebook prominently displayed on a desk in one corner.

The book claimed that the Great Eastern had once been known as the 'Savoy of the East' with luminaries such as Mark Twain and Rudyard Kipling among the roll call of guests. Gandhi, too, had stayed here, in 1896, later recalling an English journalist from the *Daily Telegraph* who'd invited him to dine at the nearby Bengal Club, not realising that Indians were not admitted by that august institution. The man, an Ellerthorpe, had apologised profusely, and instead entertained Gandhi in his suite.

During World War Two, Allied soldiers had been billeted at the hotel.

A photograph of American GIs listening to a jazz band in the ground-floor bar reminded her that she was here for a purpose, and that the clock was ticking.

She picked up the receiver of the ivory-toned phone on the desk and dialled the hotel reception, then asked for a call to be placed through to Calcutta police headquarters at Lal Bazar.

A short conversation later, she had secured an evening appointment with the contact ADC Shukla had given her back in Bombay.

28

The route to the police HQ was less than a kilometre away, a short walk along Old Court House Street, past Dalhousie Square, and on to Lal Bazar Street.

The humidity struck them as soon as they stepped outside of the relative cool of the hotel. Persis, freshly showered and dressed in a lime-green polka-dot cotton dress and elegant shoes, was lathered in sweat before she'd had a chance to hail a tonga.

The tongawallah, a spry chap in a dhoti and dirty turban, grinned at them, and then clucked his horse into gear. The wretched-looking beast lifted its tail and squirted forth a jet of excrement. A further round of clucking, combined with several passionate entreaties by the tongawallah, finally convinced the animal to break out into a gentle trot.

Seema, resplendent in a mango-coloured sari, had brought the hotel guidebook along, and leafed through it, pointing out various sights along the way.

Around them, street lamps lit up a frantic scene.

Chevrolet taxis charged by with bearded Sikhs honking manically at the rear ends of buses; a tram clanked along, marked fore and aft by distinctive yellow circles, maudlin, sweat-sheened faces peering from the windows like caged prisoners being transported to jail; crowds frothed along the street, homeward-bound or headed towards the local restaurants for an early supper. The city burgeoned with life. She could see why, once upon a time, Calcutta had attracted such adulation. There was a tumultuous beauty to the place that reminded her of Bombay.

The area was dotted with massive stone buildings built in the colonial style, as if a giant had been at work building a model city for the Gods of Olympus. Looking across the vast Lal Dighi pond, Persis saw the monument that was the Writers' Building, once the most famous edifice in the whole of India, stretching across the bottle-green pool's entire northern reach. Writers', as it was affectionately known, now housed the bureaucratic apparatus for West Bengal, but had originally served as the headquarters of the East India Company, and later the seat of government of the Raj.

From here the British had cracked the whip of influence across the length and breadth of the country.

In an earlier time, Writers' had also marked the centre of White Town, the southern half of Calcutta that had once housed English officers, merchants, and bureaucrats, delineated from the city's dilapidated northern districts – known as Black Town.

Although the British had been shown the door, that demarcation, in terms of wealth and influence, remained, the noblemen and chancers that had once occupied the mansions of Alipore and the garden houses of Ballygunge now supplanted by Calcutta's homegrown elite.

After all, if there was one thing Indians believed in above all else, it was upward mobility. Reincarnation might transform your fortunes in the next life, but in this one, lording it over the masses by slipping into the still-warm shoes of the country's erstwhile rulers was a far safer bet.

The Lal Bazar station was another monstrous edifice from the colonial era, anchored to the street by the weight of a century.

They entered a bustling lobby, introduced themselves, and, in due course, were sent with a peon upwards into the building's vast interior, along several corridors that might have doubled as high-ways, eventually to be ushered into the office of Assistant Commissioner of Police Diwan Kasturi, head of Calcutta CID.

Kasturi was a large man, seemingly made up of a series of round balls, like a brown snowman. A round head sat on rounded shoulders, with an enormous round belly sticking out above a well-padded bottom. He was one of those overweight men who made a virtue of attempting to squeeze into clothing several sizes too small for them, as if they could fool the body into believing it should shrink itself in order to fit. The buttons of his uniform looked ready to shoot off like champagne corks at the slightest provocation.

The policeman sat behind a desk so large it belonged in a medieval castle. A brass inkwell in the shape of an elephant stood on a crescent-shaped blotter; beside it were several red-backed case files.

Kasturi ordered refreshments, and then listened as Persis explained the case.

'Amit is an old friend,' he said, once she'd finished. She knew that he meant ADC Shukla. 'He asked me to help you, and so I shall, though I'm not convinced it will do you any good. Nor am I convinced of the justness of your cause.'

'You don't think James Whitby deserves to be treated fairly?'

'The man has been tried by a jury of his peers. That's more consideration than most Indians received.'

'Being tried by one's peers doesn't necessarily mean justice was observed.'

He nodded out of the window. 'You must have seen the Writers' Building as you came up? Back in 1930, a trio of freedom fighters from the Bengal Volunteers shot dead the then inspector general of police there, a Colonel Simpson. Simpson was a brute, notorious for torturing and executing political prisoners without due process ... Can you blame us if there's a lingering sense of injustice, Inspector? Some wounds take a long time to heal.'

She dipped her head. 'Nevertheless ...'

A broad smile lit up his pleasant features. He picked up the files from his desk. 'I tracked down the officer who investigated the case you were interested in. Unfortunately, he's no longer available to answer your questions. He died last year – dengue fever. These are the case files. You're welcome to examine them at your leisure, but please return them before leaving the city.'

'Thank you.'

He plucked at his collar. In the terrible heat, the rattling ceiling fan was about as useful as a chocolate hammer. 'I should warn you: the accused in that trial – Azizur Rahman – is a very powerful man in this city. Not the type you want to cross. My suggestion is that you act with discretion. In fact, if you'll listen to an old policeman, I'd advise you to drop the whole thing and go back to Bombay. Rahman doesn't take kindly to being investigated. The man is a law unto himself.'

29

The mansion rose from the water's edge, a fairy-tale keep fashioned from the fevered dreams of Englishmen with too much money and no one to stop them from acting out their wilder impulses. Even by the standards of Alipore, the structure was magnificent. High white walls, an excess of Doric columns, and a lawn so plush you could have played polo on it.

Located on Judge's Court Road, where it met the Tolly Canal, the home had once belonged to a Scottish businessman who'd made a killing in jute and tea. Now, like many of the abandoned mansions of the Raj, it had become a ward of the state, stuck in a bureaucratic limbo until some government panjandrum keen to line his own pockets managed to sell it off to a private buyer, perhaps one of the nouveau-riche natives eager to relocate from the city's less salubrious northern half.

The guard who greeted them at the gate wore a liveried uniform with pipped epaulettes and so much gold braid he might have been mistaken for a four-star general. They were handed off to an equally resplendent house servant, who led them through a riot of white marble and Burma teak to a magnificent drawing room located on the first floor, overlooking the creek. The room had the general dimensions of an airport, with a dining table that looked as if it might need a runner to relay messages from one end to the other. On horseback.

A dozen well-heeled individuals milled about, a mix of natives and whites, some out on the balcony, others examining the grandiose wall art. A few sat at a sofa arrangement at one end of the room.

A waiter bearing a silver tray bore down on them, closely followed by Dinaz. 'You made it!' A cloud of perfume buffeted them backwards.

Dinaz, dressed in a magnificent bottle-green sari with gold trim, swept a pair of champagne flutes from the tray and thrust them into their hands.

'But I don't drin—' Seema began, only to be shushed into silence.

'When in Rome, old girl,' hooted Dinaz. 'Chin, chin!'

The girl looked at Persis, who simply shrugged.

She watched as her young ward took a tentative sip. The girl's cheeks flushed, but she seemed sufficiently impressed to continue.

'Let me introduce you to Ari,' said Dinaz, hooking an arm around Persis's elbow and steering her towards a knot of people standing beside a piano in one corner of the room.

Ari Menon was a small man, almost a head shorter than Dinaz, with the look of a well-thumbed book, one that might have been passed around from hand to careless hand, with the occasional pet getting in on the action. A good deal older than either of them, he had the sort of rumpled look that even the finest tailoring could do nothing to set right.

He greeted them warmly, his peppery moustache crinkling above a generous mouth. 'Delighted to finally meet you, Persis. Dinaz never stops talking of you. India's very own lady policeman!'

Persis felt her cheeks tingle. She glanced at Dinaz, who merely shrugged.

She knew that her friend had been *involved* with Menon for some time now. The fact that the man was married appeared to have discouraged neither of them.

'Come, let's step out on to the balcony.'

He led them towards the French doors and out on to a canti-levered expanse of white marble. Clouds of midges danced around flickering torches. A warm breeze blew in from the canal, carrying a faint hint of fried hilsa. On the far bank, whitewashed buildings glowed in the moonlight. By the water's edge, dark shapes stood half immersed, seemingly communing with the gentle current flowing from the nearby Hooghly.

'Tell me,' said Menon, 'what brings you out to Calcutta?'

'I – I've never been this way before. I thought I'd come out and see Dinaz.'

'You're a terrible liar, Persis. I hope you don't mind me saying that?' He grinned like an amiable shark. 'Political power may have drifted westwards, but we're not exactly a provincial backwater. We get the news just like our cousins over in Bombay.'

She flushed. Dinaz had warned her not to be fooled by Menon's avuncular exterior. He was a highly intelligent man with the instincts of a politician.

'Besides, the Mazumdar case is close to the heart of many Calcuttans. He was, after all, a local.'

'Did you know him?'

'Not personally. But I knew *of* him. He'd made a name for himself before defecting to Bombay.'

'How so?'

'He defended several revolutionaries during the latter years of the independence movement – "terrorists", as the British called them. He was successful enough to have caught the eye of Saleem Ansari.'

'Ansari?'

'Yes. The current deputy chief minister of West Bengal. Though deputy doesn't do the man justice. He's a shoo-in for the top role in next year's elections. Many would rank him as the most power-ful man in Bengal, the éminence grise behind the CM.'

'What do you mean when you say Mazumdar caught Ansari's eye?'

'I mean just that. Ansari was the driving force behind a number of forums promoting the revolutionary cause. Industrialists, polit-ical stalwarts, free-thinkers. They were instrumental in funding the defence of several locals accused of treason. Ansari hand-picked Mazumdar for a few such cases. I believe he was lining him up for a senior role in the state legislature. By all accounts, they became close friends.'

She hesitated. How much should she reveal of her real reason for being in the city? 'There was a case Mazumdar fought back in 1946. A man named Azizur Rahman was accused of using the riots to commit murder. The victims were a native woman and an American. Mazumdar won the case, but left Calcutta shortly afterwards.'

Menon was nodding. 'Yes, I remember it well. It caused a bit of a stink. You see, Rahman is what you'd call an old-fashioned goonda. A thug. But he's plugged into Black Town's Muslim community. The man's a walking vote bank. What I mean is that as far as the locals are concerned, if you don't vote the way Rahman tells you to, you're liable to wake up in the Sundarbans with a tiger putting on a napkin and asking for the salt.

'He was instrumental in helping Saleem Ansari into power. I suppose one good turn deserves another. So when Rahman was hauled in for those murders, he appealed to Ansari. Who, in turn, prevailed upon our friend Mazumdar.'

She digested this, then: 'Have you any idea why Mazumdar would leave Calcutta immediately after winning the case?'

Menon swirled his tumbler around. 'I suppose there's a line every man draws for himself. This far I shall go and no further.'

'So you think Rahman was guilty?'

'The Americans have a wonderful saying. If it walks like a duck, swims like a duck and quacks like a duck . . .'

They were interrupted by the arrival of a gaggle of guests, among them a glamorous couple, the man in a white tuxedo, the woman in a risqué low-cut evening dress.

The flock opened out and Persis got a proper look at the pair.

Her eyes widened in astonishment. For a moment, the only sound she could hear was the gentle murmur of the city across the water – four million Calcuttans going about their evenings – and the shriek of a langur down in the mangroves.

The man seemed to recover first. His shoulders straightened. 'Hello, Persis. How are you . . . Cousin?'

30

'*What is he doing here?*'

'Well, I invited him, of course.'

Persis had pulled Dinaz aside and the pair of them now stood beside a black Steinway, beneath a portrait of a chinless white man draped in a toga, holding a trident, and standing in front of the Ochterlony Monument thrusting phallically into a bright blue Calcutta sky.

'For God's sakes, why?'

'I thought it would be a hoot. Putting the pair of you in a room together. Of course, I had no idea he'd turn up with that lipsticked flamingo.'

Words formed in her throat, but, like sheep trying to squeeze through a gate, struggled to push past each other.

'Look, he's not the man you remember. He's been dashed civil to me. When I first came out here I hardly knew anyone. He went out of his way to show me around.'

'You know *exactly* why he was doing that.'

Dinaz frowned. 'Of course. How silly of me. It was all a dastardly plan to get to *you* through me. Heaven forfend that a man might actually enjoy the company of lumpy old Dinaz.'

'That's not what I meant and you know it.'

Dinaz flapped her hands at her as if warding off a flock of geese. 'Think what you like. But Darius is a rising man in these parts. You could do a lot worse.'

'You sound like Aunt Nussie.'

Dinaz gave her a sour look.

Persis had to admit that not everything her friend had said was without merit.

Darius, by all accounts, was no longer the gormless fool she'd known growing up, the butt of every joke, and a mama's boy to boot.

Calcutta had been the making of him.

Her cousin had joined a managing agency and risen up the ranks at meteoric speed, so much so that, if her aunt's testimony was anything to go by, Darius would soon be lording over the sort of empire that would have made Clive of Plassey green with envy.

It also hadn't escaped her notice that he'd filled out.

With his waxed moustache, granite chin, and impeccably tailored suit, there was little doubt that *this* version of Darius wasn't the kind that ended up in the duck pond in his underclothes being pelted with bruised mangoes by his cousins.

A cough at her shoulder.

She turned to find Darius looking down at her. Of his companion, there was no sign.

Dinaz took the opportunity to melt away, leaving them in a sudden vacuum.

'I suppose this was Dinaz's idea of a wheeze?' His tone was mild. 'It's good to see you.'

'And you,' Persis managed. She took a deep breath. 'How are you?'

'I can't complain. Calcutta has been good to me.'

'So I hear.'

He smiled, then pulled a packet of Capstans from his pocket. Lighting one, he took a long draw, then blew the smoke sideways.

'I see you brought a lady friend along,' she said.

'A colleague. I'm a patron of several foundations. Aparna runs an art colony for the blind. Really quite inspirational.' His eyes rested on her, and she had to force herself not to look away. 'How is that English friend of yours? Blackbird?'

'Blackfinch,' she said automatically. 'He's touring the country. Setting up forensic laboratories at the Centre's behest.'

'How ... industrious of him. India owes him a great debt.' His sarcasm could have melted a hole in the marble at their feet.

'To answer your question, I have no idea how he is,' she said stiffly. 'I haven't seen him in some time.'

Something passed behind his eyes. Why had she said that?

A bubble of conversation approached them, led by Menon. 'We didn't finish our conversation,' he said to Persis, as he drew alongside. 'I'm curious to know exactly how this case you mentioned – the Rahman case – ties in with your current efforts to save James Whitby from the gallows.'

'I'm not trying to save Whitby from anything,' she replied, allowing a hint of irritation to enter her voice. 'I was tasked to review the case – no more, no less.'

'Vae victis!' He grinned, then: 'Apologies, Inspector. The curse of a classical education. I can be a frightful bore in at least three different languages. The Whitby case intrigues me. We Calcuttans have a Gallic flair for scandal. There's little else to do, sitting here in our princedoms by the Hooghly.'

'What's this all about?' said Darius.

Before she could reply, Menon explained, also mentioning Persis's interest in the 1946 case involving Azizur Rahman.

'Rahman?' said her cousin, frowning. 'He's a nasty piece of work.'

'You know him?' she said.

'Only by reputation. He's been consolidating his power base in the centre of the city –the Muslim enclaves. He likes to think he's a sort of political fixer, but the truth is, he's a gangster, by temperament and by deed. The man's practically running a criminal state up in Chitpore.'

'A few years ago, he was tried for murdering two people during the Direct Action Day riots,' said Persis. 'Apparently, your deputy chief minister, Saleem Ansari, helped him out. Why?'

'That's an easy one. They're fellow Islamists. Besides, Ansari's the type of politician who gives corruption a bad name. He struts around pretending to be a man of the people, a champion of the poor, but he's just another well-educated thug.'

'Careful, young man,' cut in Menon. 'Ansari has long ears.'

Darius shrugged. 'McDermott and Glover's the oldest managing agency in the city. We control a good chunk of the exports flowing out of West Bengal. Ansari needs men like me. In fact, I'll be face to face with him in a couple of days at a business reception he's throwing at Government House.'

'You're meeting Ansari?' said Persis.

'Yes.' Something in her tone encouraged him to continue. 'Why don't you come along? I mean, if you're so keen to take a closer look at the man.'

Her instincts told her to refuse, but the opportunity was too good to pass up. 'Thank you. That would be . . . helpful.'

'I'm still not clear how all this ties in with James Whitby,' interrupted Menon.

'That makes two of us,' muttered Persis, and tossed back her drink.

A brooding silence reigned for a few moments, and then Menon dispelled it with a wild laugh that threatened to crack a nearby marble pillar. 'Look at that picture up there, Inspector.' He pointed with his tumbler at the painting of the white man in a toga. 'That fellow was the former occupant of this mansion, the district engineer before me. Consider the absurdity of the image. He's posing as Jupiter – in Calcutta! But that was how the British saw themselves in India. Gods in all but name.'

'They weren't all like that,' said Darius. 'I've known some fine Englishmen in my time.'

'What you mean is that you've *learned* to like them. It's like learning to enjoy cigarettes. At first you throw up because your body knows they're bad for you. But eventually you absorb the nicotine into your system and you begin to crave them. You become an addict. The British were an addiction *forced* upon us.' His eyes glinted. 'It will take us years to unlearn the lessons they drilled into us. Wearing suits and ties in the heat, for instance. Or learning how to stomach the occasional slaughter.' The horseshoe of guests that had formed around them exchanged uncomfortable glances. The tone had turned maudlin. 'I was in a jeep during the worst of the Direct Action Day rioting,' Menon went on, directing himself to Persis again. 'We were up in Cossipore trying to make it back down south. We came across a gang of men – I couldn't tell if they were Muslims or Hindus, not that it mattered. They'd got hold of a pair of boys – they were brothers, I think. Certainly, they looked very alike. They couldn't have been more than eight, clutching at each other, weeping pitiably. I watched as they pulled them apart and then bludgeoned one of them to death. They kept hitting him until his head split open. They forced his brother to watch. And then they slit his throat.'

A silence spread around the room like a cold mist. Despite the muggy warmth, Persis shivered. Beside her, Seema appeared transfixed.

'It's quite a thing to witness grown men murdering children,' Menon continued. 'The brute carnality of it. It's something you can never un*see*.' He tapped a finger against the side of his glass, beating time to a rhythm only he could hear. 'Some say the British aren't to blame for our tendentious natures, and perhaps they're right. But the fact is that without the Raj, and the manner in which it ended, India would still be a single, undivided nation.'

'Do you really believe that?'

'Yes, Inspector, I do.' He met her gaze head-on. 'This man, Rahman – he's a cold-blooded killer. Be very careful.'

31

The clock on the wall said five minutes to midnight.

A dull ache was complaining like a fishwife between her shoulder blades. She glanced at Seema, sat cross-legged on the bed with a field of papers spread before her, an empty bowl of ice cream at her elbow.

They'd returned from the party unable to sleep. She suspected that her young ward's excess of energy was in no small part due to the half a dozen flutes of champagne she'd managed to knock back. It was a wonder the girl was still upright, let alone lucid enough to help her go through the case files she'd obtained from the Lal Bazar station.

For her own part, the evening at Menon's kept returning as a mosaic of clashing emotions. Her shock at bumping into Darius. Her cousin's invitation to attend a reception where she might have the opportunity to confront the politician Saleem Ansari. Seeing Dinaz with her fancy man ... This last thought lodged in her throat like a wishbone. *How did her friend justify it to herself?* Parading around publicly with a married father of two!

And yet ... the way Menon looked at Dinaz. As if he'd scoop her up and bounce her on his knee, if there wasn't a serious risk that it would flatten him in the process.

They were clearly besotted with each other, and had made the decision not to give a damn what anyone thought.

Dinaz, who'd always been the sensible one!

Her thoughts turned wretchedly to Archie Blackfinch.

Where was he now? Probably fast asleep, dreaming of faraway England, with a soppy grin on his handsome face.

Her heart burned in her chest.

She'd asked him to keep his distance; *she'd* told him there could be no future for them.

What she hadn't realised was just how much she would miss him.

His response had been to tell her that he loved her. Or rather, in that typically English way that seemed to regard romantic feelings as some sort of heroic shame, that he *thought* he did.

She'd been unable to say the words back to him. Why?

'Your cousin is very handsome.'

Seema was looking at her, spectacles perched in her hair, flexing the tiredness from her fingers.

'Who? Darius?'

'Yes.'

She sensed something lurking beneath the girl's words. 'I suppose so. If you like that sort of thing.'

'You mean there are women who *don't* appreciate handsome, well-dressed, articulate, successful men?' Seema raised an insouciant eyebrow. 'That woman he was with . . . is she his fiancée?'

'No.' The word came out a little too quickly.

'She looked like a film star,' said Seema wistfully.

'Well, she wasn't.' Why did the girl's curiosity make her irritable? What did she care who Darius was stepping out with? A moment ago, she'd been thinking about Archie Blackf—

The clock chimed gently, interrupting her train of thought.

Seema stretched into a yawn.

'We should probably finish up,' said Persis. 'What have you learned?'

They exchanged notes.

From the files Kasturi had given them, they'd gleaned basic details of the victims in the Rahman case.

Rita Chatterjee had been a dancer who'd worked at a club – the White Tiger Club – in Chitpore, a Calcuttan enclave north of their hotel. Walter 'Kip' Rivers had been based at the US consulate on Harrington Street, again within a stone's throw of the Great Eastern.

They had both been found dead at Chatterjee's home in nearby Burra Bazar.

Their killers had been seen exiting the building by Chatterjee's housemate, a Lata Tiwari.

Persis noted down the address. The chances were that Tiwari would have moved on in the intervening years, but if decent accommodation was as hard to find in Calcutta as it was in Bombay – particularly since the post-war and post-independence influx – then she might still be there.

Scanning the pathology report, she noted that the victims had been killed in different ways. Chatterjee had been strangled, while Rivers had been murdered with a bladed weapon. No rhyme or reason had been given as to why the killer should have used differing methods of dispatching his victims.

Like many of the other gaping holes in the case, this too had remained a mystery.

'So . . . what's the plan for tomorrow?' Seema was scooping up papers from the bedspread and stuffing them back into the folder.

Persis had been thinking on the matter. 'I want you to go to the National Library. It's over on the Belvedere Estate, not far from here. Dig up whatever you can on Saleem Ansari. I want to be fully prepared when I meet him. They should have back copies of the *Statesman* and the *Hindu*. Start there. And while you're at it, see what you can find out about Azizur Rahman.'

Seema nodded. 'What will *you* do?'

'I'm going to try and put some flesh on the bones of our victims.'

32

The van trundled down Chowringhee Road, its side emblazoned with the words MOSQUITO CONTROL DEPARTMENT. A bored-looking driver with one hand draped out of the window looked out at the road through a fly-splattered windshield.

She'd taken a tonga from the hotel. Her driver, a wizened homunculus in a dhoti and a torn vest, wheezed like a pair of bellows as he pulled the cart along, a bidi stuck out of the side of his mouth. Every hundred yards or so he'd stop, regain his breath, then haul in another lungful of smoke, as if taking in oxygen like a man climbing a mountain.

Early monsoon in downtown Calcutta.

The city was a furnace, intermittently cooled by the occasional deluge that left the air as fetid as a pool of stagnant water. No wonder Mark Twain had complained that the local weather was either melting brass doorknobs or turning them mushy.

Traffic congested the broad thoroughfares around the Maidan, the city's colonial-era hub, and the site of Fort William, built during the early years of the Bengal Presidency. The road was lined with banks, retail emporiums, and houses of commerce – the old temples to Kali replaced by newer shrines to the goddess of wealth: Lakshmi.

Women in designer frocks and brightly coloured saris, accompanied by men in pinstripe suits and sports jackets, stumbled from offices and public buildings like the exhausted survivors of a Roman bacchanalia. The ferocious heat and the oppressive humidity had done little to dampen the spirit of enterprise and industry that had characterised the city since the arrival of independence.

The concierge at the Grand Eastern had given her directions to the US consulate. She'd called ahead, and made an appointment for eleven.

While waiting for the hour to come around, she'd reviewed her notes over a leisurely breakfast.

In order to establish a link between Fareed Mazumdar's murder in Bombay and the case that he'd defended in Calcutta back in 1946 – if such a link even existed – she needed more information about the players in that trial. She'd sent Seema off to find out more about the politician Ansari, the man who'd pressured Mazumdar to take the case, and Azizur Rahman, the man who'd been accused of the murders.

Now she needed to piece together the victims' backgrounds, and the facts surrounding the killings.

On the face of it, these facts appeared straightforward.

In July 1946, Mohammed Ali Jinnah, future Prime Minister of Pakistan, and leader of the All-India Muslim League, had publicly called upon Indian Muslims to engage in a day of 'direct action', a nationwide strike in pursuit of a separate Muslim homeland.

On August 16th, a large gathering had taken place in Calcutta, at the Maidan, in response to Jinnah's call. Tens of thousands of Muslims came together to hear incendiary speeches – including a firebrand declaration made by the leader of the Bengal arm of the Muslim League, Saleem Ansari, future deputy chief minister of Bengal.

Within hours, gangs of Muslims and Hindus were fighting in the streets. Men, women, children – anyone caught out in the open was fair game. Bodies were left to rot where they fell.

Over the course of the next three days, more than four thousand were killed, touching off further rioting around the country, later enshrined in history as the Week of the Long Knives.

Azizur Rahman, a resident of Chitpore in the northern half of the city, was accused of entering a townhouse in the nearby Burra Bazar district on the afternoon of August 16th – in the company of a man named Mustapha Siddiqi – and murdering the two individuals present therein, namely, Rita Chatterjee and Walter Rivers.

Rahman and Siddiqi were subsequently arrested for the crime but released on bail pending trial.

Two weeks later, Siddiqi was found murdered in a back alley in Chitpore. His throat had been slit. A month after that, Rahman went on trial accused of the Chatterjee and Rivers murders.

Who *were* the victims? What had they been doing together at Chatterjee's Burra Bazar townhouse?

The defence case advanced several theories.

They alleged that Chatterjee was a sex worker, a high-class escort, and that Rivers had called on her that day for this reason.

They conceded that although it *was* possible the pair had been murdered by rioters, the rioters in question could not have been Azizur Rahman and Mustapha Siddiqi. They presented alibis from a club in Chitpore – the White Tiger Club – the same club that Rita Chatterjee had worked at – who swore under oath that Rahman and his co-accused had been in the place at the time of the killings. The prosecution countered that the alibis were worthless – the witnesses were locals in an area run by Rahman; they'd clearly been strong-armed into testifying. The fact that the alibis came from the White Tiger Club proved that Rahman must have known Chatterjee.

In his defence, Rahman did not deny having seen Chatterjee sing at the club; but that was as far as their acquaintance went. His defence team argued that the murders might instead be the work of locals who disapproved of a native woman and a black man consorting.

Persis knew that such an argument would hold sway among some of the jurors. Prejudice didn't just extend to relations between whites and natives. Ingrained preference for fairer skin, a prejudice against darker, was deeply entrenched in Indian society.

Finally, the defence pointed out that there was no physical evidence linking Azizur Rahman to the murders. No murder weapon. No forensic artefacts. And, furthermore, no clear motive.

The prosecution claimed to have an eyewitness, a woman by the name of Lata Tiwari, Rita Chatterjee's housemate.

And yet, by the time the witness took the stand, Tiwari had changed her tune. Her testimony became blurry, uncertain. Fareed Mazumdar demolished her in a brutal cross-examination.

The jury had been left with little choice but to acquit, Rahman's reputation notwithstanding.

Denver Jackson was a tall, rugged-looking black man, with close-cropped hair flecked with grey, and a trim moustache. His tie was wrenched down to the second button of his shirt, sweat stains the size of discuses visible under his armpits.

'Damned air conditioner is on the fritz,' he complained, ushering her into a seat. 'Can I get you something to drink?'

The US consulate on Harrington Street wasn't quite what she'd expected. A grim, grey-white concrete building with vertical slits slashed into its flank and ranks of recessed windows, the place looked more like a bunker than a diplomatic mission. An American flag hung from the roof, limp in the torpid heat.

Inside, she was led through long, carpeted corridors, largely silent, punctuated by white doors every few metres. The place reminded her of an asylum.

She accepted a glass of water from her host, then watched as he guzzled at his own glass like a camel at the end of a lengthy trek across the desert. Sated, he wiped his mouth with the back of his hand, then said: 'So . . . I understand you want to talk to me about Kip Rivers?'

Jackson was the US consulate's military liaison in West Bengal. During the war, he'd coordinated the American army's presence in the region. He was also one of the few black men Persis had ever met. In metropolises such as Bombay and Calcutta, they could often be seen as part of jazz quartets at the larger hotels. But they were few and far between, as rare as diamonds.

Jackson had a file in front of him, which he flicked through as he spoke. 'Walter – Kip to his friends – wasn't exactly a soldier. What I mean is, he'd enlisted, but suffered a combat injury in 1942 that meant we couldn't put him on the front line any more. Turns out Kip had an eye for photography – a lifelong passion – and a childhood ambition to become a journalist. The army paid for him to brush up his skills and he ended up working for the OWI – the Office of War Information – out here in India. The OWI's job was to foster a sympathetic attitude among the natives towards the presence of American soldiers on Indian soil. There were almost one hundred and fifty thousand GIs out here in Bengal alone.' His moustache twitched. 'Were you in the city back then?'

'No. This is my first visit.'

'Well, it was quite a sight! Chowringhee was crammed with GIs; you couldn't take three steps without some enterprising native selling you a copy of *Life* magazine or begging for a bottle of Coke or a Hershey bar. Kip's job was to document their experience – especially the black troops; there were about twenty thousand of them here too. He was posted to Calcutta in December 1942, around the time the Japs were bombing the docks and the tram depots.'

'So Rivers was in Calcutta more than three years before his death?'

'Sure. Don't look so surprised. Hell, I've been here since 1940. And this consulate has been around since the late 1700s, if you can believe that. George Washington sent a Massachusetts trader named Benjamin Joy out to Calcutta as the very first American consul. The British refused to recognise Joy's authority, but he hung around anyway, acting as Uncle Sam's commercial agent.' He reached into a pocket, pulled out a pack of cigarettes, and lit one from a matchbook.

'Why was Rivers *still* here in 1946? Why didn't he leave after the war ended?'

'He fell in love with the city. Managed to wrangle a commission to stay and work on assignments for the OWI across South Asia. He was a damned good photographer, and a more than capable journalist. I guess someone thought it would be useful having him based out here.' He smiled, reliving an old memory. 'He was always looking for the big scoop. A sort of black Lois Lane, though I kept telling him there was no Superman out here to save him – or anyone else for that matter. You only had to live through the Partition years to see that.'

'Rivers's body was discovered with that of a woman named Rita Chatterjee. What was his relationship to her?'

Jackson pulled a handkerchief from his pocket and wiped the back of his neck. 'Look. You seem like a woman of the world. It won't shock you to know that the first thing soldiers look for when they're stationed overseas is female companionship. Given the transitory nature of such postings, that usually means the type of company that's billed by the hour. From what I understand, Chatterjee was a ... woman of negotiable affection, if you'll pardon my French.'

'Don't you think it strange that, in the middle of a riot, Rivers would venture out on such an errand?'

He shrugged. 'I knew Kip. He was a good man, but he lived life on his terms. I guess he thought he'd be safe. After all, the natives were intent on killing *each other*. The rest of us were non-combatants, especially a news hack.'

Persis leaned back in her seat. 'Why didn't the US government pursue the case more vigorously? I mean, Rivers was an American citizen. Didn't they want justice for him?'

'How do you think it came to trial in the first place? Frankly, if it hadn't been for me pushing our friends over at Lal Bazar, we wouldn't have had any sort of meaningful investigation. Thousands died in the riots. Almost none have received justice.' He looked at his cigarette as if he couldn't work out how it had arrived in his hand. 'I can almost understand it. I wouldn't want to be the poor schmuck tasked to find out who did what to who in all that madness. Kip was just in the wrong place at the wrong time. Of course, there's also the fact that he was a *black* man.'

She said nothing. He took it that she hadn't understood his point. 'Come on, Inspector. I'm sure that an Indian can't be unfamiliar with the politics of race.' He waved the cigarette around. 'You know, when I first came out here, hardly anyone I met had ever *seen* a black man. You can imagine the fuss when thousands of black troops landed. Hell, some of the locals actually thought we ate human flesh, if you can believe that.'

He stood up and walked to a cabinet. Opening it, he took out a bottle and returned with two glasses. 'Kentucky bourbon,' he announced. 'Best in the world!' He poured himself a glass, then tipped the bottle at her.

'No. Thank you.'

'You're not in uniform.'

She hesitated, then nodded.

He poured a generous measure, then handed the glass to her.

She took a sip; the amber liquid set fire to her throat and she had to resist the urge to cough.

'We Americans love to self-mythologise. The defenders of democracy and the free world. But we have our own problems and we tend to take them with us wherever we go. In Calcutta, white and black soldiers were segregated in separate barracks and ate at separate canteens. Heck, we weren't even allowed to use the swimming pools on the same day. Kip spent a lot of time with the grunts and he didn't like it any more than I did. He worked on a propaganda film for the OWI featuring the lives of black troops out here. Kip used it to take a poke at race relations back home. The powers that be pulled it, of course.'

'Was Rivers – Kip – close to anyone else in Calcutta? A friend? A lover? Someone who might have held a grudge against Fareed Mazumdar for defending the man suspected of his killing?'

'You're clutching at straws, Inspector. Why would anyone blame Mazumdar for defending Rahman? Why not blame Rahman – the man accused of the actual killings? But, to answer your question: Kip was a loner; or at least, he hated the idea of being tied down. I can't think of anyone who'd care enough about his killing to make a federal case out of it.' He took another sip. 'It was an odd time and it affected us all in different ways. You have to remember, we were out here when the famine hit in '43. We saw what it did to the locals. Dead lying in the streets for days. Children and women reduced to walking skeletons. There were so many corpses, so many bodies being burned in the ghats, you could smell the city from twenty miles away. I guess we felt some measure of responsibility – if it hadn't been for the war and the decisions made to secure the Allied food supply, millions of Bengalis would still be alive today. We tried to share whatever rations we could spare – but it was a hopeless gesture.' He stopped. 'It hit Kip pretty hard – he was out in the streets cataloguing the horror. It's one of the reasons he decided to stay on. He blamed a lot of what he saw on imperialist attitudes. The idea that native lives were expendable. He sided with India's fight for freedom, I guess. Said it was no different to the fight we blacks had on our hands back home.'

'And yet his empathy didn't save him when the riots swept the city.'

'Since when has empathy been an antidote to the evil in men's hearts? I'm told neighbours butchered neighbours here once the party started.' His eyes dimmed. 'Twenty-six Americans died in Calcutta during the riots. Most of them were black.'

She reached into her notebook and took out the Star of David note. 'Does this mean anything to you?'

'Nope. I'm a Christian. Caught the Holy Ghost early in my mother's church.'

'Does it have any connection to Rivers?'

He threw back his head and laughed. 'Rivers was the most irreligious man I ever met. He used to say that if God really created man in his own image, then he had a lot to answer for.'

33

It wasn't often you saw excrement being sold next to a dietary staple.

The woman squatted over a basket of cow dung cakes; beside her, a man roasted maize over a charcoal fire. Persis wondered, with a dull horror, at the possibility of a sudden gust blowing dung particles on to the cobs. Then again, with the amount of black salt and chilli being applied to the maize, she doubted anyone would notice.

The White Tiger Club was located on a throbbing stretch of the Chitpore Road, within walking distance of the ancestral home of Rabindranath Tagore, though it was anyone's guess as to whether the late Nobel laureate and former first poet of the nation had ever set foot inside the place.

Persis had taken a taxi from the US consulate, inching the five kilometres northwards in heavy traffic. The driver, a genial chap from Assam, wittered on in an endless stream of one-sided conversation, neither waiting for, nor seeming to need, a reply.

The Chitpore Road ran north directly through the heart of the city, stretching from Lal Bazar in the south to the Chitpore Bridge, and passing through the crowded Burra Bazar neighbourhood, where the sidewalks were crowded with everything from shoe stands, to booksellers, to on-the-spot wigmakers.

Standing beside the maize and cow dung vendors, a small boy was carrying a basket on his head loaded with loaves. The basket and loaves were several times larger in volume than the boy, so that at first glance, his outstretched hands seemed to be welcoming onlookers to a magic act.

But there was nothing illusory about the look of hunger in his eyes, or the way his protruding ribs made it clear that the bounty of loaves was intended for stomachs other than his own.

The White Tiger Club was a graceless building, like a wedding cake that had wilted in the sun. The exterior whitewash was cracked, and the whole place looked as if it should have guards manning the ramparts with machine guns and a searchlight. A series of posters plastered to the outer wall proclaimed the touring marvels of Professor Ram Ram Singh and his genius for biting the heads off live kraits.

An otiose, pot-bellied guard in once-white livery and a red turban, with a scimitar at his hip, waved her through, a cigarette lodged at the corner of his mouth.

Inside, she found herself in a dimly lit antechamber with a threadbare carpet and a succession of faded posters in glass frames. The space smelled strongly of liquor, cheap tobacco, and a ground-in misery that no amount of cleaning solution could shift.

A man lurked behind a box-office counter.

Lounging in a seat, the top of his head – as threadbare as the carpet – barely made it into the frame. He spotted her and hauled himself upright, an act he imbued with a sense of endeavour akin to a labour of Hercules.

'The club doesn't open until the evening,' he drawled.

'I'd like to talk to someone in charge. I'm investigating a murder case. I'm a police officer,' she added.

He could not have seemed more astounded if a giraffe had

wandered in and told him it had taken over from Nehru as the new Prime Minister.

'Wait here.' He sloped off, returning minutes later to direct her through the darkened club to an office at the rear. The club floor, only marginally less seedy-looking than the reception, had the deflated air of a man returning to sobriety after a heavy night in his cups.

A stage lurked at the back of the space, framed by a proscenium arch.

On the arch, a succession of light bulbs made the outline of a shape. Due to the fact that the lights were off, it took her a moment to realise that they depicted a resting tiger.

In the office, she was introduced to the club's manager, a Sudeep Burman, an obese fellow sporting a wig so laughable it looked like a dead beaver flung casually on to his skull. He was dressed in a pinstriped waistcoat, flung open to reveal a white shirt soaked in sweat.

He greeted her cordially and gestured for her to sit.

'Inspector.' He rolled the word around his tongue like a mouthful of bad wine. 'How may I help you?'

'Have you worked here long?'

'Ten years now, though the club has been around longer than that. Why do you ask?'

'I'm looking for someone who remembers a woman who sang here a few years ago: Rita Chatterjee.'

He stiffened, and a look of panic flitted across his face. He seemed to flirt with denial, then said, 'Yes. I knew Rita.'

'I'm investigating her death.'

He nodded, his jowls wobbling. 'They never found her killer, as I recall.'

'Two men were charged. One went to court. Azizur Rahman. He was acquitted.'

'Well, that's because he was innocent.'

'Being found not guilty isn't the same thing as being innocent. At his trial, Rahman presented several alibis from this club. He must have known Chatterjee, or at least met her here.'

His pupils moved around like rats trying to escape a cage. She sensed his discomfort. She wondered why he'd immediately leaped to defend Rahman.

'Tell me about her.'

'What is there to tell? She was a dancer and a singer. A good one. I hired her back in, oh, early 1946, I should think. She was very popular with our customers.'

'Who *are* your customers?'

'Well, during the war, we catered to a lot of the American soldiers. Mainly the black ones. They were banned from entering the clubs and bars frequented by the whites. But our doors have always been open to all. The only colour I care about is the colour of a man's cash.' He smiled as if this sentiment elevated him to the sort of saintly pedestal reserved for men such as Gandhi. 'After the war ended, we had a *reputation*. Civil servants, managing agency men, Europeans stuck in the city … For a while, we attracted a clientele of well-heeled professionals.'

'Where was Rita from?'

'I have no idea.'

'You didn't ask?'

He flapped a hand. Each finger modelled a lavish ring, giving him the look of a cut-price maharaja. 'My girls come from everywhere and nowhere. Some come with happy stories, some with sad. I've learned not to pry. All I get is lies, in any case. They're here to work. That's all that matters.'

'What sort of work do they do?'

There must have been an unconscious inflection in her tone, because he frowned, and thrust out his chin. 'I understand what you're getting at. But you couldn't be more wrong. I run a clean place. My girls dance, sing, entertain the men, but that's it.'

'And yet Chatterjee was accused of being a high-class escort.'

He shook his head curtly, the wig moving in a countervailing direction, like a hedgehog fleeing the scene. 'Once they leave my premises, I can't stop them from doing as they wish.'

'The man she was found dead with – Walter Rivers – did you know him?'

Another hesitation, and then a nod. 'Yes. He was a regular here.'

'Were they friends?'

'No more than any of the other men who admired her. She was an attractive woman. She left an impression.'

'And yet you claim to know nothing about her.'

Sweat had begun to run down the side of his bulbous nose. He squirmed on his chair, clearly discomfited by her questioning. Yet there was something about him that gave her pause. She sensed a goodness in him, despite his obvious attempts at obfuscation. A man caught on the horns of a dilemma: to speak or not to speak?

'For what it's worth, I don't think you had anything to do with Chatterjee's death,' she said. 'But *someone* killed her. And, till date, no one has answered for the crime. Anything you can tell me may be of help.'

He looked down at his desk, his gaze alighting on a small photo frame. Even at an angle, she could see a woman and a young girl imprisoned by the frame's silver borders. 'My wife and daughter,' he said. His chin sank into his neck, and he contemplated the picture, before heaving a great sigh. 'All I know is that she came to us via a talent agency. I can point you in their direction. Beyond that, I cannot help.'

34

Thankfully, the agency was only a short tonga ride away, out beyond the western perimeter of Burra Bazar, occupying an office on the third floor of a canary-coloured building overlooking the Hooghly.

The afternoon sun blazed from the monumental steel girth of the Howrah Bridge and the roofs of vehicles packed bumper-to-dented-bumper upon it. A hazy corona of vehicular emissions and soot from the factories lining the river's banks hung over the bridge like a small mushroom cloud.

Directly across from the foot of the building, on the far side of the Strand Bank Road, stone steps led down to the Armenian ghat, one of many such gathering places on the banks of the river. The Calcuttans were a littoral people, as comfortable on the water as camels in the burning sands of the Thar Desert.

The Star of the Orient talent agency was run by an American named Fanny Drake.

Persis found the woman sitting on the roof of the building, in a deckchair, smoking a cigarette from a black slimline holder, like a movie siren from the twenties. The air of an ageing – and slightly eccentric – film starlet was enhanced by a black satin dress with shoulder pads you could land a pair of planes on and a gold belt patterned with fish scales. The ensemble wouldn't have looked out of place on Lauren Bacall.

The outfit was completed by oversized sunglasses and a flapper turban with elaborate beadwork.

Persis introduced herself and explained the reason for her visit.

For a moment, it seemed Drake hadn't heard her. And then she said, 'You're probably wondering why I'm dressed like this? Funeral. An old friend. I'm trying to decide if I should go. Never really seen the point of them. Once you're dead, what does it matter? You don't see goldfish wailing and carrying on when their friends move on to the great goldfish bowl in the sky.'

Persis looked around and saw a stack of deckchairs leaning against the low concrete wall encircling the roof.

She walked over, picked one up, returned, untangled it, and then perched herself on the edge of the striped seat.

From this vantage point, she could see far out over the Hooghly, the river traffic moving gently upon the water, flat-bottomed sampans propelled by poles, launches puttering along in a diesel haze, a logjam of riverine vessels that mirrored the thronged roads of the twin cities on either side.

'I'm told that Rita Chatterjee arrived at the White Tiger Club via your agency.'

Drake pulled her sunglasses down an inch and looked at her over the top of them. Her eyes were blue and bloodshot. Persis became aware of the waft of alcohol.

'Rita was on my books and went to the White Tiger Club. What of it?'

'What can you tell me about her?'

'What makes you think there's anything to tell?'

Persis said nothing. Drake continued to stare at her, then looked away, drawing deeply on her cigarette holder. 'I get a dozen girls a day walking through my doors. All with stars in their eyes and fresh air between their ears. *I can dance! I can sing! I can act!* Please, madam, make me famous!' Her voice was low and husky. 'And then, once in a while, a girl turns up with something else. Charisma. Presence. Rita *was* beautiful, but when you've got a city this crowded, beautiful faces are a dime a dozen. Rita could dance; she could sing. But the way she wore a dress ... Men were enchanted by her.'

'If she was as talented as you say she is, why did she end up at a dive like the White Tiger Club?'

A sharp look. 'You call it a dive, but there was a time not too long ago when that joint was jumping. A lot of VIPs moved through the place; money and power, it's a heady cocktail.' She fell silent, reliving a private memory. Persis guessed it wasn't just the British who remembered better days before independence. 'The truth is, *I* didn't send Rita to the White Tiger. I had grander ambitions for her. I thought she had a decent shot of making it in the talkies. I was on the verge of getting her her first role. But the girl wouldn't wait, wouldn't listen.'

'Why not?'

She puffed on her holder again, the smoke drifting away on a warm breeze. 'She was talked into it by a friend. A man she couldn't say no to.'

'Who?'

'The shyster lawyer who defended her killers. Fareed Mazumdar.'

35

Broken bones grow back stronger.

The man who'd told her that had been a kindly neighbour. He'd said the words to her a day after her father had broken her mother's jaw and right forearm. That was the day he'd left, taking with him the meagre savings her mother had set aside for her daughters' school fees.

Seema had never told anyone why her father had attacked her mother that night. Her mother had seemed content to draw a veil over the matter. As a nine-year-old, Seema had known even then that there were some things adults never talked about openly.

The years since had passed in a blur. Her mother's arm had never quite recovered – nor had her mind, Seema suspected – and so it had fallen to Seema to become the family's principal bread-winner. Hard years. She'd ended up finding a semi-permanent job with the railways, cleaning station latrines, a horror she would not have wished on her worst enemy.

Tying a cloth around her nose and mouth, galvanised-steel bucket in hand, twice a day she'd venture into concrete bunkers stinking of shit and piss, an odour so foul it could knock out a rampaging bull. And the careless disregard with which her fellow citizens – men, in particular – vacated their bodily effluent, liberally spraying walls and floors as if they were avant-garde artists of the type she sometimes saw in discarded magazines ... A night shift in hell might have seemed paradise by comparison.

Over time, she became conscious of another feeling, one that rose insidiously to engulf her. Shame. Not shame at her chosen role – it was honest work – but shame at the notion that she had ended up at the very place society had allotted to her kind since time immemorial.

The Untouchables. The Dalits.

She knew that Gandhi had called her people the Harijans – the children of God. Hollow words. If they were truly the children of God, why did God treat them so? Why did he allow others to treat them so?

The trajectory of her life had changed when a retired teacher had spotted her on a station platform, sitting outside the latrine, attempting to read a discarded newspaper.

Intrigued, he'd engaged her in conversation.

A week later, he'd enrolled her in evening classes that he taught for slum children; he'd even bought her a set of second-hand textbooks.

Karnik. That had been his name. Narayan Karnik. A good man, a man of vision.

The classes gave her the impetus she needed. He couldn't teach his wards everything, but he'd lit a fire inside her that continued to rage a decade later. *If you wish to know where you must go, first you must understand where you've come from.*

It had taken years for her to truly understand his meaning.

In the new India, every community, every faction was fighting for its place in the sun. The Dalits, too, would have to fight.

And the first step in that fight was to arm themselves – with education, with ideals, and with courage.

The National Library was grander than she could possibly have imagined, with all the trappings of a palace, the sort peasants might burn down during a revolution. Once the home of the

lieutenant governor of Bengal, the neoclassical milk-white building – with green-painted doors and window frames – was set
within grounds so vast and lush they could have doubled as a
safari park.

Inside, she found an intimidatingly cavernous reading room
with a vaulted ceiling held up by Roman beams and supported by
Corinthian pillars. A grandfather clock hung on one wall. Her
guidebook informed her that it had been made in London and
transported to the tropics, presumably because the locals – despite
creating an ancient civilisation rich in science and literature – had
somehow managed to neglect the tricky business of learning how
to tell the time properly.

Her heart skipped a beat as she noted the packed reading tables.
These people – young men, for the most part – looked as if they
belonged. Could the same be said of her?

It took her ten minutes to approach a librarian at the main desk
and to be directed to the newspaper section. She gathered a stack
of issues from the past decade, and then walked up a broad flight
of steps to a mezzanine where reading desks were laid out between
floor-to-ceiling shelving.

As she turned a corner, a figure coming the other way stumbled
into her, sending her sprawling, newspapers flying in all
directions.

A moment of blankness, and then she felt a hot rush race up
her throat and to her cheeks.

A youngish man looked down at her from behind square-
framed spectacles. 'I'm so terribly sorry!'

She ignored him and pushed herself to her feet, then crouched
down again and began to gather the newspapers together. Her set
of pencils – sharpened that morning to the point where they
might have served as kebab skewers – had embedded themselves
in the carpet.

The man dropped into a squat and began helping her.

'You don't need to do that,' she said, without looking at him.

'It's the least I can do.'

When they'd collected everything together, he gestured her towards a nearby desk.

Setting the stack down, he pushed his own book – a thick, red-bound volume entitled *The Criminal Law Journal of India: Volume 52, 1949* – under one arm and held out a hand. 'My name's Haresh. Once again, allow me to apologise for my clumsiness.'

She found it difficult to meet his eyes. He was of middling height, uncommonly handsome, with glossy black hair, shining cheeks, and a debonair moustache. His white shirt went well with his tan brogues and khaki trousers.

'Do you have a name?'

She cleared her throat. 'Seema. Seema Desai.'

He smiled. 'You're not from Calcutta, are you?'

She looked at him sharply.

'Your accent. You're not Bengali. Let me guess . . . Bombay?'

She nodded.

'In that case, allow me to welcome you to our fair city. *Shagatom!*' He nodded at the stack of newspapers. 'Are you studying at the university?'

She hesitated, then shook her head. 'It's research. For a personal project.'

'A personal project?' He pushed his spectacles back up his nose. 'Well, now I'm *really* intrigued.'

She watched as he took the desk beside her, set down his textbook, then removed an exercise book from a satchel. He beamed at her. 'Why don't we study together?'

36

The houses on either side of the road seemed to grow right out of the pavement; a screen of trees marching down the road secluded much of the façades from prying eyes.

The taxi came to a halt halfway along the leafy lane.

Persis disembarked, and asked the driver to wait.

He watched as she made her way to the nearest home, pushed through the unattended gate, walked to the entrance, lifted a brass lion's head knocker, and crashed it against the door.

Moments later, the door swung back to reveal a young woman in slacks and a crumpled, low-cut blouse that bared just enough skin to make the taxi driver sit up in his seat.

'I'm looking for Lata Tiwari,' said Persis.

'She's not here.'

'Where can I find her?'

'She's at work.'

'Do you have an address?'

'I do.'

Persis waited. The girl said nothing.

'May I have it?'

'That depends.'

'On what?'

'On who you are and why you want it.' She thrust her jaw out belligerently.

Persis bit back the sudden desire to blast the chit of a girl into the middle of next week. Quickly, she explained the reason for her visit – namely, that she was investigating the unsolved murder of Rita Chatterjee and wished to talk to the woman who'd appeared in the trial as a material witness.

The girl's eyes became round. 'You're the famous policewoman, the one from Bombay!'

'I really need to speak to Lata.'

'Of course. I'll write the address down for you. Please come in.'

As the girl scrabbled around for a pen and paper, she introduced herself as Tiwari's housemate. 'The murders happened right here. But I suppose you knew that?'

'Yes.'

'You know, when I moved *in*, I asked Lata why she hadn't moved *away*. I mean, how could she carry on living here, in the house where her friend was killed! Do you know what she told me? She said she owed it to Rita to stay on. Isn't that strange?'

Lata Tiwari worked for a small outfit that provided administrative services to the Burmah Oil Company. Located at the northern tip of Diamond Harbour Road in Kidderpore, within walking distance of the Alipore zoological gardens, the firm maintained offices on the third floor of a modern corporate tower, a vision of dressed concrete and rectangular windows.

Having taken an elevator from the lobby, and negotiated her way past the receptionist, Persis found herself parked in a tiny office waiting for Tiwari. The office was so small, she would have struggled to smuggle Akbar in, let alone swing the poor cat around.

In the interim, her mind circled back to the revelation that Fareed Mazumdar had not only known Rita Chatterjee prior to the trial in which he'd defended her murderers, but had been instrumental in convincing her to work at the White Tiger Club.

Why had he done that? How had they known each other? To

her frustration, Fanny Drake, Chatterjee's agent, had been unable or unwilling to elaborate.

She knew that she'd finally grasped the tail of something, a first sighting of the path that might lead to the truth. But where would that trail take her, and how might it help in proving James Whitby's innocence – if indeed he *was* innocent?

The door to the office opened and a woman walked in.

She was small, slender, with hair cut short to the shoulders, and wearing a smart white office dress with navy piping. Horn-rimmed spectacles sat on her nose, contrasting bookishly with the elegance of her outfit.

'I'm Lata Tiwari. I'm told that you wish to see me?'

Persis rose from her seat. Without ceremony, she explained why she'd tracked the woman down.

She watched as the colour drained from Tiwari's face. The woman seemed to buckle, then collapsed into a chair. Persis waited.

Finally, Tiwari spoke. 'I can't speak to you.'

Persis pulled a chair close and sat down beside her. 'I've read the initial statement you gave to the police. You said that you'd been away, out of Calcutta. You returned on the day of the killings, August 16th, and had just reached home – the home you shared with Rita Chatterjee – when you saw Azizur Rahman and Mustapha Siddiqi exiting the house. When you went in, you found the bodies of Chatterjee and Walter Rivers. Based on your statement, the men were arrested and later released on bail.' She stopped. 'Yet you changed your testimony at the trial. You claimed that you were no longer confident in your identification of either man.'

'You don't understand.'

'I think I do. Rahman – or his thugs – threatened you. You believed he'd already killed Rita. Mustapha Siddiqi had since been murdered – you assumed Rahman had been behind it, to prevent Siddiqi from being turned against him by the authorities. You were frightened for your life, and you had every right to be.'

She realised that the woman was weeping.

She sat back and waited, understanding that an internal dam had burst. How long had Tiwari waited for someone to find her, to ask her these questions?

When she had recovered herself sufficiently to speak, she said: 'Ever since, I've wondered if I did the right thing. Rita was my friend and I betrayed her.'

Persis took her hand. It pulsed warmly inside her own.

'They say unabsolved guilt rots the soul,' Tiwari continued, miserably. 'It's why I never moved away. I felt – still feel – her presence there.'

'I came to Calcutta to discover the truth behind Fareed Mazumdar's murder. I don't know if it's linked to Rita's killing, but I'm not going home until I know one way or the other. Will you help me?'

Tiwari pulled a handkerchief from her pocket, took off her spectacles, and dabbed at her eyes. She gave a curt nod.

'I'm told that Mazumdar convinced Rita to work at the White Tiger Club. How did they know one another?'

'They were childhood friends. They grew up in the same orphanage. Fareed's mother died during childbirth and his father was killed when he was still a boy. Fareed ended up at the St Nicholas orphanage in Dum Dum. Rita was already a resident there. I don't know much about their time there, except that they became close. They stayed close after they left the orphanage.'

'Were they lovers?'

'No. It was more like brother and sister. Fareed became protective of her at the orphanage. I know Rita trusted him. She was a little in awe of him, I think. Despite his circumstances, he'd qualified as a *lawyer*. For a boy growing up in a Calcutta orphanage, that's no mean feat. Rita set him on a pedestal. He took advantage of that to get her to agree to work at the White Tiger.'

'How do you mean "took advantage of"?'

'I mean he pressed her to do it. He was relentless. She wasn't sure that she wanted to work there, but he told her it would do wonders for her career. She trusted him and so she eventually gave in.'

'Why would he be so keen for her to work there? He was a lawyer. What did it matter to him where she worked?'

'I don't know. What I do know is that he delivered her into the hands of her killer.'

Persis straightened. 'I don't understand.'

Tiwari hesitated. 'Look. I appreciate what you're trying to do. But you must walk away from this. We can't change the past. Nothing you do will bring Rita back. You don't know these people. They're dangerous. Walk away. Go back to Bombay.'

'I can't do that.'

Tiwari's lips narrowed into a grim line. 'Very well ... It never came out at the trial. And you won't find his name on any paperwork ... But everyone knows that Azizur Rahman is the real owner of the White Tiger Club.'

37

The speed at which time passed depended on the situation.

She'd read that somewhere years ago. It had always made perfect sense to her. Five minutes in the latrine of Churchgate station could seem like an eternity.

But now the hours seemed to fly by.

It was not that she'd been short of male admirers.

In the Dharavi slum, they tended to be lecherous older men seeking a young bride, or penniless boys with no prospects, armed with cheesy lines they'd lifted from the silver screen. Either that or the occasional late-night drunk stumbling out of a railway toilet, sandals soaked in urine, pawing at her clothing as if she were a prize beast at the camel fair.

Haresh Saxena was different. His laughter bubbled around her like foam capping the waves that rolled on to Bombay's beaches. He seemed content to talk, and his smile gleamed like a hurricane lamp in the dark.

Once he'd understood her mission, he became keen to help. No fan of Saleem Ansari or Azizur Rahman, he'd told her that the two men were powerful and – in the case of Rahman – dangerous. He asked her why she was researching their pasts.

She'd deflected his curiosity by telling him that she wasn't at liberty to discuss the matter.

He'd persisted for a while, and then shrugged. 'Whatever it is you're doing, make sure you stay away from Rahman. The man has a hair-trigger temper, by all accounts.'

'Why haven't the authorities done anything about him?'

'The man's an animal. Nobody wants to get on his wrong side. You'd be better off kicking a tiger in the privates.' He stopped as she looked away, blushing. 'Besides, Rahman has political connections – namely, Ansari. And the virtue of our police officers is just as easily bought as those in Bombay.'

'Not *every* officer,' she said quietly.

'An idealist!' he brayed. Amusement glittered in his eyes, and then, sensing her discomfort, he said, 'Please forgive me. We're such snobs in Calcutta. They say even our servants were prone to correcting the king's English when King George came here in 1911.' He looked at his watch. 'I don't know about you, but I'm hungry. Would you care to join me for lunch?'

A surge of panic blocked her throat.

He stood up. 'Suit yourself.'

She watched him walk away, and then, rising slowly to her feet, she padded after him.

38

The sign above the arched brick entranceway was held up by ropes so worn it looked as if the slightest gust might bring it down on to the heads of those passing below.

The ride up to the St Nicholas orphanage in Dum Dum had given Persis time to reflect on her findings.

Multiple murders, all linked by a single thread: Fareed Mazumdar.

In 1921, Mazumdar's father, Shabaz Mazumdar, had been murdered at the behest – allegedly – of his employer, Charles Whitby.

As a consequence, the seven-year-old Fareed had ended up at the St Nicholas orphanage. Here he had met and befriended a fellow orphan: Rita Chatterjee.

Years later, as adults, Fareed had convinced Rita to work at the White Tiger Club, an establishment owned by the gangster Azizur Rahman. That same year, in August 1946, Chatterjee – and the American, Walter 'Kip' Rivers – had been murdered – allegedly by Rahman.

Yet it was Fareed Mazumdar who had defended Rahman in court, securing his exoneration.

Something about that case – perhaps his own sense of guilt? – had then led to Mazumdar leaving Calcutta and moving to Bombay, where, in 1949, the Indian government had asked him to prosecute Charles Whitby – for the murder of Mazumdar's own father.

And then, Whitby's son, James, had, allegedly, murdered Fareed – and was now sentenced to death for the crime.

Before his death, Fareed Mazumdar had been agitated, drinking heavily. Someone had been sending him press cuttings of the Chatterjee-Rivers case. Why?

Her thoughts returned to her meeting with Chatterjee's housemate, Lata Tiwari.

She'd wondered briefly if Tiwari might have been behind the mysterious articles, but had quickly dismissed the notion. In her estimation, Tiwari seemed genuine, and claimed to know nothing about the cuttings.

Persis had asked her about Chatterjee's connection to Walter 'Kip' Rivers.

Tiwari had said she wasn't aware of any relationship between the pair beyond a passing friendship. 'Rita had plenty of male admirers; but she was ambitious. Fareed had convinced her that the White Tiger Club was a stepping stone to bigger and better things. She wouldn't have given herself up to just anyone.' She paused. 'I think Rivers was interested in her in his capacity as a journalist. He was always photographing her. Rolls and rolls of film. Rita believed he was intrigued by her backstory: an orphan, now a glamorous singer in a bar where the city's movers and shakers congregated.'

Finally, Persis had shown her the Star of David note. 'Mazumdar also received this before his death. Why would someone send him a Jewish symbol?'

Something had flared in the woman's eyes, but she'd shaken her head. 'I have no idea. Rita wasn't Jewish. She was a Hindu, a devout one.'

For the first time, she sensed something evasive in Tiwari's manner. But there was nothing more from the woman.

For a moment, she reflected on the odd plurality of the investigation.

Chatterjee was a Hindu; Mazumdar a Muslim; James Whitby a Christian; Persis herself a Parsee. And here was a note bearing a Jewish symbol. If anything spoke to the melting-pot nature of the subcontinent, then surely this case was it. It was a wonder how so many chose to ignore this self-evident reality and instead incite hatred along communal lines.

She recalled something Jonathan Swift had written, in *Gulliver's Travels*: 'We have just enough religion to make us hate, but not enough to make us love one another.'

It took her a little while to find someone at the orphanage who might help.

She was led to a Sister Agnes Katz, refereeing a game of soccer at the rear of the orphanage. Katz was astonishingly mobile for a woman in her late fifties and wearing a habit. She was also considerably more vulgar than Persis thought reasonable for a nun, blowing her whistle every few seconds like a drunken stationmaster and blasting her young charges with the sort of language Persis had rarely heard outside of Bombay's docks.

Afterwards, sitting on a sun-warmed bleacher, the woman mopped the sweat from her face with a towel, and said, 'So what's this all about?'

'You're American?' said Persis.

'Canadian, actually. Though my father, may he rest in peace, was American for a short while. By way of Saxony.'

'I understand you've been here a long time. I'm looking for information about a pair of orphans who were here back in the 1920s. Fareed Mazumdar and Rita Chatterjee.'

The change in Katz's demeanour was instant. 'Well now,' she breathed.

'You remember them?' Persis prompted.

Katz reached into a pocket sewn into her habit, took out a flat tin, removed a rolled cheroot, lit it, and slotted it into her mouth. 'I remember all my charges. Many of them come back and see me when they've found their feet in the world.' She paused. 'It was horrible what happened to Rita. That murderous thug . . .'

'Do you mean Azizur Rahman?'

'Who else would I mean?'

'He was exonerated. Through Mazumdar's efforts.'

Katz clucked angrily. 'That was the hell of it. I never understood why Fareed would want to defend the man.'

'I understand he was asked to do so by Saleem Ansari, the politician.'

Katz gave an angry shake of the head. 'Ansari.' She looked as if she would say more, but fell silent.

'Do you know him?'

'Not personally, no. But the man's got blood on his hands.'

'How do you mean?'

'He's one of those politicos willing to sacrifice others for their own gain. Ansari's speciality is using religion as a weapon.'

'Don't you use religion too?' said Persis mildly. 'I mean, you're a nun. And this orphanage is the work of missionaries, isn't it?'

Katz aimed a sharp look at her. 'We don't use the orphanage to proselytise. Some would like to believe that we do, but the truth is that we're a secular institution. That doesn't mean my faith isn't important to me.'

Persis decided to change tack. 'Is there *anything* you can tell me that might help?'

Katz pondered the question. 'I don't know if this is relevant, but a woman came to see me a couple of years after Rita's death. This must have been in the spring of 1949. She claimed to be Rita's mother. Said she'd been too young, too unwed when she'd had the child, and so she'd left her at the orphanage with a note claiming the baby's parents had died of cholera.

'She wanted to know what had happened to her daughter. Had a sudden desire to find her. I told her we'd named her Rita, and then I told her that she was dead. That she'd been murdered.' She stopped. 'The woman seemed devastated. Anyway, that was the last I saw of her.'

Persis considered this. She wasn't sure how this new piece of information fit into her investigation, if at all. 'What was her name?'

'She didn't give one.'

'What did she look like?'

'She was tall, middle-aged, unmemorable. She had a slight resemblance to Rita, but only if you looked for it.'

Persis made a mental note, and moved on.

'You say that your charges often come back to see you. Did Fareed and Rita come back?'

'They did for a while. But then, like everyone else, they became busy with their own lives. Ambition, Inspector. The eighth deadly sin. But ambition is the worst of them all; in our modern world, we couch it in reverence and convince ourselves that without it our lives are wasted.'

39

Emerging from the orphanage, she checked her watch. Almost seven.

She'd asked Seema to be back at the hotel by eight. That would give her time enough to arm herself with any information Seema had discovered about Saleem Ansari and Azizur Rahman before attending the business function at Government House later that night.

She felt a moment's trepidation at the prospect of negotiating an evening with Darius, but if that was the price for getting close to Ansari, then it was a small one to pay.

She hailed a taxi and was about to tell the man to head back to the Great Eastern when another thought occurred to her.

She took out her notebook.

Flipping through it, she found the address that Arora, James Whitby's lawyer, had given her for the witness who'd come forward against Charles Whitby for the murder he had allegedly orchestrated of Fareed Mazumdar's father back in 1921, namely, a woman named Anabella Santos, a maidservant who'd once worked for the Whitby family and claimed to be able to implicate the industrialist directly in that murder.

She checked the address with the driver and was told it was twenty minutes away, in an area near the Hooghly known as Dakshineswar.

Having tracked down Santos's home – a tiny, two-room dwelling above a hole-in-the-wall cobbler's premises – she was redirected to the nearby Dakshineswar temple where Santos worked.

The temple was within walking distance, located on the eastern bank of the Hooghly.

As she moved towards it, the crowds began to thicken, until she was being borne along by a wave of what she presumed were devotees but might equally have been rioters. In India, it was often difficult to tell the difference.

The temple, when it came into view, was more spectacular than she could have imagined.

Built in the nine-spired tradition known as *navaratna*, the soaring architecture of the central temple – painted in cream and red – momentarily halted her advance. This was the sort of grandiose shrine that attracted both devotees and tourists, a building built not simply to honour a deity, but, like the Egyptian pyramids, raised to prove something about those who had built it. The sort of religious edifice that looked you in the eye and told you whether all your soul needed was a quick polish or whether you could expect a one-way ticket to a hotter place even than Calcutta.

The temple was set in a vast courtyard, thronging with visitors; twelve smaller temples lined one side of the courtyard, facing east.

She quickly located Santos in a smaller, roped-off shrine to one side of the main complex, supervising a crew of cleaners.

When she explained the reason for her presence, Santos, at first, seemed hesitant. Persis persisted until, eventually, the woman agreed to speak. Moving to one side of the shrine, she took a seat on a concrete bench and bade her visitor to join her.

A compact woman, in a close-wrapped, mud-coloured sari, Santos, a Goan, had a worn yet defiant look to her, as if she'd weathered life's vicissitudes and come out the other side. Her dark hair, pulled back into a tight bun, was streaked with grey.

'I'm told you worked for Charles Whitby,' began Persis.

'I worked for his wife,' corrected Santos. 'I was her maidservant and the ayah to Master James.'

Ayah. Nursemaid.

'How long did you work for them?'

'Until Mrs Whitby – Mary – left him.'

'You left after she vanished?'

'No. I would not have abandoned James. Mr Whitby dismissed me.'

'Why?'

'I suppose he sensed that I didn't like him very much.'

'Why not?'

Her mouth became a thin line. 'I've known many bad men in my life, Inspector. Charles Whitby was the worst. A callous brute, a man of no . . . *feeling*. Or rather, a man unable to *control* his feelings. Especially his rage.'

'Is that why you came forward as a witness in the case against him?'

'I came forward because I believe he was responsible for the death of Fareed Mazumdar's father.'

'What makes you so sure?'

The woman's eyes glittered. 'I overheard him giving the order.' She paused, forcing Persis to wait for her to continue. 'It was late one evening – this was back in 1921 – and I was passing outside his office at the Whitby home, here in Calcutta. I heard his voice – it was raised in anger. I stopped to listen – perhaps I shouldn't have. I heard him tell two men to find Shabaz Mazumdar and kill him. I heard them negotiate a price for the killing.'

'Who were the two men?'

'I don't know. I didn't see them. They were just thugs he'd hired to do his dirty work.'

'Why did you wait this long to come forward? It's been nearly three decades. Why now?'

Santos grimaced. 'What should I have done? Come forward against my employer, one of the most powerful men in Calcutta?

A white man? A man with the influence and money to bend the law to his whim?' She gave a bitter laugh. 'I was afraid, Inspector. I was a young woman, then, powerless, and with much to lose.'

'Aren't you afraid now?'

Shadows seem to swirl and coalesce in her eyes. 'They say the truth is a bird trapped beneath our hands. One day, you open your hands and the truth flies out. Independence gave us our country back from men like Whitby. We took our *power* back. It was just time, that's all.'

Persis considered the woman's words.

It seemed thin testimony for the Indian government to use as a basis for a prosecution against Charles Whitby. The word of a single employee, a recollection some three decades in the past, with no other corroboration. Then again, perhaps their reasoning was not based on the merits of the case, but on a desire to undermine Whitby.

If so, the Englishman had a legitimate grievance.

'The government has speculated that the motive for the killing was Shabaz Mazumdar taking a stand against Charles Whitby's business practices. Particularly in the way he treated his Indian employees. Shabaz became embroiled in the non-cooperation movement and agitated for strike action at Whitby's Barrackpore plant.'

Santos nodded. 'Shabaz was a man of principal. He'd worked for Whitby for a long time. He came to the house often. At first, they seemed on cordial terms, but I saw how, over time, as the independence movement gained ground, Shabaz began to re-evaluate his opinions. It got to the point where he was openly questioning Whitby's methods.'

'Why didn't Whitby just fire him? Why kill him?'

She hesitated.

'There was something more to it, wasn't there?'

The sound of the crowd outside, chanting in unison, momentarily interrupted them. They waited as the prayer reached a crescendo before breaking like a wave.

'This temple complex was built by a woman named Rani Rashmoni,' said Santos. 'We're sitting in a shrine dedicated to her. Rashmoni's husband was a wealthy landowner. When he passed away, she took over his estate, and used it to help those less fortunate than herself. One day, as she was planning to visit the holy city of Benares, the goddess Kali came to her in a dream, ordering her to build this temple. And so that's what she did.

'When she'd finished, she decreed that the temple would not be restricted to high-caste Hindus. All castes, all faiths, would be welcome here. It's why a woman like me, a Catholic, can work here.' She paused. 'Rashmoni stood up to all those who sought to stop her from doing what she knew to be right. Hindu Brahmins, the British. If I had had her courage, perhaps I might have stopped Shabaz's death.'

'Why did Charles Whitby really order Shabaz's murder?'

The woman's eyes had filled with tears. 'Shabaz and Mary were carrying on an affair. I believe Mr Whitby found out. That's why he had Shabaz killed. That's why Mary left him.'

40

The coffee shop resembled a railway platform.

Every chair was taken, a queue thronged the counter, knots of sweating bodies bellowed at each other in the spaces between the tables. The place was so crowded even sardines would have complained.

Seema looked around nervously.

She felt as out of place in this environment as a crow at a convention of peacocks.

The youngsters crowded into the shop enjoyed a social standing she could only imagine; their clothes were crisp and new, their hair, cheeks and teeth gleamed with a lustre that came from both having money and from never having had to question the fact. Even their conversation was intimidating: they slipped into French and German as easily as they spoke English or Hindi or Bengali.

'You look like a nervous pickpocket.'

She almost jumped as Haresh dropped into the seat opposite and set down two sundaes, each the size of a miniature iceberg.

She realised he was beaming at her. She blinked, and pushed her spectacles up her nose.

'Relax.' He waved at the crowd around them. 'They won't bite. Besides, we Calcuttans are known for our hospitality. When we're not hacking each other to bits, that is.' He grinned again. She'd begun to realise that he could make a joke out of anything and everything. His default setting appeared to be a world-weary cynicism far beyond his years.

She still found it difficult looking directly at him – it was like gazing into the sun.

She'd rarely been face to face with a man so handsome. Certainly, not one who'd ever paid any attention to her. Occasionally, she'd notice a good-looking man exiting a station latrine or threading his way along a crowded platform. Why would such a man give *her* a second glance?

If there was one thing poverty brought home to you, it was that, to a certain kind of person, you were invisible.

Which made it all the more confusing that this glittering young peacock sitting before her actually appeared to be enjoying her company.

'So . . . what are you doing later this evening?'

'I – I have to attend a function. With my colleague.'

'Who? The policewoman?'

'Yes.'

'What sort of function?'

'It's a – a business event.'

'By God, that sounds boring!' he bellowed dismissively, digging into his sundae with a spoon. 'If you're only in Calcutta for a few days, you really can't afford to waste a minute.' She watched him shovel a lump of ice cream into his mouth roughly the size of his own head. 'I've got a better idea. Come out with me. Let me show you my city.'

She looked down at the table. Someone had scribbled something obscene in English on the wood. 'I can't. My colleague will be expecting me to accompany her.'

'Why? I mean, what exactly are *you* going to be doing at this *business* function?'

She blinked. Conversation frothed around them, allowing her a moment's respite. 'Well, I – I—'

'I rest my case,' he said triumphantly.

41

The crowds had thinned.

She'd walked out from the temple complex to find a taxi, Anabella Santos's revelation – namely, that Fareed Mazumdar's father and James Whitby's mother had been lovers – large in her mind.

Had James known about the affair? Had he discovered the truth recently? Perhaps *that* had been the real reason he'd gone to confront Mazumdar that fateful day last year?

If so, then everything she believed about the case was a lie ... Had she misjudged the Englishman?

A bicycle whizzed by, milk churns rattling on either side. A man cleaning out an ear with his little finger attempted to sell her a slice of squashed papaya. A truck wheezed along the road, belching black smoke from its exhaust.

A shadow fell over her. She looked up to see two men, roughly the size of carthorses, blocking the pavement. It was as if a pair of trees had grown legs. Muscles rippled under their shirts, but other muscles had to move out of the way first.

'Azizur Rahman would like to see you,' growled one. He made the invitation seem as welcoming as a trip to a dug grave waiting in a nearby forest.

'Why?'

The man exchanged a confused glance with his colleague as if, perhaps, she'd asked him to explain the underlying principles of Euclidean geometry. Clearly, their prepared script didn't extend to improvisation.

'He wants to talk to you?' ventured the second man.

'And what if I don't wish to talk to *him*?'

The man's mouth flapped open. He seemed bewildered. She imagined few people spurned his advances. At least, not if they wished to keep their kneecaps where nature had intended.

She realised that she felt little fear from them. Their manner was unthreatening. They were errand boys. The same could not be said of their master.

The fact that Rahman had summoned her meant that he not only knew that she was in the city, but that she was making enquiries about him. *Who had informed him?* It could have been any of several people she'd come into contact with. She'd asked questions. Files had been pulled and given to her. She suspected that the Calcutta police was no different to her own force back in Bombay: as leaky as a bathtub shot full of holes.

Risk. That's what it always boiled down to. In life, there were moments when you were confronted with the safe choice and the reckless one.

In her experience, it was usually the latter that yielded results.

'Very well,' she said. 'Let's go.'

The ride down south in the back of a Buick stinking, for a reason neither of her escorts cared to explain, of fish, took thirty minutes.

They eventually came to a halt in the lee of the Nakhoda Mosque, the city's largest.

Having just come from the city's biggest Hindu temple, there seemed a certain symmetry to this. In a place riven by religious strife in recent years, it was almost ironic.

The sound of the azaan, the Muslim call to prayer, floated down from a minaret attached to the mosque. A street vendor with a red beard, a white skullcap, and a nose you could sharpen a knife on invited her to buy holy water direct from Mecca, guaranteed to cure all known illnesses, as well as several made-up ones.

A bark from one of her chaperones sent the man scurrying away.

She followed her escorts through a labyrinth of narrow alleyways until they arrived at an open-fronted store. The signboard above the entrance read: RAHMAN TEXTILES COMPANY.

Inside, she found a ground floor occupied by ranks of men – and a handful of women – hunkered behind sewing machines. The rattle made by their collective labours sounded like the chatter of teeth in a graveyard full of dancing skeletons.

She was led up a flight of steps and into a large space with naked floorboards and whitewashed walls. Bolts of cotton were piled against the walls.

At one end of the space, the hulking figure of Azizur Rahman sat behind a desk, bathed in lamplight falling in from a window behind him.

As she approached, he neither smiled nor stood to greet her.

A trace of fear brushed the walls of her heart. Sweat trickled down her back.

Rahman waited for her to take a seat, then sat back and took her in.

He was a big man. Even seated he resembled a bull tied down to a stake, his every feature threatening. His face was dark and pinched, the eyes dead. A lantern jaw. Grey hair, cut short and flat, like the bristles of a horse brush. His eyebrows alone looked as if they'd happily mug old ladies and leave them in a dark alley.

'Why have you come to Calcutta?' His voice was deeper than she'd expected; the growl of a tiger.

'I hear it's a beautiful city.'

'Why are you asking questions about me?'

She considered lying, but then realised it would be pointless. She was suddenly reluctant to enrage this man.

'I'm investigating the murder of Fareed Mazumdar.'

'Mazumdar was killed by an Englishman. In Bombay.'

'Perhaps. Perhaps not.'

'The case is ended. The Englishman will be executed. You have no reason to investigate further. You have no jurisdiction in Calcutta.'

'I'm investigating on my own cognizance.'

The skin around his eyes tightened. 'Why are you asking questions about the Chatterjee case?'

'Someone was sending Mazumdar reminders about the case before he died. Old press cuttings. I want to know why.'

His brow furrowed. 'That case, too, was resolved years ago.'

'Not exactly. You were exonerated. And if *you* didn't kill her, the real killer is still out there somewhere.'

He glowered at her, but, again, refused to be baited.

'I understand you knew her,' she continued. 'I mean, she worked at your club. The White Tiger?'

'I have nothing to do with the White Tiger.'

'Not officially. But it's common knowledge that you're the club's real owner.'

He blinked. 'You should be careful who you talk to.'

Was that a threat? A plume of fear rotated up from her stomach. And then something inside her rebelled. 'Why did Fareed Mazumdar defend you? Did you know that he and Rita Chatterjee were childhood friends?'

'He defended me because he knew I had no hand in the girl's killing.'

'Walter Rivers was murdered that day too. He frequented your club – sorry, the club you *don't* own.'

He swatted at the air with a hand the size of a dinner plate. 'I had no dealings with him.'

'What about Saleem Ansari? I understand you have extensive dealings with *him*. Why did he task Mazumdar to defend you?'

'Ansari is a politician. We have worked together in the past. He has done much for the Muslims of this city.'

'And you've done much for him. You helped him get elected and then, when you were accused of murder, he stepped in to help. A favour for a favour.'

The man stared at her with eyes so cold she thought her heart might freeze inside her chest.

'Listen to me and listen very carefully. Leave Calcutta. Stop what you are doing and go home.'

'And if I don't?'

His jaw turned pugnacious. 'I've known officers like you. You believe the truth is something sacred. You think pursuing it makes you virtuous. But sometimes the truth is simply a fire that will consume you. You have been warned.'

42

The first thing she did when she entered her room at the Great Eastern was to order a stiff whisky.

The encounter with Rahman had left behind a swirl of emotions. Anger, loathing, and, if she was honest with herself, fear. And what had she really learned? The truth was that Rahman had given nothing away. She'd have been better off interrogating a brick wall or, better yet, banging her head against it. Rahman had nothing to fear from her, a lone policewoman, operating outside of her jurisdiction in an unfamiliar city.

And yet . . . the man's demeanour had ignited something in her. The idea that she could be intimidated into taking a step backwards!

She did not know yet if her efforts would unravel the murder of Fareed Mazumdar, would help in either exonerating or proving that James Whitby had killed the lawyer – but she couldn't leave Calcutta until she had exhausted every line of enquiry.

She realised that she was running late. If she intended to confront Saleem Ansari at Darius's function, she needed to hurry.

She showered, then dressed quickly – a white satin dress with gold piping and a shawl collar; minutes later, she was knocking on Seema's door.

The door swung back to reveal her ward dressed in a neck-to-ankle bathrobe. Not exactly the height of fashion for a night out in the 'city of joy'.

Persis frowned. 'We're late.'

'I'm sorry, but I don't think I'll be able to accompany you.'

She was momentarily taken aback. 'Whyever not?'

The girl tucked her hands under her armpits. 'I'm not feeling too well. If it's okay with you, I'd prefer to spend the evening here. Resting.'

'What's wrong with you? Should I fetch a doctor?'

'Oh, no, no! It's just a – a headache.'

There was something evasive about the girl's manner, but Persis hadn't the time to pry. 'Fine. What did you manage to find out at the library?'

She waited as Seema retrieved her notebook.

'Saleem Ansari. He's the current deputy chief minister of West Bengal, representing the Congress Party. In his early fifties, married, with two children. He grew up here – in Calcutta, I mean – in a Muslim area called Metiabruz. He comes from a middle-class family – his father worked for the Indian Civil Service. He entered politics at a young age, joining the All-India Muslim League and becoming a prominent figure in Bengali politics during the Quit India years. After independence, he decided not to move to the newly created East Pakistan.'

East Pakistan. The territory that had once made up the eastern half of Bengal.

Like most Indians, it still felt odd for Persis to dwell on the geopolitical realities of Partition; the dismembering of a country was not an easy thing to digest. It seemed incredible that two peoples who were essentially one could not reconcile their differences, to the point that a new nation had to be birthed simply to accommodate their inability to get along.

'When did he first start working with Rahman?'

'Rahman's a little older than Ansari. Late fifties. Unmarried, though there are reports of several illegitimate children. He was already an established thug in the area around the Nakhoda Mosque, a Muslim enclave of Kutchi Memons – Muslims who came over from Gujarat. Shipping merchants, in the main. They built the Nakhoda Mosque – *nakhoda* means "captain of a ship". Rahman is supposedly from the Memon community, though possibly born on the wrong side of the tracks. He grew up on the streets.'

Persis pointedly tapped her watch.

'Rahman and Ansari met in the early thirties,' continued the girl, unfazed. 'Ansari was trying to mobilise support among the city's Muslims for his political aspirations. The trouble was that most Muslims here are from poor communities – fishermen, rickshaw pullers, jute and cotton-mill workers – whereas Ansari is from an educated, middle-class background. Enter Rahman. He helped Ansari organise trade unions for the Muslims he was wooing. You have to remember, Muslims were – and still are – the minority in Calcutta. Ansari used the unions as a platform to advocate for their rights, portraying himself as their saviour.'

'I don't suppose the rest of Calcutta was impressed,' said Persis drily.

'No. His enemies accused him of having links to the underworld – which is true if we consider Rahman's involvement in his affairs. Later, as his star began to rise, he was accused of corruption, of siphoning funds from government projects and lining his own pockets.'

'That would hardly make him unique. Embezzlement is practically a job requirement in Indian politics.'

'When war broke out, and foreign soldiers arrived here, Ansari allegedly used his relationship with Rahman to profit from all sorts of underworld activities. Prostitution, drugs, gambling.' Seema flipped a page in her notebook. 'After the Calcutta riots in 1946, he came out strongly against Partition. Made several speeches about how the horrors he'd witnessed had convinced him that Muslims and Hindus must learn to live together.'

Persis frowned. 'I seem to remember an accusation that he'd somehow *incited* the riots in Calcutta? After Jinnah's call for Direct Action, I mean.'

'Yes. He made a speech on August 16th at the Maidan. Tens of thousands of Muslim Leaguers are said to have attended. Hours later, riots were underway. Of course, both sides claim the other started the trouble.'

'And Azizur Rahman? I'm guessing he was in the thick of it?'

'Yes. It was reported that he and his thugs went into Hindu enclaves and murdered at whim. He denied this, of course. Claimed it was anti-Muslim bias on the part of the witnesses.'

'And yet it was for the murders of Rita Chatterjee and Walter Rivers that he ended up in court. Why did he target them? Why Chatterjee?' The question was aimed partly at herself.

'She *was* a Hindu.'

'That's not the answer. Chatterjee worked for him at the White Tiger Club. Why would he employ her if he had an issue with her religion?'

She saw that Seema was looking at her in confusion.

Quickly, she filled the girl in on her earlier findings, namely that Rita Chatterjee had worked at a club allegedly controlled by Rahman. 'What I can't work out is Rahman's motive in killing her.'

'Perhaps they were lovers? Or perhaps he made advances and she rejected him?'

'It's a possibility,' conceded Persis. 'But I don't think Rahman is the sort of man who would have waited for riots to murder a woman who spurned him. And what was Walter Rivers doing in Chatterjee's flat that day? One of the other things that Chatterjee's housemate, Lata Tiwari, told me was that she was certain that Chatterjee and Walter Rivers were not lovers. So why was he there? I think that's the heart of the case. If we can find out *why* Rahman killed them, we might be able to unravel the whole thing.'

Moments after Persis had left, Seema strode purposefully to the bathroom and shrugged off her bathrobe to reveal an elegant blue satin dress beneath. She slipped on a pair of stylish shoes, then spent a few minutes adjusting her hair and applying make-up, finishing with a flourish of lipstick.

She examined her appearance in the mirror, nervously settling her spectacles on to her nose.

A thunderous knocking sounded on the door to the room, sending her heart shooting up to lodge somewhere between her throat and her mouth.

A part of her wanted to hide in the wardrobe and wait for her visitor to leave.

Her reflection frowned back at her.

A month ago, she'd been cleaning railway latrines. And now, here she was, in the old colonial capital, lodged in a five-star hotel, with . . . an evening caller hammering on her door.

It was the stuff of fairy tales.

The problem was that life had taught her that fairy tales were not for the likes of her.

The hammering reached an elemental pitch. There was a real danger the door might cave in.

She bit her lip. And then, taking her courage in her hands, she strode out of the bathroom to the front door, grabbed the handle, and swung it back.

A bouquet of roses greeted her. It appeared to have sprouted legs, attached to stylish black shoes polished to a brilliant shine.

A face appeared from behind the flowers. 'Are you ready to let me show you *my* Calcutta?' grinned Haresh Saxena.

Seema hesitated, then nodded. 'Yes. I'm ready.'

43

A lion prowled above the arched gate to Government House.

It was a good thing it was made of stone, Persis thought, otherwise the stream of overweight and overdressed men being driven through the gate might have proved too tempting a meal.

The tonga clopped on, along a winding gravel path, towards the vast stone bulk of the official residence of West Bengal's governor. A parade of laburnums lined the road, interspersed with dwarf myrtles – festive lights twinkled among their branches.

The tongawallah clucked the bay mare to a halt outside the building's portico, an impressively venerable structure crowned by a triangular pediment held up by Ionic columns. A grand flight of stone steps led upwards like the stairway to paradise.

She paid the tongawallah, alighted, then, settling her dress around her hips, followed the crowd as they noisily scaled the staircase like a troupe of well-heeled mountaineers.

The party was already in full swing.

The gardens glowed with artificial brightness: manicured hedges strung with coloured lighting, Victorian lamp posts blazing brightly, attracting enough insects to rival a Biblical plague.

A live band played on a bandstand at the far end of the lawn, the strains of a recent jazz hit floating over the city's elite – a mix of white and non-white faces, all impeccably dressed in monkey suits, extravagant dresses, and navel-revealing saris – smoking, chatting and throwing back champagne as if it were going out of style. Peacocks strutted between the revellers, looking somewhat put out at being relatively underdressed for the occasion.

Her eyes scanned the crowd for Darius, but her cousin was nowhere to be seen.

'Are you alone?'

She turned to find a large man in a badly fitting tuxedo, with a square beard that looked as if it had been hacked into shape with a machete, peering at her. His pinched face was as easy on the eye as a sharp stick. 'The name's Junjunwallah. I run a shipping company. Second largest in the country, as a matter of fact.'

He said no more, as if this statement in and of itself was all that was required for her to swoon at his feet.

He advanced closer, enveloping her in a cologne so virulent it could have revived a corpse.

'Ah, there you are!'

She turned to find Darius at her side. 'May I borrow my fiancée?' he said, beaming at the frowning magnate.

He grabbed her elbow and steered her away.

'Fiancée?' she muttered.

'Would you rather I'd left you there?'

He led her to a row of cloth-covered trestle tables so laden down with delicacies their legs appeared to be buckling. A heady aroma arose from the buffet – she picked out the rich coconut and prawn miasma of *chingri malai* curry and the sweet jaggery scent of *nolen gur*; the odours collided violently with the not unpleasant waft of Darius's aftershave.

She couldn't help but notice that in his black tux and red cummerbund, her cousin once again looked the picture of elegance.

She shook the thought away. 'Is Ansari here?'

He raised an eyebrow. 'Business first, as always. Yes, he's here.'

'Can you introduce me?'

He hesitated. 'Are you sure you want to do this? I mean, I'm no fan of Ansari's, but the man's a politician. I doubt he can tell you anything about Rahman's activities.'

'Rahman murdered two people and got away scot-free. Ansari helped him to do that.'

Darius gave a half-smile. 'Rahman has probably dispatched more people than Attila the Hun.'

'So another couple make no difference?'

He raised his hands in surrender. 'I was making a point. You're trying to convict Ansari of guilt by association. Ansari may be a little crooked, but he's no gangster. Rahman, on the other hand, is a dangerous man. And this is *his* city. I'm not sure it's wise for you to poke the bear.'

'Too late,' she said. 'The bear's wide awake.'

She told him about her earlier meeting with the underworld don.

Darius's demeanour changed. 'He *threatened* you?'

'Not in so many words.'

'When a man like Rahman threatens you, it doesn't matter how many words he uses.' He squared his shoulders. 'You need to go back to Bombay. Tonight.'

'I'm not leaving until I finish what I came here to do.'

'Always the stubborn one! Ever since we were kids.' He ran a hand through his hair, a gesture of exasperation.

'We're not kids any more,' she said stonily.

Sweat sparkled at his temples. 'I'm not trying to tell you what to do. I just don't want you to get hurt. I – I care about you.' He hesitated. 'I know, these past few years, my mother has been a bit of a bore. She's always had this idea that you and I would one day—'

'I know.'

'She's old-fashioned. But it doesn't necessarily mean she's wrong—' He held up a hand. 'I'm merely making a point.

Sometimes, the best companion for life isn't the one you think you want. And familiarity isn't necessarily a bad thing.'

She stared at him. There was something about him, in this setting, in that suit, that forced her to reappraise the man she'd rejected time and again. Cousin Darius. A figure of fun for longer than she cared to remember. But, here and now, he was . . . something altogether different.

The heat seemed to seep into her via the pores of her skin, inflaming her from the inside out.

'Ansari. Are you going to introduce me or do I have to track him down myself?'

Saleem Ansari was holding court at the centre of a knot of partygoers.

Dressed in a black achkan and tight white trousers, embellished with a karakul cap of the type once favoured by Tagore, he looked every inch the debonair statesman who'd snake-charmed the cobra of Bengal politics for the past two decades.

'The problem, Mr Shaw, is that you British can't abide a political vacuum. At least one where *you* are now the missing element.'

A bulky white man, with a face like a drunk walrus, waved a crystal tumbler in the air. 'Look around you, sir. Before the British came along, this place was a swamp. And with your zamindars sucking the life out of anyone with two paisa to rub together, and tigers eating the rest, it's a wonder the average Bengali made it past puberty.'

'That swamp, as you call it, is one of the most fertile regions in the world. As for the zamindars . . . You know as well as I do that the Raj was complicit in upholding the zamindari system. It was to your benefit to keep the "average Bengali" yoked to the feudal plough.'

Shaw snorted, and threw back his Scotch, before casting about for another.

Persis took the opportunity to insert herself into the fawning horseshoe, Darius at her elbow.

'But with Nehru becoming more of a communist with each passing day, where do you see us headed, sir?' This was uttered by a tall, scrawny gentleman who looked like the lovechild of a plucked chicken and a hatstand.

'Nehru is no more a communist than Hitler was a pacifist,' replied Ansari mildly. 'The Prime Minister is merely trying to uphold the ideals of our dear departed Mahatma. Rest assured, he is no enemy of capitalism.'

'The man's busy stripping the feudal class of their ancestral landholdings,' piped up another voice. 'What assurances do we have that he won't come for us next?'

'That's Jairam Balaji,' whispered Darius. 'He runs Empire Tobacco. The woman beside him is his wife. Tabitha. Heiress to a Scottish jute fortune.'

Balaji looked like a depressed beagle. He was half the size and twice the age of his wife, and seemed to be wearing a suit designed for a man three times his bulk. Standing awkwardly arm-in-arm with his better half – a blonde white woman dressed in a green and gold silk sari with a daringly exposed midriff – he resembled a convicted prisoner being toured around the provinces before his execution.

Ansari turned to the man. 'Come now, Balaji. Surely the Cigarette King of Calcutta isn't frightened by a little land reform? The man who once shot three tigers before lunch and still had time to stop for a gin and tonic in the jungle?'

'If he's ever been within fifty miles of a tiger, then I'm the King of Siam,' muttered Darius. 'They're all reprobates with the hides of rhinos and the morals of hyenas.'

'May *I* ask a question?'

Ansari's gaze swung towards her. 'I don't believe we've had the pleasure, Miss . . .?'

'Wadia. Inspector Persis Wadia.'

A rustle of interest went through the gathering like a mild electric current.

For an instant, Ansari seemed perplexed, and then: 'Ah. Bombay's famed police*woman*! What brings you to Calcutta, Inspector?'

'I'm investigating an old case, one you may be acquainted with. Almost four years ago, your friend and ally, Azizur Rahman, was put on trial for the murders of Rita Chatterjee and Walter Rivers. You helped him evade justice. Why?'

The music drifted away. A gasp sounded from Tabitha Balaji; her husband choked on his drink.

Beside her, Darius cursed under his breath.

For a moment, Ansari seemed frozen to the spot. And then his lips cracked into a parched smile. 'Your directness is most refreshing. One expects no less from a Bombayite. Here in Calcutta, politesse is everything. Open a door for a Bengali and you might be there for all eternity dithering over who enters first . . . You say I helped Azizur *evade* justice? As I recall, he was proven innocent, a verdict arrived at by a jury of his peers. As to *why* I helped him – well, as you yourself put it, he has been an ally.'

'A known underworld gangster? Ally to a political aspirant?'

'Come now, you mustn't believe everything you read in the newspapers. Azizur Rahman is no gangster. We are far too quick to judge those who chart their course through the shoals of our world without recompense to a family fortune or the benefits of an Oxbridge education. I have never denied my friendship with him. Why should I? We share the same ideals. A strong, vibrant Calcutta where Muslims and Hindus can live and work peaceably side by side. Gandhi's vision made real – communal harmony in the new India.'

'Hear! Hear!' bellowed Balaji to her right.

'Communal harmony? Some say *you* instigated the Direct Action Day riots.'

His face hardened. 'You're an outsider to Bengal, Inspector. You cannot know what it was like in those days. It's true that I spoke to a crowd of my fellow Muslims on that fateful day. But all I did was articulate our legitimate fears – the fear that Muslims stood to become second-class citizens in an independent India if certain safeguards were not put in place. I had no idea of the chaos that would later ensue.'

'It wasn't chaos. It was a bloodbath.'

He blinked. 'If we are talking openly, then let us be honest. The riots were not about religion, per se. They were about who would control Calcutta once the dust settled. The grisly manner in which the killings were executed; the targeting of women and children. These were the acts of men attempting to hammer home a point.'

'Azizur Rahman was one of those men. An eyewitness stated that he left the residence of Rita Chatterjee at the height of the rioting – shortly before her body was discovered.'

'An eyewitness who later recanted.' Ansari's voice had tightened. The crowd was bobbing their heads between the pair like onlookers at a game of tennis.

'She recanted because she was threatened.'

The politician's face twitched, but he said nothing.

Persis pressed on, heedless. 'You asked Fareed Mazumdar to take the case. Why? At the time, he was a relative unknown.'

'Fareed was a capable young lawyer. He'd already defended several young men accused of anti-British activities. His reputation was growing. I was considering asking him to join the state's judicial reform unit – I knew we'd need capable men to overhaul our judiciary once independence became a reality. I thought the Chatterjee case might be a good test of his abilities.' He paused.

'Besides, I merely *recommended* him to Rahman. But I believe Fareed justified my faith.'

'He left Calcutta shortly after the verdict. Why?'

'My understanding is that he wished to practise law in your fair city. Don't they call Bombay the "city of dreams"?'

'He was murdered last year. His alleged killer is due to hang in six days' time.'

'Alleged? James Whitby was convicted. The decision was unanimous, I believe.'

'Just before he died, Mazumdar received anonymous press cuttings about the Chatterjee case. Have you any idea why someone would send him those articles?'

Ansari seemed momentarily rooted to the spot.

The swollen air pressed in around them.

Finally, Ansari's lips stretched into a smile, but the smile failed to reach his eyes. 'Have you had a chance to walk around Calcutta, Inspector? There are areas here where the streets are so closely packed that even light struggles to enter. But it was the very impenetrability of these neighbourhoods – these *paras*, as we Bengalis call them – that assisted us during the insurrection.

'I have seen those same gullies run red with blood. I have seen the British murder with impunity; I have seen Hindu kill Muslim and vice versa. But that is the past. Our task now is to lead India into the future. The British are no longer our enemies. Hindu and Muslim are no longer foes. Fareed Mazumdar – and his murderer – are no longer relevant.' His eyes glittered. 'And now, if you will excuse me, I have a speech to deliver.'

44

'What was the point of that?'

Darius was wearing a groove on the lawn, like a bull with a bad case of dysentery.

'I wanted to see what he would say.'

'It was foolish. Ansari's not some common criminal that you can just brace on a whim. The man's our future chief minister!'

'He's in bed with a murderer. Doesn't that bother you?'

He flashed her a dark look. 'Rahman could bring this city to a standstill with a word – and Ansari knows it. He *needs* Rahman. How else do you think a Muslim can aspire to the highest political office in a Hindu-majority state? The Brahmin elite despise Ansari. But with Rahman stirring up the city's poor in his favour – both Muslim *and* Hindu – Ansari has managed to build a power base. Quite a feat given what happened here during Partition. Sometimes one is left with no choice but to work with the devil.' He threw his cigarette onto the ground and crushed it savagely underfoot. 'I need a drink.'

She watched him vanish into the crowd, her mouth a tight line.

Was he right? What had she really achieved by accosting Ansari? She was no further forward than if she'd simpl—

'Persis? What the devil are *you* doing here?'

She turned . . . to find Archie Blackfinch staring at her with an expression that wouldn't have looked out of place on a stunned herring.

*   *   *

She'd heard it said that the British came to India in waves.

First to arrive had been the traders of the East India Company, pursuing the lucrative oriental spice trade, inveigling their way into the courts of successive Mughal emperors with heady promises of mutual enrichment and brandied tales of British kings and queens. Next had come the likes of Clive Plassey and company, buccaneering chancers willing to employ violence and ruthless cunning to acquire political power that could be parlayed directly into obscene wealth. Finally, with the crushing of the uprising of 1857, had come the martinets of the Raj – for the most part, glorified bean counters – establishing an administrative structure, the Indian Civil Service, that gradually strangled the remaining sparks of rebellion out of the country.

What cannons and navies couldn't quite achieve, a system of chits and registers managed in a few short decades. If there was one thing the British had learned, it was how to suck the fight out of a local populace by the simple expedient of forcing them to fill out forms. In triplicate.

And now, following independence, there were men like Archie Blackfinch, invited in as advisers as India retook the reins of her administrative offices.

'I thought you were in Jaipur,' she said, still stunned at the sight of him.

'I left two days ago. Didn't you get my postcard?'

'I've been travelling.'

'Yes, I can see that.' He blinked behind his spectacles. Dressed in a dashing black suit with a cream bow tie and silver cummerbund, black hair Brylcreemed back, he looked as if he'd just stepped out of a Jane Austen novel. 'So ... what *are* you doing here?'

'I'm pursuing a case.' She took a deep breath. 'What are *you* doing here?'

'This is the Calcutta leg of my grand tour. I'm meeting the police commissioner tomorrow to discuss the new lab.'

A waiter glided by with a tray. Persis grabbed a pink gin and slugged a large mouthful.

'What brings you to this' – he waved his glass around – 'soirée?'

'I came to talk to Saleem Ansari.'

'The deputy CM?' His eyebrows lifted. 'Funnily enough, I'm here for the same reason. An acquaintance of mine thought it would be useful for me to put a flea in his ear about the lab. Never too early to start politicking, apparently. What did you want to talk to him about?'

'Murder,' she said simply.

Before he could reply, Darius returned. The motor powering his legs seemed to give out as he spotted Blackfinch; he stuttered to a halt. The two men eyed each other like pie dogs encountering one another in an alley. Finally, Blackfinch winched out a hand as if it were being pulled from his body by a team of wild horses. Darius stared at it as if a stick of dynamite had been extended in his direction.

'Blackbird, isn't it?' he said eventually, taking the proffered hand and shaking it with all the enthusiasm of a dead fish.

'Black*finch*,' said the Englishman stiffly. 'You have the better of me. I cannot recall *your* name.'

'Darius.'

'Ah. Yes. Persis's cousin.'

'And you're her . . . colleague.'

'A bit more than that, I dare say,' said Blackfinch. He caught her eye and coughed. 'What I mean is, we've become friends.'

'Friends,' echoed Darius. He tugged at his wing collar as if it were a noose. 'And what brings you to Calcutta?'

'Work.'

Persis stared between them, wondering if they were about to urinate on the lawn to mark their respective territories. She'd never had time for this sort of thin—

A feedback whine emanating from speakers strung from poles around the lawn cut through the babble of conversation. A compère urged them to make their way to the bandstand where the guest of honour was about to make his speech.

'Shall we?' she said, and then, not waiting for an answer, turned her back on them.

Saleem Ansari looked down from the bandstand on to rows of sweating faces. His own face was ablaze in a cascade of electric light streaming down from bulbs entwined around the bandstand's canopy.

'We Bengalis are a sentimental lot, easily swayed by romantic gestures. When Gandhi shed his suit for a dhoti, he won our hearts, enjoining us to the great struggle. But today, we are faced with a new dilemma.

'The truth is that India, like ancient Rome, is a republic ruled by despots. The British have gone, but, in their stead, we breed crooked middlemen and politicians who think nothing of stealing the crumbs from a beggar's plate. Can any of us truly say that the India of today is the place we imagined when we ousted our colonisers?

'I hear some speak of past times, of strife between the many factions of our great city.' His eyes picked her out, and she was suddenly overcome by the feeling of standing in the centre of a great beam of light. 'I hear talk of corruption in the capillaries of government, of the rise of Hindu revivalism, of the lack of Muslims in Nehru's cabinet. But the fact is that *we* have willed this nation into being. Together. It is now ours to make of it either a paradise or a hell. I will not allow *anyone* to divide us. *Jai Hind*.'

45

A noble death.

Is there such a thing? Arora and I talked about it once.

The best that we can hope for, I told him, dimly recalling long ago church sermons, is to die in a state of grace. To die having lived a good life. Even better, to die in the service of others. The soldier who dies on the battlefield. The man who gives his life to save his family.

Arora flashed that wry smile of his and told me that men who gave up their lives for others were operating on something other than selflessness. Usually, they were caught in a situation that left them with no other option. Did I really think those poor saps fed into the meat grinder of war went happily to their ignoble ends?

If he was trying to cheer me up, he was doing a damned poor job of it.

I asked him how it would happen. The mechanics of the actual execution.

His fingers tapped against his knee.

'In ancient Rome,' he said, 'the position of public executioner was called *carnifex*. The man's role was to torture and execute slaves – the literal meaning of the word is "butcher". It was a lowly position and the carnifex was forced to live outside the city limits. But now, now we've formalised the process of execution, sheathed it in bureaucratic ritual, to allow ourselves the illusion that what we are doing – in the name of a just, civilised society – is no longer a barbaric act.'

I've had a great deal of time to think on his words; a great deal of time to examine my life and the world I will soon depart. A part of me thinks that perhaps Arora's original supposition might be for the best; that we are all mindless creatures caught in a great web of events over which we have little or no control. Motes of dust in a high wind.

But if man is not a teleological construct, then what was our Creator thinking? What *is* our ultimate purpose?

Here's the truth: for all my philosophical hand-wringing, there is only one thing that truly holds any meaning.

I am afraid of dying.

46

Persis floated out of sleep like a dead fish rising to the surface of a lake.

She was spread-eagled on the bed in her hotel room, face set hard against the headboard.

She flopped over and hauled herself up. A shaft of sunlight battered at her eyes, sending splinters of pain jabbing into the fogged recesses of her brain.

She became aware of two things: firstly, that she was still wearing the previous night's dress, and, secondly, of the sound of a thunderous knocking, like a giant hammering on a wooden drum.

She staggered across the carpet and opened the door.

Blackfinch stood there, looking unbearably chipper. He was dressed in a starched white shirt with a red and yellow striped tie, holding a jacket in one hand and a folded newspaper in the other. 'Good morning,' he said. 'You look as if you've been run over by a herd of wild horses.'

It took her fifteen minutes to shower, standing under the shower-head until her head had cleared.

When she emerged, having changed into a cream half-sleeved crêpe de Chine blouse and grey trousers, Blackfinch pressed a coffee mug into her hand. 'Any stronger and it would probably stop your heart.'

She sipped at the coffee, shuddered as it hit her like a lead pipe to the skull, then collapsed on to the Chesterfield.

The previous evening returned to her in shards of electric memory.

Following Saleem Ansari's speech at Government House, she'd hung around a while longer, hoping to catch the politician off guard, Blackfinch and Darius dancing around her like a pair of lancing knights.

But Ansari had remained engaged by Calcutta's hawkish mavens of industry, before dashing off.

By that stage, she'd lost count of the number of pink gins and whiskies handed to her by the ever-complaisant waiting staff.

'What are you doing here?' she finally managed. Her head felt as if it had been used as a football all night. By men wearing hobnailed boots.

'You wanted me to look at some case files,' he said, brightly. 'Don't you remember?'

She gritted her teeth and walked to the desk on fluttery legs, then returned to hand him the Chatterjee and Walter Rivers case files.

She watched him flip open the first folder. 'Frame the problem for me.'

Quickly, she explained why she'd come to Calcutta and the possible connection between the murder of Fareed Mazumdar in Bombay and the Chatterjee and Rivers killings in Calcutta.

'You think James Whitby is innocent and that Mazumdar's real killer is the man who killed Chatterjee and Rivers? That's quite a leap.'

'I think there's some *connection* between the killings. Mazumdar and Chatterjee grew up in the same orphanage. Chatterjee worked at the White Tiger Club, a place frequented by Rivers and owned by Azizur Rahman, the man accused of Chatterjee's and River's murders. Mazumdar then defended Rahman in court, but after doing so – successfully – he immediately left the city for Bombay.'

'I take it you suspect Rahman had Mazumdar killed? Why?'

She leaned forward, eyes suddenly alive. 'What if Mazumdar *knew* Rahman was guilty of the Chatterjee and Rivers murders? What if he had proof – perhaps something he discovered during the course of Rahman's trial – and his conscience had finally got the better of him? Don't you think Rahman would kill to ensure his silence?'

'I don't know enough about Rahman to make that call.'

'This wasn't Rahman's first brush with the law,' she countered. 'He's a known villain.'

He conceded the point with a nod. 'And Ansari . . . What has he to do with all this? Why did you confront *him* last night?'

'He and Rahman have been associates for years. He's the man who basically tasked Mazumdar to defend Rahman in court.' She tapped the side of her cup. 'Someone sent Fareed Mazumdar the press cuttings of the Chatterjee killings in the weeks before he died. I believe it was his murderer.'

'You think *Ansari* sent those letters? The deputy chief minister?' His tone was incredulous.

'I think it was Rahman. Possibly instigated by Ansari. If Mazumdar *had* decided to tell the truth about the Chatterjee killings, it would have been bad news for more than just Rahman. Being associated with a killer could have proven fatal to Ansari's political career. Especially given that he was the man who'd tasked Mazumdar to defend Rahman in the first place. How would it have looked if Mazumdar had revealed to the world that Rahman was guilty after all and Ansari had known all along? I think Ansari or Rahman got wind of the fact that he was about to break his silence. The clippings were an oblique threat: don't talk or this could happen to you.'

'You don't know that Mazumdar was actually planning to say anything. Or that Rahman had found out about his desire to do so.'

'Mazumdar was in touch with a journalist just before his death. I think he wanted to tell him what he knew. A confession, of sorts. Rahman may have been keeping tabs on him and found out.'

Blackfinch absorbed this.

'I think it's a sound working hypothesis. Why else would anyone send him those cuttings?'

He considered the question, then shrugged and went back to the files.

She watched him work, his tall frame hunched over in the wing chair, folder balanced on his knees. The memory of the Englishman sparring with Darius the night before filled her with a strange disquiet.

It was no easy task disentangling her emotions.

'How is that lady friend of yours? Davenport?'

He looked up. 'Jane? She's well enough. Why do you ask?'

'I wondered whether you'd made wedding plans yet.'

He gave her a flat look. 'You know very well Jane and I were never a serious proposition.'

'And why is that?'

'You know why,' he said quietly. He held her eyes, but when it became clear she wasn't about to say anything, he returned to his scrutiny of the files.

She pushed down on her disappointment. A part of her had hoped he'd say something, *anything*, just so that they could get it out in the open and lance the boil once and for all.

But they seemed to have ended up in a tar pit of their own making; the more they thrashed, the further they sank.

Ten minutes later, a frown appeared on his brow. 'Wait a minute. Look at this.'

He stood and walked to the desk. She followed him, then looked on as he laid out several photographs from the files. They were photographs of the bodies, both in the morgue – stretched out on the pathologist's table, front and back shots of the naked corpses – and at the murder scene.

Next to the photos, he set down a page from the folder. She saw that it was from the pathologist's notes on Walter Rivers.

'The post-mortem states that Walter Rivers was killed at Rita Chatterjee's apartment. The hypothesis states that rioters entered the apartment, found the pair in bed together, and killed them. One of the attackers stabbed Walter Rivers, while another strangled Rita Chatterjee. That would explain the different methods of killing used.

'Rivers was stabbed through the heart, fell back on to the bed, and died there on his front.' He stopped. 'But if you look at the photos of his body' – he pointed at the 6 x 8 shots – 'the lividity doesn't match that scenario.'

'Explain.'

'Lividity is how blood settles in the body after death. It refers to the bluish-purple discoloration—'

'I know what lividity is.'

'– that occurs when blood pools at the lowest point of the body due to gravity and loss of blood circulation after death,' Blackfinch continued, without breaking stride. 'It can also help to tell us if the body has been moved, post-mortem.'

'Are you saying Walter Rivers' body was moved around inside Chatterjee's home after he was killed?'

'I'm saying there's a real possibility that your crime scene was staged.'

47

The Medical College Hospital had been an institution in Calcutta for over a century, its principal claim to fame being that it had served as the venue for the first modern dissection of a human body by an Indian.

The Indian in question, Madhusudan Gupta, had been honoured with exultant write-ups in British newspapers celebrating the arrival of 'real' medical practise to the subcontinent, which had somewhat bemused Gupta and his colleagues, perhaps unfairly.

After all, Ayurveda, India's homeopathic medicine, was only a *few* thousand years older.

What the cadaver he'd dissected had thought about its place in history went unrecorded.

The hospital was located on College Street, just a couple of kilometres from the Great Eastern hotel, in an area considered the city's intellectual hub, a maze of coffee shops and dusty bookstores, where, the tongawallah informed her, customers could sit and read for as long as they wished without buying so much as a pamphlet.

Persis wondered, briefly, what her father would make of such wild generosity; she suspected his heart might literally implode at the thought of his own clientele wantonly thumbing the Wadia Book Emporium's merchandise before leaving without a purchase.

They alighted and paid the tongawallah.

She glanced at her watch.

The late start had put her behind schedule. A cocktail of anxieties churned inside her.

Time was rapidly running out for James Whitby.

Meanwhile, Seema had begun to worry her. The girl hadn't answered her room phone, nor opened the door when Persis had hammered on it on the way out. Persis suspected she was probably still labouring under her illness, but she didn't have time to wait for the hotel staff to open the door so that she could check. Instead, she'd tasked the concierge to ensure that her young ward was tended to when she eventually awoke.

As she'd left, another thought had occurred to her.

Seema was a fiercely independent young woman. Perhaps she'd come knocking on Persis's door while her mentor was still deep in her own slumber, given up, and wandered off for a few hours to explore the city on her own?

It seemed an unlikely scenario.

Anxiety continued to edge her thoughts as they made their way towards the Medical College Hospital's entrance.

The building was another of the city's hulking Greco-Roman edifices with columns so tall they might have held up the sky instead of the enormous pediment that capped them like a giant bicorne.

Inside, they quickly found their way to the office of a Dr Pankaj Chakraborty, the pathologist who'd conducted the post-mortems of Rita Chatterjee and Walter Rivers.

Chakraborty was seated behind a cluttered desk, a tower of files at his elbow so high it was in danger of burying him. He was an older man, balding, with pinched eyes peering out from behind bottle-bottomed spectacles. He had a snub nose, spoke out of a lopsided mouth, and, every few seconds, scratched at various parts of his anatomy like an itchy dog.

The walls of the office were covered in vivid botanical prints and plaques testifying to Chakraborty's expertise. A polished human skull sat on the desk, doubling as a paperweight.

As they outlined the reason for their visit, panic took up residence on his features. 'But this is old news!' His pupils oscillated wildly, as if looking for a way to flee the scene while leaving the rest of him behind.

Blackfinch set the file he'd been carrying on to the desk. He took out and arranged the Chatterjee and Rivers autopsy photographs, together with the post-mortem reports.

The remaining colour drained from the pathologist's face. He looked as if he might faint.

And then something inside him seemed to rally. He stood up and placed his knuckles on the desk. 'If you do not leave, I shall be forced to call security.'

'Be my guest,' said Blackfinch brightly. 'I'm sure the directors of this fine establishment will be intrigued to hear why you falsified a post-mortem report.'

He may as well have landed a blow to the smaller man's solar plexus.

Chakraborty tumbled back into his seat like a vaudeville clown.

'The lividity evident in these photographs demonstrates that Walter Rivers died on his back,' Blackfinch continued. 'You can see this from the discoloration on the back, buttocks, and backs of the legs, and from the blanching where he was in direct contact with the ground. And yet, if you look at this crime scene photograph, he was discovered on his front. Ergo, the body had been moved.' He beamed at the stricken doctor. 'And yet you mention none of this in your analysis. A pathologist of your experience – it's impossible you would not have noticed.'

Chakraborty had picked up a gold fountain pen and was juggling it between his hands. 'I can't speak to you. It will – it will ruin me.'

'Do you still believe you have a choice?' growled Persis.

'You don't understand.' Pitiful tears squeezed from between his eyelids. His shoulders shook. 'He'll kill me.'

'*Who* will kill you?'

He held his head in his hands. 'Rahman. Azizur Rahman.'

Persis exchanged glances with Blackfinch. 'Explain.'

Chakraborty snivelled. 'It's true that I was the pathologist tasked to carry out the Chatterjee and Rivers post-mortems. But before I was able to do so, Rahman's goons paid me a visit. They told me exactly what my post-mortem reports should conclude. I objected, of course, but they – they threatened my family. And then, to ensure that I wouldn't have a change of heart, they broke two of my fingers. How they expected me to complete the autopsy with two broken fingers, I don't know. But I did so nonetheless.'

Blackfinch seemed sceptical. 'Didn't it occur to them that the prosecution team might easily see through your notes if they took a close look at the photographs?'

'They told me I needn't worry about that. The prosecution would be spoken to.'

'So the fix was in from the very beginning.' The Englishman turned to Persis. 'Looks like you might have been right. Perhaps that's what turned Mazumdar's stomach in the end. Knowing he'd been a puppet in Rahman's scheme.'

'Or Ansari's.'

At the politician's name, Chakraborty seemed to go into spasms, as if struck by a series of minor heart attacks. 'Please, you can't do this to me.'

'You did this to yourself,' said Persis.

'There *is* a way to save yourself,' said Blackfinch.

Chakraborty looked up in absurd hope.

'Tell us everything you know.'

* * *

'So what now?'

They'd made their way outside and stood beneath the portico, watching a tide of chattering students flow by into the building.

It was a moment before Persis replied. The facts revealed by Chakraborty tolled in her mind. 'She was pregnant.'

Blackfinch's gaze rested on her face, but he said nothing.

'They murdered a pregnant woman,' she repeated, as if perhaps he hadn't heard.

'They?'

'Azizur Rahman and Mustapha Siddiqi. And Saleem Ansari helped them get away with it – with Fareed Mazumdar's help.'

'Do you think Rahman was the father? Perhaps that's why he killed her.'

'He doesn't strike me as the sort of man to be worried by an unwanted child.'

'We don't know him well enough to make that judgement.' When she said nothing, he continued: 'What interests me more is that Chakraborty lied in his post-mortem about the *time* of Walter Rivers' death. His examination revealed that Rivers didn't die at the same time as Rita Chatterjee; he died the day *before* Chatterjee. What does that tell you?'

'That you were right. They staged the crime scene. They *brought* Rivers' body to Chatterjee's home. Then forced Chakraborty to doctor his report to match.'

He grimaced. 'Doesn't make sense, does it? Why go to all that trouble?'

Neither of them said anything, until finally, Persis spoke: 'We have enough to reopen the case.'

He shook his head. 'You'll never get Chakraborty to testify against Rahman. Besides, Rahman never personally threatened him. At best, you have enough to go to the chief justice of the Calcutta High Court or, possibly, the advocate-general for West

Bengal. They'll promise to look into it with about as much intention of following through as a Frenchman taking his marriage
vows.'

'The Chatterjee crime scene was *staged*. The AG will have no
choice but to push for a reinvestigation.'

Blackfinch spoke slowly, as if to an idiot child. 'There's no
earthly chance that the AG will step on the toes of the future
chief minister. Remember, the AG serves at the behest of the CM,
as does the police commissioner. You won't get anyone to risk
upsetting Ansari.' He forestalled her next outburst by raising a
finger. 'I'm not suggesting you abandon your investigation. Merely
pointing out that butting your head against a wall isn't going to
help James Whitby. He'll be dead long before you get anywhere
near reopening the Chatterjee case.' He stopped. 'Besides, the first
thing they'll ask you is why? *Why* would Rahman murder Walter
Rivers? Why would he then take Rivers' body to Chatterjee's
home, murder her, and then make it look as if they'd both been
killed by rioters?'

Persis leaned back against a column, suddenly hollowed out.
She had no answers for the Englishman ... Why *had* Rahman
targeted the pair? Both victims had frequented the White Tiger
Club, a club Rahman ran, but what had propelled him to commit
murder? And how did it all link to Fareed Mazumdar's killing in
Bombay, three years later?

A stray thought flew into her mind like a bird flying in through
an open window.

She recalled something Lata Tiwari, Chatterjee's roommate
had told her. *I think Rivers was interested in her in his capacity as
a journalist. He was always photographing her. Rolls and rolls of
film.*

Why had Rivers been so interested in a woman he wasn't
involved with? ... What if Rivers had been interested in Chatterjee

not as a woman, but as a *story*? Something she knew or had seen that would give him a scoop, a shot in the arm for his journalistic ambitions?

Where *were* those rolls and rolls of film?

Persis didn't know, but had a hunch where she might start looking.

48

'The place is a maze down here.'

Denver Jackson threw a glance over his shoulder.

The corridor was lit by strip-lighting reflecting harshly from bare walls.

They were deep in the bowels of the US consulate, their footsteps echoing from the grey floor tiles as Jackson led her towards a repository situated well below ground level.

She ran a hand along the wall to her right; there was a coolness to it that made her want to stop and place her forehead against the whitewashed surface.

She'd arrived an hour earlier and had been made to wait until Jackson had finished with a meeting. Blackfinch hadn't accompanied her – he had another critical meeting to discuss his putative Calcutta lab. As ever, he'd urged caution, though his eyes seemed to convey his doubts that she'd listen. In truth, she'd tuned his voice out almost as soon as he'd begun to speak. The image of James Whitby, sitting in his cell, counting down to his execution, spurred her on.

When she'd explained to Jackson what she was looking for, he'd stroked his thin moustache. 'I know Kip kept some stuff down in our stores. I can't say exactly what, and I can't guarantee it's not been cleared out since he died. But if you'd like to take a look, I'd be happy to take you down there.'

They arrived at the storage room to find a burly white guard sitting behind a counter reading an American comic, eyeglasses perched on the end of a crapulous nose. He lumbered to his feet with the grace of a rhinoceros attempting to climb a stepladder.

Jackson explained the situation. The man took off his eyeglasses and chewed the end of one arm. 'I remember Rivers. Black fella.'

'Yes,' said Jackson. His lips twitched.

The man nodded sagely. 'Came in here every so often. Not much of a conversationalist, as I recall.' He reached under his counter, pulled out a ledger, licked a thumb, and leafed through it. 'Could you both sign here, please?'

He led them into the interior of the storage room, a labyrinth of bracket shelving glowing softly beneath tube lights. Neatly labelled boxes, of different sizes, were arrayed on the shelves.

There was a soulless precision to the place, at odds with the mouldy, rat-infested nature of most storerooms she'd been in. She wondered if Americans were always this neat.

The guard finally stopped, placed his hands on his knees and wheezed down into a crouch. Setting his glasses back on his nose, he painstakingly read the label on a box on the lowermost shelf. 'Here we go,' he muttered, then lifted the two-by-two box out and handed it to her. 'After Rivers got his clock punched, we put his things into this box. Usually, someone would come and claim it, but I guess he didn't have anyone who cared enough.'

Persis set the box on the floor, dropped to her haunches, lifted off the lid and looked inside.

The contents of the box were neatly arranged.

On one side was a stack of notebooks. She lifted out the topmost one and flicked through it. The feint-ruled pages were crammed with cursive, all but illegible handwriting. The little she could make out suggested that these were journalistic stories that Rivers had either worked on, or – judging from the half-finished state of most of them – had begun before abandoning.

It took her thirty minutes to make her way through the note-books and set them to one side.

In the meantime, Denver Jackson had vanished upstairs, leaving her with the thickset guard. She'd thought the man might return to his post, but he seemed intent on watching over his boxes with the grim dutifulness that Cerberus had applied to guarding the gates of Hades.

She turned her attention to the remaining contents of the box – several cloth bags.

Lifting out the bulkiest one, she undid the knotted string, and took out the object inside.

It was a camera. The body was light, made from aluminium alloy, with black wings and a silver midsection housing the lens. A finder hood jutted from the top of the device, inscribed with the word *Exakta*, and beneath that, in smaller font: *Dresden*.

'German.' The man's voice, coming after a protracted silence, startled her. He peered over her shoulder, a furrow carved into his brow. 'I asked Rivers about that once. Why would an American use a German camera in the middle of a war with the Nazis?' His voice radiated disapproval.

'Perhaps it was the best?'

His lips pursed as if she'd just declared an undying love for Adolf Hitler.

She set down the camera and reached back into the box. A second cloth bag was filled with lumpy shapes.

She opened it and discovered five rolls of film.

'It's thirty-five-millimetre film. How old did you say it was?'

The shop attendant was courteous and dressed in the manner of a banker: an expensive pinstriped suit complete with a waistcoat and a pocket watch. His hair was plastered to his scalp with oil and parted right down the middle. He looked like a porcelain doll.

His slim-fingered hands clutched the roll of film tightly, as if he were about to hurl a grenade.

She'd been reliably informed that the shop was the best photographic services outfit in downtown Calcutta.

'No more than four years.'

'We have a darkroom here. We shall be happy to develop the photos for you, madam.'

'How long will it take?'

'Well, developing the negatives won't take long, but waiting for the reels to dry will take at least two to three hours. And then if you wish for us to prepare prints, another hour.'

She bit back her disappointment. 'Very well.'

'Would you like to return in a few hours?'

'No. I'll stay with the film.'

He gave a small smile as if she'd suggested that she might climb on to his head and dance the fandango. 'I'm afraid our darkroom is off limits to the general public.'

'I'm not the general public.'

His mouth opened and closed in confusion. He noted her expression. Realising that a tactical surrender might be in the best interests of his continued well-being, he nodded, and said, 'As you wish.'

In the darkroom, she was introduced to a thin, lugubrious gentleman named Kumar, who stared at her with an awful fascination, as if a drooling tiger had been led into his domain. Judging from his pallid appearance, he looked as if he'd already spent too much time in the dark on his own.

She watched him as he prepared a cocktail of developing chemicals, his nervousness at her presence forcing a jerky commentary from his moist lips. 'Film is a technological miracle, don't you think? No wonder primitive tribes believed the white man was attempting to steal their souls.' He gave a high-pitched giggle that sounded as if someone had held a gun to his head and asked him to laugh.

He wore gloves as he mixed his chemicals; the whiff of fumes stung Persis's nostrils but Kumar seemed not to notice.

Once the mixture was ready, he carefully took out a roll of film from its canister and loaded it on to a reel. This part of the process was conducted with his arms plugged into a lightless changing bag. 'The film must not be exposed to light,' he explained.

With the film loaded, he set the reel into a development tank, then poured the developing fluid into the tank. He agitated the tank, and then, following further rinses, removed the film.

She followed him as he walked into a small adjoining room and hung the strip on to a thin wire using clips.

He then repeated the process for the remaining four canisters of film.

By the time he'd finished, she was able to view the dozens of images as they dried on the lines.

'I'm afraid some of the images have been underexposed and others have been overexposed. That's why they're either washed out or too dark.'

Her eyes roved over the photographs. And then she stopped.

She pointed a shaky finger at one of the strips of film. 'That image. Can you print it for me?'

'Have you found what you're looking for?'

He waited for her to answer, but she'd already bent back to the strip of film.

49

As before, Persis was made to wait in a tiny room, so stiflingly warm that it was all she could do not to tear off her clothes. She walked to the window, open to let in even more of the muggy heat, and looked out over the teeming ant heap of the surrounding city.

Bombay and Calcutta. In some ways, they were two halves of a whole, both having played their part in the great tapestry of modern Indian history. Both were glamorous in their own way, both youthfully iridescent, and yet something about them suggested – at least to the casual onlooker – that here was a city that had lived to excess, waking up each morning like a man who'd had too much to drink, trousers missing, and not knowing precisely what had transpired the night before.

Revelations swirled around her, as formless and shrill as dreams.

The texture of the case had changed. Her encounters with Rahman and Ansari had thrown a darkness over everything, a fine mesh through which she parsed her own emotions.

Anger. That was the dominant feeling that now commanded her. She was wise enough to know that this was a poor substitute for the analytical reserve that a good officer needed. But the *idea* of saving James Whitby had become large in her mind. She could almost feel his terror, his composure beginning to slip as death approached.

The door opened behind her and Lata Tiwari entered.

The young woman had shed the western outfit of their last encounter and wore an olive-green sari edged with white. 'I'd hoped not to see you again.' Her eyes blinked sadly behind her horn-rimmed spectacles.

'You lied to me,' said Persis. She walked to the table, took a sheaf of photographs from her notebook, and set them down, snapping the edge of each as it struck the wooden tabletop.

Tiwari's eyes roamed over the pictures; her face grew still.

The photographs showed three individuals, sitting at a table laden with glasses and bottles of wine. The table appeared to be set in a shadowy corner of a large venue populated with similar group- ings of individuals – a stage was visible in the background.

The proscenium arch above the stage was studded with light bulbs. They blazed a brilliant white, picking out the silhouette of a tiger.

The White Tiger Club.

The photographs appeared to have been taken from a short distance away from their subjects, and at odd angles, as if the photographer had taken them surreptitiously – one was half obscured by what might have been a pillar. None of the partici- pants faced the camera or seemed to be aware that they were being photographed.

The individuals in the prints were Azizur Rahman, Saleem Ansari, and Rita Chatterjee, the men dressed in formal evening wear, Chatterjee effortlessly beautiful in a strapless black dress.

In several of the pictures Ansari and Chatterjee were sat close together, all but entwined. In one, Chatterjee had her hand in his; in another, he stood behind her, fastening a pendant around her milky neck, a cigarillo sticking out from the side of his mouth.

'They were lovers. Why didn't you tell me?'

'I didn't know.'

Persis watched the woman closely. The rattle of truth lay beneath her denial. 'Why should I believe you?'

Tiwari continued to stare at the photographs, seemingly hypnotised. A shiver ran through her. 'I knew she was seeing someone, but she refused to tell me who. I'd guessed she'd met him at the White Tiger Club and that perhaps it was someone important or married – or both – but I had no idea it was Ansari.' She stopped. 'He – he's married. He has children. And he's a Muslim.'

'Would that have mattered to Rita?'

'Not necessarily. She was a devout Hindu, but she had no issue with Muslims. She loved Fareed as a brother and he was a Mohammedan, too. But for Ansari, the same wouldn't have held true. Muslims and Hindus were at each other's throats back then; the spectre of Partition was hanging over the country, particularly so here in Bengal. Ansari was a Muslim politician – for him to have been revealed as consorting with a Hindu, a nightclub dancer, it would have undermined his standing with *both* communities.'

It was Persis's turn to retreat into a momentary silence. When she spoke, it was with a sense of conviction. 'Here is what I think happened. Fareed Mazumdar convinced Rita Chatterjee to work at the White Tiger Club. He was already working for Saleem Ansari and knew that Ansari would find it difficult to resist Chatterjee should she extend her charms in his direction.'

'Why would Fareed do that?'

'Why does any junior man seek to curry favour with a senior? Advancement. Fareed came from an orphanage; he had no benefactor to ease his progress through Calcutta's legal firmament. Ansari had swung into his orbit, had begun to take an interest in him. But Fareed wanted more. He decided to find a way to ingratiate himself with Ansari – either that, or compromise him.

'But something went wrong. After Chatterjee and Ansari began their affair, the atmosphere soured. The growing problems between Muslims and Hindus – particularly after Jinnah made his pronouncement – made the relationship untenable for Ansari. My guess is that, perhaps, Rita had her own ideas of advancement. Perhaps Ansari sought to end the relationship and she threatened him with a scandal – she'd become pregnant by him. That would explain Walter Rivers.'

'I don't understand.'

'Walter Rivers was a reporter on the lookout for a big story. He frequented the White Tiger Club. He knew Rita. My guess is Rita recruited him, promised to give him the scoop he was looking for.'

'You can't be sure of that.'

'No. But I found these photographs on *Rivers's* camera.'

Tiwari blinked, taken aback. 'Are you suggesting Rita and Walter Rivers conspired to blackmail Ansari?'

'Possibly. And possibly Fareed Mazumdar was involved too. Or perhaps it was all Mazumdar's plan or Mazumdar's and Chatterjee's, and they simply used Rivers to pin down the story by gathering photographic evidence.'

She was shaking her head. 'No. I can't believe that about Rita.'

'The facts speak for themselves. Walter Rivers was murdered on August 15th – the day before Rita was murdered, the day before the riots. We now know that he wasn't murdered at Rita's home – *your* home. Instead, he was brought there the next day.

'Under cover of the riots, Rita was murdered and Walter's body placed there to make it look as if they'd been lovers. In the chaos following the riots, who would have cared about a native nightclub singer who'd been involved with a black man?

'But the plan went awry when *you* saw Azizur Rahman and his accomplice leaving the house. You reported this to the police and the two men were arrested. They were released on bail and the accomplice, Siddiqi, was murdered – I suspect at Rahman's behest. Before the trial, *you* were threatened into changing your testimony. Otherwise, Rahman might well have been convicted of the murders.'

Tiwari's legs seemed to give way. She grasped the edge of a seat and lowered herself into it.

'Fareed Mazumdar defended Rahman in court,' Persis continued. 'He was asked to take the case by Saleem Ansari. Asked or forced. Perhaps Ansari believed Fareed had had something to do with Rita's blackmail attempt and wanted to punish him for it by making him defend her killer. Or perhaps Fareed convinced him he'd be the best man for the job – perhaps his ambition took precedence over the murder of his childhood friend. Either way, shortly after the trial ended, he left Calcutta for Bombay.'

'Why?'

'I suspect he was sent packing by Ansari and Rahman. Or, alternatively, he was sickened by his role in the affair. Sickened that it was by his efforts that the man who'd murdered the woman he'd always thought of as a sister had walked free. Sickened by the thought that if he hadn't forced Rita to work at the White Tiger Club, she would still be alive.

'Ultimately, *he* was the one responsible for her death.'

This final thought hung in the air. Persis felt something stir at the back of her mind, but couldn't quite grasp it. Fareed Mazumdar's culpability in Rita Chatterjee's death ... Could that hold the key to everything? To Mazumdar's own murder?

Tiwari, meanwhile, seemed to be absorbing her words. Her fingers traced the edge of one of the photos before her: Rita smiling as she looked into Ansari's eyes. Unwitting victim or calculating blackmailer?

'In Bombay, I believe that Mazumdar came to be haunted by his role in what had happened to Rita,' Persis went on. 'For three years, he managed to keep her ghost at bay. But, shortly before his death, he'd finally made the decision to go public with what he knew. He'd contacted a journalist, but was killed before he could say anything.'

Tiwari looked up. 'Why would he do that? It would have ruined him. Professionally, I mean.'

'I don't think it mattered to him any more. According to his friends, he was drinking heavily; he was obsessed with notions of sin and redemption. The man was being eaten from the inside out by a guilty conscience.' She paused. 'I believe Ansari got wind of this and sent someone to kill him. Or rather, he handed the problem to Rahman. Rahman arranged for Mazumdar's murder. It was just James Whitby's bad luck that he was in the wrong place at the wrong time.' She reached into her notebook and set the sheet with the Star of David on the table. 'The last time I showed you this, you claimed you had no idea why anyone would send this to Mazumdar.'

She turned and tapped the photograph of Ansari fastening a pendant around Chatterjee's neck.

The shape of the pendant was a Star of David.

'Why would Ansari give Rita a Jewish pendant?'

Tiwari didn't reply, at first. Finally, as if weary of resistance, she said, 'It's not a *Jewish* pendant.'

50

The giant tortoise might have been carved from stone.

In the time Persis had been standing there, together with a family of locals, it had barely stirred, hunkered down in its grass enclosure in a state of near-terminal torpor more usually found in the state legislative assembly. The plaque stated that the animal, an Aldabra tortoise named Adwaita, had arrived from the Seychelles as a gift for Robert Clive of the East India Company. The tortoise had celebrated its two-hundredth birthday recently, making it the oldest resident of the city.

She'd left Tiwari's office and walked to the nearby Alipore Zoological Gardens.

Dusk had fallen and she found herself swimming upstream against the daytime crowds filtering out towards the gates. Inside, a few stragglers hung on, walking beneath Victorian lamp posts as they circumnavigated the forty-acre complex.

The ticket seller had pressed a guide into her hands.

She flicked through it, unseeingly, as she mentally worked around the facts of the case.

There was now little doubt left in her mind that Fareed Mazumdar's death had resulted from the events of three years earlier in Calcutta. The woman he'd grown up with, Rita Chatterjee, had been murdered by the thug Azizur Rahman. Fareed had felt responsible – it was he who'd introduced her to the White Tiger Club.

And yet he'd found himself defending Rahman in court.

243

That guilt had eaten away at him for years. At some point he must have decided to go public with his knowledge – that's why he'd contacted Aalam Channa at the *Indian Chronicle*. The cuttings suggested to her that someone knew this; she suspected they'd been sent to him as a warning.

The likely suspects were obvious: Rahman and Ansari.

A confession would have destroyed Mazumdar, but it would also have sunk the political ship of Saleem Ansari, the man who'd carried on an illicit affair with Chatterjee before her death.

But before Mazumdar could act on his impulse, he'd been murdered.

She was now certain Rahman had organised the killing. Perhaps he'd sent an assassin from Calcutta or reached out to his under-world contacts in Bombay. She doubted he had travelled to Bombay himself to carry out the task.

For a brief instant, her thoughts turned to Youssef Sabri, the Bombay gangster who'd threatened Mazumdar after the lawyer had failed him. Sabri had claimed innocence in Mazumdar's kill-ing; at the time, she'd been inclined to believe him – but now, she was not so sure. If there was one thing men like Azizur Rahman and Youssef Sabri had in common, it was a finely tuned sense of moral relativity.

When it suited them, they lied, cheated, and, if needs be, killed.

She realised that she'd walked on from the tortoise pen, past the Reptile House, and arrived at the tiger enclosure.

The enclosure was deserted – the last of the crowds had shuf-fled off towards the distant gates.

Her eyes moved around the space searching for the beast—

The tiger was sitting in the lee of a palm. She saw that it was a white Bengal tiger.

Her guidebook stated that only months earlier one of the tigers from the zoo had escaped, to be duly shot and killed. The tiger in question had been a notorious man-eater. Apparently, it had racked up more than fifty victims, preying on humans even when it had no need to do so.

She wondered how much truth there was to the story.

When animals and men came into conflict, it was rarely the former that survived to tell the tale. Perhaps, by putting the tiger on display, humans sought to prove something to themselves: that they had conquered their fear of an adversary greater than themselves.

Perhaps a similar dynamic was at work in the James Whitby case.

Whitby *was* the white tiger. For three hundred years, men like him had terrorised the natives. Now, he, too, was locked away. Soon the fear that he and his ilk had inspired would be nothing but a distant memory.

She heard footsteps on the gravel path and turned to find a youngish, well-dressed man approaching her. He was a handsome youth, in a white shirt and khaki trousers.

'Inspector?'

She stared at him. 'Have we met?'

'No. My name is Haresh Saxena. I'm a friend of Seema's. She sent me to fetch you.'

'What are you talking about? Seema doesn't have any friends in Calcutta. She's never been here before.'

'We met at the National Library yesterday. We've been spending the day together. But, well, she's in a spot of trouble. She thinks she's being followed by some unsavoury characters.'

Her mind flashed to the thugs Rahman had sent to escort her to see him.

'She asked me to bring you to her. I tried to persuade her to come with me, but she was adamant.'

'Where is she?'

'Close by. In a café.'

'Impossible. Seema was ill. She's back at our hotel.'

He hesitated. 'I'm afraid she wasn't quite honest with you. She – uh – felt you might not give her permission to step out with me, so she feigned being unwell. She's perfectly fine,' he added. 'But she wanted to stay where there were plenty of people.'

Persis pushed down on her anger. There would be time for that later. 'Take me to her.'

They walked out to the entrance, her stomach churning. She followed the boy down a side street and towards a waiting car, anxiety fogging her mind ... And then the thought that had been struggling to make itself known suddenly burst through like the sun penetrating a cloud bank.

'How did you find m—' she began.

A hand clamped itself over her mouth. A cloth was forced against her lips. An acrid, chemical smell invaded her nostrils.

She was gripped by a howling sense of panic.

She struggled furiously, but it was no use.

Consciousness faded.

And then there was only darkness.

51

Bombay, 1950 – James Whitby

Today Arora asked me if I believed in heaven. In life after death.

For a Hindu, the matter is far simpler: a cycle of reincarnations until the soul's ultimate release to join with the great Oneness of Brahman, creator of the cosmos.

I must have been in a contrary mood. 'What if it's all a lie?' I said. 'What if God is just a gleam in a madman's eye, a disembodied voice in the darkness?'

Arora seemed uncomfortable. I hadn't pegged him as a spiritual man. The hard-nosed factuality of the legal profession has always seemed at odds with a belief system rooted in deism.

Perhaps he's hoping that I might take solace from my faith.

My mother would have approved. She was an ardent churchgoer, a lusty chorister in her youth.

Sometimes, I dream of tracking her down. But what would I say if I found her? This woman who abandoned me to my fate?

My thoughts have become hallucinatory as the end nears. I cannot seem to hold on to any one thing for any length of time.

I've lost weight. Food turns to ash in my mouth.

Arora joked that I might try going on hunger strike. He cites Gandhi's example, though forgets to mention that it was during one such effort – in protest at the continuing Partition violence – that the great man was shot dead.

I replied that I lacked the ideological stomach for a prolonged fast. No pun intended.

Arora forced out a weak smile. During the monsoon, even the jokes feel damp.

There are moments when my anger overcomes me and I rail at my jailors.

Yesterday, I managed to cross swords with Arora. I accused him of making allowances for the prejudice that has seen me brought low. I called the new India an uncivilised society, a society of hyenas.

'The British always claimed *they* came here to civilise us,' he responded. 'Tell me, James, if you were here to civilise us, why did a million Indians die at each others' hands during Partition?'

'You're really going to stand there and blame the British for *your* murderous instincts?'

'No,' he conceded. 'I just want you to admit that you failed. On every level. You failed because you cannot build a better world on the basis of a lie.'

I knew then that I'd upset him. I apologised and we resumed our cordial comportment. I think he understood that the strain of my predicament had finally breached the walls of my seeming equanimity.

The truth is that no man can escape Death's terrible audit. The realisation of the coming end seeps into you, like smoke.

Pindar wrote: 'A shadow in a dream is man.'

That's how I feel, have felt for most of my life.

A shadow in someone else's dream, trying desperately to find something to believe in, to hold on to.

Too late now.

52

Persis awoke to the sound of a gentle hammering.

It was a moment before consciousness fully returned. Her eyes snapped open into darkness. She realised that she was laid out on a cot, set hard against a wall of wood that reeked of tobacco and a briny smell she associated with the sea. Scrabbling to her feet, she found the top of her head scraping against a lowered ceiling. She was in a confined space ... and the space was in motion.

A boat. She was aboard some sort of launch, and the hammering sound was the sound of an engine. The stench of diesel fuel cut through the cabin smells.

Her eyes had begun to adjust to the gloom. Light filtered in from a small porthole window set into the wall opposite the cot. The cabin was claustrophobically narrow, with a bucket in one corner and a heap of coiled rope in another.

She stepped across to the window, listing slightly as residual grogginess gripped her legs, and looked out into the night.

Moonlight silvered a watery surface. Some half a kilometre in the distance rose an impenetrable wall of vegetation, silhouetted against a night sky dusted with stars. In among the foliage, hundreds of tiny lights glowed.

Glow-worms. She'd read about them in her Great Eastern guidebook.

She was in the Sundarbans.

Fear bloomed inside her chest.

Where were they taking her? Why?

Florid passages floated up from her guidebook.

The Sundarbans: a vast mangrove archipelago in the Gangetic delta, stretching from the mouth of the Hooghly to the mouth of the Meghna; thousands of square miles of watery jungle cut through by a tracery of river channels, the largest of which were mighty waterways. Poets – many of whom had ventured into the Sundarbans in search of inspiration – described the place as ephemeral, a land where a thousand islands, some no bigger than sandbars, flickered like desert mirages. The tides here flowed hundreds of miles inland, swallowing thousands of acres of forest and regurgitating them hours later, reshaping the islands on a daily basis and rendering them all but inhospitable to human life.

Persis knew that Dinaz had spent the past few years working for the Sundarbans Forest Division. She'd told stories of tigers, crocodiles, snakes, and a terrain so hostile to man that only fools or the abject poor made the mistake of attempting to live there.

By the particular quirk of irony that distinguished the Bengalis, they'd named the region *sundar ban* meaning 'beautiful forest'.

She knew that the Sundarbans were a few hours south of Calcutta. Too soon for anyone to notice her disappearance.

She heard a wooden rattle behind her and turned to find the door to the cabin wide open and a man standing there holding a hurricane lamp. A sarong was entwined around his heavy midriff, and a grimy white vest glowed against the dark nuttiness of his skin. Crystals of salt flecked his beard, and his anvil-shaped head seemed too large for his squat body.

A machete hung from his shoulder in a makeshift sling.

'Nomoshkar, bibi.' Sarcasm dripped from his voice, rendering the respectful greeting a thing of menace.

Terror boomed out of the darkness. 'Who are you? Where are you taking me?' She spoke in Hindi, her Bengali not proficient enough for the task.

He said nothing. There was a hunger in his eyes that chilled her.

He took another step into the room, the lamp swinging in his hand, flinging shadows in all directions.

She reacted instinctively, rushing at him, raising her fist as if to strike him, waiting for him to lift his hands to protect his face, then feinting and slipping around him to duck through the door. She stumbled along a narrow gangway, then clambered up a ladder set into the wall, and found herself on the launch's foredeck, the cockpit looming behind her.

A shape was visible at the wheel.

Her head swung from side to side ... Her stomach dropped away.

The launch was motoring gently down the middle of a waterway at least a kilometre in width. To either side, as far as the eye could see, the riverbanks were lined with thick foliage. She knew she could make it to shore, but then what? And what lay beneath the river's surface?

Crocodiles killed hundreds in these waters every year.

A shout from the wheelhouse made up her mind.

She moved towards the hull. As she did so, she heard the engine skip a beat. Without warning, a shape materialised from behind a water butt set against the side of the boat. She saw a rake-thin adolescent form, a raised arm, a wooden club ... She cried out, a guttural gull-like sound, just before the blow landed, whirling her back into darkness.

53

'What do you mean, she hasn't returned?'

The hotel's night manager, a habitually genial man with an orange beard that gave him the look of an apologetic orangutan, swept a handkerchief over his brow before neatly folding it back into his pocket. 'I'm afraid I can tell you no more, sir. Madam left the hotel this morning and has not returned. As for Miss Desai, as far as we can ascertain, she was not in her room last night and has not returned to the hotel today.'

Blackfinch goggled at the man. 'And you haven't informed the police?'

The manager quailed. 'We have no reason to assume foul play.'

'Two women vanish and you think there's no need to worry?'

'I believe the ladies are first-timers to Calcutta. Perhaps they are simply exploring all our fair city has to offer? Our guests are often out till the early hours. Sometimes, they do not return until the following day. Especially when they encounter company to their liking.' He coughed genteelly.

Blackfinch instantly grasped the man's meaning. He leaned over the counter with a murderous glint in his eye. 'If I were you, I'd pray they return soon.'

He turned and would have marched off imperiously, if he hadn't immediately run slap bang into Darius. The two men fell to the floor in a heap, untangled themselves, leaped to their feet, smoothed out their ties, and endeavoured to pretend that absolutely *nothing had happened.*

'Blackbird? What are you doing here?' Darius's question had teeth.

'The name's Blackfinch. And I could ask you the same thing.'

'I – I came to see if Persis needed anything.'

'What could she possibly need from you?'

Darius bristled. 'I thought she might wish for a late supper. Or a nightcap. We are cousins, after all.'

'Yes. *Cousins.*'

A short, grim silence.

'Anyway, she's not here. So you can toddle off.'

'Toddle?' Red spots appeared on Darius's cheeks. Through gritted teeth, he said, 'What are *you* doing here? This is a little outside office hours, don't you think?'

'Persis and I had some business to attend to.'

'What sort of business?'

'Police business. Nothing for a civilian to worry himself about.'

'My understanding is that you're not a real police officer. You're a chemist.'

It was Blackfinch's turn to swell up. 'You seem to be ill-informed. I have every authority accorded a police officer. For instance, I could arrest *you*, should I choose.'

The two men glared at each other.

Finally, they stalked off towards the hotel's entrance in lockstep, as if joined at the hip.

In the street, they watched each other lower themselves into their respective vehicles.

A few moments later, the cars moved off.

54

This time when Persis floated up from the murk, it was to find the dark oval of Seema's face hanging above her own, anxiety evident in the girl's searching look.

A sense of relief flooded through her. It had all been a dream, the sort of dark visitation her mother would have called a *fever dream*.

She smiled fuzzily . . . and then a grenade went off at the back of her skull.

She sat up, clutching her head. It felt as if a mad tabla player had been banging out a symphony on her cranium.

'Madam, are you alright?'

Persis grunted, unable to answer. She felt the girl pull at her hand, push a steel cup into it. The brackish water offered a momentary distraction, but was hardly an effective cure for being thumped on the head with a wooden club.

Gritting her teeth, she surveyed her surroundings.

The room was spacious, with the dimensions of a Victorian drawing room. Cracked cement walls were blotched with damp spots and ancient stains. On one side, a barred window looked out over a few bare metres of earth to a low stone wall, beyond which lay forested darkness. A single bare bulb hung from a high ceiling. The only light came from a candle on a low shelf. Below the shelf stood a steel jerrycan.

The iron bedstead on which they sat dominated the room, its thin mattress rubbed raw by the weight of untold bodies.

'Where are we?' she finally managed.

'I think we're somewhere in the Sundarbans.'

'How long have I been here?'

'They brought you in an hour ago.'

She turned to face the young woman. 'How long have *you* been here?'

Seema turned away. 'This is my fault.'

Persis hesitated, then reached out and took the girl's hand.

The story spilled out of her in a torrent. The handsome boy she'd met at the National Library. His invitation to show her around Calcutta. How he'd turned up with a car, driven her to a secluded spot, and then . . .

Persis felt her stomach hollow. 'Did he . . . interfere with you?'

Seema shook her head quickly. 'No. I think he drugged me. The next thing I knew, they were pulling me off a motorboat.'

Relief flooded through her. The idea of Seema at the mercy of a predator did not bear thinking about. 'What did you see?'

'I – I was groggy.'

'Anything you can remember might help us.'

She seemed to take heart from this. Persis could only imagine the girl's terror. 'There was a wooden jetty. Set a few hundred yards back from it is this house, a large bungalow, with a pitched roof and a wall running around the compound. French windows with shutters and bars.'

'What did you see around the house?'

'Forest. Nothing but mangrove forest.'

'Did you see guards? How many?'

'I don't know. There's definitely one. He came in with a woman earlier today. She gave me food.' Seema pointed at a steel plate on the floor beside the bed.

'Was he armed?'

'Yes. He had a pistol. And a large knife.'

'A machete?'

The girl nodded.

'Did you see any boats? By the jetty?'

Seema considered this. 'Yes. There were a couple of small rowboats tied up there. But – but there's no way to get to them, no way to get out of this room.'

Persis squeezed her hand. 'There's always a way,' she said, with more confidence than she felt. A sudden pressure in her abdomen prompted her to ask: 'Is there a bathroom?'

'Yes. There.'

She followed the direction of Seema's pointing finger and saw a door to the right of the bed.

Hauling herself off the mattress, she walked to the door, pulled it open, and entered.

The bathroom was surprisingly well appointed. A porcelain toilet with a wooden seat. A cast-iron bathtub with feet in the shape of tigers' heads. A small window – barred – was set high in one wall. A bucket of water stood next to the toilet, a steel mug floating on the surface, together with the corpses of several insects. Incongruously, a towel lay neatly folded over the bath's curling rim as if this was not a prison but a hotel room somewhere in hell.

When she returned to the bedroom, she paused by the window and tested the bars.

Unyielding.

The thick silence of the mangroves poured through the ironwork. She'd read somewhere that few creatures lived in the mangroves; the saltiness of the soil and the constant tidal activity made life a precarious business here.

She found it hard to focus her gaze. The vegetation was so dense it defied the eye's ability to discern detail, like an optical illusion.

She felt the bottom drop out of hope.

She walked to the jerrycan, poured another glass of water with shaky hands, and calmed herself. She knew that she would need all her strength, all her reserve. She knew that they were both in mortal danger. The only reason they were still alive was because someone wanted something from them.

That gave them half a chance.

55

The turbaned servitor had been staring at him unblinkingly for so long Blackfinch had begun to think the glorified peon had been replaced by a wax mannequin.

It was eleven o'clock and he'd been waiting outside the deputy chief minister's office for over an hour. According to the officious peon, Saleem Ansari was in an important meeting and could not be disturbed.

The Englishman had arrived at the politico's office having visited the Great Eastern that morning to discover his worst fears confirmed.

There was still no sign of either Persis or her young ward, Seema Desai.

He'd rung Persis's friend Dinaz and discovered that she, too, had no idea where her friend was. For the past couple of days, Dinaz had been engaged in important work of her own, but had dropped everything and come charging over.

It had been almost painful to watch her maul the hotel manager, like a rampant tiger savaging a small goat.

Afterwards, Dinaz had accompanied him to file a police report. Using their combined connections, they'd managed to meet with a senior member of the Calcutta constabulary – not that it had done much good. The man had been singularly unimpressed. 'What you're telling me is that an off-duty officer from Bombay has been running around *my* city carrying out an investigation without *my* knowledge and butting heads with gangsters? And now she's missing.' His tone indicated that even a fool could draw a line between point A and point B on this particular map.

'Are you saying you won't help?' There was a dangerous rumble in Dinaz's voice.

The man had sighed and promised to do what he could. But Calcutta was a big city. Where would he even start? If harm had befallen the two women, it was likely they would never be found again.

It was all Blackfinch could do to restrain his companion.

After Dinaz had left, he'd considered the situation.

It was the feeling of helplessness that clawed at him.

He should have known Persis would not listen. Some people heard screaming and ran in the opposite direction. Persis found the nearest burning building and plunged right in. It was the part of her persona that most frustrated him – and yet he adored her for it.

His desire for her was like a badly written raga. Out of tune, poorly worded, and yet a song nonetheless. He wished he could free himself from the hold she had over him; he wished he could go back to being plain old Archie Blackfinch, an Englishman abroad, with one bad marriage behind him and a solemn vow taken to never again have anything to do with a member of the opposite sex.

But there was no accounting for the secret gods that ruled men's hearts.

His thoughts turned to Azizur Rahman and the encounter that Persis had recounted to him, Rahman's thinly veiled threats . . .

He turned as a body fell into the seat beside him.

He stared in astonishment at Darius. 'Dinaz told me you were here.'

They said nothing for a while. The peon looked between them as if two exotic beasts had emerged from mythology to take up residence in his waiting room. A burra sahib and a burra babu sat side by side.

'Do you think she's . . . safe?' Darius eventually said.

Blackfinch took a moment to compose his reply. 'I don't know. I hope so.'

The Indian fumbled in the pocket of his jacket and emerged with a packet of cigarettes and a lighter. He offered the packet to the Englishman.

'I don't smoke.'

Darius lit a cigarette, then said, 'Even when we were young, she was always the wild one. Never knew when to quit, when to take a backward step. She was born with a point to prove and, by Jove, she'd prove it even if it killed her.

'I remember one time we'd gone on a family trip to Elephanta Island. One of our cousins happened to mention that he'd once swum from the island back to Bombay. Fourteen, fifteen kilometres. So, *of course*, Persis had to prove that she could do it too. She's always been a good swimmer, but the sea was rough that day. We followed her in a boat, begged her to pull out. She wouldn't listen. She almost drowned. Not that I think that would have stopped her.'

Blackfinch said nothing.

'It's funny, you can know someone your whole life and not really know them at all.' He leaned back, blew smoke into the air, and closed his eyes.

56

They spent a restless night. Halfway through, Persis had awoken to the sound of something scrabbling along the floor. Slipping out of bed, she'd discovered a small fish dying by the window. She recognised it as a tree perch, a species of spiny fish that could drag itself along the ground, even scaling small obstacles.

Why had it made its way into this barren room?

Something about the creature's meaningless death struck her deeply, and she found the room spinning around her, panic clutching at her throat. It was all she could do not to cry out. She bent over double, nausea forcing her to retch.

And then Seema was beside her, soothing her, leading her back to the bed.

They spent the rest of the night clutching each other, a lutulent terror seeping in through the barred window, as oppressive as the sweltering heat, held at bay only by the strength of their combined will.

In the morning, guilt consumed her. That her own life was in peril, she could accept. She had *chosen* to pursue this investigation, chosen to walk into danger.

But for Seema to be in the same predicament was unforgivable.

She should never have allowed the girl to accompany her; she should never have placed her in harm's way.

Her father had admonished her many times for her recklessness. She'd always believed it came with the territory, came with being who she was.

She could no more change her nature than a snake.

But now she realised that to think like that was not strength but weakness, a peculiar kind of arrogance that she'd long employed to defend the indefensible. Seema's life now hung in the balance as a direct result of that arrogance, that unbending commitment to her own mythos.

The woman arrived at precisely twelve, carrying a blackened earthenware pot. From this she ladled out a thick fishy curry on to steel plates, adding generous helpings of rice from a second, smaller vessel.

A burly guard – the same thickset man who'd entered Persis's cabin aboard the launch – stood behind her, a pistol grasped in his hand. His eyes locked with hers. For a moment, she thought he might attack her, but he said nothing, merely waiting as his colleague completed her task.

Persis returned her attention to the woman.

She wore a drab white sari, the hem whispering against the bare floor. Grey streaked the tight bun of her hair, and lines marked the edges of her mouth. Her face held a sense of eternal sufferance. Yet her eyes were astonishing, amber in colour, tiger's eyes.

'What's your name?' asked Persis.

The woman said nothing. They watched as she replenished the water in their jerrycan from one she had brought with her.

When she'd finished, she paused a moment and looked directly at Persis. For an instant, hope flared. But then Persis saw that there was nothing in the woman's gaze. Not pity, not sadness, not cruelty. Not even curiosity.

The woman left, escorted out by the guard.

His eyes lingered on Persis as he left; a shiver ran through her. There was no doubting the unspoken message.

Unfinished business.

The door closed. She heard the sound of a latch bar falling into place.

They heard the pair's footsteps move down the corridor, come to a halt, the sound of another latch bar scraping upwards, and then a voice – a woman's cry – rang out, to be swiftly silenced by a bark from the thug.

'There's someone else here,' breathed Seema.

Persis said nothing. A shroud-like dread had fallen over her.

There was something about that voice that had sounded horribly familiar.

57

The peon's demeanour changed as he led them inside Saleem Ansari's office. The door seemed to act as a magic portal. As he passed through, he transformed from self-important lackey to bullied dog.

Blackfinch's first impression was of the great machinery of state rumbling to a halt. Several men were gathered around a desk, staring grimly at the newcomers as if he and Darius had just walked into a wake while playing musical instruments and dancing the conga.

The office was vast, large enough to serve as an infantry barracks. One wall was dominated by an oil painting of a bullock yoked to a plough, a bare-chested and scrawny man in a grubby turban standing beside the bored-looking animal.

Ansari was sat behind a desk inlaid with mother-of-pearl, its sides engraved with an arabesque picked out in brass and gold. He stood to greet them as his visitors filed out, casting curious backward glances in their direction.

'Forgive me, gentlemen, you seem familiar, but I cannot recall where I might have made your acquaintance.'

Blackfinch made the introductions. 'We met, briefly, at a business function at Government House two days ago.' His tone was mildly admonishing. How could Ansari not remember them?

Ansari's handsome face broke into a smile. 'Ah, yes, of course. You're the Englishman who's going to teach us how to solve crime.' He chuckled. 'I suppose you know that it was a pair of Indians who invented the fingerprinting system which your Scotland Yard is now so enamoured of? Right here in Bengal, as a matter of fact. Not that my compatriots received much credit for it. Please, have a seat.'

The peon was sent scurrying for refreshments; Ansari listened patiently as Blackfinch explained the matter, Darius twitching impatiently beside him.

When the Englishman had finished, Ansari leaned back in his seat, his face thoughtful. The ceiling fan stirred his thick black hair. A few streaks of grey were visible among the lustrous foliage. 'Yes, I remember your colleague. The policewoman who seemed to believe that Fareed Mazumdar's murder in Bombay was somehow tied up with the old killings of Rita Chatterjee and Walter Rivers in Calcutta.'

'That's her.'

'She seemed to believe that Azizur Rahman was guilty of the Chatterjee and Rivers murders – despite the fact that he'd been cleared at trial.'

Blackfinch said nothing.

Ansari pursed his lips. 'Forgive me, but I also received the distinct impression that she felt my own role – in recommending Mazumdar to Rahman as his defence counsel – was somehow worthy of censure.'

'She's a . . . a passionate woman.'

Ansari's moustache crinkled as he permitted himself a small smile. 'I suppose she must be quite something to know in person.'

'She is.'

Blackfinch waited as the Indian reached out to a carved wooden box, opened it, and emerged with a cigar. They watched him remove the end using an ornately engraved gold cigar cutter, light it, then take a thoughtful puff. 'What is it that you think I can do for you?'

The Englishman hesitated. 'I believe that Persis and her companion might have been abducted. I believe that Azizur Rahman might be behind it.'

Ansari stiffened. He lowered his cigar. 'You have evidence of this?'

'No.'

'Yes,' blurted Darius. 'What I mean is, sir, that Persis confided to us that she'd been forcibly summoned to meet with Rahman. I think his intention was to intimidate her.'

'And why would he do that?'

'He wished for her to drop her investigation and leave the city.'

For a moment, Ansari sat silently, smoke misting around his eyes, his thoughts inscrutable.

Blackfinch began to wonder if he'd made a mistake. He recalled Persis's own belief that Ansari and Rahman were as thick as thieves, that Ansari had had as much to lose as Rahman in the event that Fareed Mazumdar had managed to go public with the truth about Rita Chatterjee's killing. Persis had gone so far as to conjecture that Ansari might have been involved in *ordering* Mazumdar's killing.

But she'd found no evidence for such an assertion. That was Persis all over. Leaping to wild conjectures and *then* setting out to prove them. Now, sitting here in front of the man, Blackfinch couldn't tell how much of her claims had been based on fantasy and how much might be cold hard reality.

The truth was that he'd come here because he could think of no one else who might help or who had the *power* to help. If Rahman *had* abducted Persis, then Ansari might be the only man in Calcutta who could convince him to let her go.

Unless, of course, Ansari had been the one to order her kidnapping.

That, too, was a possibility.

In which case, he and Darius were sitting before the lion asking him not to eat the deer he'd already made a meal of.

Ansari finally stirred. 'Very well, gentlemen. Let me see what I can do.' He set the cigar into a brass bowl, then picked up the receiver of his telephone. 'Get me Azizur Rahman.'

Moments later, the call was connected. A short conversation ensued, and then Ansari replaced the phone.

'Azizur is indisposed at present. It appears that he's out of the city.' He picked up the cigar. 'He's not the man you think he is. It's true that Azizur lives by his own code. Occasionally that code deviates from what you and I might find acceptable. Yet it's equally true that without him, I would not be here today enjoying the fine trappings of this office.' He waved his cigar around. 'But the Azizur I know is an honourable man. And just because he has helped me in the past does not mean that I would condone an act such as you describe.' He seemed to arrive at a decision. 'I shall follow up with the police commissioner. We will make every effort to find these women. You have my word.'

The man was either a consummate actor or genuinely innocent in the matter. Blackfinch couldn't make up his mind.

As Ansari led them to the door, he placed a hand on the Englishman's shoulder. 'Let us pray that this is a misunderstanding. Perhaps the women have become so engrossed in their mission that they have simply lost their way? Calcutta can be a difficult city to navigate. Wasn't it your own Kipling who compared Calcutta to Dante's *Inferno*, with its various circles of hell?' He shook his head ruefully. 'Rest assured, I will do everything in my power to find your colleagues.'

58

The woman returned that evening.

This time, the guard accompanying her stayed out in the corridor.

Persis watched her squat down to ladle out the stew and rice.

'What's your name?'

The woman ignored her.

'Do you know *our* names?'

Silence.

'Why are you helping them?'

The only sound was the soft clank of the ladle on the plates.

'What will they do to us?'

Silence.

'If you help them, then whatever happens to us is on your head too.'

The woman stopped and looked at them with those strange eyes. When she spoke, her voice was gravelly, almost mechanical. 'Who are you to me? Outsiders. City folk. This is the Sundarbans. What do you know of me, of my life?'

Persis leaned forward, lowering her voice to an urgent hiss. 'I came to Calcutta to find a killer. To save a man from being put to death by our government for a crime he did not commit. Justice. Does that mean anything to you?'

Something shifted in the woman's eyes. Or perhaps it was just a trick of the light.

'This is Seema. Her father abandoned her when she was a child. She has a younger sister and a mother who need her. I brought her with me because I thought I could keep her safe. But I was wrong. I was arrogant. We need your help. Please.'

The woman transferred her gaze to the girl.

For what seemed an eternity, she seemed to hover on the horns of indecision, and then the stiffness went out of her slender frame. She set down her ladle, then leaned in. 'My name is Mahima,' she whispered. 'I don't know what they intend to do with you. That is the truth. They ask me to make food and to bring it here. I know nothing of why you're here.'

'Who's in the other room?'

'Another woman. I don't know her name.'

'Is there a way you can get in touch with the authorities?'

She shook her head. 'I cannot do that. They will know that it was me.'

Seema broke in. 'Please. You *must* help.' The girl was on the verge of tears.

The woman rose to her feet, her sari rustling.

'If you won't contact the authorities,' said Persis desperately, 'then at least help us to get out of here. Give us a fighting chance.'

'What would you do if you escaped? Do you know the water-ways, the jungle? Have you any idea what it takes to survive out here? This is Bon Bibi's land, mistress of the tides, queen of the tigers.' Her voice was tinged with an inexpressible sadness. 'I'm sorry. But there's nothing I can do.'

59

The sarangi player appeared lost to the music, plucking at his instrument with his eyes closed, dishevelled hair matted to a sweat-soaked forehead.

To Blackfinch, the raga sounded less like a tuneful rendition of a Bengali folk classic and more like the sound of a soul in torment.

Either way, it mirrored his mood.

Following a fruitless day spent chasing up with the police commissioner's office – Ansari had been as good as his word and contacted the man, and all but ordered his cooperation – Blackfinch had circled back to the Great Eastern in the evening on the off-chance that Persis had returned. The only thing he'd found out was that Persis had met with a Diwan Kasturi, head of Calcutta CID, when she'd arrived in the city. It was from Kasturi that she'd obtained the Chatterjee and Rivers case files.

The man had now taken personal charge of the hunt for the missing women.

Having found no sign of Persis at the hotel, Blackfinch decided to wait it out in the Great Eastern's Maxim's Bar.

He was on to his fourth beer when a shadow fell over the table.

He looked up to find Darius standing over him, tie at half mast, sleeves rolled up, jacket over his arm, patches of sweat spreading across his chest.

'May I join you?'

Blackfinch stared at him, then waved his glass at a seat.

Darius lowered himself into a chair, crooked a finger at a hovering waiter, ordered a gin and tonic, then lit a cigarette.

For a moment, they listened to the wretched sarangi player, who seemed oblivious to the grimacing faces of his audience – mainly men, all with the look of shell-shocked soldiers under aerial bombardment.

'It's the feeling of helplessness I can't abide,' said Darius eventually.

Blackfinch pursed his lips. 'When you join the force, they tell you that you have to learn to be phlegmatic. You can't solve every case. You can't prevent every crime. It's like trying to stop the tide. But you never get used to it.'

'It's different in my line of work. *We* decide who to work with. *We* set the rates. We oversee everything, from start to finish. To a great extent, we control our own destiny.'

'Or perhaps you allow yourself the illusion that you do.'

Darius lifted his glass to his lips. 'So ... you and Persis?' His words were picked with the care of a man dancing across a minefield in lead boots.

Blackfinch locked eyes with him, expecting him to expand, but the Indian said no more.

'Are you intending to stay in India?' continued Darius eventually. 'I mean, once your work here is done, I presume you'll return to England?'

There was an edge to his tone.

It wasn't that Blackfinch hadn't dwelt on the matter. What had seemed straightforward when he'd first arrived here, more than a year earlier, had now acquired the contours of a problem so thorny his mind simply bolted in the opposite direction whenever he thought of it.

There was no doubting it – this land, these people, they'd found their way under his skin. Fattened as a child on tales of the glories of empire, he'd revelled in his own ignorance. But, in just a short time, he'd come to understand the appalling weight of his inheritance.

How had the Indians borne it for so long?

He'd mused on an image of the first white man in India to come face to face with a tiger. A moment of fear, of wonder, long-dismissed native myths crystallising into a magnificent reality. And then he'd raised his shotgun and blasted the poor beast to kingdom come.

Had anyone stopped to consider what the tiger must have thought? Truly, who was the savage beast in that moment?

The Indians he'd met had been nothing but welcoming. He'd sensed so little in the way of recrimination or bitterness that he found it hard to believe these same people had laboured under three centuries of bondage. He'd marvelled at their warmth, their dignity, the sheer unfettered exuberance of their headlong charge into the future.

Heaven help him if he hadn't begun to fall a little in love with them.

And then there was Persis . . .

'I suppose one day I'll go back.'

Darius was silent a moment. 'Wasn't it George Bernard Shaw who said that when an Englishman wants something he never admits to wanting it? Instead, he becomes inflamed with a burning conviction that it is his moral duty to conquer those who possess the thing he wants?'

Blackfinch didn't rise to the bait. 'I never came out here to change the world. Like most Englishmen, I suppose I thought of India as a romantic abstraction. An exotic jewel we'd once possessed and now lost. My father kept a copy of Stoddard's *The Rising Tide of Color* on his bookshelf. He was a man who believed in the primacy of the white race and was terrified that we would soon be overrun by vast waves of yellow, brown and black men.'

He stopped. 'But I'm not my father. The horrors I saw during the war ... There's no such thing as a master race. Only men and the things they do, both good and bad.

'I needed to get away from England, to get away from myself, and so I accepted the posting to India. I wasn't prepared. I don't think anyone can truly prepare themselves for this place. The more I learn, the less I feel I know. Persis has been a ... a question to which I don't have the answer.' He sighed. 'What I *do* know is that I can feel the shape of my life changing, like glass in the hands of a glass-blower. India has done that.'

He saw that Darius was staring at him with surprise.

An uncomfortable silence reigned into which the sarangi player inserted another torturous raga. A man on a nearby table cursed loudly, threw a handful of notes on to the table, and stumbled from the room.

'I work for one of the top managing agencies in the country,' said Darius eventually. 'It's been three years since independence, yet every post on the board is still filled by an Englishman. My father would have approved. He loved the British. If he were alive today, he would probably be labelled a quisling. But the truth is that every one of those Englishmen earned their spurs out here, not by subjugating anyone, but by running a successful business that gave many Indians the makings of a solid career – including me. Why should they step aside simply because political expediency now dictates that they must do so?' He stopped. 'The world *has* changed. But sometimes I don't think it's changed as much as we'd like to believe.' He seemed about to say more, but then subsided.

'Another gin?' said Blackfinch, eventually.

'Yes. Why not?'

60

The candle had guttered out. Without the faint moonlight falling in from the barred window, they might have been consigned to pitch darkness.

Persis listened to Seema breathe beside her. Something buzzed by her ear; she bit down on the urge to slap at the air.

A sudden shift in the girl's breathing told her that she'd jagged out of her fitful sleep. For a while, Seema said nothing, and then, 'Are we going to die here?'

'No.'

'How can you say that? You can't know that.'

'If they wanted to kill us, why would they imprison us?'

'How can they possibly let us go?'

That same thought had reverberated in her mind, growing larger and larger until it pushed everything else to one side. She'd controlled her panic and attempted to analyse the situation dispassionately.

The truth was that Seema was right. If Azizur Rahman was behind this, then there was little chance that he would let them go. What would he gain by doing so? An act as dramatic as kidnapping two women – one of them a police officer – had an air of finality to it, like a man setting a revolver to his temple.

'We still don't know exactly what they want,' she said. 'Once we give them whatever it is they need from us they'll let us go.' She understood instinctively that Seema *needed* reassurance, needed her to show strength, even if they both knew it was only a façade.

A silence fell on them, each woman lost to her own thoughts, until Seema spoke again. 'When I was nine, my father attempted to molest me. My mother intervened and he broke her arm. But she stopped him. She told him that if he ever touched me again, she'd pour kerosene over him in his sleep and burn him alive. That's when he left us.'

Persis remained still, allowing the awful words to wash through her.

She felt the girl's fingers entwine around her own.

'I'm not afraid of dying. I'm afraid of dying without having lived.'

An inchoate feeling – part sorrow, part anger, part helplessness – bloomed inside her. She gripped the girl's hand fiercely, hoping that she might communicate her feelings by touch alone.

Time passed, and then she let go Seema's hand, and slipped silently from the bed.

Walking to the wall, she began to rap on it with her knuckles, a dull, repetitive Morse code.

After what seemed an eternity, an echoing knock sounded from the far side of the wall.

She grimaced in the darkness, triumph glowing momentarily in her eyes.

Dropping to her knees she bent down to a breeze-block vent in the bottom corner of the wall. Placing her mouth to the vent, she hissed, 'Can you hear me?'

Seconds passed, and then, 'Yes.'

'Lata, is that you?'

A pause. 'Yes. It's Persis, isn't it?'

'Yes.'

Another silence, then, 'You're the reason I'm here.' It was a statement, not a question.

'Yes.'

'What do they want from me?'

'I don't know. But my guess is they want to stop my investigation into Rita's death. They were following me.'

'And you led them straight to *me*.'

'I'm sorry. I – I should have thought of the possible consequences.'

More silence drifted through the vent, and then: 'I can't believe this is happening. Two days ago, my life was . . . normal . . . Are we going to die here?'

'No! We'll find a way out. I promise you.'

'Aren't you tired of making promises you can't keep?' The woman's voice sounded hollow, shot through with anger. 'I told you to stop. I told you to walk away. You practically dared them to do this.'

Persis swallowed, then said, 'Have they mistreated you?'

A pause, then, 'No.'

'That's good. We have to stay alert. Tomorrow, when the woman comes with our food, I'm going to try and disarm the guard.'

'He has a gun.'

'I'm a trained police officer.'

This seemed to give Tiwari pause. 'Do you really think you can overpower him?'

'Yes.'

'And if you fail?'

'I won't fail.'

A soft shuffling sound came through the vent. Persis had a vision of Tiwari sitting back on her haunches.

'Did you solve your case? Fareed's murder?'

'No.' She stopped. 'I keep thinking it's tied up with what happened to Rita. But that might be wishful thinking.'

'A woman came to see me last year,' said Tiwari. 'She claimed to be Rita's mother. She'd been to the orphanage where she'd left

Rita as a baby. They'd told her about Rita's murder. She'd dug up the newspapers and followed the story to my door. She had a million questions, wanted to know everything about the daughter she'd never met. She wanted to know the "truth" about Rita's death. I told her about Ansari and Rahman. I told her about Fareed Mazumdar. I found it cathartic talking to her. But now, now I feel responsible. For her grief. As if, somehow, I let her down. If I'd been more alert, I might have saved Rita.'

Persis said nothing. She recalled Agnes Katz at the St Nicholas orphanage mentioning Rita's mother. She wondered what had become of her, this woman so overcome by remorse that she had tracked down the daughter she'd abandoned so long ago.

Had she eventually confronted Azizur Rahman, her daughter's murderer? And if so, what had become of her?

A knot of fear settled in Persis's stomach.

It was not beyond the bounds of possibility that Rita's mother might have followed her daughter into the darkness. Azizur Rahman was not the sort of man who left loose ends lying around.

Her thoughts returned to Rita's relationship with Saleem Ansari.

The last time she'd spoken with Tiwari, she'd shown her the photographs of Ansari and Rita at the White Tiger Club, Ansari slipping a pendant around Rita's throat, a pendant in the shape of a Star of David.

Tiwari had resolved the mystery for her. 'The symbol isn't just used by Jews. The six-pointed star is a part of Hindu tantric tradition, used to represent the union of male and female. It's known as the *shatkona*. Rita was a devout Hindu. When I first saw her wearing it, I asked her who'd given it to her. She wouldn't tell me.'

'Why didn't you tell me this when I first showed you the Star of David note?'

'Because I didn't want to become involved. I'd always suspected it might have been given to her by Rahman or someone she'd met at the White Tiger Club. I had no desire to cross paths with Rahman again.'

Perhaps Persis should have understood then the fear that Tiwari had lived with, ever since Rahman had first threatened her, prior to his trial for Chatterjee's killing, forcing her to change her testimony, namely that she had seen him leaving Rita's house on the day her housemate had been murdered. If she had, she might have walked a more careful path, might have prevented the situation they now both found themselves in.

Tiwari spoke again. 'I've heard that gangsters sometimes bring their rivals out to the Sundarbans and leave them staked near the water's edge. The crocodiles leave no trace of the bodies.'

'It won't come to that.'

'I hope not,' came the reply. 'I've never liked crocodiles.'

61

At the academy, Persis had excelled in hand-to-hand combat.

As the only woman, there'd been a certain satisfaction to wiping the condescending smirks from the faces of her fellow trainees. It was amazing how a well-placed jab or a spinning kick to the ear could revive chivalrous instincts in her male colleagues. More than one, in the grip of a judo chokehold, had vouchsafed his suddenly arrived at opinion that it was high time for a female Prime Minister, or, even better, an entire cabinet of women.

She'd barely slept.

Dawn had arrived and, with it, a sense that she was hurtling towards a precipice. Despite her bravado, she knew there was a very real chance she might come off second best in the coming encounter.

Her unease must have communicated itself to Seema. The girl had been silent for much of the morning, as if realising that further discussion was pointless.

From the room next door, there came only a deathly quiet. Persis imagined Lata Tiwari praying, eyes closed, lips moving feverishly.

She hoped someone up there was listening.

The sound of the latch took her by surprise.

It was too early for Mahima's lunch round.

She tensed, setting herself on the balls of her feet, and readied herself for action.

Her father's face passed briefly before her eyes. *What would he make of her now?* Standing here, in a pair of torn trousers, a dirty blouse stinking of sweat, hair dishevelled, ready to take on an armed man. If she failed, she might die in this room, her remains cast to the watery labyrinth of the Sundarbans.

Sam would never know what had happened to her; never know how it had been at the very end.

A clew of emotion lodged in her throat. Her eyes blurred.

Focus.

The door swung back. Her fingers folded into fists—

A young man walked through the door.

Astonishment set her back on her heels. She heard a gasp from Seema behind her.

It was the same man who'd approached her at the Alipore Zoological Gardens; the same man who'd beguiled Seema, before abducting her.

He must have sensed the danger, because he reached behind him and emerged with a revolver. Pointing it at Persis, he said, 'Whatever you're contemplating doing . . . don't.'

Behind him, the squat guard entered the room. He, too, held his gun in readiness.

And then, ducking into the space, came a third figure.

'Inspector,' said Saleem Ansari. He raised his hand to touch his forehead in mock salute. 'And you must be the young apprentice. Seema, I believe?'

Persis heard the girl stir. She resisted the urge to turn around.

'Ladies. Allow me to apologise.' He waved a hand at the two men brandishing weapons. 'But I learned a long time ago that a caged animal is a creature not to be taken lightly.'

'*You* had us abducted,' spat Persis. 'Why?'

'Is there any point asking a question to which you already know the answer?'

'Rita Chatterjee. Walter Rivers. You don't want the world to know the truth.'

He gave a pained look. 'The first thing you learn in politics is that truth is a matter of perspective.'

'Rahman killed them on your orders. Rita was threatening to go public with your affair, with the fact that she was pregnant with your child. Walter Rivers would have made you front-page news. Your career wouldn't have survived that, not in the climate of the time.'

A flutter passed across Ansari's features. He seemed flustered.

'And then, later, when Fareed Mazumdar decided he would tell the world what he knew, you threatened him. You sent him clippings of the case, hoping it would remind him of his own complicity in the verdict that had cleared Rahman of wrongdoing.'

Ansari sighed. 'Yes, I had the clippings sent to him. I'd hoped they would bring him to his senses. He called me, you see. A few weeks before his death. He told me that he was struggling with his conscience. He blamed himself for Rita's death. He'd introduced us, hoping that it would help him curry favour with me. He knew that I frequented the White Tiger Club. He knew that I had a weakness for beautiful singers. I admit, Rita dazzled me. And so yes, in return, I helped Fareed in his career. He was an ambitious and intelligent young man. A talented lawyer. I had use for him. But he should have remembered the old saying, Inspector: *be careful what you wish for*. After Rita and Walter died, I felt it was only fair that Fareed handle the case.'

'He had no idea that Rita would end up dead.'

'He made a conscious choice to set his own ambition above her safety. Whether he knew that she would try to blackmail me, I don't know. He claimed not. It was, ultimately, irrelevant.' He paused. 'When he left Calcutta, he did so with my blessing and a warning. Forget. Leave everything behind. The past is a country that it rarely pays us to revisit.'

'But he couldn't do that, could he? He thought of Rita as his sister. They'd grown up together in that orphanage. It ate away at him. My guess is that, after he called you to tell you he was thinking of coming clean, you knew it was only a matter of time before he'd crack. That's why you had him killed.'

'You're mistaken. I had no hand in Fareed's death.'

'You suspected that the warnings you'd sent him, in the form of those cuttings about Rita's case, would only delay the inevitable. I presume you also sent him the Star of David note? The *shatkona*?'

He blinked rapidly. A hand rose to caress his throat. She caught the flicker of light on silver. A chain around his neck. A thought snagged at the back of her min— 'Yes,' he said. 'I thought that, together with the clippings about the case, the sight of the *shatkona* might jolt him from his path. You see, it was *his* idea I buy the pendant for Rita. He'd told me that her Hindu faith was important to her, and that she'd wanted that same necklace for some time. I thought if I sent him the picture of the *shatkona* symbol, it would remind him of what had been lost already, what we had both lost. And what more might be lost. But I did not have Fareed killed.'

Her thoughts churned. The chain around Ansari's neck . . . She'd seen it before.

Without warning, she stepped forward, then pretended to stumble. As she fell, Ansari reached out, instinctively, bending at the waist as he did so. She looked up, saw the flash of silver inside his open-necked shirt, caught the dangling outline of the *shatkona* pendant.

At the last second, the politician stopped himself from intercepting her, and she fell to the floor.

A stillness descended on the room.

Slowly, she got to her feet, wiped her hands on her blouse.

A single thought tolled in her mind.

Ansari was wearing the pendant he'd given to Rita Chatterjee.
She was certain it was the same one.

Why was he wearing it? How had he got hold of it?

She mentally went back over the case files, the inventory of items found on Rita Chatterjee's body and in her home.

The pendant had not been on that list.

Had it been taken from the crime scene? Had *Rahman* taken it after he'd killed her? Had Ansari asked for it back? Why? As a reminder of the woman he'd had killed? Why would a Muslim walk around wearing such a pendant? Why take the risk of it being seen and misconstrued?

An idea began to form in her mind, a monstrous revelation that threatened to overturn all that she had so far surmised about the case.

Finally, she spoke. 'You say you didn't kill Fareed. By that, I take it to mean you tasked Rahman to handle the matter.'

He was shaking his head. 'Neither of us had anything to do with it. As far as I'm aware, it was the Englishman, James Whitby, who killed him. He appears to have beguiled you with his pleas of innocence.'

'I don't believe you.'

His face folded into a frown. 'You're not a native of Bengal, are you? We are a people who understand the principles of *shomaj sheba* – service to society. I have never sought high office for personal gain. Perhaps this is hard for you to comprehend.' He searched for the right words. 'I saw the horrors of the riots with my own eyes. I walked the streets, between bodies piled high. At that moment, I vowed that I would not leave India. I would not run away to Pakistan. I would stay and fight. Fight for the cause of oneness and brotherhood.'

'How? By murdering innocents?'

Her scorn clearly pained him. 'Don't you understand that it's because of those ideals that I couldn't let Rita live? She was threatening to derail everything I had achieved or hoped to achieve. I loved her without malice. She was a Hindu; I was a Muslim. Yet I treated her as an equal. All I asked of her in return was discretion. I had no idea that she would betray me.' He beat the air with his hands, anguished beyond words. 'I loved her, Inspector. And I believe she loved me. She asked me to marry her. But how could I?'

'She was carrying your child.' A flat assertion. But she saw it strike home, an arrow to the heart.

His shoulders slumped. 'She placed me in an impossible position. What would I have said to my wife? To my children? Even had I acquiesced to her demand, her faith would have come between us – the timing simply wasn't right, not back then. It's only in fairy tales that love conquers all.'

The thought jolted her. For a brief instant, Blackfinch floated before her eyes, grinning stupidly, looking as perennially out of place as a camel at a dog show. She wrenched herself back to the moment. 'And now what? More bodies to add to your tally? More dead just so you can protect your *ideals*?' She spat the word.

Sadness reshaped the contours of his face. He reached into his jacket and emerged with a notebook. *Her* notebook. They must have taken it from her when they'd abducted her. In the time since, it had slipped her thoughts.

From inside, he took out the photographs from the White Tiger Club.

His gaze lingered on the images.

And then he fished in the pocket of his jacket, emerged with a lighter, and set the bundle on fire. He watched the prints blacken and curl inwards, and then dropped them to the floor as the flames advanced hungrily towards his hand.

Finally, he met her gaze again. 'Believe me, Inspector. I did not want this. How I wish you had listened to Azizur and returned to Bombay!'

She frowned. '*You* ordered him to threaten me, didn't you?'

'It was not a threat. I was simply trying to save you from yourself.'

She looked at him through a blaze of red. 'Rahman's nothing but a common murderer. And so will you be if you allow this to happen.'

'I have no wish to see you die. I *could* keep you here, indefinitely.' There was a note of wistfulness in his voice.

A bitter laugh escaped her. 'You know as well as I do that you can't afford to leave us alive. What if we escaped? Perhaps you're trying to convince yourself that your hands won't have blood on them if Rahman makes the decision for you.'

He sighed. 'This house belonged to an Englishman. He was a contemporary and disciple of a man named Daniel Hamilton, a Scotsman who made a fortune with the P&O shipping line, then decided to buy ten thousand acres of the tide country so that he could build an Eden for the poor. Hamilton's efforts brought people here – but what he hadn't counted on was the land fighting back. Hamilton dreamed of a utopia, but what he created was a lesser hell.' His gaze rested momentarily on the barred window. 'There's nowhere to go. Escape is impossible.'

62

By the time the woman, Mahima, returned, a wind had arisen outside, and the first flecks of rain had begun to slant in through the barred window.

The confrontation with Ansari had left Persis in a state of agitation. Any hope that she'd had that they might yet leave this place alive had been dispelled. Despite the politician's prevarication, she'd sensed an unspoken finality behind his words.

She'd also seen a desolation behind his eyes, the haunted guilt of a fanatic.

She believed she now understood why. The key was the *shatkona* pendant . . .

She'd attempted to console Seema, telling her that Ansari's mention of an indefinite confinement gave them hope. But the girl was too bright for that. She'd withdrawn, retreating to sit on the bed, hollow-eyed, hugging her knees. Persis saw her now as she should have seen her all along. Seema was a child, and like any child, fear and the subliminal workings of uncertainty had undermined her resolve. It had been Persis's duty to protect her, and she had failed.

Mahima entered with the squat guard close behind her. His pistol was in his hands and there was a wariness about him that convinced Persis he'd come prepared for her to act.

Perhaps the man wasn't as stupid as she'd thought.

She chafed, watching him as he kept his distance, eyes not leaving her face.

Meanwhile, Mahima set out two clean plates, and ladled out their food. The woman said nothing, too embarrassed to meet their eyes.

When she'd finished, she turned back towards the door, then stopped, and said, 'A storm is coming. Don't be afraid.' Her mouth began to shape itself around further words, but then she simply turned and walked out.

The guard lingered a moment, then he too turned and left.

They heard the latch bar fall into its keep.

Outside, the sound of the wind had flattened to a steady roar, the noise of the rain rising and falling inside it like the breath of a giant.

Anger pulsed through her as she moved around the room.

How had she allowed this to happen? She recalled something her father had told her a long time ago. *There's only a hair's breadth between confidence and hubris, Persis. When you fall from one to the other, that's when fate punches you on the nose.*

A scream rose inside her, and suddenly she could hold it in no longer.

She yelled, a great smear of rage and frustration. She lashed out unthinkingly with her foot at the plates of food Mahima had left for them on the floor.

The steel vessels clanged against the cement wall, the rice and fish mixture splattering in all directions.

She stood there, nostrils flared, breathing wildly, a trickle of sweat snaking down her back.

Finally, her senses returned.

She saw that Seema had sat bolt upright and was staring at something.

She followed the girl's gaze to the base of the wall.

She blinked, then lurched forward, bent down, and scooped up the object. Wiping the rice from it with shaking fingers, she held it up to the light.

It was a thin sliver of beaten metal, no more than five inches in length, tapered at one end.

A shim. Or the nearest thing to one.

She understood instantly why and how this object had reached her, and the incredible risk the woman, Mahima, had taken.

She walked to the door and dropped to her knees.

There was a gap between the door and the frame, no more than an eighth of an inch. Inserting the shim beneath where she guessed the latch was, she slid it upwards, and felt it bump against the bottom of the latch bar.

Gently, she lifted the bar out of its keep.

She pushed on the door; it swung back smoothly with a soft creak.

She turned to Seema. 'Let's go.'

63

It took them only moments to collect Lata Tiwari from her room.

The young woman was dazed but defiant, still dressed in the olive-green sari that Persis had last seen her in. Judging from its torn and dishevelled state, she'd put up quite a fight when they'd taken her.

Tiwari had enough sense not to waste time with questions.

She followed them as they barrelled down the hallway, endeavouring to make as little noise as possible.

The corridor ended at a heavy-set wooden door.

Grasping the handle, Persis took a deep breath, then swung it back and charged through . . . into a spacious, wood-floored room, incongruously furnished with an eight-seater dining table, a rattan sofa, and a portrait on one wall of a white man sporting a handlebar moustache, knee breeches and a buttoned-down frock coat. A candelabra chandelier hung above the table, the stumps of half-melted candles still visible in their holders.

She stood a moment, surveying the strangely domestic scene, and then pushed onwards.

The room let on to another, smaller space, and then they were into an anteroom, a wide-set door before them.

The door opened on to a shaded veranda.

They were outside.

Directly before them a path of mossy flagstones led down to a wooden jetty. A brace of rowing boats bobbed on the sluggishly flowing river, tethered against the current to mooring posts on the jetty.

She looked around for signs of the guard, her heart galloping. But they were alone.

As soon as they stepped off the veranda, the wind caught them, tugging at their clothes and flinging a barrage of rain at them.

She heard Seema gasp behind her; the sound of her stumbling to the ground.

She turned, blinked the rain from her eyes, and half helped, half dragged the girl to her feet.

They hurried down the path.

Behind them, the house loomed large against a gathering darkness. To either side, the forest was a wall of green, a monochrome vista of whispering mangroves. There was something indescribably louche, almost antediluvian about the forest.

They reached the boats, unslung the mooring rope on the nearest vessel, and clambered aboard. The boat rocked gently in the wind-whipped water. A coil of bait rope lay in one corner, almost submerged beneath a few inches of warm rainwater.

Persis fell on to the wooden oar seat, grasped the oars – lashed to their tholes with fraying lengths of rope – and leaned into the effort with a grunt.

The boat slid out into the river.

Minutes later, the house had vanished into the grey mist.

64

Blackfinch was finding it hard to focus.

Each time he tried to return to a semblance of the work that had brought him to Calcutta, his thoughts plunged into blackness. Finally, he'd abandoned the effort, and had instead chosen to spend the day with Dinaz, tagging along as she'd made the rounds of the offices of various senior policemen and politicos, savaging one after another, until word began to spread, and they began to discover that the man they'd come to accost had either moved out of the state in the past few minutes or inexplicably succumbed to a mysterious illness.

He knew that Dinaz's aggression stemmed from the same cocktail of fear and worry that powered his own anxieties. If there had been any doubt before, there was none left in his mind now.

Persis was in trouble.

The thought churned his stomach. Memories of the time they'd spent together, the unhappy trajectory of their relationship – if that was what you could call it – pressed down on him. He'd always believed himself to have an assured grasp of the world, and his own place within it. But now he felt untethered, floating freely in the unsettled sea of his own emotions.

He'd suggested to Dinaz that they might want to get in touch with Sam, to inform him of the situation. But the truth was that neither of them knew precisely where Persis's father might be found. All they knew was that he was on honeymoon, and making life miserable for all those unfortunate enough to encounter him on his travels.

What would they say to him even if they *could* find him?

Where the hell was she?

65

The sky had closed in.

Sails of rain broke over them in continuous sheets. The wind continued to rise, howling around them, buffeting the boat as they churned along the narrow waterway.

Seema was a dark silhouette perched at the boat's tapered prow, peering into the murk.

At the stern, Tiwari looked behind them. But the rain made it impossible to see further than a dozen metres.

'Can you see anywhere to come ashore?' Persis shouted. The wind snatched the words from her lips.

Her clothes were plastered to her skin; water ran in rivulets down her face. Her feet were ankle-deep in briny water; it sloshed against the gunwales each time the boat was buffeted by the storm. *How much longer could they stay afloat?*

Her first and only thought had been escape; now, she began to understand the true nature of their predicament. Without help, they would be lost in the swampy embrace of the Sundarbans. *They had to find Mahima's village.* She was certain that the woman lived nearby – the food she'd brought with her had always been warm. But in which direction did that village lie? Was it on the same island as their makeshift prison or a nearby one?

Her shoulders ached, lightning bolts of pain lancing down into her forearms with each stroke.

Focus.

She heard a shout behind her, and then something fell hard against her back, toppling her forward in her seat. Her hands sank beneath the water, scrabbling for purchase against the slippery wood. She caught herself, then twisted around, and found Lata Tiwari in her lap, clutching at her stomach, a bloom of blood visible between her fingers.

She looked up.

Bearing down on them was a second rowboat, their jailor balanced between the oars. He'd allowed the boat to temporarily coast in the slow-moving current so that he could stand and aim his pistol.

She saw him raise his arm again, his squat form shimmering in the mist of rain.

A sudden squall rocked the boat.

For an instant, he remained poised there, in the centre of the boat, like a dancer on the tip of executing a particularly difficult pirouette . . . and then his balance deserted him and he tumbled sideways into the boiling water.

He vanished beneath the whitecaps.

Moments later, his head reappeared, breaking the surface like a porpoise, water sluicing from his dark, leathery features. His hands scrabbled at the side of the boat . . . and then he had it. He twisted his neck to look at her.

A look of triumph. *I'm still here. And now I have you.*

A pair of massive jaws shot out of the water.

Persis had a fleeting vision of a dark snout, flared nostrils, a twisting and lunging motion; hard yellow teeth locked around the thug's head, and with a powerful wrench, he was pulled beneath the water.

The attack couldn't have lasted more than a few seconds. There was nothing left behind to suggest that man or beast had ever existed.

She looked down at Tiwari.

The woman's face was slick with rain. Her eyes had closed, and it was impossible to know if she was still breathing.

Persis looked desperately around her.

The channel had narrowed; they seemed to be sliding down a gullet thick with mangroves on either side. She shielded her eyes against the near horizontal rain—

There.

A narrow tongue of mud between the water and the encroaching vegetation.

She set Tiwari gently to one side, resumed her position on the oar seat, and began to row towards shore.

Seema turned from the prow. Her eyes widened as she saw first Tiwari's prone form, and then the second boat rolling rudderless in the current behind them.

Persis had no time to explain.

She locked her jaw against the ripples of agony in her shoulders, and rowed for all she was worth.

The current fought her, but soon they were only metres from the shore.

She let go the oars, and leaped out of the boat and into the shallows. She immediately lost her footing, and the muddy brown water rushed up to meet her. For a steep second, she was cocooned in a briny murk. Her hands sank into mud; her feet scrabbled for purchase. Silt invaded her nose, her throat. Panic clutched at her; her limbs thrashed, windmilling in the turgid water.

And then she found her equilibrium, thrusting up from her haunches, corkscrewing in the current to burst through the surface, water streaming from her mouth and shoulders.

She blinked and her senses returned.

She looked around, squinting through the curtain of rain.

Carried forward by its own momentum, the boat had ploughed up on to the mud spit.

Seema had already begun pulling Lata Tiwari out of the vessel.

Persis joined her and, between them, they manhandled the woman on to the mud.

Tiwari's face was bleached grey by the ashen light, the land all around bathed in silver.

She slipped her hand into the dying woman's, watched her as the last glimmer of life ebbed away.

She heard Seema shouting from a long way away.

She looked up to see the girl pointing behind her.

Twisting her head around, she saw the dark, flat shape skimming along the mudbank towards her.

Time seemed to slow. Her limbs had frozen; she saw the beast moving in a series of flashes, each one bringing it closer.

And then it was upon her.

A shriek rose from the centre of her being.

The oar hammered into the croc's head just as it lunged at her, the impact turning its gaping jaws away to graze against her shivering body. A second blow, just above the right eye, sent the beast shimmying into the water.

A flick of its tail and it plunged out of sight.

She squatted there, adrenalin coursing through her, until she felt Seema tugging at her arm, her other hand still clutching the oar.

She stared at the girl with something akin to awe, then allowed Seema to pull her to her feet.

Persis took a last look at the boat. The bait rope floated free in the rainwater. Acting on instinct, she bent down to scoop up the rope, and slung it over her shoulder.

Minutes later, they were deep into the tangled thicket of the mangroves.

66

Bombay, 1950 – James Whitby

My father took me to a hanging once. I was six years old at the time. He told me it was for my own improvement.

The hanging took place inside Alipore Jail in Calcutta – it was where they kept political prisoners during the Raj. I don't know why my father was given permission to attend – he had no connection to the convict, no reason to be there – but he was a powerful man, and the less powerful men who ran the judicial system in Bengal went out of their way to accommodate him.

My mother was out of the city and so I was left with no choice but to accompany him.

I'm not sure what I had expected.

An ogre, perhaps, a big, sullen, rough-hewn Indian of the type you saw caricatured in the English magazines my parents received from London. The kind that illuminated the pages of *Punch* or *Vanity Fair* above captions denigrating the independence movement.

Instead, what I saw was a small, timid-looking man, bespectacled, with beads of sweat sparkling in his thinning widow's peak. He was dressed in a simple white kameez and drawstring trousers. Holy threads hung around his neck and at his wrist, and a caste mark was prominent on his forehead.

My father remarked to a man sat beside us that Mitra – for such was the condemned man's name – was what they called a 'gentleman revolutionary'. My father's friend, a white man the colour of a boiled crustacean, with whiskers like twin horse's tails either side of a very red mouth, chuckled.

Mitra, as I would discover many years later, was a middle-class dilettante from a well-to-do Calcutta family, a poet whose poetry was so bad it had been known to induce nausea, a man of impeccable manners who had been bitten by the revolutionary bug, gulled into believing that, for men of his class, it was all high games and adventure, romantic grist to the mill of his literary ambitions.

He had become embroiled in a conspiracy case, arrested shortly thereafter, and hurtled through a special tribunal ordered by the viceroy – a trial at which Mitra himself was not present. The kangaroo court had been presided over by three prominent white judges – Mitra had been summarily sentenced to death by hanging.

On that day, I knew none of this, of course.

All I saw was an uninspiring man, sweating profusely in the furnace-like heat of the prison compound, staring out at us with the look of a stunned porpoise.

The Alipore warden gravely asked Mitra if he had any last words.

The prisoner seemed bemused; his eyes had taken on a dull glow. He looked owlishly out at the crowd – almost entirely composed of po-faced white men – perhaps searching for some inkling of how this had all come to pass.

When he spoke, it was in a voice withered by terror.

Why does a man have to die for expressing a desire to be free?

The words fell from his lips as if being pushed from a cliff. And yet they echoed loudly in that dusty prison courtyard, bouncing from the walls, gathering power, until they boomed and reverberated like the beat of the surf on a rocky shore.

Although I wouldn't have been able to name the feeling then, I felt shame, shame that this man was being made an example of. I was too young to fully understand what was taking place, but later I would realise that to the men gathered in that prison, Mitra's hanging was the ultimate enactment of British justice. Mitra was a symbol of a national cancer that had to be purged, and in doing so they were merely fulfilling their God-given duty. We had lived so long with the idea of the white man being 'exalted among the heathen', with the idea of enlightened despotism, that we had become indifferent to our own cruelties and the moral vacuum left in their wake.

Why does a man have to die for expressing a desire to be free?

The question has haunted me all these years and I've yet to find a satisfactory answer.

Now, as I sit here awaiting my own date with the gallows, I find myself thinking of Mitra. Did he dream, as I do, of a last-minute reprieve? Did he believe that he might awaken from a nightmare to discover that his ordeal had been nothing more than a cosmic jest?

Perhaps. But it was to no avail. His life ended not in a crescendo, but in a whimper.

That's what I remember most.

The absolute silence as his frail body swung from the gibbet beneath the punishing Calcutta sun.

67

A womblike darkness enfolded them.

Deep inside the mangrove forest, their sight lines were reduced to a matter of yards.

The sundari trees, with their twisted, stilt-like trunks and tangled prop roots, crowded thickly on all sides; the leathery-leaved canopy filtered what little light fell from the darkening sky above. The earth underfoot was damp, coated in a blanket of seedlings and root protrusions that tripped them up and grabbed at their ankles.

Persis's limbs had begun to quiver. She was shivering hard, her clothes matted to her body with the salty river water.

Her legs swung below her, seemingly of their own accord. She knew that it was important to keep moving. They were alive; they were free: that was all that mattered.

But, as time passed, she began to realise her error.

They would never find Mahima's village simply by stumbling around in the dark.

They should have climbed back into the boat and taken their chances on the water, despite the storm, and despite the very real possibility of the boat sinking beneath them.

'We have to go back.'

Seema halted beside her. Her mouth opened, but before she could give voice to her thoughts, a shape shot out of the murk, jagging her words into a yelp of fright.

It was a wild boar, zigzagging crazily, battering past them with a high-pitched squeal, before vanishing into the darkness.

Persis's heart was pounding. She'd instinctively fallen into a crouch. Now, as she sat back on her haunches, she noticed something at her feet. An impression in the clay earth, as clean as a stencil engraving.

A giant paw print.

A shiver danced through her. Dinaz's voice poured into her ears. The dangers of the Sundarbans: scorpions, arboreal snakes, giant Asian honeybees, crocodiles, and, above all, tigers. An animal that could break a man's neck with a single swipe of its paw. The king of the forest, a silent, deadly hunter who, it was said, killed men not just for food, but out of spite. Because they had invaded his land, had broken the ancient pact whereby men stayed away from the *bhatir desh* – the tide country – and the tigers left them alone.

'We need to get back to the shore,' she said, shouting to make herself heard above the ever-rising wind. 'There might be a passing fishing boat, or a forest patrol.' She had the sudden image of Dinaz, in her Forest Division uniform, standing at the prow of a motorboat, peering into the gloom, spotting them on the mangrove shore, a great smile of relief blooming over her broad features.

A roar from somewhere deep in the forest shattered the fantasy. She surged to her feet. 'Let's move!'

Twenty minutes later, it became obvious that they were lost.

The storm had continued to rise, whipping the trees into a frenzy, creating a steady, powerful droning, so loud it drove coherent thought from their heads.

She thought of another danger Dinaz had told her about, a phenomenon Persis had believed – from the vantage of distance – to be fanciful.

A cyclone.

The tide country of the Sundarbans was intermittently wracked by these destructive storms, surging up from the Bay of Bengal, so powerful that they could pick up boats and hurl them kilometres inland.

Terror galvanised her.

She ignored the mechanical ache in her muscles, and practically shoved her exhausted ward along.

The storm was gradually giving full vent to its fury. They were carpet-bombed by a continuous stream of projectiles – a flying soup of leaves, seedlings, decayed bits of wood.

And then, out of the corner of her eye, she saw something: a flash of black and gold.

Fear bloomed inside her and she stood stock-still, peering into the tempestuous gloom.

But there was nothing.

An image came to her, of her father, reading to her from a book of poetry as a child: *'Tyger tyger, burning bright. In the forests of the night.'*

They staggered into a grassy clearing.

She realised that Seema was pointing at something. Persis followed the direction of her arm and saw, lodged in the upper branches of a tree, a small wooden box, a shrine, inside which was an idol of a female deity sitting astride a tiger.

Bon Bibi. The lady of the forest. Goddess of the Sundarbans.

Without conscious thought, she found herself praying to the goddess, guardian spirit of the tidal land, venerated by Hindus, Muslims, and anyone else foolish enough to set foot in her domain.

And in that instant, she knew that here is where they would have to make their stand.

It was pointless to continue in the teeth of the tempest. They would not survive.

As the thought came to her, she began to turn, and saw Seema go down, felled by a projectile that struck her at high velocity on the temple.

Persis bellowed, and fell to her knees, scrabbling to turn the girl over.

Blood seeped from Seema's forehead. Her glasses had cracked. She attempted to revive her, but it was no use.

Focus.

She stuck her hands under the girl's armpits, then, leaning into the wind, dragged her to the tree housing the shrine. Setting her among the exposed roots with her back to the trunk, she slipped the bait rope from her shoulder, entwined it around the tree, then sat down next to Seema, and tied off the rope around both their midriffs.

She hugged Seema closely to herself, setting the girl's face into the crook of her own neck. Tears burned her eyes. She twisted her torso to face the tree's silvery trunk, shielding the girl with her own body.

The storm's roar had become deafening.

Minutes later, something hit the back of her head and the world went silent.

68

'I advised her to return to Bombay.'

Blackfinch thought the man looked genuinely sorrowful.

Sitting in the Lal Bazar police HQ office of Diwan Kasturi, he was conscious of the fact that he was very much out of his element.

His dealings with senior Indian policemen over the past year had largely involved attempts to explain to them either the merits of modern forensic science or the need to approve expenditure for them.

To be called in to speak about the fate of someone he cared deeply about was a new experience.

Dinaz had no such qualms. 'Why don't you just tell us what you've discovered?'

Blackfinch glanced at the woman, perched on the edge of the seat beside him.

He'd thought it only fair to invite her along when the call had come through from Kasturi.

The older man seemed unperturbed by Dinaz's belligerent manner. 'We have a possible sighting,' he said. 'Two days ago, late in the evening just outside the Alipore Zoological Gardens. An eyewitness claims that a woman matching Persis's description was seen being manhandled into a car.'

A low groan escaped Dinaz. Blackfinch felt a blast of terror at the back of his skull.

'Do you have any details about the car?' he asked.

'I'm afraid not. It was white. That's all our witness can recall.'

'And her assailant?'

'Nothing useful. I think our witness believed the woman may have been the worse for drink.' He coughed. 'He – uh – believed she might have been a lady of the night, picked up by a customer. It was only later that he began to have second thoughts and reported the incident.'

'A lady of the night,' breathed Dinaz.

Blackfinch tried to imagine what Persis would have said at being described in such a way. He'd have advised the witness to move out of the state; better yet, the country. And to leave no forwarding address.

The macabre humour failed to lift his spirits.

'So what do we do next?'

Kasturi made a steeple with his fat-fingered hands. 'I'm afraid there's little we *can* do. We've searched Rahman's known bases of operation. She's not being held in any of them. His men deny any knowledge of the matter.'

'And Rahman?'

'Still not traceable.' Kasturi's eyes were full of sympathy. 'We shall keep searching. In the meantime, all we can do is pray.'

69

She awoke into an eerie silence, the ghost of a gunshot ringing in her ears.

Her eyes flickered open. A moment of disorientation, an insensate calm, and then she snapped back.

They were still strapped to the trunk of the mangrove, Seema out cold beside her.

The storm had vanished; a sulphurous light flowed down from the canopy, denuded in places by the tempest's fury. She hoped – *prayed* – that the storm had spent itself. Hot on the heels of this thought came another: she recalled Dinaz speaking of the 'eye of the storm' and wondered if they'd entered that strange cone of silence, stretching upwards to the heavens.

Untying herself from the trunk, she subjected Seema to a cursory examination.

Aside from the swelling bruise at her temple, the girl seemed fine.

She stood up. Pain bloomed around her back and shoulders; her battered arms were so stiff it was as if they were encased in sleeves of wood. Her body felt as if it had been used as a piñata by a gang of lathi-wielding thugs. Her face had been lacerated by projectiles and she could taste blood in her mouth.

She looked up, into the tangled branches of the tree, and saw that Bon Bibi had vanishe—

A gunshot rang out, impossibly loud in the hush.

She dropped to her haunches, her heart leaping into her gullet.

The earlier shot that had brought her out of her slumber hadn't been a dream.

Someone was out here.

Someone armed with a rifle.

For an instant, she simply crouched there, blood beating at her temples. Conscious thought had been replaced by instinct. She couldn't allow any harm to come to Seema. Everything else was secondary, including her own life.

Focus.

She looked around, then bent down and picked up a stout length of wood.

Standing, she began to move as silently as she was able, headed towards the sound of the gunshot.

Moments later, she found herself against the trunk of a tree, peering around it at a figure moving through the shadows some thirty metres distant.

Rahman.

The big man was clad in a brown safari suit, a rifle in his hands, a bandolier slung around his shoulder and chest.

Was he alone? Who had he been firing at?

Terror powered her thoughts.

She knew she couldn't allow him to reach Seema. Yet she couldn't attack him head-on. He'd cut her down before she could get near him.

She breathed deeply, fought for a centre of calm.

Kneeling down, she picked up a small rock, then slowly scrabbled up the gnarled trunk of the mangrove. Settling herself in the lower branches, she hesitated, then threw the rock directly downwards.

It made a hard sound as it hit the mangrove's exposed roots.

From behind a cover of leaves, she saw Rahman whip around, raising the rifle to his shoulder.

He peered into the gloom, then began to move towards her.

Her heart pounded in her chest. Sweat rolled down her forehead and into her eyes. She found herself suppressing the urge to laugh at the ridiculousness of her predicament. If she did, she thought she might shake the very stars from their orbits.

Rahman was now directly beneath her, searching for the source of the sound.

She blanked out rational thought and leaped, crashing down on to him, flattening him face first into the dirt, the rifle flung from his grasp.

She scrabbled atop him, hefted the length of wood, and struck him across the shoulders, then the back of his head.

He twisted beneath her like a giant reptile. His strength was extraordinary. Lifting his body, he swatted her aside, grabbed the rifle, then surged to his feet.

She scrabbled backwards until her back fetched up against the trunk of the mangrove.

Staring down the rifle's barrel, she braced herself for the shot.

But Rahman did not fire.

Instead, he lowered the weapon fractionally, and said, 'Why didn't you just leave?'

His expression was inscrutable.

'Because it was my duty. Because a life is at stake.'

His face was so still, he seemed carved from wood. In his eyes, she saw not anger or hate, but sadness.

Words stumbled out of her. The theory that had crystallised into place after she'd seen the *shatkona* pendant around Saleem Ansari's neck.

'You didn't kill Rita Chatterjee. Ansari did. You just cleaned up his mess.'

His face twitched. A complicated shadow moved across his features. He seemed to arrive at a conclusion: *what harm could the truth do now?*

'He called me from her home that day. The day of the riots. He'd spoken at the Maidan that morning, to a large crowd, and had then vanished. None of us knew where he'd gone. It turned out he'd gone to see Rita.

'He'd already asked me to take care of Walter Rivers, the day before. I wasn't sure about killing an American – they don't take kindly to that sort of thing. But Ansari was adamant. He assured me he'd take care of any investigation – even back then he had enough clout with the police commissioner for me to believe him.

'I killed Rivers at the White Tiger Club. He was there on the evening of August 15th. He stepped out back for a smoke; I followed him and stabbed him. He died quickly.

'I drove his body to one of my godowns, ready to be taken to the Sundarbans the next day where the crocodiles would get rid of any evidence.

'But then, the next afternoon, just as I was about to have him taken away, Ansari called, telling me that *he'd* killed Rita.'

'*Why* did he kill her? Why then?'

'He didn't intend to.'

'Is that what he told you?'

'Yes. I believe him. He loved her. Or perhaps it's more accurate to say that he was *infatuated* by her. She became his weakness. But when she threatened to go public with the fact that she was about to have his child – unless he agreed to marry her – that she'd had Rivers photograph them together . . . *that's* when he decided Rivers had to be killed. But he had no desire to kill *her* . . . That's why he went to her that day. She'd telephoned him. Told him she was going to make a statement to the press. He tried to reason with her. She wouldn't listen. He found his hands around her throat. By the time he returned to himself, she was dead.'

The silence beat around her like the wings of a bat.

'When he telephoned me, I told him to stay put, to wait for me.

'Siddiqi and I arrived with Walter Rivers's body. I sent Ansari away, and then we staged the scene. I knew riots had begun in the city and I knew we could create a story about Rita and Walter. I'd seen them at the White Tiger Club. I knew that they were friendly and had been seen to be so. Ansari agreed to go along with the plan, even though it hurt him to think of Rita smeared in that way. But he knew he had no choice. It was the only plan that made sense. For both Walter and Rita to go missing without explanation might have led to a greater investigation. In a way, the riots proved a blessing. Frankly, if Siddiqi and I hadn't been seen leaving the home, it would have ended there.'

'But you *were* seen. By Lata Tiwari.'

'She wasn't supposed to be there. Rita had told Ansari that her housemate was out of the city and not due back for several days. That's why he agreed to meet her at her home. Tiwari returned early.'

'And now she's dead too.'

'She's dead because of *you*.' The words were said with a finality that brooked no dispute. The weight of truth fell on her, crushing what remained of her resistance.

Persis felt tears leak from her eyes. Tears of anger and self-recrimination. How many would perish because of her precious sense of mission? 'Did Fareed Mazumdar know the truth?' she blurted. 'Did he find out? Was that why you and Ansari had him killed? Because he was going to tell the world that Ansari was a murderer?'

Rahman grimaced. 'He didn't *know* the truth. Not at first. But I believe he guessed it. He defended me in court because Ansari threatened to ruin him if he didn't. And because he was ambitious. In the end, it turned out that he couldn't reconcile his ambition with his conscience ... But I didn't kill him. As far as I am aware, the white man, the Englishman, did.'

Through a blur, she saw him raise his rifle.

Her final thoughts were not of herself, or of James Whitby, but of Seema. It wasn't fair that the girl's life would be cut short because of *her* foolhardiness.

She heard her father's ghostly cackle in her ear. *Since when was life ever fair, daughter of mine?*

Rahman's lips seemed to move. She fancied he'd said *I'm sorry*, but that might have been her imagination.

She closed her eyes.

70

Blackfinch was back in his hotel room.

A thunderous knocking raised him from his helpless stupor, and the nearly empty bottle of whisky set before him.

He stumbled to the door, swung it back . . . to find Dinaz standing there, a wild light in her eyes.

'We've received a message at the Forest Division. It could be nothing.'

'Tell me.'

'The message was anonymous. It simply said that three women were being held captive on an island in the Sundarbans.'

'Three?'

'No names were given. I don't know who the third woman might be.'

'Is the tip-off credible?'

'I have no idea.'

He felt sobriety fall on him like a guillotine.

'How long would it take to get out there?'

'A few hours.' She hesitated. 'There's a problem. There's a storm. A big one. None of my colleagues will venture into the Sundarbans until it clears.'

'Can you pilot a boat on your own?'

'Yes. I'm going out there now. I can't ask you to come with me. Only a fool would go.'

His fingers curled around the glass in his hand, so tightly he thought it might shatter. 'Let me get my jacket.'

71

The roar struck her as a solid wall of sound, echoing pneumatically through her inner cavities, and stunning her into senselessness.

What she retained afterwards was the incredible speed and power of the animal, the litheness of its leap, the way Rahman fell beneath its enormous bulk – the beast was larger than anything she had ever imagined – his rifle blasting ineffectually into the canopy.

The tiger clamped its jaws around the fallen man's shoulders and dragged him backwards out of the clearing, the muscles of its mud-splattered flanks rippling, the earth rustling as it moved.

And then it was gone. All that remained was an after-image on her retina.

She'd heard Dinaz say that the tigers of the Sundarbans were called ghosts of the forest. They were so rarely seen, that to do so often meant you were caught directly in the path of their murderous intent.

Few saw a tiger up close and lived.

The wind had begun to howl. The storm was returning.

They were almost out of the eye.

She staggered to her feet, picked up the rifle, realised that it had been rendered useless by the tiger's attack, then stumbled back towards Seema.

She fell to her knees beside the girl and slapped her across the face, once, twice, thrice.

Finally, she stirred, her eyes fluttering beneath her eyelids. Her mouth moved, and then a cry escaped her, and she leaped out of the darkness.

Persis hugged the girl to her chest, then pushed her back against the trunk of the tree.

They'd lived through the storm once. Now they would have to do so again – this time without Bon Bibi standing watch over them.

She was overpowered by the idea of survival. Not for herself, but for Seema, and Lata Tiwari, and James Whitby, and Fareed Mazumdar. The dead – and the soon to be dead. They were her warrant, her charge, and she could not, *would not*, betray their faith.

It was then that she saw the beast.

The tiger was sitting on its haunches, wreathed in the shadows just at the limits of vision. Its tawny eyes glowed in the dark. As the shadows moved, it seemed that those glowing eyes had become detached from the creature and floated freely in the murk.

She heard Seema's breath catch in her throat. Terror seeped from the girl and into her.

She leaned down, picked up a length of wood, then pushed the girl behind herself.

'We mean you no harm,' she heard herself whisper. 'You are the lord of this forest and we pass through this land by your grace. But if you come for us, you'd better brace yourself for the fight of your life.'

A sound rose above the wind, a clashing of metal upon metal, and the shouts of many voices.

Her head whipped around.

A dozen points of light, materialising out of the inky darkness to her right, gradually crystallised into hurricane lamps and flaming torches held by a line of lungi-clad men, led by a woman.

Some of the men banged on pots and pans; others wielded machetes and sharpened staves; all were bellowing at the top of their lungs.

The woman who led them was Mahima.

Persis looked back and saw that the tiger had vanished. She felt her knees buckle. She had to resist the urge to swoon into the woman's arms as she arrived at her shoulder.

'You have survived the *bāgha*. The tiger. Both the tiger of the forest and the human one. Bon Bibi has smiled on you.'

Yes, thought Persis. They had survived.

But she would see the tiger's eyes glowing in the darkness of her dreams for the rest of her life.

The village was a collection of mud, thatch and bamboo dwellings, from the very centre of which rose a single brick structure, built like a blockhouse on brick stilts, with external steps leading upwards.

Evidence of the havoc already wrought by the storm was every-where. Roofs denuded of thatch; the smashed timbers of fishing boats; breached tide embankments; nets and crab lines tangled in the surrounding mangroves; pottery shards and metal utensils scattered and embedded in the clay earth like the discarded dregs of an archaeological dig.

Mahima led them to the brick building.

Persis felt Seema's hand slip into her own as they climbed the steps.

They entered a large room, lit by hurricane lamps and packed with bodies: women and children, with a smattering of elderly men. Their glistening faces held fear, and a sense of awe.

How many had lived through a storm like this before?

'What about the men?' she found herself asking.

Mahima did not answer. The answer was obvious. There was not enough room for the entire village in the storm bunker.

She led them to a corner and bade them hunker down beside an elderly woman who looked at them as if they were apparitions newly emerged from the forest.

In a way, they were.

'We have always been out of sight of the city dwellers,' said Mahima. 'Out of sight, out of mind. People talk of the Bengal famine, but we live in a state of constant famine. Everything here is our enemy. The soil, the tides, the creatures of the forest. When the storm comes, the tide devours everything, destroying the little we have built.' She stopped. 'My husband was lost to such a storm. I work for men like Rahman and Ansari so that I can feed my son. They began coming here when the government began pouring money into the islands – for schools, hospitals, wells, permanent estates. They collude with the managers of those estates, and those controlling the flow of funds locally. Little reaches those who the funds are meant to help. Anyone who protests is beaten or vanishes.'

'Why did you help us?'

Mahima looked away, her eyes finding a boy huddled beside the old woman. 'I helped you so that I could look my son in the eyes again.'

72

Hours later, when the storm had abated and Persis had walked down to the water's edge, to see the patrol boat nosing its way downriver, and then recognised Dinaz on the launch's prow, the shock had almost sent her reeling back to the storm refuge.

The vision of her friend in her bottle-green uniform, smiling broadly at her, was so uncannily like the one she'd dreamed of while lost in the forest that it was akin to déjà vu.

Of course, in her dream, there'd been no sign of a grinning Blackfinch manning the boat's wheelhouse.

The village had survived the storm. Barely.

When the temporary respite occasioned by the storm's eye had finally ended, the settlement had cowered beneath a cascade of water, thunder and lightning raging overhead like duelling gods, the tide surging inland until it lapped at the walls of the brick redoubt at the centre of the village.

Persis, unable to still her anxiety, had peered out from a port-hole and witnessed, first-hand, the storm's elemental fury. Even above the ear-splitting roar of the gale, she could hear the cracking of bamboo as many of the village's huts were obliterated, the wreckage joining the horizontal fusillade of debris borne aloft by the wind and a mixture of sea and rainwater.

She'd felt Seema's presence beside her. She turned and looked at the girl, wondering if she was reliving the storm's first onslaught and the miracle of their survival.

*　　*　　*

Afterwards, the bodies of two men had been discovered tangled in the battered mangroves; two others could not be found at all.

They'd left shortly afterwards, to make the slow journey back upriver to Calcutta.

Before leaving, she'd attempted to express her thanks to Mahima and the residents of the village. That was when she'd discovered that it was Mahima who'd sent a man back to the city to make the anonymous phone call that had led Dinaz and Blackfinch to them.

Words failed her. She thought of the incredible risk the woman had taken in helping them, the possible consequences of her actions. Would Ansari blame her? Would she face punishment?

Anger came unheralded, a great roar of rage, pulled from deep inside her.

She vowed to herself that Saleem Ansari would never be given the chance to harm this woman, would never again be given the opportunity to harm another living soul.

Depravity must have its consequences.

Upon reaching Calcutta, Dinaz had insisted on taking them to a hospital, overruling Persis's objections. If the cyclone had been an irresistible force, Dinaz proved to be an immovable object.

They'd both been examined by a moon-faced doctor that Dinaz had bullied into a gibbering state of terror. By the time the man had reassured them that no lasting damage had been done, Persis was champing at the bit to get away.

But it was too late into the night for anything meaningful to be achieved. They had no choice but to wait until the morning.

Sitting in a chair beside Seema's hospital bed, watching the girl breathe gently in her sleep, she returned her attention to Saleem Ansari.

That the politician was still able to move freely around the city seemed a perversity to her. She could not erase the image of Lata

Tiwari's lifeless body from her mind, stretched out on the mud spit back on the island.

Following the cyclone, they'd searched for the body – but it had vanished by the time they'd turned Dinaz's launch back to the riverine shore. Crocodiles or the tiger: it was anyone's guess who'd found the corpse first.

Blackfinch stayed with her, while Dinaz, exhausted by her efforts, was eventually persuaded to return home.

'We seem to spend a lot of time together in hospitals,' the Englishman remarked, as he settled into the seat beside her.

She sensed a mild criticism, but was too weary to argue. Tiwari's death was a heavy torus of guilt that hung around her neck. Persis knew that she could not rest while Ansari remained free. Everything else was secondary.

'I remember a tutor at the police academy,' he continued. 'He told us that justice was like a river; sometimes it simply takes its own course.'

She looked at him sharply. 'Are you suggesting I do nothing?'

'Not at all. Merely, that—' He hesitated, searching for the words. 'Most people live in a world of light and order. But that world is surrounded by darkness. For those of us who enter the dark in order to discharge our duty, we cannot expect to return unchanged.'

She continued to stare at him, but he seemed to have run out of words.

They sat in silence, and then, unexpectedly, she found his hand on hers. For a moment, she thought of shaking it away, but then decided to let it remain there.

73

The next morning, they found themselves at Calcutta police head-quarters at Lal Bazar, sitting before ACP Diwan Kasturi.

Having discussed the situation with Blackfinch – and having been apprised of the various lacklustre policemen he'd met with in his search for her – she'd convinced him that Kasturi was their best bet. She'd sensed some sympathy – to her original mission – in the veteran detective when first they'd met; she knew, instinctively, that without the support of a senior officer, her chances of successfully bringing Ansari to brook would be greatly undermined.

Dispassionately, she recounted her story.

When she'd finished, Kasturi sat back, took out a pipe, and began the complicated process of tamping tobacco into it, lighting it, and executing a series of exaggerated puffs.

She sensed that he was playing for time. She was about to urge him on when she felt Blackfinch's hand on her arm. Patience.

Finally, Kasturi spoke. 'Do you have any evidence against Ansari?'

Persis reached into a satchel and set down a sheaf of photographs.

From the hospital, she'd directed Blackfinch to the photographic studio that had developed Walter Rivers's negatives. Here, she was relieved to discover that no one had come looking for the rolls of film. She supposed neither Ansari or Rahman had felt the need to tie up that particular loose end yet, not with Persis trapped on the island.

Neither man had expected her to return to Calcutta alive.

Kasturi picked up the photographs tentatively, as if they might explode in his face.

When he'd scanned them, he set them down again, and said, 'This isn't enough. These prove nothing.'

She fought for self-control. 'Those photos prove that Ansari and Chatterjee knew each other. Besides that, you have the testimony of two people, myself and Seema Desai. Ansari came to the island, the island where we were being held captive. At *his* behest. He confessed to involvement in Rita Chatterjee's murder. Before his death, Azizur Rahman confirmed – to me – that Ansari was the one who actually killed Chatterjee.'

'Rahman, as you point out, is dead. We have only your word that he accused Ansari.'

Blackfinch cleared his throat. 'With all due respect, sir, I've never known Persis to lie. She's a police officer. If *her* word doesn't count, then what's the point of any of us?'

Kasturi continued to rattle the pipe between his teeth.

'At the very least, you have Ansari for involvement in a double kidnapping. I'd say that's a good start.'

Kasturi seemed to debate internally with himself, then said, 'Very well. Allow me to make a few calls. I'll have to inform the chief minister and the commissioner of police. It's not every day you arrest a deputy chief minister.'

Persis spoke up. 'I want to be the one to arrest him.'

He waved her request away with a flourish of his pipe. 'You have no jurisdiction in Calcutta.'

She'd anticipated the refusal. 'In that case, I'd like to accompany the arresting officer.' She saw that he was about to object. 'Please. It's important. I – It's my fault that Lata Tiwari is dead. I pursued this investigation. I led them to her.'

Kasturi set his pipe carefully down into a silver ashtray, then locked eyes with her. 'Humans are savage, unpredictable creatures,

Inspector. We are ruled by emotions as intemperate as the storm you barely survived. If you insist on holding yourself responsible for the actions of others, you will never be able to discharge the oath you have taken. Your allegiance is to your uniform, never forget that. God knows there are few enough who believe that any more.'

Above them, the ceiling fan creaked slowly around in ineffectual circles, like a geriatric peon.

'I want to be there when the cuffs are put on Ansari. I want – I *need* to look in his eyes.'

Kasturi sighed and picked up his pipe again. 'Tell me, how does your commanding officer in Bombay put up with your ... determination?'

'Whisky,' she said. 'Lots and lots of whisky.'

74

Six hours later, Persis – with Seema beside her – arrived at the Dum Dum airport to board a plane bound for Bombay.

This time the flight was provided courtesy of the West Bengal government. Her conscience had rebelled at the idea of accepting further help from Charles Whitby, despite the fact that his son's fate had begun to weigh heavily on her mind.

Time had almost run out.

James Whitby's execution was scheduled for the following day. Any delays in the flight and they would barely make it back to Bombay in time.

Then again, what good would it do him even if she were to be present for the final act?

She was under no illusions. Nothing that she'd discovered would secure Whitby's release. Appeals to reason had long since been exhausted by those better placed to make them.

Her failure clung to her like a shroud. Added to her complicity in the death of Lata Tiwari, she found her emotions scoured out. There was a hallucinatory quality to the journey the investigation had forced her to make. In some ways, it felt like a pilgrimage to the darkest corners of her own being.

She wasn't the same person who'd taken on the case in Bombay.

Perhaps she never would be again.

Hours earlier, following her meeting with ACP Diwan Kasturi, the arrest of Saleem Ansari had proceeded with a simplicity that had seemed out of step with recent events.

Accompanied by a retinue of officers, including an experienced senior man – an assistant deputy commissioner of police named Ganguly – they'd arrived at Ansari's office to find him immersed in a budget meeting. The incongruity of seeing this man – who, only days earlier, had ordered her kidnapping and murder – engaged in the mundane minutiae of political office momentarily stunned her, so that she could only stand to one side as Ganguly read out the charge sheet.

Perhaps she'd expected fireworks. But Ansari simply stared at them, as a man of whom something impossible had been asked might have done.

His eyes never left hers and she knew that he hadn't expected to see her alive again. The fact that she was here, now, to testify against him, had crumbled what remained of his resolve.

When he finally spoke, it was in a distant voice. 'Last month I met a man who'd survived the Direct Action Day riots. He told me that he'd gone out that day to buy a cake for his daughter's birthday. He encountered a mob. They told him a story, and before he knew what he was doing, he'd joined them. He killed three people that day. Two men and a woman. Later, he could scarcely believe it. He called it an out-of-body experience, as if his soul had momentarily gone away, and the blind machinery of his body had carried out the acts.' He stopped. 'He'd told no one. He'd gone back home that day, locked the doors, and celebrated his daughter's birthday. And then, three years later, he began to suffer from waking dreams. Not of those he'd killed, or even the act of killing them, but of finding himself alone in a desert, stumbling blindly towards a horizon that came no nearer no matter how long he placed one step after another. In the end, he simply walked into a police station and confessed his guilt.

'I attended his execution. He asked to speak with me before they hung him. I expected that he wished to apologise, but all he said was that he hoped his daughter would remember him as he'd lived, not how he'd died.'

In that instant, Persis was overcome by an image of him as a depraved infant, guilelessly complicit, yet yearning to be forgiven, to be told that the fault for his crimes lay elsewhere – at the feet of others, or the ungovernable laws of circumstance; perhaps even in the stars above.

She wondered how a man could compartmentalise his actions so perfectly in his own mind. The same man who'd beguiled the masses on his way to high office had, time and again, unleashed the monsters in his own nature.

Then again, he wouldn't be the first maniac to have found his way into power in this ancient land.

'Who killed Fareed Mazumdar?'

He seemed puzzled by the question. 'I don't know.'

Her last words to him: 'You have the chance to save James Whitby. It's the least you can do.'

He looked down at his hands, a wry smile playing over his lips. 'There's to be no atonement for me, Inspector. You won't believe me, but I never meant to kill Rita. I loved her. It's why I held on to the *shatkona*, why I wear it still. It's my last memory of her. When I strangled her, I could feel it beneath my hands.' He shuddered. 'Prince Saleem, Akbar's son, was willing to give up an empire to marry his Anarkali. But I could not do the same. I owed a debt of service to my people, you see. I promised to lead them into the new world. What would they have done without me?'

The roar of the aeroplane's engines pulled her out of her thoughts.

Beside her, Seema, her head still bandaged, was asleep, in part due to the medication churning through her system. Persis had tried to convince her to stay until she was in better shape, but the girl had no more desire to remain in Calcutta than Persis herself.

She knew that they would have to return to testify against Ansari, but that moment was a long way away. Ansari would be forced to rot in prison before his eventual court date – his political opponents would ensure that.

Such was the fate of those toppled from the dizzying heights of power.

Her thoughts floated free as the plane taxied to the start of the runway.

She marvelled at the chain of events that had led to Fareed Mazumdar's death, the intertwined nature of so many lives.

Almost three decades ago, Charles Whitby had ordered the murder of Fareed Mazumdar's father. That act had led to Fareed ending up in an orphanage, where he had met and befriended Rita Chatterjee. Years later, as an adult and an ambitious young lawyer, he had all but forced Rita to work for Azizur Rahman at the White Tiger Club, knowing that she would move into the orbit of a man who might further his own career: Saleem Ansari.

He could not have predicted the fate that lay in store for Rita, yet, in the fullness of time, he'd nonetheless held himself accountable. And, once his conscience finally moved him to the precipice, to the brink of a public confession, he'd been murdered, the killing pinned, by the cruel machinations of fate, on Charles Whitby's son.

There was both a cosmic irony to the situation, and a sense of infinite balance, of events coming full circle.

Persis suspected that, somewhere up there, Fareed Mazumdar might be taking a measure of satisfaction from James Whitby's impending death. Would it make up for his own father's murder at Charles Whitby's behest?

A question that would never be answered.

Her thoughts lingered on James Whitby and his predicament.

Both Saleem Ansari and Azizur Rahman had denied any hand in Fareed Mazumdar's killing. They'd had no reason to lie. She'd been entirely at their mercy.

But if not them, then who?

Her thoughts turned once more to the mysterious man James Whitby believed he had seen fleeing the scene ... Could he have been mistaken? He'd admitted that the lighting in the car park had been out. And he'd been drinking all afternoon.

For the first time, it began to seep into her that perhaps James Whitby's recollection of events could not wholly be trusted.

On the heels of this thought came another: *were Whitby's memories purposefully obscure?*

A chill swept through her.

What if the Englishman had lied to her? What if she'd allowed herself to be gulled by his pleas of innocence? That would mean that her entire pursuit of the case, including her visit to Calcutta, had been both in vain and entirely unnecessary.

If James Whitby had lied, then Lata Tiwari had died for nothing.

She knew this was unreasonable. Regardless of Whitby's guilt or innocence, her investigations in Calcutta had led to Rita Chatterjee and Walter Rivers's true killers receiving a measure of punishment.

But at what price?

She found herself agitated beyond measure. Her anxiety over the coming flight vanished, to be replaced by a churning of emotions that left her writhing helplessly in her seat.

She found herself back in the cell with James Whitby, listening to him as he spoke of his childhood, his father, his mother—

A discordant note clanged in the cacophony of her thoughts.

James Whitby's mother.

All of this had begun there. Her affair with Shabaz Mazumdar had been the catalyst for Charles Whitby ordering Mazumdar's murder and the subsequent orphaning of Mazumdar's son, Fareed, and the winding path that had led from there to Fareed's own murder, three decades later.

Her mind fastened on to a single memory.

She recalled her second meeting with James Whitby, something he'd said about his father's reaction to his mother's flight from their home ...

She stood up and stumbled to the front of the craft.

Crashing into the cockpit, she shouted, into the startled face of the pilot, 'Stop the plane!'

The man looked at her in mute astonishment, then nodded, and turned back to his controls.

She knew that the delay would cost her valuable hours, and might mean she could not make it back by the hour of James Whitby's execution.

She could only pray that that would not be the case.

75

The mansion was bathed in late afternoon sunlight. A fragrance of jacaranda blossom floated over the walls.

The ragtag retinue came to a halt before the gates.

A somnolent guard stared at them as if the inhabitants of a nearby graveyard had come alive and now stood before him, presumably intent on asking him to join them.

'Are you sure about this?'

Persis turned to Blackfinch. The man looked decidedly put upon.

Held in Calcutta by his own commitments, the last time he'd seen her had been at the airport. He'd imagined that he'd seen her safely off back to Bombay, his duty – as a friend and colleague – discharged.

When she'd turned up at his office, and all but ordered him to help her in a new quest, he'd at first thought he might be locked in a nightmare from which waking was proving particularly difficult.

They'd driven through the city to find Anabella Santos.

Persis had explained why. Blackfinch had decided to keep his own counsel. He knew, from past experience, that there was little point in trying to dissuade the policewoman when she was in this mood. It would be like trying to persuade a Cossack to relinquish his last bottle of vodka.

Having located Santos, and explained their mission, they'd then driven to the Calcutta home of Charles Whitby.

Knowing Persis's intent, Blackfinch had taken the precaution of speaking to ACP Diwan Kasturi.

Kasturi, though sceptical, had sent a brace of officers to assist them.

With the guard negotiated, they entered the empty mansion.

Walking through the shadowy corridors, led by a hesitant Anabella Santos, Persis found herself wondering at the life James Whitby had endured here, particularly after his mother had vanished.

They passed the German grandfather clock Charles Whitby had mentioned. It ticked in the silence like a woodcutter's axe in a forest.

Out in the gardens, she allowed Santos to lead them through the manicured grounds to a squat pomegranate tree at the very rear.

The woman held out an open palm, taking in the flowering shrub with its crown of red flowers.

'This is the one.' A question hovered in her eyes. Persis had explained to her only the bare outlines of her thoughts, but she suspected an inkling of her own suspicions had begun to filter into the woman.

Or, perhaps, those suspicions had been there all along, and now there was simply a sense of relief that someone else had had the courage to voice them.

Persis turned to the two officers accompanying them.

Pointing to the base of the plant, she said simply, 'Dig.'

76

Twelve hours later, she walked into the Arthur Road Jail in Bombay, to be once more led deep into its interior.

She'd arrived back in the city less than four hours earlier, with barely time to shower and fall into a fitful sleep, before rising, wolfing a hurried breakfast, and heading for the prison.

If she'd expected to find a haggard and terrified James Whitby, she was to be disappointed.

The cell door creaked back to release a cloud of sweet-smelling pomade.

Whitby was standing by the bookshelf, thumbing a small volume, resplendent in an immaculately tailored, grey chalk-striped three-piece suit. He'd had a shave and a haircut and there was a brightness in his eyes completely at odds with the situation.

He seemed like a man about to attend his nuptials rather than the gallows.

'I thought I might dress for the occasion,' he said, the ghost of a smile playing over his lips. She sensed a weight of feeling behind the words, a dam holding back his true emotions.

'You look . . . good,' she managed.

He tapped out a soft staccato on the book's spine. 'It would be too much to hope that you've found a way to get me out of here?'

She took a deep breath. 'No. But I have news.'

She saw the air go out of him and realised that, somewhere, down in the depths of his being, he'd retained a slight glimmer of hope – hope that she, or the system, or blind dumb luck might rescue him from his predicament.

He sat down on the bed, gingerly, as if it might collapse beneath his weight.

She saw that the volume in his hands was the Book of Psalms, a finger stuck between the pages. He opened the book, bowed his head, and read from it: 'Yea, though I walk through the valley of the shadow of death, I will fear no evil: for thou art with me; thy rod and thy staff they comfort me.' He looked up. 'I've heard those words many times but never stopped to wonder what they really meant. They sent a priest to see me this morning. He told me that those lines are an allusion to the eternal life promised by Jesus. Do you think there's such a thing? Eternal life beyond the grave?'

The machinery of her throat had rusted. 'I don't know.'

'The priest enquired whether there was anything he could do for me. I asked him if he would mind very much switching places.' He gave a sad smile. 'So, what is it that you've come here to tell me?'

She recounted for him her investigations in Calcutta. He listened without interruption, only raising an eyebrow when she described how she'd survived her kidnapping at the hands of Saleem Ansari and Azizur Rahman.

'That's how I'd like to go,' he said. 'Mauled by a tiger. In the belly of a croc. There's a little glamour in that, at least. Swinging on the end of a rope seems so-so . . .' Terror moved in his eyes like a monster of the deep. 'They say you soil yourself. At the end.'

Persis leaned forward. 'I discovered something in Calcutta. Your mother . . . She didn't abandon you.'

He blinked. 'I don't understand.'

'Your father told you that your mother left you. It's not true . . . Did you know that your mother and Shabaz Mazumdar were having an affair?'

His brow furrowed. 'I was seven years old.'

'*That's* why your father had Shabaz killed.' She paused. 'And that's why he killed *her*.'

His mouth formed a small O, but no sound emerged.

'He killed her, then buried her in the grounds of your Calcutta home. The tree that you told me he planted in her memory the day after she left? He planted it above her grave, so that no one would question the dug soil.'

'The pomegranate tree,' he whispered.

'Yes.'

In the silence, she could almost hear the beating of his heart. And then he bowed his head. It was a moment before she realised that he was weeping.

She wondered if perhaps he'd suspected all along but, like a man who refuses to face his worst fear, had shied away from the truth.

'Your mother found out that your father had been behind Shabaz's murder. Your ayah, Anabella Santos, told her that she'd overheard your father order the killing. That's why your mother made up her mind to leave him. But he couldn't bear the thought of her humiliating him any further. She'd had an affair with his subordinate, an *Indian*. The thought of her now leaving him, of word of his status as a cuckold spreading, it was too much for him. He snapped.'

He remained stooped in grief; she wondered if he was grieving for his mother or for himself.

'James. There's not much time left. I need to ask you a question.' She took a deep breath. 'Did you kill Fareed Mazumdar?'

His head came up slowly. He looked at her wondrously through glazed eyes. 'You're really asking me that? After everything?'

'Yes. I must know.'

He continued to stare at her, then said simply, 'No. I didn't kill him.'

She nodded. In that instant, she made her choice. James Whitby hadn't lied to her.

He hadn't killed Fareed Mazumdar.

Everything that had happened since she'd taken on the case – it was fate, no more, no less.

Somewhere behind her, the ghost of Lata Tiwari turned and evaporated into the ether.

'Is there anything you can tell me about that evening, anything you might have recalled since last we spoke? Something to help us figure out who really killed him?'

'It's too late.'

'Perhaps. But what have you got to lose?'

He seemed to steady himself. 'What do you want to know?'

'Let's go over what happened in the car park.'

'We've been over it.'

'Lead me through it again.'

He sighed, then recounted how he'd arrived, swept past the guard, entered the darkened car park, and seen a shadowy figure.

'Close your eyes. I want you to focus on that figure.'

He seemed sceptical, but did as she'd commanded.

'Describe him to me.'

'There's not much to describe. As I said, I saw a tallish figure in the shadows, dressed in black, possibly with a close-fitting hat pulled down low over his head.'

'And that figure ran when you entered the car park?'

'Well, not exactly ran.' She waited. 'He moved quickly, but, well, the movement was odd.'

'What do you mean?'

'He limped. It was only slight and it didn't really register at the time.'

'Are you certain?'

'Yes. But, like I said, it was dark and I only saw him for a few seconds before he vanished.'

She sat back, her thoughts aflame. She'd spent the best part of a day considering and rejecting alternate suspects.

Owain Price, for one, Fareed Mazumdar's disgruntled former employee.

He'd been working at the high court that evening, barely ten minutes' walk from Mazumdar's home. He'd told her that he bore no grudge for Mazumdar's poor treatment of him, but she'd sensed the chip on his shoulder. Mazumdar's aide Victor Salazar had been convinced that Price was due to be dismissed – could that have been the final straw? Might that have triggered Price to violence?

But Price had no limp, at least none that she had seen in the short time she'd spent with him. And she was still reluctant to believe that the thought of dismissal would have incited him to murder his employer.

Who else?

Could the Bombay gangster Youssef Sabri have sent someone to kill Mazumdar merely for losing a case, a case that had seen Sabri's lieutenant, a close friend, locked up?

He'd claimed not. How far could she trust a man like that? And yet ... she realised that she *did* believe Sabri. In this matter, if nothing else.

Her mind whirled in loops. The killer had to have motive, means, opportunity. There were plenty with motive and several with opportunity.

That left means.

She focused now on the knife. Something about the weapon had nagged at her for a while now.

A killer with a limp, wielding a distinctive knife.

Her thoughts roamed back over the entirety of the case, the various players involved, the myriad testimonies. She saw Mazumdar as

335

a piece on a chessboard, the king, at once the centre of everything *and* the most vulnerable. She hovered above the board, mapping the trajectory of each piece, each player in the game, watching the game play itself out . . .

And suddenly she had it. A blazing revelation illuminating the murk.

She stood up. 'I have to go.'

His face opened in surprise. 'You're not staying for the show?'

'I have an errand to run.'

He seemed crestfallen. He stood up and coughed, straightening his tie. 'Of course. Far be it from me to get in the way of an errand. I mean, I'm only dying today.'

77

The store had occupied the same spot for almost a century, a high-ceilinged showroom with black Corinthian columns out front and octagonal glass cabinets inside, ranged across a marble floor so vast battles might have been staged upon it.

Samuel's Antiques had enjoyed a brisk trade in recent years with a glut of Raj-era artefacts finding their way into the store via Englishmen fleeing back to Blighty and maharajas hocking the family silver as Nehru's government stripped them of their privy purses and ancestral holdings.

Persis walked past the sort of furniture that wouldn't have looked out of place at the Dorchester.

At the counter, she discovered an impeccably dressed Indian, prosperously round, with a bovine jaw and a trim, waxed moustache hovering below a gaze of mild reproof. She supposed that, for an establishment that relied on reputation, it must be disconcerting to see a uniformed officer on the premises.

'May I help you, madam?' the man enquired, in the sort of tone that actually meant: 'May I have you thrown off the premises?'

She reached into the satchel at her shoulder and set a parcel on to the counter, wrapped in white cotton. It settled on to the marble with a dull clink.

He looked down at it, a not inconsiderable feat of athleticism, given that he was looking so far down his nose at *her*, he had all but completed a backflip.

She unwrapped the parcel to reveal the knife found at the scene of Fareed Mazumdar's murder. 'What can you tell me about this?'

His interest quickened. Setting a monocle into his eye, he bent to the knife, picking it up and cradling it in his hands as if it were a baby.

Moments later, he set it down, stepped backwards, turned smartly on his heel, and marched away.

Persis stood there in mute confusion.

Nearby, a well-heeled white couple exchanged animated whispers as they examined a bronze of a tiger. The beast was caught with its jaws open, one paw raised, claws extended, eyes rolled back.

It looked nothing like the silent, ghostly killer she'd seen in the Sundarbans.

When the store manager returned, he placed a red-bound volume on to the counter.

Thumbing through it, he arrived at a page that depicted a knife very similar to the murder weapon.

'Your artefact is an example of a *katar* knife,' he said. 'Katars are push daggers that originated in south India, possibly with the fourteenth-century Vijayanagara Empire. They were often employed as ceremonial weapons, worn by kings as a mark of respect for the soldiers who laid down their lives for them. Later, the katar became a status symbol, and was given by superiors to loyal subordinates. Some nobles even hunted tigers with the katar, for to do so was the highest sign of bravery. After all, only a madman or a true warrior would tackle a tiger armed with just a dagger.' He smiled indulgently, as if there was no accounting for the eccentricities of the rich.

She considered his words.

On the face of it, nothing he had told her would advance the wild theory that had sprung into her mind during her meeting with James Whitby.

'Is there anything else you can tell me? Anything at all? A man's life is at stake.'

He seemed taken aback by her words.

Sensing her earnestness, some of the stiffness melted from his shoulders.

He bent once more to the volume.

When he straightened, he peered at the knife, then said, 'The specimen you have is relatively unique. This falcon is a family crest, a cognisance. The sacred *garur* of the solar Rajputs. On the other side of the hilt is this inscription in Sanskrit ... Do you know what it means?'

She shook her head.

'It says: *"The Lord of Bundi will protect the bearer of this dagger, for when it pierces a foe it is like the tongue of death".*'

She couldn't see how that was significant.

Sensing her disappointment, he said: 'The Bundi reference, taken together with the crest, means that this blade was not forged in *south* India.'

'Then where was it made?'

He smiled. 'Allow me to explain.'

78

The subterranean car park was brightly lit. All the bulbs had been replaced.

Persis tried to imagine the space as it had been that night.

A small sliver of ambient light trickling in from vents in the concrete brickwork near where she stood would have dully illuminated the area directly before James Whitby, but the rear of the car park would have been almost entirely dark.

She walked the forty-odd yards to the point where Whitby said he had seen the intruder.

From here, the intruder could have ducked into the narrow passageway at the rear of the car park – screened by a thin wall – walked up a slope to the back of the compound within which the apartment tower stood, and then made his escape over the compound wall.

Standing inside the passageway, she scanned the route the figure might have taken.

Her gaze halted as she encountered the doorway that fronted the stairs leading upwards into the building.

Her initial assumption had been that the man Whitby had seen had fled the car park, scaled the wall at the rear of the compound, and vanished into the night.

But there was another possibility.

The door chime sounded loudly through the wood.

When the door finally swung back, Lavinia Mathur blinked at her in mild astonishment. 'Inspector?'

'May I speak with you, Mrs Mathur?'

'What is this regarding?'

'James Whitby is due to be hanged today. I have some follow-up questions.'

At Whitby's name, her face became still. A timeless moment passed, and then, finally, she turned, and moved inwards.

Persis watched her limp towards the sofa in the centre of the room, and lower herself into it. Her hands clutched the cane between her legs.

'How can I help you?'

Persis looked closely at her face. Now that she knew what she was looking for, it was obvious.

She reached into her notebook and set a photograph on to the table. 'That's Rita Chatterjee. She is – *was* – your daughter. You abandoned her as a child to the St Nicholas orphanage in Calcutta. When you returned, years later, looking for her, they told you she'd been murdered. And so you began to follow the trail – of her life, and her untimely death.' She stopped, observing the woman's stunned reaction, before continuing. 'You blamed Fareed Mazumdar. You blamed him because he convinced Rita to work at the White Tiger Club. You found all of this out when you spoke with Lata Tiwari, Rita's housemate. Lata convinced you that it was Azizur Rahman who'd killed her. And he would never have met her if Fareed hadn't introduced her to the club.'

Mathur seemed about to speak, but then sat back.

'I have testimony from Agnes Katz at the St Nicholas orphanage. She can place you there – it won't be difficult for her to identify you. Lata Tiwari is no longer alive to do the same. James Whitby, on the other hand, remembers Fareed's killer that night walking with a limp.' Persis stopped. 'But none of that will be necessary.' She reached into her satchel, took out the katar dagger, and set it down on to the table beside the image of Rita.

'This is the knife that was used to kill Fareed Mazumdar. It's a katar dagger. This type of knife originated in south India. But here's the thing: I consulted an antique dealer to identify its provenance. He told me that this particular knife is known as a Bundi knife. Bundi knives are a distinctive set of katar daggers that were tooled at Bundi in Rajasthan during the eighteenth and nineteenth centuries, mainly for decorative purposes. They were exhibited at the Great Exhibition of 1851 in London and became popular as ceremonial artefacts with both the British elite and Indian nobility.' Persis pointed up towards the framed painting that she had noted on her prior visit to Mathur's home, the canvas of her husband, outfitted in traditional Rajasthani court attire.

Hooked into his belt was a katar dagger.

Mathur seemed to quiver in the centre of a fierce wind. 'You can't prove that that's the same knife.'

'No. Not categorically. But you told me that your husband worked for the maharaja of Jodhpur's administrative offices in Rajasthan. I presume that's why he's posing in that outfit. Katar knives have traditionally been given by kings to loyal employees. I suspect your husband was given one by the maharaja. How difficult would it be for me to track down the provenance of that dagger?' She paused. 'You may rightly believe that much of the evidence against you is circumstantial, but it is, nevertheless, damning.' Persis allowed this to sink in, then leaned in. 'Your daughter was murdered by men who had done terrible things. But James Whitby has never harmed a soul. He's an innocent victim. As was Rita.' Her eyes bored into Mathur's. 'If it's any consolation, Azizur Rahman is dead and Saleem Ansari under arrest. He'll hang for your daughter's murder. You see, it was Ansari who actually killed her. Rahman merely helped him cover it up.'

The woman's eyes widened. Seconds passed as she seemed to evaluate the truth of these words.

Finally, a deep sigh fell out of her. Tears glistened at the corners of her eyes.

'The first time we met, I told you that my husband had recently passed. That was true. He died just over a year ago. We'd never had children – we couldn't. And so I began to think about the daughter I'd left behind. In the end, I decided to return to Calcutta to find her.' Memories unspooled in her eyes. 'But when I finally pieced together what had happened to Rita, how her life had ended, I was overcome by a rage I couldn't explain. I blamed myself and I knew that the only way to set right my own crime – in abandoning her – was to avenge her death.

'Yes, I spoke with Lata Tiwari. She told me everything. I came to believe that Rita had been murdered by Azizur Rahman.'

'Then why didn't you go after *him*? Why come after Fareed Mazumdar? After all, Rahman was the one put on trial for Rita's murder.'

'I tried. I couldn't get near Rahman.'

'So Mazumdar died because he was the easier target?'

'Someone had to pay for her death.' Her jaw tightened. 'But it was more than that. Without Mazumdar, she would never have come into contact with Rahman. Rita told Lata that she thought of Mazumdar as her brother. Yet he betrayed her. For his own ambition. If anyone was responsible for her death, it was him.'

'Some might argue that you had a hand in her death too. If you hadn't abandoned her all those years ago . . .'

Her eyes flashed and her grip on the cane became white-knuckled. 'You don't know a thing about my circumstances!'

Persis waited. Her remark had been purposefully blunt. She hoped to shake loose further revelation from the woman.

Mathur's ire dimmed. 'When I was seventeen, I became involved with an older man. Of course, it transpired that he already

343

had a wife. He abandoned me. I gave birth to Rita, but I had no way of raising her. And so I gave her to the orphanage and left Calcutta. It was the worst thing that I have ever done.'

'Not the worst,' said Persis. She leaned forward. 'In another hour, James Whitby will be executed. For *your* crime. You're right in that I don't have enough evidence to arrest you. By the time I find such evidence, Whitby will be dead. Only you can stop that from happening.'

The woman squirmed in her seat.

'Ask yourself, would Rita have wanted that? An innocent man dead because of her?'

At the mention of her daughter's name, Mathur looked up. For the longest moment, Persis thought the woman would reject her plea, but then she nodded.

And with that, a calmness seemed to descend on her, as if the worst was now over.

Persis had no doubt that Mathur had been wrestling with her conscience for a very long time.

The woman's voice was thick with emotion. 'When I first arrived in Bombay to track Mazumdar down, I had no idea of what I truly intended to do. I was just an ordinary woman, not a calculating murderer. I simply wanted to confront him, to hear from his own mouth the exact circumstances of my daughter's death.

'I even went to his law office, posing as a potential client with a fictional case. Over several meetings, I began to get a feel for him. I learned where he lived. As fate would have it, within a month of arriving in Bombay, the flat beside his own became available. I immediately took it up.'

'How did Mazumdar feel about that?'

'He had no say in the matter. Besides, he was a very solitary man. I don't think he even registered my presence, though no doubt the idea of a future client living beside him proved disconcerting.'

'When did you decide to kill him?'

Mathur hesitated. 'It was one evening when I caught him on the terrace smoking. I mentioned Rita's case, pretending that I'd come across it as I'd looked into his background while attempting to decide whether or not to hire him as my lawyer. I asked him who he felt had killed Rita if it wasn't the man he'd managed to exonerate. He looked at me for the longest time, then said: "Fate killed Rita. Blind fate."'

She drew a deep breath. 'By that time, I'd discovered that he was a slave to routine. Every evening he'd return to the car park at the same time. I knew the car park was always deserted at that time. It seemed as if circumstances were conspiring in my half-formed plans, pushing me to the precipice.

'On the day that I finally decided to act, I did so with more than a little doubt. I dressed in dark clothes, went down to the car park and smashed the lights. I waited for Fareed behind a pillar. I had my husband's dagger with me.

'I remember feeling as if I had become disembodied, watching myself from a short distance away.

'When Fareed arrived, I didn't hesitate. If I had, I might never have gone through with it. I walked up to him and stabbed him, before he could utter a word, before I might lose my nerve.' She paused, reliving the horror of that instant. 'I remember him falling to the floor, the knife still in his chest. I hadn't intended to leave it behind. But I heard a noise and panicked. It was James Whitby.

'For an instant, I froze. Then I turned and fled, stumbling my way to the rear of the car park and then back up the stairwell. Halfway up, I stopped. I calmed myself and realised that I needed to go back and assure myself that Fareed was dead. I needed to know if I'd been seen.

'I went up to my apartment, quickly changed my clothes, and came back down. That's when I saw Whitby by the body, the knife in his hand. I screamed. It wasn't a planned reaction; the scream was pulled out of me. I think it was an acknowledgement of my own crime. The unreality of it was beginning to hit me. I stood there in a daze, and when the security guard arrived, seconds later, I did nothing to disabuse him of the idea that it was Whitby who'd stabbed Mazumdar.'

Persis absorbed the confession in silence, and then said gently: 'But the guilt has been eating away at you, hasn't it?'

Mathur closed her eyes. Tears squeezed out between her eyelids. 'Yes. That's why I stayed in Bombay after the murder, after Whitby was arrested. I attended each day of his trial. I hoped that he might be exonerated without the need for me to be implicated. Following his conviction, I've stayed on, each day hoping that something might come to light that will overturn the verdict, stop his execution. But I was too much of a coward to come forward.'

Persis leaned forward and placed a hand over the woman's, still fastened to her cane. 'If you allow Whitby to die, you will never find peace. And neither will Rita.'

A silence trembled in the room; the walls seemed to close in on them.

Finally, Mathur opened her eyes. 'Tell me what I must do.'

79

Legend had it that the monsoon was the result of an ancient battle between the god Indra and the demon-king Vritra, bringer of drought, chaos, and general bad tidings. The killing by Indra of Vritra unleashed the first monsoon. Had Indra known the heaven-directed curses the annual deluge would later engender in cities such as Bombay, he might have walked away from the confrontation and left the land to parch.

The drive to the Whitby mansion became a nightmarish peristalsis, navigating potholed roads, overflowing sewers, and the occasional half-drowned drunk. The rain beat on the roof of the jeep with such ferocity that for an instant Persis was transported back into the teeth of the cyclone.

By the time they arrived, the rain had relented.

The mansion sparkled in a sudden burst of sunshine.

They were led through the house to the gardens at the rear. The houseboy seemed subdued; even his resplendent busboy uniform appeared to have lost its lustre.

They found Charles Whitby slumped in his wheelchair beside a square pond decorated with lily pads, tadpoles darting in the turgid water. The pond was situated in the centre of a wide, brilliantly green lawn, edged with a tracery of spider lilies. A myna bird sang in the branches of a tamarind tree.

A glass was clutched in Whitby's hand, a bottle set beside the right wheel of his chair.

In comparison to his previous, neatly turned out appearances, there was something almost louche about the man before her. His shirt was open at the throat, revealing an emaciated, mottled neck. He hadn't shaved and a hoary glimmer clung to his cheeks and chin.

He twitched as they approached, then looked away again.

For a moment neither she nor Birla spoke. The sub-inspector shifted nervously beside her. It wasn't often a man like Birla came calling on wealth and power. The idea of arresting an Englishman of Whitby's influence had almost made him pass a kidney stone when she'd asked him to accompany her.

'My son came to see me,' said Whitby, sparking into life like the twitching leg of a vivisected frog. 'I suppose I should thank you. I've rarely seen him so ... animated.'

She could only imagine the things James Whitby had said.

'I suppose one reaps what one sows. If James cannot see the world for what it is, the fault is mine. My own father inculcated in me the necessary virtues of the blue-blooded Englishman. Cunning. Courage. Resolve. The type of resolve it takes to win an empire. James imagines me to be a moral monster, but the truth is that there are no such absolutes. Given enough time, history will denounce us all.' He coughed, the sound of a stuttering motor. 'I loved her. But love demands obedience. Loyalty. The price of betrayal must be prohibitive, else all would be chaos.'

Persis realised that she'd been expecting contrition, or some form of it. But Charles Whitby was another of those men who'd succumbed to his own mythology, the limitless self-deception of the narcissist. His claim to have loved the woman he'd killed seemed contemptuous to her, the boast of a vainglorious general after the battle had been lost.

Her thoughts fastened briefly on Saleem Ansari.

What motivated men like Whitby and Ansari to destroy the very thing they professed to worship?

She suppressed the urge to rail at him. In the end, she said simply, 'Charles Whitby, I am arresting you for the murder of your wife, Mary Elphinstone.'

After Birla had left with Whitby, she stood for a moment by the statue of Hypatia.

She recalled now that Hypatia's life had ended in violence, at the hands of a band of early Christians, her murder ostensibly attributed to political machinations in the ancient city of Alexandria.

Dragged from her carriage in broad daylight by a baying mob, she was carried into a pagan temple that had been converted into a church, stripped, murdered, her eyeballs gouged out, her body torn into pieces and set on fire. Thus ended the life of a woman described by Christian historian Socrates of Constantinople as one who had "made such attainments in literature and science as to far surpass all the philosophers of her own time".

A weariness overcame Persis at the idea that some things were destined to be endlessly repeated. If even the soaring philosophies of the ancients couldn't light the darkness at the heart of men's souls, then what hope was there for a modern age rife with anarchy?

Perhaps all that anyone could do was to stay true to one's own convictions.

A bird landed on the statue's shoulder. She watched it a moment.

Her mind flitted between a carousel of faces. Lata Tiwari. Rita Chatterjee. Seema. She realised that she'd discharged her duty as best as she'd been able; if she'd made mistakes, there was little she could do about it. To move forward, she would have to let go.

Self-recrimination was unproductive, and had never been a trait she'd particularly admired.

Her thoughts circled closer to home.

Her father would be arriving back in two days' time. A gladness bloomed inside her, shaded by the thought of the coming confrontation with Aunt Nussie. She'd had little chance to talk to Nussie since arriving back in the city; she had no idea how the bookshop had fared under her vigilance. But it was a sure bet that seeing Nussie behind the counter might cause her father to spontaneously combust.

Meanwhile, Seema, safely back at home, had asked for a few days to recover herself.

It was too early to know whether her brush with death had hardened her resolve or drained it. Persis hoped that the girl's natural resilience would see her through, but would she be able to ever again trust Persis's judgement? With responsibility came a duty of care. And regardless of Seema's assurances on the matter, Persis knew that she had failed her ward.

Only blind luck had prevented a tragedy.

She thought of Darius and Archie Blackfinch back in Calcutta, two question marks that hung over her future. Her feelings were hopelessly tangled, as impenetrable as the mangroves back in the Sundarbans.

And, finally, her thoughts moved to the envelope in her pocket. She'd typed out the resignation letter that morning. A few simple lines, addressed to ADC Amit Shukla.

The envelope burned against her heart.

Bitterness, anger, humiliation: it took all her strength not to be overwhelmed by a wave of negative feelings. The idea of voluntarily quitting, of giving in to those who'd never wanted her on the force in the first place, seemed the greatest foolhardiness of her life.

But how could she continue in an institution that treated her with such contempt?

Her self-respect was worth more than a uniform.

She watched the bird ruffle its feathers.

Her mind unspooled and she found herself back in the forest, the tiger's glowing eyes seeking her out in the darkness.

Gently, it began to rain.

80

Bombay, 1950 – James Whitby

It was Arora who came to tell me the news. Just moments before they arrived to usher me along my final walk.

He stood for a moment in the doorway, his slight figure imposing in a way that had nothing to do with size. I assumed he was simply capturing a last image of the condemned man, a memory that would either haunt or sustain him in the coming years.

He'd tried his best, and maybe that would be enough.

His gaze took in my last meal – a handsome steak with a medley of vegetables, a glass of wine as accompaniment, a frangipani tart for dessert, the food delivered piping hot from the kitchens of the Taj Mahal Palace Hotel.

The plate remained untouched, a solitary fly crawling over the cooling victuals, unable to believe its luck.

I was stretched out on my bunk, feet crossed at the ankles, polished wingtips gleaming. My gaze was unfocused, roving over a crack in the ceiling. My mind was light years away.

Registering Arora's presence, I pushed myself into a seated position. 'Has my father arrived?'

'No.'

I gave a wry smile. What did it say about me that I had imagined the old man might enjoy a ringside seat for the spectacle of my death?

'I have news,' said Arora.

*   *   *

How did it feel? To come so close to death and survive?

The question they now all feel obliged to ask me. The same newspaperwallahs who were so eager to convict and hang me are now my greatest sympathisers, demanding that *someone* be taken to task for the miscarriage of justice that almost cost me my life.

But the truth is that I harbour no ill will. The whole experience has flicked a switch inside me. It seems both pointless and indescribably petty to seek vengeance against the monolithic bureaucracy that has crushed so many before me.

I am one of the lucky ones.

Arora had his own questions. *What will you do now?*

After my father's arrest, his assets – those that remained – became mine. He signed the papers willingly.

I saw him only once. Our discussion was brief. He remained defiant. There was no remorse, no apology. No acknowledgement that his actions had been anything other than righteous.

They say that if a man bathes in the Ganges, the sins of his ancestors will be forgiven. I'd have to bathe a long time to wipe the slate clean of my father's sins.

My first act will be to return to Calcutta and to bury my mother anew.

A Christian burial, with all the pomp and ceremony that I know she would have loved.

And then . . . then we shall see.

The one thing I am sure of is that I will not leave India. This is my home. If fate decrees that I die here, then so be it.

My identity is not up for debate. I am a white man and I am an Indian. A strange bird, but this is my forest and if I am to fly, then it shall be here.

THE END

Author's Note

Although this is a work of fiction, many of the ingredients have been culled from fact:

- The Direct Action Day riots (also known as the Calcutta Killings) took place in Calcutta on 16 August 1946. The brutality of the violence shocked the country and quickly spread to other regions. At least four thousand died: men, women, children. Hindus, Muslims, and Sikhs were all culpable. Very few were ever brought to justice.
- On the morning of 16 August, just prior to the rioting, a large gathering did take place on the Maidan in Calcutta. A Muslim politician named Huseyn Shaheed Suhrawardy spoke to the crowd. Today Suhrawardy is remembered in different ways. In Pakistan, he is considered a founding father (he served as Prime Minister of Pakistan); in Bangladesh (formerly East Bengal), he is remembered as a mentor of Bangladesh's founding leader Sheikh Mujibur Rahman; and in India, he is a figure of controversy, with some suggesting he did not do enough to prevent the riots. Others disagree and say the riots were beyond anyone's control.
- During World War Two, 150,000 American GIs did indeed arrive in Bengal, and 20,000 or so were black/African-American. They were largely segregated, as I have described.
- Gandhi and Kipling did indeed stay at the Great Eastern Hotel, also as described. The hotel still exists – though is now (officially, at least) known as the LaLiT Great Eastern Kolkata.

- The Jews of India have had a small yet storied history on the subcontinent. Few now remain, the population having gradually dwindled since the birth of Israel. However, those that remain strive to maintain the traditions of their culture and religion, and there are wonderful synagogues that may be visited around the country. The Cochin Jews were written about in Salman Rushdie's award-winning novel *The Moor's Last Sigh.*

- The Sundarbans is one of the most intriguing natural habitats in the world and the domain of the Bengal tiger. Bon Bibi is indeed a local goddess, and cyclones do indeed regularly strike the region, causing havoc. Organised criminals have been operating in the Sundarbans for decades, much in the manner that I describe.

- I am indebted to Amitav Ghosh's wonderful book *The Hungry Tide*, which is set in the Sundarbans and helped me immensely in getting a lie of the land.

Acknowledgements

These books are my way of learning about the historical heritage of my parents – and grandparents – and the shared history, both good and bad, of India and the West, especially Britain. I hope the books are as much fun – and as informative – to read as they are to write.

The books wouldn't be possible without many other cooks helping out in the kitchen. Luckily, I don't feel the need to shout at them, like some TV chefs...

So, thank you to my agent Euan Thorneycroft at A.M. Heath, my editor Jo Dickinson, my publicist Steven Cooper, Helen Flood in marketing, and assistant editor Sorcha Rose.

I would also like to thank the others involved at Hodder, namely, Inayah Sheikh Thomas in production and Dom Gribben in audiobooks. Similar thanks go to Euan's assistant Jessica Lee. And thank you once again to Jack Smyth for another terrific cover.

Thank you also to the many critics, reviewers, bloggers, book-groupers, and word-of-mouth enthusiasts who have helped give this series a real headwind. Your kindness is hugely appreciated.

My gratitude, as ever, to the endlessly entertaining – and distracting, especially when deadlines are looming – Red Hot Chilli Writers, namely, Abir Mukherjee, Ayisha Malik, Amit Dhand, Imran Mahmood and Alex Caan.

READ MORE OF THE HIGHLY ACCLAIMED MALABAR HOUSE SERIES

'A hugely enjoyable book'
ANN CLEEVES

'The Da Vinci Code meets post-Independence India. I'd be surprised if I read a better book this year'
M.W. CRAVEN

And the fun never stops... Listen to bestselling crime authors Vaseem Khan and Abir Mukherjee on the Red Hot Chilli Writers podcast

A podcast that discusses books and writing, as well as the creative arts, pop culture, risqué humour and Big Fat Asian weddings. The podcast features big name interviews, alongside offering advice, on-air therapy and lashings of cultural anarchy. Listen in on iTunes, Spotify, Spreaker or visit WWW. REDHOTCHILLIWRITERS.COM